STACY M. JONES

Mad Jack

First published by Stacy M. Jones 2022

Copyright © 2022 by Stacy M. Jones

This novel is entirely a work of fiction. The names, characters and incidents portrayed in it are the work of the author's imagination. Any resemblance to actual persons, living or dead, events or localities is entirely coincidental.

Stacy M. Jones asserts the moral right to be identified as the author of this work.

Stacy M. Jones has no responsibility for the persistence or accuracy of URLs for external or third-party Internet Websites referred to in this publication and does not guarantee that any content on such Websites is, or will remain, accurate or appropriate.

Designations used by companies to distinguish their products are often claimed as trademarks. All brand names and product names used in this book and on its cover are trade names, service marks, trademarks and registered trademarks of their respective owners. The publishers and the book are not associated with any product or vendor mentioned in this book. None of the companies referenced within the book have endorsed the book.

First edition

ISBN: 978-0-578-36886-3

This book was professionally typeset on Reedsy.
Find out more at reedsy.com

For Ed - for sharing his valuable insight into cults

Acknowledgement

Thank you to detectives, special agents, and forensics teams I've had the pleasure of working with through the years and the knowledge and expertise you have shared with me. Special thanks to 17 Studio Book Design for bringing my stories to life with amazing covers. Thank you to Dj Hendrickson for your insightful editing and Liza Wood for proofreading and revisions. Thank you to my readers who enjoy these stories and continue to be excited by this series. Your messages are a source of encouragement.

CHAPTER 1

FBI Special Agent Kate Walsh leaned against the windowsill and peered out between the slats of the custom white wood shutters to look across the street at her neighbor's perfectly manicured front lawn. "Nothing is happening. Not even a blade of grass is out of place."

"That's one of the problems, Kate." Special Agent Declan James sipped from a martini glass then sucked an olive from a stainless-steel cocktail pick into his mouth. His dramatic slurp and sigh of satisfaction elicited a groan from Kate.

She gave up her post and sat down in a lounge chair across from where Declan sat with his feet up on the couch. She toed off her flats and pulled her feet under her. Kate knew her frustration was evident all over her face. "This is the most boring assignment we've ever been on. No one has even talked to us let alone tried to get us to join a cult. We weren't even invited to the community BBQ last weekend."

"Patience, kid," Declan said, offering a smile. "They need to sort us out first and make sure we're one of them."

Patience wasn't high on the list of Kate's qualities. After wrapping a case in Miami, the two had been contacted by their FBI supervisor and handler, Martin Spade. He informed them that they could have a few days of vacation and then it was wheels up to Los Angeles. That was two weeks ago.

Spade, as he was known, decided what cases Kate and Declan took. They rarely saw the man outside of his underground office suite at the FBI headquarters in Washington D.C. – where neither of them was stationed. Spade, an enigma at the FBI, had run the specialized unit Kate and Declan were assigned to for nearly all thirty years of his career. If Spade wanted them on a case, they were on the case.

Declan worked undercover assignments and was more prepared for this assignment than Kate, who had given television news interviews during her career. Her forensic psychology and forensic linguistic specialties were what made her unique in the FBI and a boon for television news interviews, which she mostly avoided. Undercover wasn't her gig. While Kate was sure no one knew her name, she was concerned someone might remember her face.

Kate had told Spade that, but it didn't seem to matter. An FBI specialist had shown up in Miami and three days later, Kate looked like someone else. Her hair had been cut a few inches, her brown tresses highlighted a shocking blonde, and colored contacts turned her brown eyes a striking shade of green – not too unlike Declan's seafoam green eyes, which caused nearly every woman he met to swoon.

Kate also sported a full face of makeup and dark black glasses. It was enough that one might think Kate looked familiar but different enough that no one would know her unless they had studied her past interviews extensively. Even then Kate could claim she had "one of those faces" and divert the conversation to something else.

They were given new identities too – husband and wife, Kate and Declan Murphy, which had the same Irish-American bent as their real last names. They had been able to keep their first names for simplicity's sake. Kate knew if she had to call Declan something other than his first name, she'd mess it up for sure. Kate was a photographer and Declan a lawyer. It gave a plausible explanation for why both worked at home.

Once the details were in place and a moving truck of furniture and clothes for the new couple secured – they were off to a small community outside of Los Angeles known as Mulberry Grove, known simply as the Grove to locals. The community, which had been developed ten years ago, had close to five thousand homes and a population of just under ten thousand. It was a mecca for young working professionals without children. Since they arrived, Kate hadn't seen one child or community playground or anything to indicate the community was even child-friendly.

The community had a large wooden white fence that ran the perimeter and right in the middle sat Mulberry Grove Town Center, which featured a small-town square and a few streets of shops, restaurants, and a 1950s looking movie theater that had two screens. The community even had its own small grocery store. No one working in any of the shops or restaurants could afford to live there, but outsiders frequented Mulberry Grove Town Center because it was a little like stepping back in time with its quiet and peaceful streets.

Few knew the danger lurking in the community.

The target of their investigation – Jack Harlow, otherwise known as Mad Jack. That's what the FBI agents first on the case had been calling him. His followers called him Luminary as if it were his first name.

The man was in his fifties, with movie-star good looks and a bank account to match, and had been a successful investor turned life coach. He had launched a successful personal development program, which he sold to unsuspecting people for hundreds of thousands of dollars. Like similar scams before his, members paid more to move up the ladder of enlightenment. Each level became more secretive and more expensive than the last. This had been going on since the founding of Mulberry Grove, and it was only in the last year that a handful of people began breaking free of him and telling their story. All faced legal reprisals for breaking their iron-clad non-disclosure agreements. Some people thought it was worth the risk.

Jack Harlow, according to the reports, was more than a kind man interested in wellness and personal development. He was being accused of running a cult. Worse still, over the last five years, five couples had mysteriously died in Mulberry Grove. All of the homicides remained unsolved, open cases.

No one knew for sure if the cases were connected to Jack. Even local detectives assigned to the cases had been squirrely about considering Jack a suspect. He was a well-known investor who was praised for his business savvy. It was why he attracted so many people to join his program.

When they did break free and go to the cops, they were written off as crackpots who couldn't hack it in Jack's program and decided to badmouth the man.

Suffice it to say, no one was taking it seriously – except the FBI. It had all the hallmarks of a cult. The reports from former members indicated that Jack Harlow was a manipulative, conniving cult leader who intimidated those who didn't do what he said. He promised those who sought his help professional and personal success. What he did though was destroy their lives.

Jack Harlow bought one of the first homes in Mulberry Grove. He built his business on the backs of the Grove's residents. Young professionals with money were the perfect target for Jack. They were up and comers and had disposable income, but young enough to still be seeking advancement and impressionable enough to be taken in by him.

At one point, Jack even demanded to vet and approve anyone who bought a home in the Grove. He positioned himself as the homeowners association president and played it off that it was good for the community to know who was moving in to make sure the Grove maintained its serene beauty and perfect aesthetic.

Los Angeles County officials put a stop to it, so Jack found another way. Rumor had it that Jack's members pressured people to sell their properties below market value to those he hand-selected. Jack also scooped up several homes in the community that he rented out to his followers. No one was quite sure how he always got his way.

Kate assumed it was good old-fashioned blackmail, but she didn't have proof of that – yet. Some of the defectors had hinted at that, but most were so fearful of Jack even their statements to the cops weren't complete. Access to credible information was one of the biggest challenges to the case – hence the undercover assignment. Kate and Declan had to get close to Jack and understand what was happening from the inside.

Not all who lived in Mulberry Grove were members of Jack's program. But few didn't know him and didn't know the rumors. Most, at least, tried to stay on his good side even if they didn't buy into his personal development program.

Always on the lookout for new unsuspecting marks, Jack ran open seminars at his home as the first gateway into his business. The seminars, while free, were by invitation only. No one, not even Spade, seemed to know how to score an invite. It was part of the allure – people loved exclusive things.

Jack's home, a ten-bedroom estate, took up the largest back corner lot of Mulberry Grove and overlooked the Grove's man-made lake on one side and the back nine of the community's private golf course on the other side. Even his home had an air of exclusivity and mystery.

On their third night in Mulberry Grove, Kate and Declan put on exercise clothes and power-walked their way through the neighborhood. They ended up at Jack's house hoping to catch a glimpse of the man. No such luck that night. The driveway had been lined with golf carts, the typical mode of transportation of residents who traveled inside the fence of Mulberry Grove. Kate assumed the man was hosting one of his famous seminars.

They had turned back that night planning for a different strategy.

Two weeks later, they still didn't have much of a strategy. Each thing they tried had failed to gain them traction. The few times Kate had tried to speak to her neighbors about Jack Harlow, it was either met with silence or glowing praise. There was no middle ground.

"Declan, we are wasting time," Kate said, pushing herself off the chaise chair. "I'm surprised Spade hasn't pulled us out of here yet."

Declan glanced over at her and smiled. They knew each other too well at this point. They had met while attending the FBI academy and had become partners soon after. "Spade planned for this, Katie," he said, calling her by the nickname she hated and didn't allow anyone except Declan to use.

"You think he knew it would take this long?"

"Spade knows what he's doing. We have to become a part of this community before anyone is going to accept us, and more importantly, trust us."

Kate put her hands on her narrow hips. "We need to start making inroads into this community."

Declan raised his eyebrows. "What do you propose we do?"

"We need to get out there and start meeting people. It's been long enough that no one should be suspicious of us. They have seen us on our nightly walks. We've answered all the welcome to the neighborhood questions. We have kept up on all the HOA regulations and have proven to be good, quiet neighbors."

Declan sucked down the last olive. "We had no plans tonight so I had a martini. You really want to bring me out there drunk?"

Kate rolled her eyes. She had tried to have a no drinking policy but they had been so bored, she had slipped up and had a few glasses of wine. "You aren't drunk. You're not even slightly buzzed."

Declan raised his eyes to her like a child who'd been scolded. "What's your plan?"

"Let's go get dinner at the Mulberry Town Tavern. We need to get out and mingle more with people. I can enjoy a lobster roll and a bowl of chowder while you work your charismatic personality."

The hint of sarcasm in her voice made Declan show his pearly whites. "I've always fashioned myself more cult leader than a follower."

Kate had no retort and gestured for him to move it along.

The Mulberry Town Tavern was the place to be most nights. The restaurant offered traditional New England fare and had a good wine and beer menu along with comfortable indoor and patio seating. It was the place in the Grove to see and be seen.

Declan stood and offered Kate his hand, which she brushed away. "You've been my wife for two weeks and we have yet to consummate our marriage. I'm fairly certain that would qualify us for divorce." The corners of Declan's eyes crinkled as he teased her.

"Nothing is being consummated." Kate walked through the living room into the kitchen to find her purse where she had left it earlier. Declan remained in the living room, arguing the merits of sex and the good it could do for their undercover assignment.

On her way down the hall toward the front door, Kate stopped briefly at the hallway mirror to reapply lipstick. When she was done, she bent down and looked directly at a photo of her and Declan at the beach with their arms wrapped around each other. They had taken it in Miami after they knew their assignment. It was staged, after Kate's appearance had been altered, to look like a honeymoon photo. They appeared on the surface to be a happily married couple – an attractive one at that. She had no idea if they could pull it off though.

CHAPTER 2

Kate sat at a table in the far corner of the patio that offered a good view of the sidewalk in front of the restaurant. She could see anyone who entered. Declan had gone to the bar after the hostess directed them to their seats. He said he wanted to read the menu even though there had been a bar menu on the table. Kate knew what he was doing. He was good at convincing bartenders to make them drinks that looked like normal alcoholic beverages without the alcohol. It brought up fewer questions in social settings when everyone else was drinking.

A few minutes later, he returned with what looked like a Cape Cod – cranberry and vodka – for her and something with coke for him. Kate took the drink from him, sipped it, and noticed the hint of ginger ale. She side-eyed the people sitting around her.

Declan sipped his drink and then joined Kate in assessing their surroundings. The tables on the patio were filled with couples having dinner. Some were paired with other couples, while others sat together in large groups. "Do you see any inroads?" he asked, placing his drink on the table.

Kate scanned the crowd and then landed on a table with two couples. Both were more plainly dressed than the others on the patio. One woman had a store-bought box dye job, no manicure, and a beaded bracelet. The other woman was slightly chubby and tugged at her shirt as if she were uncomfortable. Neither man was completely clean-shaven. All four of them looked out of place in Mulberry Grove.

"Them," Kate said, hitching her jaw toward them. "Let's find out their deal."

Declan angled his body and peered over the rim of his glass. Kate knew he was seeing what she saw. If anything, Declan probably picked up more. Where Kate excelled at human behavior and the criminal mind, Declan excelled at picking up clues from the scene.

A server interrupted their planning with a request for their food and drink order. Declan explained he left his tab open at the bar and he'd handle their drinks. Kate ordered exactly what she had planned and Declan ordered a scallop roll instead of the lobster roll and a bowl of chowder.

As the server left, Kate stood from the table. "I'm going to say hello."

"Signal me if you'd like me to join you."

Kate threw her shoulders back and navigated through two tables until she reached the foursome. "Excuse me," she said on approach, looking down at the slightly chubby woman with short dark hair. She introduced herself and said that she was new to Mulberry Grove. "I thought I'd come over and say hello. We are trying to meet some of our new neighbors."

The woman smiled up at Kate and extended her hand. "Is that a friend of yours?" she asked pointing to Declan.

"No," Kate laughed, "my husband."

"Oh," the woman said with surprise on her face that Kate didn't understand. "I'm Natalie and this is my husband, Andrew. Our friends Frank and Molly. We've only been in Mulberry Grove a few months."

Kate pointed between them. "Did you know each other before moving?"

"Natalie and I were teachers at the same school," Molly said quietly.

"My husband, Declan, is a lawyer and I'm a photographer. What brought you to Mulberry Grove?"

The four of them shared a quick look.

Andrew grunted. "You might as well tell her. It's why we're here in this stupid place."

Frank laughed to ease the tension. "Ignore him. He hasn't eaten yet. We were fortunate to attend one of Jack Harlow's seminars. I'm a documentary filmmaker and Jack is interested in me telling his story to reach a broader audience."

Kate's eyes lit up. "That's exciting. I've not had the pleasure of meeting Jack Harlow yet. We only recently heard of him. Declan and I are quite eager to attend one of his seminars. I heard they are hard to get into."

"Nearly impossible," Frank said. "I was fortunate that my agent made a connection for me. I dragged my wife along and Natalie was interested too. After the seminar, we made the quick decision to move and join Jack's program."

Andrew looked away and shook his head. He was the holdout. Kate assumed that Natalie had talked him into moving. "Andrew, what do you do for work?"

He took a sip of his drink and didn't make eye contact with Kate. "Construction."

Natalie glanced at her husband and then at Kate. "What brought you to Mulberry Grove?"

"Declan and I were living in the northeast and tired of all the snow. We were out here for one of his work meetings and stumbled upon Mulberry Grove. I fell in love with the place." Kate gave the answer they had practiced, but the words didn't feel like her own. She stepped back from the table. "It was nice to meet you. We are at 55 Primrose Lane if you'd like to stop by sometime."

Natalie and Molly said they'd love to get together. Frank waved goodbye and she headed back to her table without Andrew turning to look at her or comment again. She sat down and took a sip of her drink and updated Declan about the meet and greet. "They uprooted their lives to move here and join Jack's program."

Declan took it in and then glanced in the couples' direction. "That's exactly what Spade said people do. They leave everything behind. The one guy seems like he isn't too happy to be here."

Kate leaned into the table. "If he's disgruntled now, that's probably only going to grow. We might have an inroad there."

"He looked like he didn't want to talk to you."

"He didn't want to talk to me, but maybe you can reach out to him. His name is Andrew, worked in construction and doesn't want to be here. It was his wife's decision."

"At least I can relate to that." Declan considered himself blue-collar from south Boston but was anything but. He had attended a prestigious college and was recruited quickly into the FBI.

"I gave them our address and told them to stop by. The ball is in their court now."

Declan raised his eyebrows. "Did you get their address or phone number?"

Kate shook her head. "I didn't want to push too hard or seem too eager. No one likes people who come on too strong."

Declan's eyes sparkled as he bobbed his eyebrows up and down. He looked around the patio as the crowd thinned out. They were far from anyone who might overhear their conversation. He laughed. "I never mind when women come on too strong."

Declan had been out of the dating game for a long time. He had been quite the player in the FBI Academy but married against advice from Kate. Now he was staring down the barrel of a divorce.

"You're not dating while you're here. I'm not dealing with a cheating fake husband."

Declan reached for her hand. "You're my one and only." He brought her hand to his lips and kissed it.

Kate drew her hand back. "Natalie was surprised we were married. She thought you were a friend. That doesn't bode well. What do you think is wrong with us?"

"It's one person, Kate. I wouldn't worry about it."

Luckily, the server chose that moment to deposit their food on the table. Kate wasn't sure where to start first. Steam rose off the chowder but the lobster looked delicious.

Declan looked down at his food. "If I'm stuck leading this celibate life then at least I have good food."

Kate wondered even before this case if he was lonely. After leaving his ex, Declan had moved into her brownstone in Boston's Back Bay. Neither of them had much time to date. They had gone from one case to the next – even though Kate had planned to take a nice long break to reevaluate her life and career. Mid-thirties and not married and no children, fully committed to her work. Kate wasn't sure that's the headspace she was in anymore.

After taking a bite of scallop, Declan pointed at her. "You have that line on your forehead when you're pensive about something. What gives?"

Instinctively, Kate reached up and ran a finger across her forehead. "Spade never gave me the vacation he promised me months ago. It's been one case after the other, and I still have personal things to sort through."

"We all have personal things to sort through." Declan popped another scallop into his mouth. "We have this time, Katie. Lean into it."

"What does that mean?"

"It means we've been here for a couple of weeks and we'll probably be here much longer. We've had plenty of downtime. Take the time to sort through whatever it is that's on your mind. That's what I'm doing. Time is finite and we are in beautiful surroundings. Use it while we have it."

Kate offered a shy smile. That was one of the things she liked most about Declan – his ability to calm her down and offer practical, rational sense she sometimes overlooked. "I've been avoiding talking about your divorce. I thought you didn't want to talk about it."

Declan shook his head. "I don't want to talk about it, but I'm dealing with it. I already signed the papers."

Kate dropped her spoon with a clang on the table. "You signed the papers? You're not going to fight her ridiculous demands?" His ex was asking for serious financial compensation, more so than what was common and Kate thought she deserved.

Declan blew out a breath. "I want it done, Kate. I don't want to waste money to fight it out in court. I want the marriage to be over so we can both go our separate ways. My lawyer negotiated a better settlement for me. She can have the house. I wash my hands of it." He smiled over at her. "I'm broke though so I'll be living with you until we are old and gray."

That was fine by Kate. Her brownstone was too much for one person. She'd never sell it though. Her parents had been killed in a terrorist attack overseas when her father was an ambassador. Kate was about to graduate from Harvard at the time and she inherited the house and their entire estate, which was worth millions. Kate didn't have to work at the FBI if she didn't want to. She was financially set for life.

"You know I enjoy the company." Kate ate a spoonful of chowder and thought about what Declan said. "You're right though. I need to take this time and get my head right."

"If you want to talk it through, you know I'm here for you."

"I was thinking about marriage..." Kate's voice trailed off when the echo of sirens wailed in the distance. She turned her head in the direction of the noise. "I wonder what's going on."

Declan dropped his spoon next to his plate and reached for his cellphone. "I missed a text from Spade. He said there's been another murder. A couple was killed three blocks from us. A housekeeper found their bodies."

Kate scooted her chair back. "We should go."

Declan shook his head and gestured for her to sit. "We can't go, Kate. We're undercover. Spade is sending some agents in who will update us."

Kate sighed – there were so many reasons not to like undercover work. Being kept out of an active crime scene made the top of the list.

CHAPTER 3

Two days later, a man in his late fifties with dark hair and dressed in khakis and a blue dress shirt made his way up the sidewalk to Kate and Declan's house and knocked on the door. Kate stood on the other side ready to answer. "Come on in, Bob. Declan has been expecting you. He's in his office," she said, standing back so he could enter. Kate waved to her neighbor across the street who seemed to watch carefully whenever they had visitors.

After Kate closed the door, her posture relaxed. "What took you so long?"

Bob Carver was a seasoned undercover FBI Special Agent from the Los Angeles field office. He ran the Mad Jack investigation and was their local contact on the ground and their only official source of information from the outside world. He had spent years undercover and was the only one who could make face-to-face contact with Kate and Declan. During the investigation, he wasn't working out of the FBI field office but rather a rented office in a non-descript building in downtown Los Angeles. They had created a dummy corporation to make it look official.

Bob shook the file folder in his hand. "It took the medical examiner and crime scene investigators a minute to process everything. We still don't have toxicology back yet."

Kate led Bob down the hall and through the kitchen to a back office. After the FBI secured the home for the case, agents posed as construction workers to create a soundproof room with a special phone line. The FBI had also swept the place for bugs and left Kate and Declan the equipment to do the same any time they left the house. The FBI wasn't going to take any chances.

What they knew about the murdered couple, Winnie and Ned Stockton, was limited. She had been a ballet teacher after years of performing and he was in finance. Both were thirty-four years old. Declan had told Kate and Bob that he hadn't found anything in their backgrounds that would provide a motive for their deaths. They had been waiting for Bob with the crime scene information before they made any judgments.

Declan stood from behind the desk and shook Bob's hand. "Coffee?"

Bob declined. "We don't have much time. If I'm supposed to pass for a business meeting, I can't be in here all day." He slapped the file folder down on the edge of Declan's desk and took a seat. Kate pulled up a chair next to him.

Bob flipped open the file and handed Kate a stack of crime scene photos. The couple had been found dead in their home at six-thirty that evening. Winnie was in her bed and Ned on the floor of his office. The housekeeper had left at four that day but returned because she had forgotten the sweater Winnie had asked her to drop off at the dry cleaner. She found the couple and called 911 immediately. Local cops arrived on the scene to find the woman hysterical in the front yard.

Kate studied each photo in as much detail as her eyes could take in and her mind could process. Winnie was found face down on her bed with a bullet wound just behind her ear. Her husband had been shot in the back of his head as he was sitting at his desk. The earbuds sticking out of his ears told Kate he probably never saw or heard the killer coming. When Kate finished with each photo, she handed it over to Declan for further inspection.

"Cause of death was the gunshot. Do we know about any other trauma on the bodies?" Kate asked, handing the last photo over to Declan.

"The medical examiner didn't see anything," Bob confirmed. "They had no defensive wounds and no sign of a struggle. He had earbuds in and she was sleeping, maybe napping since it was so early in the evening. There was no forced entry and the housekeeper said the back door had been unlocked."

Declan finished off the pile of photos and then handed them back to Bob. "We have any information about anyone they had trouble with?"

Bob shook his head. "Nothing so far. They were both working from home. Ned didn't have any meetings, and Winnie wasn't scheduled to be back in the studio for a class until today. The housekeeper said they were in good spirits and had an easy workload that day."

Bob explained there were no calls for help or arguing heard from the home. There was nothing to indicate any domestic violence between the couple and no enemies had been uncovered yet. He added, "Their families live back east and there were no friends close-by, except for other neophytes."

"Neophytes?" Declan and Kate asked at the same time.

"That's what Jack calls his members. He is Luminary and they are all neophytes."

"I had been wondering if he had a name for them," Declan said, leaning back in the chair. It hadn't been a term provided in the case notes. He said as much to Bob.

"We didn't know about it either," Bob confessed. "I heard the term when we called Winnie's sister to notify her of the deaths. It was a term that Winnie had used with her sister and then told her not to tell anyone because she wasn't supposed to tell anyone outside of the community."

Kate narrowed her gaze. "I thought people came forward to

complain about Jack after leaving his program. No one else used the word in their statements?"

"No. They had no problem telling the FBI what Jack was doing to them, but when it came to disclosing anything about the program itself, they were all closed books. Jack's reach runs deep and many of them are living in fear while he's still operational. Don't forget he's suing two of them for breach of the non-disclosure agreements."

"How did he know they talked?" Declan asked what Kate had been wondering. "It's not like any journalists have run their stories. We didn't see anything in the news about Jack Harlow, other than positive stories about his investment business and personal development business."

"There's an underground blogger who has been putting out some stories. It's hard to find online and doesn't come up in a search." Bob rattled off the website address and Declan made a note. "We don't know what's true and not true. I was surprised when we opened an investigation and they sent in an undercover team, especially from your unit. Spade must have seen something worth pursuing."

Kate started to speak, but Declan inadvertently cut her off. "We're here because of the murders. That's what Spade told us. If it had just been a few people coming forward to complain about Jack, they wouldn't have pulled us into this." Declan tapped at the case file. "I assume you believe this case is connected to the others."

"We believe it's connected," Bob explained, sitting back on his chair. "All of the couples, including the most recent murders, have been in their mid-thirties and professionals in their respective fields. Well-educated and financially well-off. The local detectives who had been assigned to the previous cases don't think they are connected, especially the first murder five years ago."

Kate recalled the cases from the briefing they had been given. "Is it because the first couple was stabbed and the others shot?"

"That's correct. It's harder to deny the connection with these last murders though. All of the couples, excluding the first, were killed with a Glock 26. The 9mm shell casings were found at the scene."

Declan shared a look with Kate. "Do the local detectives still deny a connection even with the same murder weapon?"

"There are still some hold-outs with the local detectives. Right now, there is a good deal of political maneuvering and the local cops have no idea that we have an undercover team inside. We have officially taken over the previous murder cases, and the FBI was on scene at this one. It's why we are getting information back so quickly." Bob ran a hand over his head and slumped his shoulders. "Unfortunately, this complicates things a little bit for you. No one in the community knew until the other night that the FBI was involved. Because they were on scene, the local news picked up the story and showed the crime scene techs with their FBI windbreakers going in and out of the house. They haven't run a story about the connection to the other murders yet, but it's only a matter of time. I'm sure the perp knows that the FBI is sniffing around."

Kate needed some backstory for all of this to make sense. "Spade didn't tell us much about how all this came to be. Could you walk us through how the FBI came to be involved?"

Bob spoke with authority. "Mulberry Grove does not have its own police force. It employs a security company on-site in the community, but they aren't real cops. They carry guns but have no investigative or arrest powers. Residents need to call Los Angeles Police Department if they have a criminal situation."

"They are here for security only then, enforcing community regulations rather than laws?" Declan asked, trying to clarify.

"Essentially, but there isn't much they can do if someone violates community regulations. It's all for show. The illusion of safety." Bob looked to them to see if they understood and when Kate and Declan nodded, he went on. "Because Mulberry Grove is an incorporated town in Los Angeles, you're dealing with the Los Angeles Police Department. The first murder happened five years ago and the detective on the scene never got anywhere with the case. The next murder happened a year later and it was a new detective assigned. There was never a connection made. More than a year goes by and there's a third murder and then a fourth and fifth after that. Det. Jerry Miller was assigned on the last two murder cases. He tried to connect with the other detectives but internally couldn't get a consensus that all the cases were connected. Things changed over the years. You know how it goes. People change positions, cases go cold. Even staff at the medical examiner's office changed."

Kate understood to an extent, but it still didn't add up for her. "If this were downtown Los Angeles or the murders were scattered all over Los Angeles County, I could understand not connecting them. But this is Mulberry Grove. It's like 1950 touched down and never left."

Bob held his hands up. "Kate, I understand. I'm just giving you the history. They should have been connected when the second murder happened or at least the third. After the fifth murders, three of Jack's members broke rank and came to the FBI field office in Los Angeles."

"Did they all come at once?" Declan asked, interrupting.

"No. The first person called the FBI office when the Los Angeles Police Department didn't take the report seriously and then a few months later the second and then the third person came forward, but they all told the same story about Jack. The FBI agent initially assigned took statements but didn't have much to go on. Nothing was done." Bob clasped his hands between his knees and shifted his body forward. "Somehow Det. Miller got wind of a few people coming forward and called the FBI. He reported his suspicions about the murders and wondered if it was connected to Jack Harlow. That's when the FBI supervising agent sat up and took notice. He put an agent on it, requested files from the locals, and then did some follow-up interviews."

Declan narrowed his gaze. "The LAPD detectives handed over their case files?"

"Det. Jerry Miller was willing to cooperate and handed over his files and then talked his supervisor into cooperating with the FBI. They didn't have much to lose at that point."

Kate leaned back in her chair. "I assume the FBI agent and the supervisory agent decided there was enough to pursue."

"Exactly," Bob said with conviction. "The supervisory agent called Washington and that's when Spade got involved." Bob held his hands out wide. "Here we are."

Kate asked, "Is there a task force or anything created?"

Bob shook his head. "You're looking at the task force right here. You let me know what you need and I'll pull in the resources. We've set you up here with everything. I probably should have immediately brought you the case files but Spade wanted to give you a chance to settle in and meet some people before we bombarded you with information from the previous murder investigations. Now that there's been another, we are going to need to get you up to speed. Let me work through a few things and I'll get you additional information."

Declan rubbed his forehead and squinted. "I assume the FBI officially has all the murder cases now?"

"Yeah, they are ours. Det. Miller has been assigned as a liaison from the LAPD should we need anything from them. He was at the crime scene the other night. I've spoken to him on the phone, but he does not know my real identity and he is not aware we have you both in here undercover."

Kate and Declan thanked Bob for getting them up to speed. The backstory might not be helpful to solve the murders, but it certainly helped them to understand the evolution of the murder investigations and those first on the scene.

Bob pointed between the two of them. "The only thing you two have to focus on is keeping your cover." They went over a few more things and then he stood and headed toward the front door with Kate and Declan right behind him.

Before he left, Bob turned back to them. "A word of advice from an old guy who has done undercover for years – work on your marriage. No one is going to buy that you two are married. There's no intimacy."

Kate took offense. "It was a work meeting, Bob. Should I have sat on Declan's lap?"

"It's a vibe, Kate. Trust me. I'm not going to question your expertise so please don't question mine. Fix it before someone starts to question you two." Bob walked out the door leaving them both stunned into silence.

CHAPTER 4

Kate was unnerved by what Bob told them. She considered Declan one of her closest friends, and if she couldn't pull off being married to him, they were in trouble. After Bob left, Declan sensed Kate was upset and tried to reassure her, but she didn't want to talk.

Kate left the house alone, walked around the neighborhood, and then found herself sitting on the patio of a coffee shop in Mulberry Town Center. She sipped her coffee and caught up on the news on her phone. The sun warmed her face and she relaxed into the chair, letting the time pass by.

"Excuse me," a voice said a while later, drawing Kate's attention. "I'm Natalie. We met the other night."

Kate raised her head from her phone and squinted, the sun blocking her view of the woman's face. She leaned her head slightly to the side and saw Natalie's uncertain look. "Care to join me? I was thinking about getting another cup of coffee."

Natalie turned her head to the side and hesitated. "I'm supposed to be going for a walk, but I have a few minutes. No coffee for me though. I'm off caffeine." She pulled out the chair and plopped down with a slight bounce.

Kate picked up her cup. "I don't think I could ever give up coffee."

Natalie chewed on her lip. "It's part of the program."

"You have to give up all caffeine? What else?" Kate asked, her voice going up slightly.

Natalie's voice grew quiet. "We aren't supposed to talk about the program with people who aren't involved."

"I won't tell anyone," Kate assured her, taking a sip of what was left of her coffee. "Sometimes it's nice to be able to confide in someone who isn't so connected to the experience. We are still thinking about Jack's program but would need someone to recommend us so we get an invite."

"You should consider it. I'm more into the program now and soon I'll be well on my way to meeting my weight loss goals."

Kate wouldn't have guessed Natalie was any more than twenty pounds overweight. "Is losing weight one of the goals you came here to achieve?"

Natalie sucked in a breath. "It is now."

"What does that mean?"

Natalie leaned into the table. "Luminary," she blushed and corrected herself, "Jack makes health recommendations. He said if we can't get our bodies healthy, then there is no way we can work on our minds."

Kate's instinct was to debate that the opposite was probably true. The mind had to be right before the body could follow. "Do you have to call him Luminary?"

"That's what he prefers." Natalie shifted in her seat and looked over at Kate. "I know it's silly and it feels silly to call a man that, but it's part of the program – surrendering my control and letting Jack guide me."

Kate would be hard-pressed *surrendering* to anyone. "How much weight do you have to lose?"

Natalie lowered her eyes to the table. "Fifty pounds. It's going to take forever. I thought at most I'd have to lose twenty-five pounds, but it's fifty. I guess with the program I just started, I should drop it quickly."

Kate had an athletic build with long thin limbs, a flat stomach, and only a slight curve to her hip. She had never struggled with her weight, but dropping fifty pounds didn't seem like something a person could do quickly – in any healthy way, at least. "What kind of program are you on?"

Natalie picked at her fingernail. "I'm on a liquid protein shake diet for breakfast and lunch and then I can have a small dinner of chicken and vegetables. That's it for the day. It's less than one-thousand calories and then I have to walk at least seven miles a day and lift weights. I weigh in every morning."

Kate cursed under her breath and Natalie's head snapped up. "I'm sorry. I'm not trying to be rude, but that's not even healthy. What does your husband think about it all?"

Natalie offered a wry smile. "If I were being honest with myself, Andrew doesn't even want to be here. Frank was all in and excited. Molly, of course, had to come with him. She didn't want to be out here alone so we had Frank recommend us. Andrew came along because I didn't give him a choice."

Kate wasn't sure how to broach the question she most wanted to ask. She leaned in a little and rested her head in her hand. "This is a terrible question, so forgive me for asking. I've heard the program is expensive. How are you affording the move, this community, and Jack's program? That must be a lot on a teacher's salary. Your husband said he worked construction. Is that correct?"

Natalie confirmed and then admitted, "My husband was frustrated about the money. He was just about to start his new business and this came up. We used some of the money we had set aside for that to come here." Natalie had a wistfulness in her voice that made Kate wonder if regret wasn't already setting in. "Frank is going to work for Jack, and Molly and I teach English. I've been a freelance writer for some time now, so we are also working on the documentary. Andrew is going to help Jack with a few construction projects. We are being paid a stipend and have our housing free for now. We are in Jack's rental houses."

The couple had made their entire lives beholden to Jack. Kate wondered how many others did the same. "What about the cost for the program though? I heard that's incredibly expensive, especially as you advance."

Natalie nodded. "We used our savings and the money we received from the sale of our house in Maryland – which is where we are all from."

"You're all in then," Kate said, offering a smile but wanting to tell the poor woman to run. "I wish I could be that committed to something."

"How long have you been a photographer?" Natalie asked, relaxing back in the chair. "You said you were a photographer the other night. Do you run your own business?"

"Yes, I do." When Kate lied in any context outside of an interrogation room, she became hyper-aware of her body language. It was one of the things she looked at to assess when someone was being untruthful with her. Kate had to remind herself that not everyone had her skills. She forced her body to sink into the chair and drop her shoulders, which had grown tense with Natalie's question.

"How long have you done that?"

Kate forced a smile. "I come from a family of artists. I didn't even consider doing anything else. I've been making a living from my photography for the last ten years. I occasionally do couples photos, engagement and weddings and such, but mostly I focus on nature shots and anything that captures my interest."

"Would I have seen any of your work?"

"Possibly. I've had some showings in Chicago, New York, San Francisco, Los Angeles, and in London." Kate's website showed all of her work. She was proud to say most of it was actually hers. Kate had few hobbies in her life, mostly due to lack of time, but photography had always been one of them. When she had to pick an alternative career that she'd know enough about, that's what she chose. Someone from the FBI went to her house in Boston and found photos she had taken – enough to make it look good for a website. Many of them were iconic historical sites in New York City and Boston. Others were from her travels with the FBI around the globe. The website even impressed Kate. It made her look like a legitimate photographer.

Natalie's face lit up. "That's exciting. I can only dream of living such a glamorous life. That's part of why I'm here. I have goals I want to meet, but I stop myself each time."

"It's not as glamorous as it seems. What other goals are you trying to meet?"

Natalie waved her off. "They'd probably seem silly to you. I'd rather not share, but I'm hopeful that Jack's program can help me get there."

"Hopefully, it can." Kate looked around to see if anyone had come near them, and when the coast was clear, she locked eyes with Natalie. "Are you worried about the murder the other night? I heard that makes the sixth couple killed in this neighborhood over the last five years."

Natalie's eyes got wide. "I had no idea. We heard those sirens at dinner and then we heard our neighbor say they had found someone dead. I figured it was a heart attack or something."

Kate shook her head. "The news said a couple was murdered. I don't know much more than that. I heard from friends who live locally that other couples had been murdered, too. It might be connected."

"I don't know anything about that." Natalie checked her watch and then stood. "I better get going. I have more miles to cover, but it was nice to speak to you."

"Nice seeing you. I hope we run into each other again sometime."

Natalie started to walk off and then stopped and turned to Kate.

"You know, given your photography, you should see if Jack wants you to do some work for him. One of the people who works for him mentioned that they wish they had a professional photographer to capture some of the training sessions and events. That might be a way into the program."

"That sounds interesting." That certainly would provide Kate a foot in the door. The FBI had given her a range of camera equipment for her use in case she felt it important townspeople saw her out taking photos. "Is there someone specific I should reach out to?"

"Claire Adler." Natalie rattled off a phone number.

"Is she local?" Kate entered the information into her cellphone.

Natalie pointed away from the town square. "She's two blocks over on Jasmine Lane."

Kate didn't want to press too much during their first conversation, but she had several questions. "Does Jack have a lot of staff working for him? It's hard to tell from the outside the scope of his business."

"Not too many. Claire is his business manager. She is also a licensed real estate agent so she sometimes helps people find housing here in Mulberry Grove. Then he has two women and one man who are trainers for him and run group sessions. Jack calls them guides."

"Does he have a doctor on staff?"

"No," Natalie said shaking her head. "We went to a clinic not far from here. I don't know the doctor's relationship with Jack. I don't think he works for him though."

Kate didn't need to ask anything else right then. "Enjoy the rest of your walk. I'm going to sit here a while longer and enjoy more coffee – which I'm never giving up." Kate laughed good-naturedly and waved as Natalie walked away.

After Natalie walked out of sight, Kate got up and went inside to get more coffee. She stood in line and then got her refill.

"You're new around here, aren't you?" the young woman behind the counter said as she handed Kate her cup.

"My husband and I moved in a couple of weeks ago. You must get a lot of regulars in here."

"We do." She pointed toward the cup. "If you're drinking coffee, I assume you're not one of Jack Harlow's zombies."

Kate looked down at her cup. "I'm not one of them, no."

The young woman didn't look any older than twenty. She raised her eyebrows. "Are you planning to join Jack's program?"

Kate wasn't sure what to say. "It's something my husband and I discussed, but we are on the fence. Is there something wrong with his program? I've heard good things."

"Stay away from it." She fixed another customer a cup of coffee as Kate stood there watching her. When she was done, she extended her hand across the counter. "I'm Alison Brady, most people call me Ali. My father, Liam, and I moved to Mulberry Grove a few years ago. My father has been doing some research on Jack and can't understand why the cops haven't arrested him yet."

Kate drew back in surprise. "Aren't you worried about speaking against Jack like that? I've heard no one crosses him."

Ali laughed. "My father has crossed him many times and has lived to tell the tale."

"I'm surprised you'd tell me all this. I could be one of Jack's spies."

"I can tell who is connected to Jack. You're not a dead-eyed zombie. All of Jack's people have a certain look about them. You'll see." Ali shrugged. "If I can stop someone from joining Jack's program, I consider it my good deed for the day."

"Duly noted. Nice to meet you, Ali."

Ali watched Kate walk out the door to the table on the sidewalk. Kate felt the young woman's eyes on her as she sat down. Kate wasn't sure if the girl was serious or if it had all been a test.

CHAPTER 5

"Hi, honey, I'm home," Kate sing-songed jokingly as she walked through the door. Declan didn't respond so she called for him again. "Where are you?"

Kate went to the office where he had been when she left the house more than two hours ago and found it empty. She called him again and got no response. Kate walked back to the front of the house and climbed the stairs to the second floor to the bedroom that they were sharing.

Kate had wanted separate bedrooms, but Spade argued that if anyone came into the home and found the spare bedroom bed rumbled or noticed two upstairs bedroom lights on in the evening or even got the hint that they weren't a real couple, they could blow their cover.

Nearly everyone in the community had a housekeeper, so they had to hire someone to keep up appearances. Kate didn't understand why it couldn't be someone the FBI brought in, but they weren't taking any chances. Kate had gotten a recommendation from her neighbors. Now, she had the same housekeeper as everyone on the block, which only drove home Spade's decision they share a bedroom.

"People are observant in Mulberry Grove, Kate. Sharing a bed with Declan won't kill you," Spade had argued.

When Kate told him that if Declan had been assigned with a male agent, they'd never ask them to share a bed, Spade had shut her down quickly. "If I told Declan to share a bed with a man for the good of the case, you best believe he'd be snuggled up with him every night." There was no room for discussion after that.

So, the two were not only sharing a bedroom but a king-sized bed. Declan stayed to his side and Kate to hers. She slept on her back and Declan slept on his side facing away from her. That's exactly where Kate found him. He had his shirt tossed on the chair and a throw blanket from the closet pulled up to his waist. His soft snores filled the room.

Kate checked her watch. It was nearing four in the afternoon. She went to her side of the bed, kicked off her shoes, and climbed in. She sat back against the headboard and rested her eyes for a minute. She wasn't tired, but she wasn't fully rested either.

"We can snuggle if you want to," Declan said softly, rolling onto his back. He reached over and pinched her thigh.

Kate lowered her head to look him in the eyes. "Why are we so tired?"

"Lots of sitting around. We're used to more action." Declan yawned for good measure. "I'm tired because I didn't sleep well last night considering the murder. I feel a bit hamstrung to do anything about it, even though it's why we are here. This whole 'catch the bad guy from the inside thing' isn't *my thing* anymore."

"It's never been my thing." Kate recalled what Natalie said earlier about surrendering control. She told Declan about the chance meeting. "Natalie told me Jack's program is all about surrendering control to let him guide and make decisions for them. Part of what we're dealing with right now is surrendering our control over the case to the FBI agents who can go out there and view the crime scene and interview witnesses. We aren't used to having to rely on anyone else."

"I rely on you all the time."

"That's different." Kate said the words but stopped and considered how exactly it was different. It wasn't the first time she came to realize that she considered Declan an extension of herself. "We trust each other unquestioningly. Neither of us has that with anyone else."

"We are going to have to quickly put our trust in someone though." Declan pushed himself upright. When he did the blanket came down and his blue and white striped boxer briefs peeked above it. Declan noticed Kate looking and put a hand on his waistband. "I'd be happy to show you him if you want a better look."

Kate smacked his arm. "I've seen him and he's not that impressive."

"Oh, Katie, you saw him asleep. Just wait until he roars to life." Declan roared like a lion and then giggled when he looked over at her.

Kate couldn't help but laugh, grateful that Declan could always lighten the mood. "Let's keep him tame for now."

Declan shrugged it off and sat up and pulled the blanket around his middle.

Kate explained more of her conversation with Natalie including her extreme weight loss endeavors "It's not healthy, Declan. I felt bad for her and had to hold back from giving her any advice. If I start doing that, then I'm another person she'll need to pull away from. I feel a weird sense of protection over her now."

"I don't think it's weird, Kate. If we could find a way to tell her and her husband and friends to run and not blow our cover, I'd be all in. We can't though. Right now, all we can stay focused on is the task at hand and hope no one else gets hurt in the process."

"I might have an in with Jack besides joining the program," Kate said evenly, finally letting the biggest news slip out. She had been worried about telling Declan because she assumed he wouldn't think it was a good idea. "Natalie suggested that Jack might be looking for a photographer. She mentioned that his right-hand woman, Claire Adler, would be the one to speak to. If we can get that close, it's a definite win."

Declan ran a hand down his face. "Do you think that's a good idea? I know we want to be close, but…" he trailed off not finishing his thought.

Kate knew what he was thinking. "You're wondering if I have the photography skills to come across as a professional?"

Declan looked at her "Are you that good? I've never seen you be anything other than Kate Walsh, FBI agent extraordinaire. You've never struck me as artsy."

Kate wasn't sure she could pull it off. Photography had been a hobby. In college, friends had told her that she should sell some of her black and white prints of interesting architecture and nature scenes, but she had never pursued it. She wasn't sure that she had the lingo down or the demeanor to pull it off. She admitted to Declan that he might be right, but it still might be worth a shot. If they didn't like her, they didn't have to hire her.

"It is a good in with them though," Declan said, backtracking.

"I'll give it more thought. I'm going to make contact with Claire and have a conversation at a minimum. Maybe you can schedule a routine physical with the doctor that Natalie mentioned to me. Jack makes all his newbies go through a thorough physical. Even if we can't interview him, I'd like to get eyes on him and do a little background research."

Declan ran both hands down his chest. "I'm the perfect male specimen in good health. Why do I need to go to the doctor?"

Kate held back snickering. "You two can discuss how perfect you are then. He might want to include you in a medical journal or something," she said with sarcasm dripping from her voice. "What did you do here today besides nap?"

Declan rested his hands in his lap. "I read through the file Bob left us and did some background research on Winnie and Ned Stockton. They both came from serious old money. She was a dancer in several

Broadway productions in her twenties and then she taught dance. He was successful in the finance sector working on Wall Street. About five years ago, they quit their old lives, moved here, and started Jack's program. They cut off nearly everyone they knew."

Kate snapped her fingers. "Just like that?"

"Just like that. Their friends and families were confused. Winnie's father cut off her trust. Ned's family tried numerous times to get them to leave here."

"Not surprising at all." Kate had read statements from other people who had lost family members to cults. One of the surest signs of being in a cult was breaking away from family and friends. Many people break off toxic relationships in their lives, but that isn't what Kate had seen with cults. It's breaking apart good relationships and lifelines people had – particularly people who are watching out for those who had joined the cult.

Anyone who says anything even questioning the cult leader or the fact that the person is distancing themselves from everyone they once loved is labeled a suppressive or another similar word. It's encouraged and sometimes commanded that the newly converted cut off ties with those people. This had happened with parents and children and other loved ones. It's one of the biggest hallmark signs of cult activity.

"I can't even imagine it, Kate," Declan said, pulling her out of her thoughts. "My brothers and I are distanced because of their criminal ways. They keep away out of respect for my work with the FBI. They know I'd turn them in and they don't want to compromise me. If Mom calls for Sunday dinner though, we are all there."

Declan had a large Catholic family in South Boston. His brothers were constantly in trouble with the law for petty crimes. Declan's drive and intelligence had gotten him out of the old neighborhood and into a respectable career. It just so happened to be at odds with his brothers. Kate knew his brothers would do anything for him though and Declan wouldn't hesitate to do the same.

Kate thought about her life. "You know I'm the kind of person cults look for. If it wasn't for the FBI, I'd be the perfect target – alone, no family, few friends, and lots of money." Kate didn't think she'd ever question herself or life enough to join a cult, but she could understand how people were sucked into it.

Declan turned his head and looked at her. "Right, Kate, but if it wasn't for the FBI, you'd probably have a husband, tons of friends, and kids by now."

"That's a fair statement." Kate wondered if she wanted any of those things. "Regardless, I understand how people get involved. There's nothing in the Stocktons' background that gave a hint how they got involved with Jack or why?"

"Bob said he has two agents working to track down more family and speak to some of their former co-workers," Declan explained. "We don't even know how they got involved with Jack Harlow. Bob noted in the file that they have almost no one else in their lives other than members of Jack's program. If the murders aren't connected to Jack, then I have no idea what's going on."

Kate knew it would take some time to sort through the couple's connections. She wished she and Declan were the ones doing it. Kate snuggled down farther into the bed – not quite laying down but not quite sitting up either. It was an awkward position matching her awkward feelings at the moment. Without more information about the Stocktons, they didn't have much more to go on.

"I met a young girl at the coffee shop. She was vocally anti-Jack and told me that her father had been doing some research into him. They live here in Mulberry Grove."

"I thought most people who work in those stores and restaurants can't afford to live here. What's her father do?"

"I'm not sure. I didn't want to press for too much information. It's something I want to explore though. Who knows what this man has uncovered if he's been researching Jack for a few years."

Declan remained quiet for a moment. "We are going to have to walk a fine line with them. I don't know that it will be helpful for us to be seen talking to them too much. I want to know what they are up to though."

"That's a good point," Kate said absently. They would have to figure out a way to straddle both the detractors and the supporters. "I think I'm going to reach out to Claire first and go from there."

"You follow up with her and I'll schedule with the doctor." Declan yawned again and then looped his arm through hers. "So, wife, what's for dinner?"

"I don't know, husband," she teased back. "You're the one cooking."

Declan groaned. "This marriage isn't going to work for me. No sex and I do all the cooking."

CHAPTER 6

At noon the next day, Kate stood across from Claire Adler in the woman's home office. The woman's house was like walking into an airy effortless photo shoot with white furniture and splashes of blues and green accent pieces. It was paired with marble flooring, crystal fixtures and art on the walls Kate would have bet was real and not reprints. The furnishings probably set the woman back close to a hundred grand. The home was laid out on one floor with long hallways and the home office taking up much of the back of the home.

The tall, willowy redhead gestured for Kate to sit. "Your portfolio is impressive."

Kate pulled her chair into the desk. "Thank you. It's taken me several years to build."

"I saw your website, too. Equally impressive." Claire sat back and appraised her. "Why would you want to do corporate work when you should be working on a showing? You're talented, Kate. I'm not saying too talented to work for us, mind you, but a valid question nonetheless."

Kate had been expecting this and her response would play a dual role. "I've hit a bit of a block in my creative work. If I were a writer, you'd say I had writer's block. For a photographer, I guess I've lost my muse. I want to keep using my skill and talent though and figured working with Jack Harlow would certainly keep me in practice."

"I can understand that." Claire flipped through Kate's portfolio studying each picture. She stopped on some black and white portraits Kate had taken while in college. She had close-up images of facial features of some of her friends. None of the photos showed an entire face, but rather features set in shadow and light. The images were striking and Kate had won an award for the series.

Claire tapped down on a photo. "These are magnificent. I'd say we are most interested in this line of work. Close-ups of our members as they learn and grow and blossom into their own. I'd love it if the photos could be more artistic than corporate."

"That's certainly something I can do."

Claire closed the book and sat back. "What do you know about Jack Harlow? I saw that you and your husband moved here recently. Is there a reason you moved to Mulberry Grove?"

"No real reason. We were tired of living in the northeast and wanted a change. We were here for a work meeting for my husband and stumbled on Mulberry Grove. I fell in love with the location and community."

Claire narrowed her gaze. "You didn't say what you knew about Jack."

Kate brought her hand to her chest and laughed lightly. "I'm sorry. Yes, you did ask me that. I don't know much of anything at all. I had heard he runs a personal development business and that many of the people who live in Mulberry Grove are part of the program. I haven't heard much else."

"Any interest in joining the program? It's quite exclusive and we don't take just anyone." Claire stared at Kate for an answer, but when she didn't respond, Claire leaned in. "I'm trying to see if your reason for taking the job is just a chance to get close to Jack Harlow."

Kate wasn't sure by Claire's tone what she wanted to hear. "I assume he's a wonderful guy, but he wasn't my motivation. I spoke to Natalie, who I met the other night, and she is the one who suggested that if I was looking for work that you had mentioned needing a photographer. I like the idea of working locally. There wasn't an ulterior motive to it."

"Understood." Claire smiled and appraised Kate more. "You're lovely, you know that. I assume you have many men desiring you. Your husband must feel incredibly lucky."

It was such an odd comment in an interview, Kate didn't know what to say. "Thank you," she said with a hint of confusion.

"Jack likes a particular kind of woman. I know that hiring shouldn't be like that, but he likes what he likes. If you're working for him, you're a representative of his brand. He will want you to look and act a certain way. Is that okay with you?"

"I'd have to give it some thought," Kate said honestly, not sure what she was getting into. "I like how I look and I'm not planning to make any drastic changes. As far as acting, I'm always professional."

"Of course," Claire said and jotted a note down on the paper on her desk. She stood. "I'll be right back."

Kate watched the woman leave and then scanned her eyes around the home office. She resisted the urge to get up and snoop around. For all Kate knew, cameras were tracking her every movement. She couldn't blow the chance.

Claire returned a few minutes later. She walked into the room with her arm outstretched and a small blue Post-It note in her hand. "Jack will see you in fifteen minutes. This is his address. You can walk there. Do you know where it's located?"

She took the note and glanced down at the address. "My husband and I walk every evening. We have walked by Jack's house a few times. I know my way."

"I need your cellphone." Claire held out her hand.

"Excuse me," Kate said, raising her eyes. "Why do you need my cellphone?"

"It's how we do things here. If you have a meeting with Jack, cellphones are not allowed."

He didn't want to be recorded. Kate pulled her cellphone from her purse and handed it over to Claire. Thankfully, it was a cellphone she was using locally and not her personal one. The FBI had thought at some point during a training session or meeting, someone might go through Kate's phone. They had been prepared.

Kate slapped it down in her hand. "I'm not comfortable with this, but I'll leave my phone home going forward if I know I'm meeting him."

Claire's smile stiffened. "We won't go through your phone, Kate. Did you have something to hide?"

"I have banking information on my phone. I don't like it out of my possession."

Claire went behind her desk and put Kate's phone in the top drawer. "You better hurry. Jack doesn't like to be kept waiting."

Kate turned and left without saying another word. With no phone and the house too far out of the way, Kate wasn't able to tell Declan that she was headed to Jack's. She wasn't armed either. Kate hadn't planned on meeting Jack today, but the goal was to get close to him. She certainly had accomplished that.

When she reached the house, Kate climbed the steep driveway and rang the bell as nervous anticipation fluttered in her stomach. A moment later, a young woman with long dark hair and a bounce in her step answered the door and escorted her into what she called Jack's library – only there were no books on the shelves or anywhere else in the room.

"He'll be right with you. Take a seat and get comfortable." The woman hadn't introduced herself, but Kate assumed she worked for

Jack in some capacity or another. The room had a warm feel about it. There was a thick red rug with a geometric pattern, a comfortable-looking tan couch, and a chair positioned across from it. Kate stood in the middle of the room staring at the floor-to-ceiling empty shelves where most normal people would have had books. The only thing on one of the shelves was a large television.

From behind her, a man said, "Kate, thank you for waiting for me."

Kate turned to face Jack Harlow for the first time. He stood about Declan's height – six foot –and had a trim build. His silver hair was cut short and his beard trimmed close to his skin. His icy blue eyes penetrated her as his hand slipped into hers. He gripped her firmly and then dragged his fingertips across her palm as he released her. "I heard wonderful things about you. Please, let's take a seat and talk."

Kate sat down on the couch and watched the man dressed in tan linen flowing pants and a white untucked linen dress shirt relax back into the chair. He crossed his legs at his bare ankles. "Excuse me for not wearing socks or shoes. I like the feel of the floor beneath my feet. I find it grounding."

Kate nodded with a smile. "I do the same at home."

Jack didn't waste any time. "What have you heard about me, Kate?"

"Your work proceeds you that's for sure. Since I arrived here in Mulberry Grove…"

"Two weeks ago," Jack said interrupting. When he saw the surprised look on her face, he shrugged. "I'm the homeowners association president. I keep an eye on the place. Your husband's work is impressive. He's made you both quite wealthy."

"You do check out everyone," Kate said, keeping the smile on her face while she cringed on the inside. In stature, Jack Harlow was what everyone had said – tall, good-looking, and had a presence about him. He certainly carried himself with confidence. Kate wasn't a shrinking violet on her best day. "You asked me what I knew about you."

"Correct." Jack gestured for her to go on.

"I heard about your successful program and that you're quite skilled at changing people's lives. Many who go through your program make significant improvements."

Jack zeroed in on her. "What about you, Kate? Where do you need to make changes in your life?"

"I'm happy with things how they are right now."

Jack laughed lightly. "I don't think I've ever met someone content with themselves. You're being dishonest, Kate. I like honesty at all times. I'll give you another chance. What would you like to change in your life?"

Kate crossed her legs, caught off guard by the question. "I'd like to improve my photography business. That's a goal of mine."

Jack shook his head and stood. He gestured for her to stand, too, and then he closed the distance between them. "That's a goal – a professional one at that. I'm talking about something personal – an attribute about yourself, a relationship you'd like to improve." He didn't wait for Kate to answer. He locked eyes on her. "I've only known you a few minutes, Kate, and I can tell you lack emotional connection in your life. You're emotionally constipated."

Kate stared at him, unblinking and unmoving. She wouldn't give him the satisfaction of changing her body language in response.

He reached out and ran a strand of her hair through his fingers. "Your romantic relationship suffers because of that. When was the last time you were physically intimate with your husband?"

Kate wanted to smack his hand away and shove him back, but she stood perfectly still, unwavering and unresponsive.

Jack raised his eyebrows. "I'm guessing it's been a while and not because he doesn't want you. Any man would be a fool not to take you to bed every hour of the day. I don't know that I'd let you out of the bedroom."

Kate's stomach turned at the thought of Jack in that way. She stepped back from him and bumped right into the couch. "I don't see what my relationship with my husband has to do with a job with you."

"I see," Jack said, going back to the chair. He sat and folded his hands in his lap. Kate remained standing even when he gestured again for her to sit. "People who come to work for me also work on themselves. We are all a work in progress, Kate. There's no reason for you to deny your shortcomings. It doesn't make you look any better in my eyes. I'd respect you more if you were honest with me. I'll give you a pass because I don't think you're being honest with yourself. We have time to work on that though – it might just save your marriage."

Kate wasn't going to take the bait. "Does that mean you're hiring me?"

"Turn around."

Kate resisted but then the importance of building a connection with him won out. She stood there with her hands at her sides as his eye roamed over her body. She had never felt more exposed fully dressed. She turned to the side and then quickly to the back and then around to the front again. She did not stop and allow him to stare at her backside.

When she turned to face him, Jack narrowed his eyes. "Has anyone ever told you to lose weight before, Kate?"

"Never," she said with slight offense in her voice. "I've never had an issue with my weight. I'm perfectly healthy."

"That may be so, but I need you smaller." Jack stood and walked toward Kate. She stopped herself from stepping back when he reached out and wrapped his hands around her bicep. "This here, Kate. You're too muscular. It's not attractive for a woman. I'll admit that the weight lifting you've been doing has done tremendous things for your backside, but the rest of you needs some work."

Kate had nothing to say that wouldn't blow her cover. "I'll consider what you're saying."

Jack ran a finger under her chin. "Don't be sensitive, Kate. All women suffer from self-esteem issues and it's my job as a man to help you improve yourself. Trust me, follow my advice and you'll see an improvement in your confidence. You'll be more than willing to share your body with your husband."

Kate cleared her throat. "You think I don't have sex with my husband because I'm not confident in how I look?"

"I don't think it, Kate. I know it. I've seen many women like you. You're intelligent, that much is clear. You think that's the way into a man's heart. No man has ever met a woman and thought about her brain. His eyes and his intention fall a little lower."

"I don't understand," Kate said, blinking several times. "Is my unattractive body the reason men don't want me or is it that I'm not willing to be emotionally intimate? Which one is the cause of my poor sex life? I'm a little confused by what you said."

Jack stepped back, realizing that he had contradicted himself. He could play the game with the best of them, but Kate had one-upped him. He recovered quickly. "I never said your body was unattractive. That's your perception of it. As I said, it's a small change to make. We can work on the rest of your issues as we work together. I'd like you and your husband to come in for the seminar tomorrow night. Then we will see about officially inviting you into the program. Do a good job and show me some initiative and I'll give you the photography job. You need to work for it though." With that, Jack stepped toward her again, gripped her by the biceps he had just insulted, and kissed her on the cheek. He walked out of the room without saying another word.

CHAPTER 7

"I feel like I need to take a shower after that meeting," Kate said, squirming against the kitchen counter. She had left Jack's house and gone directly to pick up her cellphone at Claire's. When Kate was there, Claire told her how much she'd impressed Jack. Kate nodded and left without saying much of anything. There wasn't anything to say. She had been both taken aback by what Jack picked up about her and annoyed at his blatant sexism.

She found Declan in the kitchen when she returned home and explained her meeting in detail. When she finished, Kate watched for his reaction and was surprised that he wasn't as horrified as she felt. All he did was scold her.

"I can't believe you went there alone." Declan poured himself a cup of coffee and then sat at the kitchen table. "I figured you went to Claire's house for an interview. What if Jack had made your cover? You could have been in danger. We can't be separated like that."

Kate knew Declan was right. At the moment though, there hadn't been a lot of choice in following through with the interview once it was started. Kate pushed herself off the counter. "I know. It happened so fast though. I didn't even end up getting the job. Jack offered us a spot in his program. We attend the seminar tomorrow night."

Declan raised his cup to her. "At least it's a foot in the door. More than we had this morning."

Kate stood near the end of the table and watched Declan drink his coffee.

He raised his eyes to her. "Is there something you're not telling me?"

Kate started to speak and then stopped herself. She started again and rushed her words to get them all out at once before she changed her mind. "Do you think I'm too muscular – unattractively so?"

Declan raised one corner of his lip and looked at her like she had lost her mind. "Are you feeling okay? I've never once heard you say anything negative about your appearance."

Kate didn't think that Jack had gotten to her, but it raised a question and she wondered what Declan thought. "Jack told me that if I lost some muscle weight and had more of a feminine appearance my husband would want me. He also said that basically, I'm a cold shrew who wasn't screwing my husband enough. A bit of a contradiction he knew I caught."

"The man's right. We aren't having enough sex." Declan winked at her and took a sip of his coffee. He caught the pensive look on her face. "Katie, I'll have my way with you right here in the kitchen if you want me to prove how attractive you are. There's nothing masculine about your body. You have curves in all the right places and you're strong and healthy. Don't let him get to you."

"He didn't get to me about my appearance. I know my attractiveness, but I don't date often so I wondered if something had changed. Maybe I'm not as attractive as I used to be."

"You're talking nonsense." Declan leaned back in the chair and looked over at her. "What else did he say? You seem suddenly insecure, which isn't like you at all."

Kate grabbed a cup of coffee, debating telling Declan what was bothering her. In the end, it wasn't anything he didn't already know. Kate made her way to the table and sat down. She wrapped her hands around the cup. "Jack immediately picked up that I'm emotionally closed off. I barely said five words to the man and he picked it up. I'm not usually so easily read. It freaked me out a little."

Declan stayed quiet for an uncomfortably long time. She raised her head to him and he finally spoke. "What's bothering you more – that he picked that up about you or that it's a quality about yourself you don't like?"

Kate turned her head away from him. "I hate when you do that."

"Cut through the crap and get to the heart of the matter?"

"Yeah, that."

"I've known you for years. Sure, Jack picked up something personal, which we don't normally have to deal with in our cases. There's a reason he's good at what he does. If he wasn't able to do that he'd never be able to sell his program so effectively." Declan reached out and touched Kate's arm, drawing her attention to him. "People are leaving their entire lives behind, selling their houses, giving up stable, long-time employment, and moving across the country to be near him. There's a reason for that. If I can quickly zero in on insecurity and say that I have the cure to fix that, people will listen."

Kate knew what Declan said was the truth. There was always a draw like that with cult leaders. They were able to tap into what the person was longing for – whether it was a spiritual connection, a family connection, or some kind of self-improvement. Victims of cults tended to be people who were questioning and looked outside themselves for answers. Kate knew all that in the abstract. It was an entirely different thing when that cult leader's attention was focused on her.

Declan stared at her. "You still didn't answer my question."

Kate looked at him. "Both bother me. I wasn't underestimating Jack, but I was surprised he so quickly assessed me. Whether that's from years of practice or understanding psychology or even years of manipulating people, I'm not sure. What I do know is he's perfected the skill."

Declan raised one eyebrow. "The other thing I said?"

"Yes, it bothers me that I'm closed off emotionally. I know this about myself. I've had a hard time getting close to anyone since my parents' deaths. But you know better than anyone that this work isn't always conducive to long-term relationships. Work has to come first."

"Maybe it shouldn't," Declan said with an air of wistfulness that made Kate take notice.

"Please don't tell me you are second-guessing your divorce. Lauren wasn't right for you for a myriad of reasons. It was so much more than the work."

Declan gnawed at this bottom lip and then laughter bellowed out of him. He ran a hand over his dark, messy hair. "We have to snap out of this, Katie. This melancholy mood we are both in is going to get us sucked into Jack's program. We need to toughen up and put our personal crap aside for now."

"Normally, I'd agree with you. I don't know if that's going to be possible."

"Why not?"

"Declan," she yelled louder than she meant, "we aren't going to be able to hide who we are from him. Sure, we can pretend to be a couple and hide the fact that we are in the FBI. I don't think we are going to be able to hide who we are at heart though. I'm telling you. I barely said anything to him and he picked up the quality I most hate about myself. Even his attack on my appearance put a dent in my armor, and I knew what he was doing and why he was doing it."

The tone of Kate's voice and the force with which she spoke made Declan sit up straighter. "You're the forensic psychologist. What do you recommend we do?"

"We have to keep each other in check like you did with me today. We have to remind each other what Jack is doing and work to counterbalance that. If one of us sees the other start questioning ourselves and what we know to be true, we have to bring it up when we are back home away from him. If he corners us alone, we need to hold firm and remember who we are."

"Sounds easy enough. What else?"

Kate pointed at Declan and then back at herself. "Our fake marriage needs improvement. The couples last night noticed it and Bob picked it up right away. We aren't believable as a married couple. We are acting like we always act. Something is missing between us to make this work."

Declan smirked. "Sex?"

"We can't have sex," Kate said seriously. "It would ruin our working relationship and our friendship."

Declan drew out the words, trying not to laugh. "Or could it save our friendship?"

Kate had considered it on the walk back to the house, but there was no way she was ever going to admit that to him. "I'm not having sex with you. But I do think we need to break down this invisible barrier between us and become more affectionate in public and here in private. We have been operating as if nothing has changed between us. Jack picked that up right away – that we don't have intimacy between us. We are going to need to fake that without having sex or it's our marriage that's going to be up for discussion with Jack. That's territory we need to stay away from considering it's not real. I can't lie my way through a fake marriage, Declan. I've never been married."

Declan suddenly got serious with her. "I don't want anyone digging around in our relationship, and I agree that we need to put on a better act. I'm just not sure..."

"If you want to?" Kate asked with hesitancy in her voice. She didn't want to hear that Declan couldn't even pretend to be with her.

Declan shook his head. "It's not that at all. Never that."

"Then what?"

"I don't know that I can explain myself." Declan got up from the table and walked across the room to the coffeemaker. He poured himself another cup and then offered some to Kate, who declined. He took his time adding milk and sugar, stalling. When he came back over to the table, he set the cup down and reached across the table and put his hand on Kate's arm. "I can't lose you, Kate. You're more than my partner and friend. You're like my right arm. I don't know what to do without you."

Kate felt the same way about him. "Then what's the problem?"

"I joke about us having sex, but I don't know that I could handle it if you ever said yes. If we shift things between us and we act like a married couple, what if those fake feelings turn real – what if we fall completely in love, or what if only one of us falls in love? How will we survive that? I'm vulnerable right now, Katie, with the divorce and all. I know that you're not emotional, but marriage changes people. Even fake marriage."

Kate had never heard such emotion in his voice. Declan had always been a jokester, a rebel. He spent the majority of his time at the FBI Academy bedding every woman who came along, but Kate knew underneath the gruff exterior Declan was a softie and far more romantic than she could think of being.

"We aren't going to fall in love, Declan," she assured him, though not sure that she believed the words she was saying. "This is us, so let's not make a big deal of it. We need to act more married – playful and affectionate and loving. I need to stop treating you like you're my brother and see you how other women see you."

Declan scooted his chair closer to her. "What if you fall in love with me?"

Kate didn't want to tell him that she had long ago assumed she wasn't capable of falling in love. She didn't even admit that to herself most days. "I promise you that neither of us is going to fall in love with the other."

"Are you sure? I'm pretty irresistible and have a trail of broken hearts behind me."

"I swear, Declan. I'm never going to fall in love with you."

Declan stood and gestured for her to do the same. When she didn't budge, he reached down and pulled her up by her hand. He stood in front of her and then leaned down and caressed her cheek with the back of his hand then cupped her chin. With his other hand, he wrapped around her narrow waist and pulled her close to him. Kate stared at him in curiosity.

All at once, he leaned down and brushed his lips against hers, gently at first. Kate wasn't sure if she should push him back or go with it. Then he slipped his tongue between her parted lips and pulled her closer against him.

Kate lost all sense and matched his passionate kissing, teasing his tongue with her own. They stayed like that, kissing long enough they both lost sense of time. Kate grew aroused under his touch. Declan pressed his body hard against her middle making his arousal evident.

Then as quickly as he had kissed her, he released and stepped back.

Kate raised her fingertips to her lips as she breathed short puffs of air. Her eyes roamed over his face as a smile spread across his lips.

"Never say never, Katie," he whispered, tucking a strand of hair behind her ears. Before Kate could say anything, he rested his hand against the fly of his jeans and gave her a knowing look. He sauntered out of the kitchen leaving her breathless.

CHAPTER 8

Kate spent the afternoon trying not to think about the kiss. She had retreated to the office and called Spade to update him on their progress. He said she sounded strange and asked what was going on. She assured him all was fine and that progress had been made. He ended the call with praise for both of them – something he didn't dole out regularly or easily.

Kate had been sitting in the same spot an hour later staring across the room when Declan stuck his head in the office. "Bob is sending over case files for us to review. I wish Bob hadn't given us time to settle in and had sent this over to us at the start. Better late than never."

Kate turned to acknowledge him. "How is he going to bring all that in here and not look suspicious?"

"He's not. Bob said he shipped it all in boxes." Declan shrugged. "He said not to worry about it, so I'm not worrying."

The doorbell rang and drew their attention to the front door. As Kate passed by the front of her desk, Declan reached for her and pulled her into him. He kissed her forehead and patted her bottom. "Is this more of what you had in mind for us?"

Kate wiggled out of his arms but had a smile on her face. "No one is watching right now, but sure I guess so." She wasn't going to give him the satisfaction of acknowledging that his earlier kiss had shaken her to her core or that she had sat at the desk thinking about it for most of the afternoon.

Other than a friendly peck on the cheek, Declan had never kissed her before. She questioned whether she had made the right call in telling him they needed to start acting more like a married couple. Declan was a little too good at it.

Declan took a bow. "Ask and you shall receive."

Kate padded down the hallway in her socked feet with Declan right behind her. She pulled open the front door as the delivery guy unloaded another three boxes on the front porch.

"I have six more," he said, heading back down the sidewalk to his truck.

Kate counted twelve in all sitting in the middle of their porch. They were big enough to hold the deep rectangle file boxes that the FBI used to hold case notes, statements, and photos for each case. Each was addressed to Declan's company name and was from a man that wasn't familiar to either of them. Kate assumed Bob had made up a client.

When their next-door neighbor came out of their house with a dog on its leash, she peered over at them. Kate waved and smiled.

"I told my client to send me a few files. I guess I should have been more specific." Declan laughed and waved. The woman looked at the porch and them, then turned her nose up and walked away.

Kate and Declan carried each box into the house and down the long narrow hallway to the office. They stacked neat piles along the far wall and then one by one took the file boxes out of the shipping boxes. It was a good deal of cardboard for the recycling bin.

Kate stared down at the pile they had created of broken-down cardboard. "We can't bring this out all at once. It violates the HOA to have things above the bin."

Declan shook his head. "We'll take it out a little at a time to not arouse suspicion. You know of all the things we shouldn't have to be worried about while going undercover are HOA rules."

"Let's hope they are the least of our worries." Kate and Declan carried out the cardboard to the back porch where the bin sat. As they stacked a neat pile after filling the bin, Kate brushed her hands together. "Simple domestic bliss."

Declan laughed. "I guess it doesn't take much to make you happy. This is better than my first marriage."

"Well wait a bit before you decide. We've only been doing this real married thing for a couple of hours, but you're cooking dinner tonight." Kate walked back to the office. She knew Declan wouldn't argue about cooking. She wasn't the best cook and he was a master in the kitchen.

"We're eating early tonight. I didn't have lunch and I'm starving already. I'm going to walk down to the store and pick up a few things." Declan grabbed his keys and left out the front door. Kate double-checked to make sure it was locked and then retreated to the office to start work.

She pulled the first victims' case file and sat on the floor cross-legged. Kate tugged off the lid and then pulled out the case files. A photo slipped from a folder and landed on the floor face up. Kate reached for it and then let it go, pulling back in horror. It was a close-up photo of the woman who had been stabbed in the chest, her eyes wide open in death. Blood smeared her cheek and she stared out at Kate as if asking for help.

Kate picked up the photo with her fingertips and examined it closely. Then she reached in the file for the other photos. Together, they created a complete scene. Like the Stocktons' murder, Nancy and Ron McCann had been taken by surprise. Both of their bodies were found in the dining room with chicken and green beans still on their plates. A wine glass had been tipped over and the table stained with wine as red as their blood. Tea cups sat empty near each plate.

Kate sumised that Ron had been stabbed first. There didn't appear to be much of a struggle around his body and he hadn't been bound. He lay in a twisted heap next to his chair. Ron had one shoe on and the other had been tossed across the room. He died with one hand outstretched toward his wife who was on the other side of the table with her head partially under it.

From the photo, it appeared Ron had been stabbed once in the back and then again in the chest. Nancy had a stab wound to the chest, but that was all Kate could see in the photo. Nancy hadn't been restrained and she hadn't tried to make a run for it. The scene didn't make sense.

Kate dropped the stack of photos in a heap on the floor and reached for the medical examiner's report. She scanned through the autopsy reports, noting that her initial observation had been correct – Ron had been stabbed twice and Nancy once. Neither had defensive wounds, as she suspected.

The scene itself didn't indicate any struggle. They had been killed mid-dinner and then found the next morning by the neighbor after Ron had missed a tee-time. Nothing at the scene helped narrow down a suspect. It had been free of other people's prints and no murder weapon found. It told Kate that either the killer had worn gloves or had wiped down the scene – possibly both.

It bothered Kate that there hadn't been a struggle. No matter how she envisioned the scene playing out that night, it didn't add up for her. Most people would have fought in some capacity or another. It's not like being shot. They had time to fight the assailant. Something, or possibly someone, had stopped them.

Kate continued reading the report until she reached the toxicology section and then pulled back. She blinked adjusting her eyes and pulled the file closer to her face unsure that she had read it correctly the first time. Psilocybin – the hallucinogenic chemical in mushrooms.

Ron and Nancy had been under the influence of a psychedelic when they were killed. Kate knew that the drug wouldn't have incapacitated them. *Had they thought the killer was their shared hallucination? Could that even be possible?*

Kate wasn't sure. She had never experienced it firsthand. She flipped through the pages until she came to the case note that indicated the drug had been made into a tea. Residue had been found in the empty teacups on the table.

The front door lock clicked open and Declan called out that he was home.

"I found something," Kate shouted from her position on the floor.

"What did you find?" he asked and then pulled up short in the doorway when he saw her on the floor. "I'm gone less than twenty minutes and you've made a mess of the office."

She extended her hand with the medical examiner's report. "Page four. The first victims, who were stabbed, had ingested psilocybin tea before their deaths. Do you know how that impacts a person?"

Declan took the report. "Magic mushrooms. Been a long time since I thought about those. I took them a handful of times in college."

"You took a hallucinogenic?" Kate asked surprised.

"In college, yeah." Declan pushed some files out of the way and took a seat on the floor with Kate, who stared at him with her mouth agape. "Don't look so surprised. I wasn't into getting high, but I had read some research papers about the mind-opening effects of hallucinogens. I only tried it a handful of times. It's not like I was dropping acid on the weekends for fun. It was a controlled environment."

"How did you fit it in with all the drinking?" Kate laughed.

"I made time." Declan had been known for drinking far too much in college and that even carried over into his years with the FBI. It never impacted his work, but Kate didn't like it. After Lauren kicked him out and he moved in with Kate, the drinking seemed to have slowed.

Kate was grateful for that. "It's not as bad as it seems, Kate. It's been known to do a lot of good for some people in a controlled setting. Even the CIA and military have been testing its effects."

Kate knew the powerful positive effects of psilocybin in treating post-traumatic stress and even helping other addictions, but that was as far as her research covered. She had never been around anyone taking the drug. If there was one thing Kate didn't like it was to be out of control. If she were honest with herself, she was afraid of what she might uncover about herself.

Kate handed him some of the crime scene photos. "I don't even know if what they took is considered a high dosage. Off the top of my head, I couldn't even tell you how quickly it metabolizes. Could the psilocybin paralyze them to not react to a killer?"

"It wouldn't physically paralyze them, but if they are in the middle of the experience, I don't know what would happen if confronted with danger. Your reaction times are impaired and so is your reality. They could have thought it was a hallucination, and by the time they realized it was real, it was too late. Did either fight back?"

"No. That's what's bothering me," Kate said with force. "There are no defensive wounds at all. I assume Ron was killed first because what man is going to sit there and watch his wife being murdered and not react. He was stabbed twice so I assume someone came up behind him and stabbed him and then stabbed him in the chest. The medical examiner's report indicates that as well. Nancy was stabbed once in the chest."

Declan lowered his head to the report and read through that section. "We'll need to check this out with Bob. He'll have to follow up with the medical examiner for us or maybe there's an expert we can reach out to. I'm surprised Bob didn't mention this before. Was this found with any of the other victims?"

"I didn't get that far." Kate stood and went to the pile of boxes and opened the top of the first. She riffled through the file folders until she found the autopsy report for the second victim. She scanned through the report until she reached the toxicology report and found no drugs. She told Declan and then found the reports for the rest of the victims. As she put the last file back in the box and closed the lid, she said, "No one has had drugs in their system."

"Maybe that's why Bob didn't tell us. They haven't considered it an important factor in their deaths." Declan handed the report back to her as she sat. "Are we sure this one is connected to the others? Bob said the local detective didn't think so."

"I can't imagine why it wouldn't be. They lived here in Mulberry Grove, they were part of Jack's program, and both died together like the other cases." Kate leaned back on her arms and stretched out her legs in front of her.

"Do you think this murder is the first time they killed someone?" Declan asked, a hint of skepticism in his voice.

Kate pointed to the pile of boxes in front of them. "I'm not going to know anything until we go through all of those. When's dinner?"

Declan pushed himself up off the floor and smiled down at her. "It's coming, dear, as quickly as I can make it."

CHAPTER 9

After a hearty dinner of salad and spaghetti and meatballs, Kate and Declan retreated to the office to go through the files. He sat at the desk and she took a comfortable chair and ottoman across the room. She continued to dig through Nancy and Ron's case file while Declan took a look at the second case – the case with the first victims who died by gunshot.

In Nancy and Ron's case file all of their family and friends told a similar tale of losing them to Jack Harlow. None of them were happy with the man or saw any value in the program that he ran. Former work colleagues and friends of the victims described them as happy on the surface but underneath desperately insecure and searching for something that would make their lives complete.

In a statement, Ron's brother, Steve, described him as a man who was never content. Part of the statement read: *All Ron wanted in life was a sense of contentment. It didn't matter how wonderful his relationship with Nancy was or how much money they had in the bank – and it was a lot. It didn't matter what trips they took or the promotions he got at work – Ron always searched for something more. Something that would make him whole. When he found Jack Harlow, something changed in him. He talked to me about how he finally found what he was looking for. He was convinced that Jack was the answer.*

Kate read through more of the statement until she got to a part that caught her eye. Steve said: *Almost immediately, Ron cut off contact with his family, former work associates, and friends. When I asked him why he was doing it, Ron told me that he had to shed everything about his former life to step into his new life and that most people wouldn't be able to follow him where he was going. He spoke like he was more enlightened than the rest of us and we wouldn't get it. I tried to reason with him. We are a year apart in age and he was not just a brother but my best friend. He radically changed almost overnight. I don't know how he came to find Mulberry Grove or meet Jack Harlow, but it was a turning point in Ron's life that only led to his downfall. He became a different person and not someone likable.*

Steve went on to describe his only visit with Ron and Nancy after they moved to Mulberry Grove. *About three months after they moved, Ron invited me to one of Jack's seminars. He said part of what he needed to do was recruit more people into the program. He explained that he needed to share the gifts that he had been given. I visited not because I had an interest in the program for myself, but I wanted to see firsthand what they were involved with and it was eye-opening and terrifying at the same time. Ron and Nancy were focused on everything that had been wrong with themselves. They had lost substantial weight, even though neither was heavy or even slightly overweight when they entered the program. My brother looked sickly and Nancy looked downright gaunt. I tried to talk to them about their health, but they wouldn't hear of it. The most bizarre part of the visit was when Nancy told me she pledged herself to Jack. I didn't know what that meant. I wondered if it was some weird sexual thing the way she said it. Later, when I got him alone, I asked my brother if that's what she meant. Ron looked me dead in the eyes and told me if Jack requested that Nancy share herself like that – that's exactly what she'd do. I didn't recognize my brother anymore. The Ron standing in front of me was a stranger. That was one of the last conversations I ever had with him. They both tried hard to get me to join the program and I went to the initial seminar to learn more but didn't even make it all the way through. When I chose not to join the program, Ron told me that was my way of pushing him out of my life. I tried to reassure him that wasn't the case. It was then he told me that unless I was a part of the program, he could no longer be my brother. I was stunned and tried to reason with him. I left and that was the last I saw or heard from him.*

The statement didn't say anything about drug use or go into any detail about what the couple had been doing in Mulberry Grove for work. Kate flipped through a few more statements to find that Ron had opened a marketing consulting business locally and was only doing enough work to pay the bills. The rest of the money he and Nancy had was turned over to Jack Harlow.

Kate explained what she had read to Declan. "Is there any weird sexual stuff in the case file you're reading?"

"What do you mean?" Declan asked absently as he continued to read the file in front of him.

"Nancy McCann pledged herself to Jack Harlow. When Ron's brother asked if she meant sexually, Ron told him that she would if it was requested of her. He was willing to share his wife with Jack. What kind of husband would do that?"

Declan set the file down and turned to Kate. "Is that surprising? Isn't that usually a part of these weird cults? Charles Manson had sex with all of his girls. David Koresh did as well. It's been a part of every cult I've ever read about. Most times, it's young girls, sometimes underage. I'm sure the couples are groomed over a while to accept that it's normal. We also have no idea what these couples were into before joining Jack's program."

"What do you mean?"

Declan paused and looked at Kate waiting for her to get it, but she didn't. "An open marriage, Kate. Swingers or whatever you want to call it. We don't know that Ron and Nancy didn't already have that going on before they met Jack."

Kate sighed, feeling out of step since she'd never been in a real long-term relationship. "I forget people do that. I know with all the crap we see that I should be prepared for anything. It's not the way I was raised, and I forget sometimes that people didn't have a family like mine."

"Or mine," Declan smiled. "I can't imagine my parents having an open marriage. But people do it today more than we probably realize."

They retreated into silence as they read the reports. When Kate finished the first case file, she swapped with Declan. It was more of the same, filled with the medical examiner's report, crime scene photos, forensics, and a handful of statements from family and former friends and colleagues.

This couple had also been killed early in the evening and shot at close range. The victims had been taken by surprise or at least that's what the crime scene showed. There were no signs of a struggle and they had not been impaired by any drugs or alcohol. They were found in their family room with the television on. The husband had a gunshot wound to the back of the head and the wife had been shot in the face. The assumption was that she had heard the shot and turned as her husband was murdered. She couldn't react quickly enough to save herself. She died moments later.

Kate looked up at Declan who sat hunched over the case file. "Can I interrupt?"

Declan raised his head to look at her. "You find something?"

"I've only made it part way through the second murder case and it occurred to me there's no forced entry just like the first case. It's like the killer walked into the house and killed them both."

"That's true of the case the other night, too." Declan pushed himself back from the desk and stretched his arms out. "What do you think it means?"

Kate wasn't sure if it was significant or not. "Mulberry Grove is the kind of community where most people probably don't think to lock up all of the time. It could be as simple as that."

Declan's expression told Kate that he didn't think so. "Let's read through the other case files and see if it's the same. Then we can talk it through."

Kate agreed and stood to grab the next case file and handed another to Declan. She snuggled back into the chair and started reading. It surprised her how much like the other cases this one was in every sense including similar statements from friends and family. This couple had been killed close to seven in the evening at home. She was found in her home office and he was killed in the living room. Like the most recent victim, she had earbuds that were still in her ears and plugged into her laptop. Kate assumed that the husband had been shot first and then the wife.

That was another two patterns – the time of death in the early evening and killing the husbands first. The medical examiner indicated no sign of drug or alcohol use. Neither was on any prescription medication either. No sign of struggle or forced entry into the home.

By the time Kate made it through the case file, it was closing in on nine in the evening. She dropped the file down on her lap and looked over at Declan. "What do you have?"

Declan pushed the file he had been reading across the desk. "No forced entry and no sign of struggle."

"Same." Kate tapped the file in her lap. "What was the time of death in that case?"

"Medical examiner put it close to seven."

"That's close to the time in the other cases. Do we have a time of death in the case from the other night?" Kate strained to remember the details as information from other cases clouded her thoughts.

"About the same time. You think it's significant?"

Kate nodded. "Everything is significant until it's not. Was the husband killed first in the case file you just read?"

Declan read notes from the file. "The medical examiner can't tell for certain because the times of death match. The husband was found in the living room and the wife was found on the threshold of the kitchen and living room like she had walked in there to check what was going on. At least, that's the note from the LAPD detective – Det. Miller."

"Why did Det. Miller assume that?"

"There was a bottle of dish detergent next to her on the floor and a sink of dirty dishes. The theory is she either heard someone in the living room with her husband or rushed in when she heard the shot."

Something about the shooting cases bothered Kate. "How do we explain that none of the neighbors called the police after hearing gunshots?"

"Det. Miller noted in the fourth case file that he tried to speak to the neighbors. A handful of people in the surrounding houses admitted to hearing gunshots but never called the police and didn't go to check on them."

"Why not?"

"The people in Jack's program wouldn't respond to that question and the people who weren't said they didn't want to get involved."

Kate groaned loudly with frustration. "This place is crazy."

Declan pinched the bridge of his nose. "I feel like I'm still missing information. There's not much in these files about the victims' lives around the time of their murders. We have the statements from friends and family who hadn't been near the victims in years. There is nothing current though."

Kate didn't have any answer for him, but after reading, she needed a recap. She stretched her hands high over her head and recounted what they knew. "Jack is called Luminary, the members are called neophytes and Natalie told me the teachers who work for him are called guides. We know that it's a personal development program that almost sounds like a multi-level marketing business where people have to get others to join. Ron told his brother that. We need to better understand the structure still. But people join at the bottom level and then work their way up. They pay a fee for every level they advance. The ones who make it to the top are part of Jack's inner circle, but we have no idea what that means."

"We have no idea of cost or how many levels there are though," Declan countered.

Kate nodded. "That's still missing information. We also don't know anything about what's being taught in the program other than it's secretive and invite-only. We don't know the expectations of the members either. We know almost nothing about these couples' lives after they moved to Mulberry Grove. It's huge gaps of missing information. There is a focus on weight in the program. I'll be curious what Jack says about your body given Ron also lost weight in the program."

Declan flexed his bicep. "I'm not starving myself for anyone. What was Jack like?"

"About your height. Thin and not muscular, but he's probably one of those guys who is weirdly strong. I just got that sense about him."

"He might be starving his members so they aren't a physical threat."

Kate hadn't considered that. "I assumed that it's one more way he's exerting control over them. I was surprised to hear about Ron. At first, I thought it was just the women because that was Jack's preference or standard of beauty. The fact that Ron lost a considerable amount of weight doesn't align with that reasoning."

Declan shrugged. "No reason to believe that Jack isn't into men, too."

"That's true, but we haven't heard anything to say that he is. I don't even know for sure that there is a sexual component to this. Just because Ron made that off-hand comment to his brother about Nancy doesn't mean that's what Jack intended."

Declan agreed with her. He tapped his finger on a victim's file. "We need to understand how far up the ladder these couples were in Jack's program. Were they part of his inner circle or recently joined the program? Did they have any special job or just regular people who paid him a good deal of money to be spoon-fed nonsense information?"

"We'll need to check with Bob." Kate appraised Declan. She wasn't sure how to say what was on her mind. "We need to be careful how we talk about the content of Jack's program. We can't appear to be anti-Jack or be dismissive of the program content. They will call us out as fakes as soon as we join the seminar tomorrow."

"I'll watch my disgust." Declan checked his watch. "Let's call Bob and ask a few of those pending questions and then call it a day."

CHAPTER 10

K ate scooted her chair to the edge of the desk while Declan punched in Bob's number. He hit the speakerphone button as it began to ring. Bob answered, his voice sounding tired. "Bob, Declan and Kate here. We hate to bother you this late, but we were going through the files and had some questions."

"Shoot. I'll answer if I can." The sound of movement echoed through the phone.

Declan took the lead on questions they had compiled between the two of them. "I was surprised to see that the first victims had ingested psilocybin-laced tea before their deaths. Can you tell us more about that?"

"I was going to mention that detail and then forgot. Sorry about that, but it's not critical to their deaths." Bob blew out a breath. "We don't know much of anything, to be honest with you. The LAPD detective who investigated this case found no other drugs in the house. They didn't find additional psilocybin and there were no other reports of drug use."

"I read that in the report," Kate said. "It may not be a factor in their deaths, but it is weird."

Bob disagreed. "Who knows what people get up to at home. The medical examiner estimated that they had consumed the tea about ninety minutes before their deaths. It's probably just an unfortunate coincidence. You plan a good night of tripping at home with the missus and then you get whacked."

"They were already impaired at the time of the murder," Declan said more to Kate than Bob. "It takes about thirty to sixty minutes on an empty stomach before someone feels the effects, normally at least. That's if it hasn't been laced with anything else. I assume by their full plates that they hadn't had a chance to eat yet."

"That's right," Bob added and then became more conciliatory. "Look, guys, I know these cases are complicated. This one is five years old. They are cold cases at this point. When these were investigated, no one in Mulberry Grove was willing to talk. By the time we got the cases, we couldn't send FBI agents into Jack's program and start trying to interview people without alerting him that he's under investigation. That's why you're there. They aren't going to talk to law enforcement. You're going to have to be our eyes and ears."

Kate knew that. Her point was critical details like drug use hadn't been mentioned before, which made her wonder what else they didn't know. "None of the family indicated any prior drug use?"

"None. Those questions were asked by the LAPD detective first on the case and then the FBI agent assigned. The drugs aren't found in any of the other murder cases either. It's something we just can't explain."

"But you believe this case in question is connected to the other murders?" Declan asked again and then before Bob could answer, he reframed his question. "You told us that the LAPD detective didn't think the cases were connected. Did your office?"

"We can only assume so. Look, I know the last five gunshot cases are connected because of the shell casings and the rest of the common details. The first is close enough but does have some differences. Is there any reason you suspect it's not connected?"

Declan turned to look at Kate. She leaned forward as she spoke.

"Normally when looking at a series of murders, the killer doesn't change up how he kills. If there is a change, the killer typically wants a higher thrill so he gets closer to the victim. In this instance, he's moving away from the victims to cause the manner of death. Stabbing is more hands-on, but shooting someone doesn't require the killer to be close to the victim. In the last five cases, the victims weren't shot point-blank range. The killer stood back a few feet."

"Does that mean you don't think it's connected?" Bob asked, a hint of frustration in his voice.

"Not necessarily. My gut tells me it's the same killer. The change is significant but could be for any number of reasons." Kate crossed her legs and leaned toward the phone. "Off the top of my head, it's possible he wants to be removed from the murder. Maybe he doesn't like killing as much as he thought. Maybe he's worried about being overpowered and shooting is more efficient. It could be he had never stabbed someone before and didn't realize how easy it would be to leave evidence behind. It could also mean he had more rage toward the first couple."

"We don't know that it's a man," Bob corrected her.

"I've been assuming the killer is Jack, but we probably shouldn't get ahead of ourselves. From what I read in the files we have nothing other than his relationship with the victims to connect him to the murders."

"That's correct, Kate. No one other than Det. Miller suspected Jack Harlow, and he did have a relationship with the first victims."

"Do we have any idea how far into the program the couples were? Had they just started, were they a few years in, or had they made it to Jack's inner circle?"

The sounds of papers shifting around echoed through the phone. "I don't think anyone has ever asked that question. Do you think it's important?"

"I do," Declan said, glancing at Kate. "I want to understand how close they were to Jack. Did they know any of his secrets? Had they questioned his practice? Had Jack had sex with the wives? There is a great deal of information that's missing here."

"Got it, Declan. That's all information we have not been able to uncover from the outside."

Declan hit the mute button and raised his eyes to Kate. "That's his answer for everything. It sounds like no one even asked the question before."

"We'll figure it out." Kate reached over and clicked the button to unmute Bob. "We appreciate the information, Bob. Is there anything else you think we should know?"

"Not off the top of my head. I know this case is frustrating for its lack of information. You know how it goes."

Kate knew but that didn't mean it made it any easier, especially because they could not interview anyone or conduct an investigation like they normally did. "Keep us up to date on any developments in the most recent murder case. I'm sure we will have more questions."

Bob was about to hang up but Declan asked him to wait. "Are Jack's followers devout enough to kill for him?" He glanced down at the top photo that depicted the first victims lying face down in their dining room. The tan carpet had been soaked red with their blood.

"We don't know."

Declan tried another question. "Do you know the names of those people in Jack's inner circle?"

"Anecdotally we have a few names of people, but they have no prior criminal convictions and are clean from what we can find. They are all his staff at this point." Bob moved again sending a wave of static and noise through the phone. "What you have to understand is that people are committed to Jack and his program. There are thousands of people who credit Jack for helping them to improve their lives.

There's even been talk that a few of the cops with LAPD had joined his program. It's only been in the last year that there have been a few defectors, and they have been completely discredited by people in the program."

"That's how it goes all the time," Kate argued. "People leave and those who stay say the defectors were disgruntled. From what I read and what you've told us, this has all the hallmarks of a cult. People are isolated from family and friends, they shed everything about their old lives, they follow the leader like he's a god, they are financially exploited, and when it comes time to leave, it's nearly impossible."

"I'm not defending him, Kate," Bob said, softening his tone. "One of the agents interviewed one of the women who left. Jack took every last cent she had, starved her down to nothing, groomed her for sex, and then cast her aside when he got bored with her. Then when she wanted to move out of state to be closer to family, he told her that she wasn't *allowed* to do that. She spent a year feeling confined to her home. Every time she left Mulberry Grove, she said someone followed her."

Declan rested his hands on the desk. "Was she paranoid or was someone following her?"

"I followed her for two weeks and I wasn't the only one. I was never able to confirm the guy's identity though."

Kate and Declan shared a look. "Do you have a photo of him?"

"No, was never able to get one. You guys are against the impossible here," Bob reiterated, seeming frustrated with them or the situation. Kate couldn't tell. "That's why we had to resort to undercover work. This group is so insular that gathering intel from the outside wasn't going to work. We also couldn't get a warrant for planting any bugs. Jack's got business leaders, politicians, and judges in his pocket. He knows everyone's secrets."

Declan shook his head not understanding. "Why is that?"

"It's part of the program." Bob mumbled to himself whether he should share something else. He relented. "This is only a rumor, mind you, so don't put too much stock in it. No one, not even the people who broke rank admitted this, but it's the rumor going around. Everyone who joins Jack's program has to make videos of themselves talking about what's holding them back in life. Every teaching and counseling session is recorded. Jack supposedly has dossiers of every member. Members admit their darkest secrets in the hopes of overcoming them to become their best selves or whatever lingo they are running with today."

Kate wasn't surprised. She had already considered that blackmail was one of Jack's methods of operations. She had seen it before. "That's common in a cult."

"There's more," he said, interrupting. "I don't know how to explain this. Jack sees into their souls. One of his ex-members thought he might be psychic. She said that within five minutes of meeting her, Jack knew she had issues with her mother. She had never told anyone that before and her mother had passed away three years earlier."

A chill ran down Kate's spine. She had witnessed it herself, but she didn't believe Jack had any special powers. "He reads body language and picks up clues by what you say."

"That may be true but protect yourselves."

Kate hadn't told Bob that she had met him. She took that moment to explain the meeting to him in detail. "Declan and I will be at the seminar tomorrow night."

"You need to watch your back." Bob got quiet for a moment and then said, "I didn't mean to offend either of you earlier when I said you need to work on being a married couple. I didn't mean to criticize you, but I wanted to drive home the point that there can't be any cracks in the façade you've created. If I saw cracks, Jack definitely will too."

Kate appreciated what he said. "No offense taken. Declan and I are working on it."

Bob cursed good-naturedly. "You're both attractive people. Are you attracted to each other?"

Kate and Declan looked across the table at each other with their eyebrows raised. She had never really looked at him in that regard. When they met, Declan had been such a player that she wrote him off immediately as any sort of romantic partner.

Bob spoke through their silence. "I'm not going to make you answer me, but you need to answer it for yourselves. If you're not attracted to each other, that shines through. If you are attracted, then use that sexual energy. The best undercover jobs I had were when I wasn't faking it. If I felt real emotion in the situation, I could tap into it." When he was sure they had nothing else to ask him, he said goodnight and hung up.

Declan stacked some of the files into a pile and then stood. "Let's call it a night and head to bed." He reached for her hand and she allowed him to take it, leading them out of the room and upstairs to their bedroom.

CHAPTER 11

K ate stood against the kitchen counter and yawned for the fourth time that morning. She had tossed and turned all night, a good night's sleep escaping her. She had on yoga pants and her favorite running shirt. She needed to burn off her annoyance at herself for letting Declan get to her as he had. Kate tapped her foot while she waited for the coffeemaker, which seemed to be slower than normal.

"What's wrong with you?" Declan asked as he rounded the corner into the kitchen. He had on a simple long-sleeve blue tee-shirt and gray joggers. "I figured we could go for a run this morning since we won't have time tonight." He grabbed his sneakers from the mat at the back door and then sat down on a kitchen chair.

Kate stared at him unsure of what to say. She was annoyed that nothing seemed to have affected him. "Don't you feel like things have changed between us?"

"What do you mean?" Declan asked absently as he tied his laces. When she didn't respond, he raised his head. "Did I miss something because you've been acting weird since last night?"

There was something about the earnest way he sounded that deflated all the pent-up energy she had been feeling since last night. "I guess not," she said softly and walked across the kitchen to grab her sneakers.

Declan reached for her hand as she passed by him. "Kate, if something is bothering you, tell me. We need to be on the same page especially going into tonight."

Kate bent down, grabbed her sneakers, and sat in the chair across from him. "It's nothing. I guess I feel weird about the kiss."

Declan chuckled softly. "I've still got it. I didn't realize you'd fall in love with me that quickly."

"It's not funny, Declan, and I'm not in love with you." Kate tied her laces and then sat up, her back as straight as an arrow. She thrust her shoulders back and turned her head to him. "Don't you feel any different? Like we crossed some line we shouldn't have?"

Declan stood and reached his hand to her again. She let him pull her up. "Katie, I'm sorry if I caught you off guard with the kiss. I was nervous and figured we might as well get it out of the way. We will have to be affectionate in public and I assumed, maybe wrongly, that if we get it out of the way in private that it would be easier. Plus, what if we were horrible at kissing each other? That could have made for a seriously awkward moment in front of other people."

Kate hadn't thought of that. "I didn't mind that you kissed me. I was glad you didn't give me a chance to overthink it."

"That's exactly why I grabbed you and kissed you," Declan admitted, red creeping up his cheeks. "I kind of assumed you'd stop me, but you kissed me back. Turns out we've got some chemistry, which doesn't surprise me. I've been undercover before. Think of actors. They have to kiss each other all the time and it's not a huge life-altering thing."

Kate pointed to his cheeks which were a sure sign that he was embarrassed by what had happened between them. "You don't have to be embarrassed. I was a little caught off guard and then we didn't talk about it."

"We should have talked about it." Declan locked eyes with her.

Kate wasn't sure she wanted to admit the next part, but while they were being so open with each other, she let her guard down further. "I didn't hate it. I don't know what I was expecting but that wasn't it. You're a good kisser."

Declan looked down at his pants. "Clearly, you had an effect," he laughed. "I don't know that I've gotten aroused like that just from one kiss."

Kate tried to hold back a laugh. "I can't believe you admitted that to me."

"I can't believe I admitted it either." Declan rubbed his hand down his face. "Are we good? Can we go for a run now?"

"We're good. We need to make sure we talk about these things though. Not talking about it makes it weirder."

Together, they left the house, took a few minutes to lightly stretch, and then took off down the driveway. The way they ran was symbolic of their friendship – sometimes Declan would pull ahead a little and other times it would be Kate. Neither left the other behind though. There wasn't competition in their strides.

They ran like that for nearly forty minutes around the neighborhood. When they reached the town square with all the shops and restaurants, Kate slowed her pace. "Let's take a break and you can meet Ali. I want your impression of her."

Declan agreed so they jogged slowly to the end of the block and then stood off to the side of the door and stretched their legs. "I hope I'm not too sweaty."

Kate glanced over at him. "You look like you haven't even exerted yourself."

Declan wiped his brow on the back of his wrist and then pulled open the door. "What else do they sell in here besides coffee?"

Kate pointed to the menu. "Looks like they have a lot of options."

Declan surveyed the menu and stepped to the counter. He let Kate order first and then he ordered, paid cash for the purchase, and they both stepped to the side.

Kate surveyed the shop and saw Ali with her face buried in a book. "She's right over there," she said, pointing to a table in the far corner of the shop. "Let's try to strike up a conversation."

They waited for their drinks and when the barista slid them across the counter, Declan grabbed their drinks – a protein smoothie for him and a cup of coffee for her. They chose a table not far from Ali who had her head bent over the book. She hadn't looked up yet.

As Kate passed by, she bumped the table enough that Ali raised her head. "I'm so sorry about that."

"No problem," Ali said with a smile. "Kate, right?"

"Yes," Kate said, sitting at a table for two. She gestured toward Declan. "This is my husband, Declan. Ali is the young woman I told you about yesterday."

Ali's smile beamed wider. "You talked about me?"

"I told Declan your warning about Jack Harlow. As I mentioned yesterday, we had been considering going to one of his seminars."

Ali turned her body so she was facing their table. "That's a bad idea. People go to those things and walk out like zombies."

Declan took a sip of his smoothie. "What does that mean? Zombies?"

Ali let her gaze fall over him and she smiled more shyly this time. It was clear she found him attractive. "I don't see any reason why either of you would need Jack Harlow's help with anything. Most people who join his program have issues they want him to fix. In the process, they lose a sense of themselves. That's what Jack likes most. He likes molding people into who he wants them to be."

Declan took another sip of his smoothie and relaxed back into the chair, turning slightly to look at Ali. "That seems odd that it happens that way. I thought he was supposed to help people meet their goals and become who they want to be."

"That's not how it turns out." Ali reached for the book she had been reading and flipped it over to show them the cover. The bright red cover had gold lettering, which Kate couldn't make out given the angle Ali held it. "This is the best book available about how to break people free of cults. That's what Jack is running – a cult. You need to be careful if you meet him or join the program. It's not what it seems to be."

"Do you know someone in Jack's program?" Kate asked, sensing from Ali's tone that all of this might be personal to the young woman.

Ali shook her head. "I've seen a lot of people in this community lose everything they have."

"Aren't you worried talking about him like that?" Declan asked the question Kate had the other day.

"There's always a reason to worry when you're talking about Jack Harlow. Sometimes though you have to be strong enough to stand up for what you think is right no matter the consequence." Ali grabbed her book and reached for her bag that hung on the back of her chair. "Were you running this morning?"

"We either walk or run every day." Kate took a sip of her coffee.

"Where did you run?"

"Around the neighborhood. We usually do a few miles up and down the side streets."

Ali stood abruptly. "Meet me outside and I'll show you the entrance to the best running trail around here."

"I didn't know we had one of those around here. That would make for a much nicer run."

"It's a bit out of the way and unless someone points it out, you'll never find it." With that, Ali waved goodbye to the girl behind the counter and left through the front door.

"That was odd," Declan said, staring at the door. "I guess she wants us to follow her."

Kate leaned into the table. "I assume she doesn't want to continue the conversation in here." Kate finished her coffee and then got up with Declan following right behind.

Once outside, it took Kate a moment to spot Ali who stood staring at the coffee shop from across the square. Kate and Declan walked over to meet her. "Is there a running trail or did you want to speak to us outside?"

Ali looked at Kate. "You're not the kind of people who move to Mulberry Grove."

Declan sipped his smoothie. "What do you mean?"

Ali stood back and assessed them both. Kate's stomach dropped wondering if they weren't even capable of fooling a young woman. "I don't know what I mean. It's just a feeling – like you asking me if I wanted to get you guys alone – most people wouldn't say that."

"You rushed out of there. That's why I asked," Kate said, turning it back on her.

Ali turned and walked away, gesturing over her shoulder for them to follow. "If you want to know the truth, it was both reasons," she said when they caught up to her. "There is a trail I think you'd enjoy, but I also don't like talking at work. I run on this trail most mornings if you ever want to meet up. If you're going to join Jack's program, you might not want to be seen with me."

"No one tells me who I can and can't speak to," Declan said his voice clear and strong.

Ali tilted her head up to him. "That's why I can't see you remaining in the program. It's not how Jack works. You either follow along or you're gone."

Ali stepped between two trees to reveal a dirt path where the grass and the shrubs had been worn away. "It's through here about one-hundred yards and then the woods open up to a nice trail. It gives you a good look behind Jack's house, too."

"Thanks," Kate said looking around the area. The tree cover

provided some seclusion. "Is there something you wanted to tell me?"

Ali looked between them. "You seem like nice people but you don't seem like you belong. Get out while you can. People get hurt around here. There have been several murders, one just the other night. If you get involved with Jack, your life will be at risk."

Without waiting for them to respond, Ali walked off leaving Kate and Declan to stare after her.

CHAPTER 12

"Weird exchange, right?" Kate asked as they walked through the front door of the house. They didn't explore the trail given neither of them were armed and it seemed a bad idea at the time. Ali had led them there and they didn't know who might be on the trail waiting for them.

Declan toed off his shoes in the living room and plopped down on the couch. "I'm not sure whether to be impressed or scared that she thinks that there is something up with us."

Kate picked up Declan's shoes and put them on the mat next to hers. Then she chastised herself for cleaning up after him. She inched herself back on the recliner and crossed her legs. "That has me a bit worried but she might be a good source of information for us. It certainly sounds like she's done a good deal of research and knows her way around the community."

"I don't understand how she singled you out though."

"I ordered coffee and right away she knew I wasn't involved with Jack. She asked me if I planned to be. Sounds like she's seen so much, she can spot Jack's people a mile away."

"Either way, she's perceptive and we are going to need to be careful."

Kate didn't disagree. "She might be a wealth of information. I have the feeling though her interest in Jack is personal. I know her father has been researching him and that interests me too."

Declan raised his eyebrows. "Is there a mother on the scene?"

"I don't know. She's only mentioned her father. She didn't say anything new today. It's basically what she told me the other day."

"Did you get her father's name?"

Kate shook her head. "Her last name is Brady so I assume that's his as well. She said his first name is Liam. I figured we could do some background on Ali and her father."

Declan got up from the couch and went to get his laptop. He came back with it a few minutes later along with two glasses of water. He set everything down on the coffee table and then eased back onto the couch with the laptop.

Declan talked aloud as he typed, telling Kate what he was doing. First, he dropped Ali's name into a few social media websites and read Kate off the information he found. "It provides basic information and her birthday. Her posts seem fairly benign. I don't see anything about Jack Harlow or the program or even much about living in Mulberry Grove. She seems to have a handful of friends she spends time with doing typical twenty-two-year-old activities. I don't see a boyfriend though or any mention of her parents."

Declan tried a search for Liam Brady next and came up short. "I'm not finding him on social media anywhere. The name Liam Brady comes up but no one that I suspect is him."

"What about private profiles?"

Declan shook his head. "No. It's not too uncommon of a name but nothing private. I tried looking in Ali's friend list too and his name didn't come back." Declan tried a simple online search and came back with several research studies connected to Liam Brady. "Looks like he's a sociologist. He's been studying cults for some time. Looks like he might have a focus on the sociology of deviance and criminal activity."

That checked out from what Ali had told her. "Does it say what university he's connected to?"

Declan scanned through the list of links and then clicked one that appeared to give the man's bio. "He's from Vermont originally and was a professor at the University of Vermont in Burlington. He last taught there about five years ago. I don't see an employment history after that." Declan raised his head from the screen and looked over at Kate. "Is that around the time they moved here?"

Kate wasn't sure of the math. "Ali said when she graduated high school they moved, so that would make sense if we assume she graduated at eighteen. It doesn't say anything about what he's doing currently? No local university he's connected to?"

Declan did another search adding the word professor in front of the man's name and then he tried Ph.D. after his name. "I'm not finding anything."

Kate knew she'd have to ask some probing questions to get Ali to reveal information about her father. The young woman had been more than eager to talk about her hatred of Jack Harlow but hadn't revealed much about herself or her father otherwise. "Check the database and see if you can find any criminal history."

"Already a step ahead of you." Declan clicked one more button and pulled up the screen in the criminal database the FBI utilized. "Nothing on either of them. I checked nationally and then did a specific search for Vermont and then California and came up clear." Declan moved the laptop to the coffee table. "We can explore more and see if someone can get some background from the university."

"We'll need to wait on that. I don't want to tip them off that we are digging around. Hopefully, Ali will be a little more forthcoming with information once we get to know each other better." Declan didn't disagree with her. "I think it's going to take some time to warm her up. Going to Jack's seminar tonight probably won't help, but with her, I'm going to have to act like I'm on the fence about him. She seems to have taken a liking to me quickly though."

A phone rang somewhere off in the distance and Declan stood from the couch. "Mine is on the charger upstairs. Where's yours?"

"Kitchen."

Declan walked to the kitchen and came back with her phone. He handed it to her, but not in enough time to answer the call. Kate looked at the screen and didn't recognize the number. The cellphone was not her normal FBI phone but the one she was using locally. The only people she had given the number to were Natalie and Claire Alder, which meant that Jack would have the number, too. Kate punched in the numbers for her voicemail and hit speakerphone so both of them could hear the message.

Claire's voice came through the phone reminding them that they had to be at Jack's house at six that evening and that anyone late would not be admitted. She did not ask to be called back, but her sharp punctuated speech drove home the formality of the program.

Kate rested the phone in her lap. "What is our strategy for tonight?"

Declan relaxed back on the couch and put his feet up. "I'm not sure we get to have a strategy. It's not our meeting. We are going to have to go with the flow for this one."

Kate clicked her tongue. "I wish we had some information about what this seminar entails. I want some insight before we go in there."

Declan hitched his jaw toward her. "Call the woman you've spoken to a few times."

"Natalie?" Kate asked and Declan nodded. "I'm not sure she will tell me anything. She told me a little the other day but told me a few times she's not supposed to talk about the program."

"Give it a try. She might be excited that you are thinking of becoming one of them."

Kate scrolled through the phone to Natalie's saved contact info. She clicked the button to call her and then waited. "Hi Natalie, this is Kate from the coffee shop the other day," she said when Natalie answered.

"Kate, hi," Natalie's voice had an edge of reservation. "I'm surprised to hear from you."

"I hope I'm not bothering you. I'm sitting here with my husband and we are talking about attending Jack's seminar tonight. Neither of us is sure what to expect. I was wondering if you could give me some idea what it entails."

"Oh, well…" Natalie didn't finish her thought.

"I'm not asking about the program just about the first seminar. We haven't officially joined yet. I'm just not sure what we are walking into and want to be prepared."

"There's nothing to prepare. There should be other people at the seminar with you and then there is an overview of the program. All of Jack's guides are there."

"Is that it, just sitting and listening to an overview of the program?" Kate didn't think that sounded so bad.

"No, not exactly. That's the first part," Natalie said and then hesitated. She excused herself to someone on the other end of the phone and then the sound of movement echoed through the phone. "Kate, listen, as I said, I'm not supposed to share any information."

"I understand and don't mean to put you on the spot." Kate softened her tone almost to a whisper, "Declan wants to make a good impression and I don't want to ruin this for us. I've been so nervous today that my stomach is in knots. As you know, we only get one shot at this."

Natalie remained quiet for several moments. "All I can say is that after the initial part, the guides separate the group between couples and singles. Then based on your status, there is a questionnaire. I don't know what the single people are asked but the couples are asked personal questions about their individual goals and then goals as a couple. There are some personal questions though that we didn't feel comfortable answering."

Kate's breath caught in her chest. "Like what? What happened when you didn't answer?"

"I had to answer or leave. We didn't end up having a choice. Personal questions about your relationship – your sex life, communication style, things you fight over. It was incredibly detailed."

It was one thing to pretend to be a couple to make conversation. Kate took a breath. "Okay, thank you. I appreciate it more than you know. Will I see you tonight?"

"No, but I hope you join the program if it's right for you."

There was an edge to Natalie's voice that made Kate uneasy. "Is joining something that you're regretting?"

"I don't know, Kate. It's much different than I thought it would be. Andrew and I are fighting a lot and one of our guides today said that if he can't get on board then maybe I should consider divorce." Natalie sniffed back tears. "We didn't have problems like this back home. We hardly ever argued. I don't want to get divorced."

"Then don't get divorced." Kate wasn't sure what to say. "Natalie, don't let other people make big life decisions for you. Meeting your goals is one thing, but your marriage is something else. If Andrew loves you and is supportive of you outside of being in this program, it might be good for both of you to step back and reevaluate what's important here."

"I know, Kate." She sighed. "I've never felt so conflicted in my life. We gave up everything to come here. I don't even know what we'd have to go home to."

"How does Andrew feel about that?"

"He said we can make a new home anywhere."

"He's right." Declan stared at Kate as she tried to give Natalie more advice. She didn't know if anything she said was getting through to the woman, but at the end of the call, Kate offered, "How about we meet for lunch tomorrow and talk? It's always good to have a friend for support."

"I'd like that. I tried talking to Molly, but she is enjoying the program. Frank is all in so they aren't much help to me."

They made a plan for tomorrow and then ended the call. Kate dropped her phone back in her lap and explained about Natalie. Declan said all of the right things and offered the same kind of advice that Kate had given. In the end, only Natalie could make the decision.

"We have bigger fish to fry than that." Kate pushed herself up from the chair and went over to sit next to Declan on the couch. "Tonight, we are going to be given a questionnaire about our relationship and we need to be on the same page."

Declan shrugged as if he had been expecting it. "I don't think there's anything we can't fudge our way through."

Kate didn't think it was going to be that easy. "I hope so because if we are separated and have to answer the questions on our own, there's no way our answers will match."

"What do we need to know about each other that we don't already?"

"It's not about knowing each other. It's about knowing our marriage. How do we fight? What's our communication style? How often do we have sex?" Kate could feel her heart start to race.

Declan waved her off. "Easy. You're bossy and I'm a pushover. You win every argument and we have sex five times a week."

"Five?" Kate asked her brow furrowing.

Declan shrugged. "More? I'm in my late thirties, Kate. I don't know that I have that much stamina left."

"I was thinking less," she said, knowing that they were doomed.

Declan put his arm around her and squeezed her shoulder. "We got this, wife. Piece of cake."

Kate sighed, his reassurance not doing anything to lower the stress bubbling up inside her.

CHAPTER 13

At six o'clock that evening, Kate and Declan sat in the last of five rows of folding chairs that had been set up in a small auditorium-like space on the first floor of Jack Harlow's home. The room was on the opposite side of the home to where Kate had been before and overlooked the lake. When they arrived, they had been handed a letter-size manila envelope that was weighed down with materials and they were instructed not to open it yet.

Kate and Declan chose chairs where they could see the entire room and on the far end of the row for easy escape. Old habits die hard. Kate watched as single men and women and couples filed into the room and took their seats. All had the same deer-in-headlights look.

At six o'clock on the dot, two women and one man entered from a door in the back of the room, walked down the aisle between the chairs, and took their place at the front of the room in front of a dry erase board and large Post-It easel pads. The man, who was in his forties, had dark hair, a muscular build, and striking blue eyes. He toyed with a marker and watched the crowd of people as they quieted.

"Welcome, everyone. My name is Ethan and this is Monica and Sadie. You can refer to us as guides as we help you navigate and understand the magnificent Jack Harlow's personal development program. Trust me when I say that nothing will ever be the same for you after tonight."

Ethan proceeded to give a ten-minute overview of his background, which included a master's degree in psychology and years working in the field at psychiatric hospitals. He claimed that he grew disillusioned with the field and wanted to seek out more alternative therapies for people and that's when he found Jack. Together, they had been working for the last ten years on transforming people's lives.

Kate couldn't help but notice that the man looked like he could bench press a bus and didn't look like any therapist she'd ever seen. "Jack's muscle," she wanted to whisper to Declan, but she didn't dare speak and draw attention to them. She gently elbowed Declan in the side and when he looked down at her, they exchanged the message with a look. He had been thinking the same thing.

Ethan then went on to introduce Monica and Sadie. Each woman said only a few words and then stepped back to allow Ethan to resume the talk. "Let's start with the basics. Please open your packets and take out the first paper in the front."

Kate unlatched the small metal clip and opened the envelope. She reached in and tugged out a sheet of paper. She and Declan both drew back in surprise when they read the words at the top. It was a non-disclosure agreement specifying a five-million-dollar forfeiture if they disclosed anything they learned in the program or during their time working with Jack Harlow. It forbade them from even acknowledging they knew Jack or were in his program. It covered nearly every aspect of interaction they could have, including anything they learned about other members, the guides, or anyone they met as a result of being in the program if they were accepted.

One man sitting in the second row raised his hand. When he was called on, he said, "I don't think I should sign anything without running it by my lawyer."

Ethan went over to him and held out his hand. "Your packet please." The man handed it over with confusion on his face. Ethan stepped aside. "Monica will walk you out. You've officially been released from the program."

"But, I…" The man didn't get much else out of his mouth. Monica came over and put her hand on the man's back and nudged him toward the door. As he started to argue, Ethan moved to him, whispered something in the man's ear that shut him up quickly.

When he was gone, Ethan returned to the front of the room. "Now, let's get back down to business. Please read and sign and Sadie will be around to check your identification and collect them. If you choose not to sign them, please follow Monica out. You will never be admitted back into the program though. You will forever forfeit your spot."

Non-disclosure agreements had a time and place. Kate didn't disagree with them in theory. She had to sign several documents and pass several background checks to receive her security clearance. Non-disclosure agreements though had been used to cover up sexual harassment, sexual assault, and other high-profile crimes with some of the world's richest and most powerful. They often paid off their victims and had them sign non-disclosure agreements – stopping them from even talking about the agreement, payout, or the reason for one.

Kate didn't like this one bit, but now understood Natalie's hesitancy in sharing any information with her. There were serious legal and financial ramifications. Kate looked up at Declan. "Are we signing?"

"I don't think we have a choice if we want to stay."

Kate wasn't a lawyer and she wasn't sure the legality of signing with their fake names, but it turned her stomach at the mere thought of participating with such nonsense. She pulled a pen out of the packet and then signed her name and handed it over to Declan. He did the same, and then when it was time, they both pulled out fake driver's licenses and showed them to Sadie.

Kate watched as each person reluctantly took the same action. No one in the room appeared comfortable with the decision and a tense vibe had fallen over them. The only ones that didn't seem to notice were Ethan and Sadie. Monica appeared at the doorway a moment later but there was no one else for her to escort out.

Ethan clapped his hands drawing everyone's attention to him. "I'm glad you all decided to stay. Let's press on. You will find the next document in the packet. It's a health waiver. We ask all our program members to have a full physical and blood work and then allow Jack access to the information. Please sign that now." He looked around the room at the confused, unsure faces and then clapped his hands loudly. "These are non-negotiable. If you want to be in the program, it's a requirement. Right now, this is your chance. You either care about reaching your life goals or you can walk away from here the losers you are right now."

Kate shifted her eyes to Declan. "Losers? Is he a schoolyard bully?"

Declan held back a snicker as Ethan directed his attention at them. Kate lowered her head and handed Declan one of the health waivers. He skimmed over it and signed it. Kate knew it was part of the deal so she followed suit, choking down her discomfort.

Sadie then walked around the room and collected the documents from everyone. Three people refused and then were escorted out of the room. A meeting of thirty had now dwindled to twenty-six. People had started to get nervous about what was next. They chatted with the people next to them and a few of the singles looked around nervously.

Ethan stood in the front of the room again. "Now that we have thinned the herd of the weak, let's get started. First and foremost, you will only address Jack Harlow with the honorable title he deserves. Henceforth he is known to you only as Luminary. We are only to be referred to as Guide and then our first names. You all are neophytes, but we will call you by your first names as you can with your classmates. Anyone who does not do this will get a demerit. Three demerits and you'll face a punishment of Jack's choosing. Understood?" Everyone either nodded slowly or gave a verbal okay. Kate and Declan did neither and no one seemed to notice.

Ethan then proceeded to lecture them for the next thirty minutes about the program itself and how goal setting was essential and so was working with the guides to overcome roadblocks to their success. He detailed the five pillars of the program – physical health, emotional health, mental toughness, gender role acceptance, and sexual freedom.

When Ethan spoke about gender role acceptance and how too many women have assumed the male's role in the relationship, Declan reached over and took Kate's hand and looped his fingers through hers. She assumed he did so as a reminder that she couldn't tell anyone off. Kate had gone from uncertainty about the program to anger in seconds flat.

Declan ducked his head low and whispered in her ear. "I'm more interested in sexual freedom than any of those others. Do you think there will be an orgy? Maybe one of those 1970s key parties where we dump them all in a bowl and trade spouses for the night. I'm hoping for that redhead in the second row."

Kate had to bite her lip to keep from laughing. Declan nipped her ear gently with his teeth before straightening himself and pretending he hadn't said anything at all.

Ethan finished off his overview and then asked that people separate by singles and couples. He told the couples to exit the room and follow Monica and Sadie. Kate and Declan stood and filed out of the room with other couples. Four were taken to one room with Sadie and Kate and Declan and two other couples were taken to another with Monica. Kate couldn't help but notice that the two other women looked strong and confident like her. All of them walked with their heads held high, were dressed professionally, and their body language indicated that none of them took a backseat in their relationships.

Monica brought them into a room with comfortable couches and chairs. Declan and Kate chose a two-seater love seat in the far corner of the room. Monica shut the door and then turned to them. "I'm sure you're wondering why we separated all of you. We study all of our potential members before invites for the seminar are disseminated. You are separated based on particular issues the guides and Luminary determined that you're facing as roadblocks to your success. Please get comfortable. There is a questionnaire I need you all to complete."

Kate and Declan chatted quietly with each other until Monica brought them the document. She extended the clipboard to Declan. "You know Luminary thinks you're the most interesting couple he has ever observed. You're both alphas. With these other couples, the women are in charge. With you two, even Luminary couldn't figure out who is in control."

Declan looked up at her. "That's because our relationship isn't based on control. It's a loving partnership of two equals."

Monica broke into a wide grin. "If you believe that you're kidding yourself. Someone is always dominant and someone is always submissive. It's how the world works. I don't think you're interesting at all. To me, you're two people who are kidding themselves and living all on the surface. I think once we crack you open, you'll be as pathetic as the rest of them. And don't ever speak back to me again."

Everyone in the room had turned to look at Monica. While a few of the people showed uncertainty on their faces, no one got up and left.

Kate, for once, didn't respond to the woman who was projecting her own relationship issues onto them. She began to wonder if that was how the whole program was structured – Jack's warped projection on self-esteem, goal attainment, and relationships.

Monica looked down at Kate. "Seems you're learning already to keep your mouth shut like a good woman."

Kate sucked in a sharp breath.

Declan's hand gripped her thigh. Then he stood to his full height and towered over the woman. "Don't you dare speak to my wife that way."

Monica stood back and clapped and then turned to the room. "Now this is a couple who might make it in this program after all."

Kate reached up and tugged on the back of Declan's pants for him to sit back down. "Not worth it."

He reached behind himself and grabbed her hand while he sat. "Are you okay?"

"I'm fine," she whispered. "I think I figured out their racket."

Declan's head snapped to the side and locked eyes with Kate. "Already?"

She nodded. "I'll tell you later. Let's get to this questionnaire." Kate took the clipboard and scanned over the first page which all seemed harmless enough. It was when she got to the second page and read through the intimate questions that she swallowed hard.

CHAPTER 14

Kate filled out the first page with basic information about their relationship. How they met. How long they were dating before marriage. Their wedding date and so forth. It was all fairly routine. Towards the bottom of the page, the questions became a little more challenging. They had to list qualities they liked about each other. It wasn't difficult for Kate. She easily jotted down what she loved most about Declan – his kindness, patience, intelligence, humor, ability to admit when he's wrong and be open to others' opinions, and ability to never waver in his support of her.

When Kate finished, she turned to him. Her eyes were wide and questioning. "I'm not sure what you love most about me?"

"You don't know?" Declan asked curiously and when Kate shook her head, he took the clipboard from her. He focused on the page and wrote several things and then handed it back to her with a beaming smile. "Now you know – and none of those are made up. I'm surprised you don't know."

Kate was almost afraid to look down, but when she did, she couldn't help but feel overwhelmed with emotion. She teared up a little and then had to wipe her eye with the back of her hand before anyone noticed. Declan wrote: *Kate is the person I trust most in the world. She is beautiful, smart, kind and she can kick butt when she needs to. A perfect combination of beauty and strength. There is no one I'd rather have in my corner than her and I can't imagine my life without her.*

Kate looked up at him and rested her head against his arm. "I wasn't so eloquent but back at you."

Declan looped his arm around her shoulder. "I know how you feel. What's next?"

Kate lowered her head to the page and had reached the point of the questionnaire she had been dreading. "Now, it's all the questions I can't believe they are asking. Do we have to answer these?"

The words had barely left her mouth when a woman across the room threw the clipboard down on the ground and stood, grabbing her purse and her husband's hand as she got to her feet. "We are leaving. I'm not answering these vile and filthy questions that have nothing to do with self-improvement and achieving goals in life."

Monica calmly walked over to the couple and stood in front of them. "We figured you'd fail. You don't have what it takes to achieve anything in life. Be on your way."

The woman pulled back. "Are you kidding me? I was top of my class in law school. I've built a successful business. I have a loving and happy family."

Monica stepped closer to them. "Yet you aren't happy. You're here seeking freedom from yourself." She turned to the woman's husband. "What about you? Are you happy to be standing in your wife's shadow or are you going to be a man and tell her what you want?"

The man cleared his throat and looked across the room to Declan. When Declan gave the man a slight nod of his head, he focused his attention on Monica and said with conviction, "I agree with my wife. These questions aren't appropriate." He held his wife's hand as they stepped past Monica and left the room without looking back.

As Monica turned around with a scowl on her face, they all dropped their heads back to their papers and got back to work, except for Kate. She locked eyes with the woman defiantly and didn't look away until

Monica broke eye contact first. Kate knew it was a small victory but still a win.

She took a deep breath and tapped on the page. "Okay, let's get this over with. How often do we have sex?"

"Not nearly enough," Declan joked and then Kate handed him the clipboard and watched as his eyes grew wide. "I'm with that guy, let's get out of here."

"We can't. Come on, Declan, let's just make up some stuff and sound like the most boring couple on the planet." That's what they did – they made up answers about how often they had sex, their favorite sexual positions, the birth control they used, what kind of sex they engaged in and how frequently, how old they were when they lost their virginities, and a host of other thoroughly inappropriate questions no one should ask a couple. For their most unfulfilled fantasies, Kate wrote having sex on a boat and Declan wrote having sex on the beach.

He pointed to the answers. "I've technically done that but not with you. We don't need to tell them that though. If they thought they were getting some good answers from us, they are going to be bored."

Kate didn't care what they had written as long as they were done. The last page was all about things they argued over and their fighting style, which were fairly easy answers. The only one that stumped her, she had to ask him. "What do we fight about most as a couple?"

That one even stumped Declan. He sat there for several moments pondering the answer. The only one they could come up with was that they fought over how much the other worked. It was the only thing that seemed plausible to them both. When they were done, they sat there until Monica came over to collect the questionnaire, and then she went to the other couple and collected theirs.

Kate wondered how many others had left at that point. She relaxed back on the couch and checked her watch. They had been there nearly ninety minutes. "I'm getting hungry," she said as her stomach growled.

"We should have had a snack before we left."

Monica said a few words to the other couple and then they got up and left the room. It was just Kate and Declan sitting in the back. She flipped through their questionnaire and made her way over to them. She thrust the clipboard back at Kate. "We don't like liars here. Answer the questions on page two honestly."

Kate raised her eyes. "We did."

"No, there's no way any of that is true." She stood with one hand extended and the other on her hip. Kate refused to take the questionnaire from her. "We expect people to go deep to do the work here and explore with each other. This is surface information."

Declan squinted. "Sorry, our sex life is boring. It's probably not going to get you off, but porn is free on the internet."

"I don't think you're right for this program. I'm going to recommend that you not be allowed to join."

That wouldn't bode well for the investigation, but Kate didn't know what else they could offer. "I'm not sure what you were expecting, but we are who we are. We aren't that interesting a couple."

Monica shook her head. "It's not just that. You argue about how much you both work. That's it and your communication style is talking it out. No one is that good." She clicked her tongue and looked down her nose at them. "Maybe the problem is you both lack passion. It's possible the love has died and neither one of you can admit it." She turned on her heels and walked out the door, leaving them alone in the room.

Kate assumed there were cameras everywhere and that they were being watched. "She doesn't like us that's for sure. I don't have the energy to try to win her over."

"I don't think we'd impress her even if we tried." Declan leaned into Kate and moved closer to her like he was going to kiss her. He nuzzled her cheek with his and then nibbled at her ear. He whispered,

"This is all a bunch of head games. They want a reaction. That's what they are doing, seeing how we react to criticism. They are weeding out the weak. Play along and we'll be out of here soon enough. No matter what they throw at us, don't react."

Kate knew that Declan was right. She ran her hand against his thigh pretending to enjoy the spontaneous affection. They broke apart a moment later when Monica strutted into the room with a young blonde woman in her twenties. "Kate, it's time to go. Luminary has requested your presence."

"Alone?" Kate stood and turned to look at Declan.

"Alone. Down the hall to the left. Go now." Monica escorted the young woman over to Declan and with Kate in earshot, said, "This is Bridgit. She's here to keep you company while Kate is in the other room. Feel free to do with her what you like."

Kate reached the doorway and turned back as Declan remained sitting with an uncertain look on his face. His posture had become rigid and he had balled his hands into fists, a telltale sign of his discomfort with the situation. There wasn't anything she could do right now other than leave him with the two women and go meet Jack.

Kate navigated down a long hallway and stopped short when Jack stepped out of one of the doorways. He stood perfectly still with his hands folded in front of his body. "Monica, sorry, I mean Guide Monica, said you wanted to speak to me."

Jack gestured for her to enter the room and then he went in behind her and closed the door. "You're a complex woman, Kate."

Kate turned around to face him, unsure of the best response. "I'm not sure what you mean."

Jack smiled. "I'm sure you know what I mean, and that's exactly what I'm talking about. You're dumbing yourself down. You are an outspoken woman and certainly strong. I already told you that you're lacking in femininity so I won't cover that again. You demure to Declan though at times, unsure of yourself. It's an appealing quality."

The last thing Kate wanted was to be attractive to Jack Harlow. "My husband and I are partners, equals. Guide Monica didn't seem to like that answer. Let's be honest, she didn't like any of our answers."

"Direct, Kate. Confronting the elephant in the room. I like that." Jack walked across the room and took a seat in the comfortable oversized chair. "Please, sit and we can talk more."

Kate tentatively stepped toward a sofa and eased herself into it, not taking her eyes off Jack. "I find being direct is a good communication tool. Less misunderstanding that way."

"Why are you here, Kate? You seem resistant to the program already."

Kate crossed her legs. "I wouldn't say resistant. I'm finding my footing. There were several personal questions I wasn't comfortable answering and the health questionnaire and non-disclosure agreement seem excessive." Kate held up her hand before he spoke. "Excessive to me walking in the room not knowing much about the program. Remember, I was just here for a job, not to join. I thought I was coming here to learn about the program not already be immersed in it."

A slow smile spread across Jack's face. "You never answered my question, Kate. You defended yourself. Answer the question like a good girl."

Kate cleared her throat and counted to ten in her head. She imagined herself leaping across the room and punching him in the face. When she was done counting to ten, she started over and counted to twenty and then gave the answer she had practiced earlier. "I'm an only child, have a handful of friends, but I find it challenging to connect to people. I like to keep my circle small but would like to meet new people. I was also looking to explore some goal setting for my photography."

"You know what I see, Kate?"

"What?" She didn't want to know.

"I see a mentally tough woman. I'll concede that you're probably one of the most mentally tough people I've ever had in this program. You're intelligent, too. More than an artist. You're physically fit, although as I said, you need to lose some muscle. What you lack – is a willingness to settle into your gender role, tap into your full range of emotion, and explore sexually." Jack gestured with his hand. "You're all bottled up. You seem afraid to let yourself feel and explore."

Kate didn't say anything because she had nothing to say. Jack had hit home and she couldn't defend herself from the truth. After a moment of her not speaking, Jack stood and gestured for her to follow him to a television mounted to the far wall.

As they approached, he clicked it on and a scene happening in the other room came to life. Declan sat rigid on the couch as Brigid had her hands all over him. He took her hands and moved them out of his lap. When she launched herself on him, he stood, brushing her off again.

"I'm not cheating on my wife," Declan said as he headed toward the door.

Kate swallowed hard not understanding quite what was happening. "Why are you showing me this?"

Jack turned to her. "I figured he'd cheat when he had the chance. But look, he's faithful for now. It's not always going to be like that, Kate, if you remain as you are."

Kate didn't respond and turned to leave, but Jack's icy fingers roamed across her back and up to her neck under her hair. She stiffened against his touch.

Jack caressed the soft skin under her hairline and dipped his head to speak low into her ear, his breath hot against her face. "Don't ever cross me or question my methods again. You told another member to leave my program and I won't stand for that. You're lucky you're even here tonight. I will destroy you if I have to. Never forget that."

Kate didn't respond and refused to show any fear, but her blood ran cold. She relaxed her posture and stepped away from him and headed for the door. She turned back to him and offered only one warning. "That may be true, but you'll be destroying yourself in the process."

She left Jack standing there half-smirking, but there was fear in his eyes. Kate was sure of that.

CHAPTER 15

Once out on the street and far away from Jack's house, Kate finally exhaled. It came out in a loud groan. "There is no way we can go through with this program. I'm not sure what Spade is expecting from us, but that was seriously one of the strangest things I've ever been a part of."

Declan shared in her misery. "Being undercover in the mob, faced with daily death was easier than that last two hours. At least, we got the names of people running the program."

Because everyone left at different times, Kate had no idea how many were joining the program officially from their seminar. After leaving the room with Jack, Kate had met Declan in the hallway and they raced toward the door, both not wanting to spend another second there.

What Jack had said at the end ate at her. "I got Natalie in trouble. I don't know how Jack knew. I don't think she would have told him we spoke. I wonder if he bugged her phone."

"It's possible. We are going to have to sweep the place when we get back." Declan pointed to her pocket. "You're going to need to check that phone, too. Claire had it when you first met Jack."

"I checked it after the meeting. It was the first thing I thought of." The more Kate came to know Jack Harlow, the less she trusted him. She didn't understand how anyone could miss the early warning signs. The red flags were everywhere. He did little to hide them. She expressed as much to Declan.

"He's a good-looking guy, Kate. Look at how many people never believed Ted Bundy did what he did. Even after all these years and his confession, women think he was framed. The evil man is never the hot guy – only he is and it's the easiest cover in the world."

"That's exactly it, but I don't find Jack Harlow attractive at all. I can understand why women would. Ethan, Sadie, and Monica were attractive. It presents an image that their members probably want to attain, but also that Jack wants his members to reach. It's not realistic though." Kate didn't want to put Declan on the spot, but she hadn't asked about anything that happened while he was alone with Bridgit and Monica. She turned her head and looked up at him and bit the inside of her lip.

Declan glanced down at her. "You're wondering if Bridgit succeeded in seducing me?"

Kate shook her head. "I know she didn't. Jack has surveillance cameras in the room and brought it up on screen while I was in there with him. I watched you push her away."

Declan cursed and pounded one fist into his palm. "That man is sick. Can you imagine if we were a real couple and in love what that could do to us?"

Kate could because if she admitted it to herself, she had a spark of jealousy that bubbled up out of nowhere when she saw Bridgit trying to grope him. "Jack assumed you'd cheat on me because I'm not passionate enough or he thinks I'm boring in bed. He thinks I'm an emotionless robot."

Declan reached for her hand. "You know I'm not a cheater, Kate. Even in a fake marriage, I like commitment." He shrugged. "Bridgit isn't my type anyway. But I want to know what the heck that was about. I know it was a test, but I'm fairly certain had I been into it she would have had sex with me right there in front of Monica. That's sick, Kate. It wasn't even like she was a person, just a sex object. She took her orders from Monica and didn't do anything without express direction from her."

"That's creepy. Did Bridgit say anything?"

"Yeah," Declan said with disgust in his voice. "She asked what she could do for me. Then she tried to kiss me. When I backed away, she wanted to know my fantasies."

Kate cringed. "What did you tell her?"

Declan chuckled. "I told her the only unfulfilled fantasy I had was playing shortstop for the Red Sox. I asked her if she could make that possible."

Despite herself, Kate laughed aloud. "I'm sure that didn't go over too well."

"Neither of them knew what to do with me. We frustrated Monica more than anything. She's one creepy lady." Declan stopped about a block from the house and turned to her. "What are we going to do, Kate? We aren't going to be able to do this from the inside. It's going to take months before we can gain anyone's trust."

"I know." Kate sighed. It didn't go quite as planned and she was out of ideas for the night. The meeting had drained her of every last ounce of energy she had. "I say we give it one more meeting and then go from there. We can't quit before we get into it. Although, I'm surprised they are even asking us back."

"It's what Monica said – you're a fascination to Jack. She said it again after you left the room. She asked me how I could stand living with you." Declan paused not sure he should say more, but Kate reminded him that they couldn't have secrets. "She called you a cold shrew. I don't feel that way, Kate. The reality is we both have to shut down our emotions to do this job. I'm not an emotional guy."

"Yes, you are. I was there when you cried with joy when the Red

Sox finally won the World Series. You're far more emotional than you let on. I'm…" Kate didn't finish her thought because she didn't know what she was and it was starting to bother her in a way it hadn't before.

"You're amazing and don't question it so much. Besides, I cried more over that World Series than I did with my divorce. What does that tell you about me?"

"That you were married to the wrong person." Kate looped her arm through Declan's and they continued down the sidewalk to their house. "We are both a little screwed up," she said as he slipped the key into the lock and opened the door for her.

As soon as they stepped inside, the ringing phone sounded shrill in contrast to the quiet house. Declan ran down the hallway to the office. It was the secure line that had been set up for them. There was no voicemail attached to that line so it would ring until it was answered or the person calling gave up. Declan answered, told the caller he'd need to call them back, and then hung up.

Declan stepped out of the room to sweep for bugs. The office had a keypad entrance so even if someone had entered and planted a bug, they wouldn't have been able to get to the office. Kate went to the kitchen and got a drink of water while Declan swept the house for planted surveillance equipment.

"All clear," he called out from the office. "I'm calling Spade back now."

"I want an update," Spade demanded instead of hello, his husky voice booming through the phone. "Why didn't you call me sooner?"

Kate walked into the office, dreading the conversation, and pulled up a chair. "We are just getting home. The meeting was longer than I assumed it would be." She and Declan proceeded to update him about every aspect of the meeting including having to sign a non-disclosure agreement and the health checks that would be upcoming. Spade cursed at every turn.

"I'm going to need to check with legal," he said finally when they were done. "Those agreements won't hold up in court. You signed with fake names under the guise of investigation. I wouldn't worry about it. The issue I have is what Kate said – that you're not going to get access to people this way. That throws a wrench in our plans."

"It was just the first meeting, Spade. I don't know what comes next." Kate felt like she was walking back what she said earlier. "It might behoove us to attend one more session and get to know some people better. Tonight was supposed to have been an information session. I'm not even sure we've officially been invited into the program."

"All right," Spade said, relenting. "Go to the next thing whatever it may be if you're invited. Otherwise, bail on being in the program and start developing some outside assets."

Declan had a look on his face like he was on the brink of a good idea. He sat back and stared at the ceiling as he spoke. "I need to flesh this out more, but go with me for now. What if we wait to see if we are invited and attend the first session and then cause a scene and bail on the whole program? Something big that gets people's attention. Something that will have everyone talking. Then we sit back and see what happens. After that, we can stir up some drama in the community, and hopefully, some of those in his program might start to crack and when they do, here we are to support them. It might be people on the fence start talking. Of course, the people who believe in Jack and all that nonsense will dig in, but others might see it as their way out, especially with us right in the community. Then if other community members see us standing up to Jack, they might be more willing to do that, too. We will probably get sued though."

"I'll handle that," Spade reassured. "I like it. It's got some teeth, but you'll need to flesh it out as you said. It would have to be spectacular." Spade asked them to hold and then the sound of drawers opening and closing came through the phone. "If we are going in this direction, I want you to have a sit down with Det. Jerry Miller. Bob is great, don't get me wrong, but I want you two at the source of the information. Right now, there is no greater expert on Jack Harlow than Det. Miller."

Kate couldn't wait to interview the man. She was all in but the timing was important. She leaned toward the speaker. "Spade, we have to wait to see if we get formally invited into the program. We can't risk talking to a local cop and cutting our feet from under us right now."

"True, true. Do what you have to do and let me know if you get in and the plan. In the meantime, start background research on Jack's employees and see what you can find. Then attend the first lecture or whatever they are called and wreak some havoc. I'm sure you two must be bored as anything sitting around pretending that you're a married couple." Spade grew quiet for a moment and then his voice grew louder on the phone. "I probably should have said this before I sent you in there. I hope you two know better than to do something stupid and mess up your partnership. The FBI relies on you too much." With that, he loudly hung up on them.

Declan bobbed his eyebrows up and down. "I shouldn't have my way with you then."

Kate stretched in the chair and then yawned. "I might let you have your way with me if it will prove to myself that I'm capable of some passion."

"You don't mean that, Katie."

"I don't know what I mean anymore." Kate rose from the chair.

Declan's face contorted and the winkled crease across his forehead made an appearance. He stared at her in disbelief. "I honestly don't know what to say to you right now. You're taking all of this with Jack way too seriously."

Kate slowly nodded. "Jack is getting to me, but it's only because he is picking at things that I already don't like about myself. He's right I need to loosen up."

Declan stood and came around the desk. "Remember that you're a criminologist and an FBI agent, not a married photographer who has a boring sex life with her husband. It scares me when you talk about getting loose. I can't even picture what that would be like."

Kate rolled her eyes. "That's the problem. I never let loose even in college. When I was at Harvard, I was focused on graduating and then going to grad school and joining the FBI. It's always been the next step for me. I'm not sure I ever stop and enjoy the moment I'm in."

Declan checked his watch. It was nearing eight-thirty and they still hadn't had dinner. He held out his hand to her. "You trust me?"

Kate took his hand without giving it another thought. If he guided her upstairs to the bedroom, she didn't think she'd resist. "What do you have in mind?"

Declan guided her toward the staircase. "I could hear your stomach growling during the call with Spade. Go put on something comfortable and meet me in the backyard."

"The backyard?"

Declan nodded and smirked, allowing Kate's imagination to run away with her. Then he laughed. "I'm going to heat leftover pasta and open a nice bottle of wine and then we are going out back and relax. Who knows, I might even convince you to skinny dip with me under the moonlight."

Kate leaned into him and wrapped her arms around his waist. "Sounds like the perfect night."

CHAPTER 16

By mid-morning the next day, Kate and Declan had already gone through all of the murdered victims' files one more time. Spade had placed a call to the medical examiner's office to ask questions for Kate and Declan. The answers provided a clearer picture than they had received from Bob – through no fault of his own.

Kate appreciated the agent's efforts on their behalf but there was nothing like going to the source for information. Spade was about as close of an extension of them as they were going to get. Kate trusted him to ask the questions in the way she'd ask and dig deeper at the right times.

Kate's biggest area of interest was still the psilocybin tea the first couple ingested before the murder. Given there was no force, Kate could only assume the couple had made the conscious decision to ingest the drug.

Declan tossed a case file on the coffee table and looked over at Kate who was stretched out on the chaise. She had a thin blanket covering her legs, a bed pillow supporting her back, and a stack of case files around her. She had been that way since they left the office after the call with Spade.

Declan had made her favorite tea and she couldn't imagine a more comfortable place to work.

"You're stuck on the first case," Declan said, a statement not a question. "I'm stuck on it, too. None of the other couples were eating, and none of the other couples had ingested a hallucinogenic. It doesn't add up for me, but at the same time, I'm sure the cases are connected."

"The last five there is a clear pattern. It's evening time, the couples are relaxed, and then the killer strikes. That first one, there are too many variables."

Declan repositioned himself on the couch and reached for a case file. He flipped it open to the crime scene photos of the first victims. "Even the scene is different."

"What do you see that I didn't?"

Declan walked over to her and pulled a pile of files from her lap and set them on the floor. He inched into the chaise with her and then pointed to the photo. "They are in the middle of dinner. See, their chairs are moved back. They got up before they were killed or were in the process of. They hadn't even finished their dinner yet. The teacups are sitting empty, but their dinner isn't touched. The order is all out of whack to me."

Kate thought she understood what he was saying. "Would it make more sense if they had eaten dinner and then had the tea?"

"No, that's not what I'm saying. I'm saying they probably wanted to drink the tea on an empty stomach so it would hit them faster instead of being metabolized with a full stomach. So, they sit there and drink the tea but so much time passes and still no dinner. They are alive for approximately ninety minutes before being murdered – what were they doing sitting at that table if not eating?"

Kate didn't have a response for it.

He continued. "It would even make more sense if the teacups were found someplace else. Like they drank it in the living room and then went about making and eating dinner. The cups on the table and uneaten food tell me they were interrupted. They are sitting at that table with cold food on their plates hallucinating. It doesn't add up."

Kate hadn't thought of any of that. She stared at the elements on the table as Declan pointed them out. Serving bowls of food, full plates, empty teacups, and two dead people. She tried to imagine the scene. When she glanced up at Declan though, his expression told her he had done the math already and had a theory. "What do you think happened?"

"They had a dinner guest," Declan said, letting the revelation hang in the air.

It took Kate a moment for her to catch up with his rationale, but when she got there, it struck her like a lightning bolt. "Do you think the dinner guest drugged them or that they all took the psilocybin together?"

"I don't think they were drugged without them knowing. There are easier drugs to use to knock someone out and kill them. I don't think the killer took the drug with them though. I believe it was like what Charles Manson did to his followers."

Kate raised her eyes to him. "You think the killer suggested they all trip together but never took the drug themselves. He was trying to influence them somehow?"

Declan pointed to the serving dishes on the table. "How many couples do you know that go to the trouble to put food in serving dishes just for themselves?"

"Probably very few." Kate thought back to dinners she had with guests. Rarely did she use serving dishes unless there were a few of them at the table. They made plates in the kitchen and carried them into the dining room. There was little reason for such formality and no reason to dirty that many extra dishes. "They had a guest for dinner and then what? Why not eat?"

"Conversation, Kate. There was a distraction that kept them from eating."

"What about a third place setting?" Kate studied the table and only saw two – the ones in front of the couple.

"The killer cleaned up after themselves." Declan got up and went across the room to the coffee table and pulled another file related to that case. He flipped it open and dug through it until he found the crime scene report. "There were traces of the victims' blood in the bathtub and on the bathroom floor that are unexplained. The medical examiner noted that the victims had lost too much blood where they were stabbed to make it to the bathroom. They died where they were attacked."

"The killer took his time and cleaned up after himself," Kate said as she thought through the situation. "That meant whoever killed them had to have been comfortable in their house and confident that no one was going to interrupt them."

"It changes everything for me, Kate. This isn't someone who came in and killed them quickly." Declan sat back down on the couch and leaned back. "This crime scene is also more frenzied than the others. The man was stabbed in the back first and then the chest. Do you feel like there could be anything symbolic in that?"

Kate raised her eyebrows. "You mean literally being stabbed in the back?" Declan nodded and she thought about what it could mean. "I assumed the killer stabbed him in the back as the first strike to get him out of the chair already incapacitated. Your theory makes a good deal of sense so it's possible the killer came up behind him and stabbed him in the back as an act of retaliation and then stabbed him in the chest to end his life. If the killer was in the home with them for some time before the murder, there are several ways it could have gone down."

"Let's explore that then for the sake of argument. Do you think the killer meant to kill them?"

Kate pointed to the crime scene report Declan had next to him on the couch. "We know the murder weapon was a knife. Was it a knife from the home? Did they ever find it?"

Declan grabbed the case file and read it over. "Yes, it was an eight-inch chef's knife from the butcher block in the kitchen. They tested every knife for blood and residue was found."

Kate tried to picture the scene in her head, but she didn't know where the kitchen was situated in relation to the dining room table. She asked Declan to read her the details.

"Ron was sitting at the dining room table with his back to the kitchen. I assume then, the killer got up from the table and went into the kitchen, and then came back with the knife. He goes up behind Ron and stabs him once in the upper back near the left shoulder blade. Ron is sitting when that happens clearly from the angle of the knife attack. Then Ron gets up and as he turns, he's stabbed in the chest and drops on the spot right near the chair. The killer pulls the knife back out and advances on the wife, who is killed from a standing position and then drops to the floor. Nancy is five-foot-four and the knife had a somewhat downward trajectory so the killer was taller than that but not over six foot is what the report says. They both bleed out on the spot."

Kate recalled the responses from the medical examiner. "We know that Nancy didn't die instantly. She suffered on the floor bleeding out for at least a few minutes. She was too injured to move, so the killer either stood over her and watched her die or went about cleaning up the place."

Declan sighed loudly. "I think this was the killer's first kill and they learned how messy and complicated their method was so they changed it up."

Kate was starting to believe that was true. "You asked Bob a question that has me curious."

"What was that?"

"You asked if Jack's followers were devout enough to kill for him."

"Right. That happens in many of these cult cases. Charles Manson didn't kill the victims that fateful August. He sent his followers to do his dirty work."

"What if that's happened here? All roads lead back to Jack. It's possible he could have killed the first victims and found he didn't have a taste for the dirty work, so the next time he wants revenge or whatever the motive, he sends someone to do it for him."

"It's entirely possible, Kate. I want to talk to Det. Jerry Miller."

A bit of excitement bubbled up for Kate. "I'm sure he'll have a better perspective on this."

"Let's take a walk by the victims' house and see if we can figure out anything from the outside." He flipped to the first page of the report and noted the address. "It's on Jasmine Lane. Why does that sound familiar to me?"

"That's the street that Claire Adler lives on. What's the street address?"

Declan checked the file and then raised his head. "3320. It says here that it's the last house on the left."

"From the street number, it sounds like that might be on the far end away from Claire. At least, we can snoop around a little and she might not see us."

Declan ran upstairs to the bedroom to get his wallet and phone while Kate cleaned up the living room and pulled the files back together. She carried one stack to the office and then when Declan came back to the living room, he carried another. They stacked them neatly back in their respective boxes and then closed and locked the office door.

Kate grabbed the keys from the table near the front door and then they walked the few blocks to Jasmine Lane. They passed by Claire's house and kept walking. Kate turned her head slightly to look at the house as they passed but she didn't see the woman. They kept a pretty good walking pace until they were at the end of the block.

Declan read off the numbers of the homes as they went. They ran out of houses before they reached 3320. The homes stopped at 3318 and next to that sat a vacant lot. The grass had grown over where the house should have been.

Kate looked across the street thinking there might have been something strange with the numbering. She turned back and raised her eyes to Declan. "I don't get it," she said with confusion in her voice. "There's no 3320. Are you sure you read the report correctly?"

"It was typed. Unless it's a misprint, the house is gone." Declan stared down at the curb and then moved toward it bending to touch the cement with his hand. "See here, Kate. You can almost make out the white paint where the numbers were."

Kate bent low and followed where Declan traced the number with his finger. Sure enough, it read 3320.

While they were both bent over looking at the curb, a voice from behind them said, "Jack Harlow had the house demolished three months after the murder."

Kate whipped her head around to see a woman standing there with a small gardening rake with a green handle in her hands. "How do you know that?"

The woman pointed to the house across the street. "My husband and I have lived here since this community opened. Jack bought the house after the murder and then had it torn down. We aren't in his program if that's what you're wondering."

Declan looked up the street and stepped toward the woman. "Will you answer some questions for us?"

The woman stepped back. "Are you involved with Jack?"

"No," Kate said softly, hoping to ease her obvious tension. "We were invited to join the program and have reservations. We are trying to find out as much information as possible." She paused and then bit her lip. "We've heard rumors."

"I'll talk to you but not here on the street."

Kate and Declan followed the woman across the street and into the front door of her house.

CHAPTER 17

Rebecca Woods directed Kate and Declan into the dining room and offered them something to drink. When they declined, Rebecca excused herself to wash her hands and then joined them at the table, drying her hands on a dishtowel, which she tossed on the table.

Taking a seat across from them, Rebecca said, "I don't talk about this often. Well, really ever. My husband would be upset that I'm talking to you about this now, but we are about to put our house on the market and move back east. I figure Jack can't do much to us now, and there's something about you two that I trust."

Kate wished she could ease the woman's fears and tell her that they were FBI. She clasped her hands on the table and leaned forward slightly. She kept her voice even and low. "I know it might seem strange that we'd ask to speak to you like this, but we are new to Mulberry Grove. I heard Jack Harlow needed a photographer and that's what I do so I applied for the job. Instead of a job offer, he invited me to a seminar, which we attended last night."

"It was strange, to say the least," Declan added. "As you can imagine, experiencing it and then hearing all the rumors in the community, we got a bit curious about the murders that have happened. I don't know that it's all connected, but it's an odd thing. We had no idea there were so many murders in this community before we moved.

Had we known, we might have found someplace else to live."

Rebecca smiled back at him. "I can understand that. You're both young and you think you're moving to this amazing community and then find out all of this is going on. It's a lot to take in." She sat upright in the chair. "I can thankfully say that I've not experienced one of Jack's seminars firsthand, but I've certainly heard a great deal about it."

Kate didn't hide her surprise. "You have friends who joined?"

Rebecca nodded her head once. "Nancy wasn't just my neighbor. She was a friend. I know she wasn't supposed to share anything, but she talked to me about the program."

"Last night we had to sign a non-disclosure agreement that we couldn't talk about the program. Even mentioning that to you violates the agreement. Did Nancy come out in the open and talk about it? Maybe it was different back then."

Rebecca smiled as if remembering something. "It was the same. This might seem silly and we might have been overly dramatic about it, but it was a bit like being in a spy movie with her."

Kate narrowed her gaze. "In what way?"

"We never talked here in the community. We'd leave Mulberry Grove separately and then meet at a restaurant about thirty minutes from here," Rebecca admitted, wringing her hands. She leaned into the table and dropped her voice low, barely above a whisper. "If Nancy wanted to talk about the program or share some frustration or concern, she'd send me a sign. She'd bake me cookies and at the bottom of the disposable tin, she'd write the date and time she wanted to meet me. She'd make sure to leave the community a full two hours or more before that meeting so we wouldn't be seen leaving together. She never told Ron she was doing it either. We were careful how others in the community saw us, too. Never too friendly to make it seem like I might be a threat, but chummy enough that it would make sense she'd do a neighborly thing and bake for me."

Kate and Declan shared a look of admiration for Rebecca. Kate didn't know too many people who would have the wherewithal to come up with a plan and execute it like that. "Did anyone ever find out?"

"Not that I know of. It was a real shame, too, when Nancy and Ron were killed. They were in the process of leaving the program."

Declan withdrew his arm from Kate's back and sat up straighter. "Why were they leaving?"

"Something happened to Nancy that she wouldn't tell me. But it shook her to her core." Rebecca grew quiet and dropped her head low. "I never knew the full details so even if I had wanted to tell the police, I couldn't have."

Kate reached her hand across the table and offered it to Rebecca. "Nancy was probably trying to keep you safe."

"I tell myself that, but it feels like I should have been able to do more. She did tell me a few things, but I haven't done anything in the five years since her death." Rebecca raised her eyes to Kate. "I should have called someone. I tried to speak to the detective who was here after Nancy and Ron were murdered. I couldn't get the words out and he wasn't patient enough with me. He was rushed and then dismissive of me."

"It's never too late," Declan interjected, resting his hands on the table. "Rebecca, I might be able to help you. If you tell me what you do know about Nancy's time in Jack's program, I might be able to advise what you can do with the information. I know people and have resources at my disposal." There was context under his words that Kate caught and she hoped Rebecca did as well.

Rebecca sat quietly for a few moments and then she made eye contact with Declan. "Nancy and Ron had been in the program for a few years when we became friendly. She seemed lonely and had lost a good deal of weight. I saw Nancy in the yard one day and she just said hello and we started talking. She trusted me quickly, probably too quickly. Much like the way I am with you now."

Rebecca stood from the table, brushed back the hair from her face, and went into the kitchen. When she was out of earshot, Declan leaned over to Kate. "Luck must be on our side."

"It's not luck. She desperately needs to unburden herself. She's carried this secret for a long time and she's leaving the community. She wants to make sure Nancy's story is told." Kate checked the doorway that led to the kitchen to make sure Rebecca hadn't returned and then turned back to Declan. "We can't tell her we are with the FBI, but I'm okay going as close to the line as possible. This is the information we need."

"I agree." Declan hitched his jaw toward the doorway. "Are you okay, Rebecca?"

She held up a glass of water. "I needed something to drink. If I were being completely honest, I need to pause to steady my nerves and make sure I want to share Nancy's story." She took a sip of water and then set the glass down.

"My brother works for the government. That's not public information and not something we are sharing in the community, as you can imagine." Declan had her full attention. "I can share your information with him and make sure it gets to someone who might be able to help."

Rebecca took a sip of water and then set it back down. When she spoke, her voice was full of conviction. "Nancy told me that all the women in the program are groomed for sex with Jack. Not just Jack either, his top echelon of men – even other members of the group. Nancy told me that's why single women are a part of the program."

Kate thought back to the young woman with Declan. She didn't doubt what Rebecca told them. "Is it just the single women or married women too?"

"Not all the married women – just the ones that Jack was interested in. He explained that it's all part of the process and he's teaching them about intimacy. Their husbands don't seem to have any say in it. I don't know what happened with Nancy but I assume it was something like that." Rebecca picked up her water glass again and it shook in her hand as she brought it to her lips.

Kate had so many questions swirling in her head, she had to slow down not to overwhelm Rebecca. "Were the women willing to have sex with Jack or did Nancy say this was all by force?"

"Both. Nancy believed date rape drugs might have been involved in some instances, but she wasn't sure." Rebecca leveled a look at Kate. "The higher Ron and Nancy rose in the program, the more insider information they accessed and the more they became hesitant to continue."

"Even if Nancy didn't detail her own experience, did she tell you about others?" Declan asked hesitantly. By the look on his face, he knew where this was headed.

Rebecca ran her thumb up and down the condensation. "Nancy told me that one night she was at Jack's house for a training session and it ran late. She was there with a few other women and one of the guides. There was a commotion down the hall and a young woman went running past the doorway. She was partially dressed, makeup smeared down her face, and she was crying. They all rushed to the door but couldn't stop her. When Nancy turned back, that's when she saw Jack and one of the male guides standing at the other end of the hall watching the scene play out."

"Was the young woman running away from Jack?"

"I don't know. Nancy wasn't sure. She felt like that's what she was doing, but she was inside the room when the girl ran past so she didn't know where the girl came from. Jack wasn't shouting after her or chasing her." Rebecca lowered her head and looked at the table and mumbled something.

Kate asked her to repeat what she had said.

Rebecca pushed her chair back and got up from the table and this time went into the living room. She dug through the books on her bookshelf and pulled out a spiral hardcover journal and carried it over to the table. She flipped open to the center of the book and took out an old newspaper clipping. She unfolded it carefully, smoothed out the edges, and then handed it to Kate. "Nancy was sure the same girl who ran out of Jack's house was found murdered in an abandoned building in downtown Los Angeles not even a week later."

Kate lowered her head and read the article while Declan read it over her shoulder. Lucile Schaeffer, twenty, was found on the second floor of an abandoned building in Los Angeles that was frequented by homeless people and drug addicts. She had recent track marks from shooting heroin and had died of an overdose. The medical examiner had ruled the death a homicide because Lucile had no history of drug use, two witnesses saw her fighting with a man, and there were bruises on her wrists like she had been held down.

Kate held up the paper. "You're sure this is the same girl?"

"Nancy was positive. When she read it in the newspaper, she came running over. She didn't even wait until we were out of the community to talk about it."

Kate scanned the newspaper for the date and then pointed it out to Declan. "This is two weeks before Nancy and Ron were murdered."

"I know," Rebecca said and sniffled back her emotion. "I always wondered if it was because she came over here and talked to me about it. She was sure that Jack had something to do with that girl's death. She even called the detective on the case and told him about seeing her at Jack's house."

Declan's eyes grew wide. "What was done about it? Did they come out here and speak to her?"

Rebecca shook her head. "No one ever followed up and then Nancy was dead. I tried to tell the detective who investigated Nancy's death, but he said everything I said was hearsay and he couldn't corroborate any of it. I should have tried harder. He just wouldn't hear anything I had to say."

Kate couldn't explain the detective's actions. She handed the newspaper back to Rebecca but she wouldn't take it.

"You keep it." Rebecca turned to Declan. "Maybe you can share the story. I don't know if there's anything to it or not."

They talked for a few more minutes as Kate asked a handful of questions that Rebecca couldn't answer. When it was time to go, Kate stood from the table and walked with Declan to the door. They both thanked Rebecca for being brave enough to share the information with them. As they stepped outside, Declan turned to her and asked one last question Kate had forgotten to ask herself.

"During the time that you knew Nancy and Ron, had you ever known them to do drugs? Particularly a hallucinogenic?"

Rebecca didn't even need to think about it. "No. Never. She was against drug use. Ron too, at least according to Nancy. I never spoke to him much. He was the quieter of the two. In one of our conversations about our past, going to college and such, Nancy said that she had never even smoked pot. That was also one of the requirements about Jack's program – that they not do drugs, which also makes me wonder if the dead girl had such a heroin habit why Jack would even allow her there."

"That is certainly a good question," Declan said, tension in his voice. He reached out and shook her hand. "Thank you for trusting us. You've given us a lot to consider."

CHAPTER 18

Kate didn't say anything for several minutes after leaving Rebecca's house. She and Declan walked side by side at the same pace back toward their house. As they reached the end of Jasmine Lane, she looked up at him. "I hope we didn't blow our cover by talking to her."

"I don't think it matters. As you said when we were in there, she needed to tell her story." Declan slapped one foot in front of the other, his sneakers pounding into the pavement. It was clear his anger rose with each step. "I want to slam this guy into a wall, Kate. He's been getting away with this for far too long. Now the death of a twenty-year-old girl. It's too much, Kate. We are blocks from him and we can't do anything other than pretend like we want to learn from him. I don't know how I'm ever going to look at him again."

Kate understood his anger and she still believed it was Jack who was responsible for all of this. "I don't want to get sidetracked by this. If Ron and Nancy were the only two who were killed then it might be a slam dunk that's related to the Lucile Schaeffer murder. We need to find out if that was ever solved and see if we can speak to the detective on that case. I need more information to determine if Ron and Nancy are connected to the other murders though."

"It's connected. I feel it in my gut."

"You feel nothing in your gut except hunger." Kate couldn't help but smile.

Declan stopped walking so suddenly Kate bumped into him. He reached out to steady her. "I hate to even say this aloud, but it needs to be said. Do you think Jack is grooming you for sex?"

"What?" Kate heard the words but she hadn't processed what he said. "Me? You think Jack is going to try to have sex with me?"

"Think about it, Kate," Declan's tone implied she wasn't thinking clearly. "Nancy told Rebecca that Jack grooms some of the women for sex, even the married women. That he does it under the guise of some kind of sex therapy. His whole focus with you is about being frigid and having no passion. That's the kind of thing you say to someone to start grooming them."

Kate knew Declan was right. The thought had come to her briefly when Rebecca mentioned that's what Jack did, but it had been so repulsive to her that she shoved it to the side in her mind refusing to even entertain the idea of it. Now that Declan had echoed the same sentiment, a chill ran down her spine. "I'm not having sex with him. I'm never going to be alone with him again."

Declan slid his arm across her shoulders and pulled her tight against his side. "I'm not sharing my fake wife with Jack Harlow or anyone else. We are going to need to keep watch though and make sure you're not alone with him. I do think that's part of the reason he's been singling you out."

"When Rebecca mentioned that young single women are often used for sex, I thought of that girl that tried to seduce you the other night."

"Bridgit. Yeah, I thought of her, too. She was so robotic in her approach to me and she took orders from Monica. I'm sure, by the way she was acting, that she has done the same with others. We need to make sure she isn't being held against her will."

"How are we going to do that? It's not like you can go in there and request to speak to her." Kate wondered if Declan could do that, but that might then put her in a situation of being alone with Jack again.

"I don't know how we are going to do anything at this point, but it's going to have to be done. I know her first name. We just need a last and then I can run a background check on her and find out where she lives."

"I need to check on Natalie, too. Not that I want to get her in trouble again, but she might at least know the woman's name."

Declan ran a hand over his head and looked around them to make sure no neighbors were overhearing their conversation. "We need to check out every property where there has been a murder. I don't like that Jack bought Ron and Nancy's house after the murder and then tore it down. What's he hiding?"

"I thought that was strange. I can't believe the detective didn't question any of this or take Rebecca's concerns seriously. It is hearsay so she wouldn't have been able to testify to it in court, but he could have used it for investigative purposes. We do that all the time."

"So much was left undone that I'm starting to question if it was intentional."

Kate looked up at him again. "Like the detectives are in on it or don't want to go up against Jack?"

"Either. Both. I don't know." Declan shrugged. "There's something though. No seasoned skilled detective is this sloppy. I don't think I've ever encountered such a small community that has so many unsolved murders."

Kate didn't want to be a naysayer but there was a fact he overlooked. "Lucile Schaeffer wasn't killed here though. I know you believe it's her, but we don't have solid facts that she's the woman who went running out of Jack's house."

"Yeah, I know. We don't know what we don't know." Declan and Kate walked the rest of the way in silence. The last thing Kate needed right now was Declan brooding and the pall that had come over him since leaving Rebecca's house indicated they might be in for a long night. Declan got this way sometimes, bogged down with the things he wanted to accomplish and couldn't because of outside forces.

It was Kate's turn to cheer him up. As they unlocked the door to the house, she said, "I'll order pizza for dinner later and pick up your favorite beer."

Declan didn't say anything one way or the other about her plan. He went to the office, unlocked the door, swept the house for bugs, and then went back into the office. He pulled out the desk chair and asked Kate to join him. Together, they called Spade. They updated him with everything they had found and Spade heaped more praise upon them. Before ending the call, he assured them that within an hour or two, he'd call them back with all the details they needed about the murder of Lucile and the subsequent investigation.

When they hung up, Declan leaned back in the chair and rocked it as he stared off into space. Finally, after a few minutes, he realized Kate was still sitting across from him. He locked eyes with her. "I'm going to take a shower and go through the files again."

"I'm going to take another walk and hopefully casually run into Natalie. As I said, I want to check in on her and then see if she knows Bridgit's last name." Kate watched Declan for a moment longer, worrying he'd chase his tail for the rest of the afternoon. "Try to shake yourself out of the mood you're in. We made progress today. It brought up a lot more questions, but it's a win as far as I'm concerned. We are one step closer than we were this morning."

Declan raised his head. "I guess it's your turn to be positive."

"Don't make me come over there and put a smile on your face." Kate winked at him. It was about as flirty as she got with him. It at least elicited a smile.

"Take your gun with you when you're out," Declan called after her. "I don't like that you're going alone, but Natalie probably won't talk to you if I'm there."

Kate waved her hand over her head acknowledging that she had heard him. She made it halfway down the hall when the doorbell rang. She pulled open the front door and came face to face with a young woman with her hair pulled back in a severe ponytail.

"Congratulations," she said, handing Kate a white envelope. "Jack Harlow requests you and your husband be at his place at six tomorrow night for a welcoming ceremony." Without saying another word or waiting for Kate to respond, she turned and left the porch.

Kate closed the door and leaned against it as she opened the envelope. It was the official invitation to join Jack Harlow's program and to attend a welcoming ceremony tomorrow night. It was a small reception for new members who joined within the last month to meet and get to know current members. Kate had been anticipating the invite into the program but not the welcoming reception. She tossed the envelope down on the hall table and yelled the good news to Declan. If he heard her, he didn't respond. Kate would discuss it with him later.

Kate left the house and made a right at the end of the block. She pulled out her phone and plugged in the first address she had written down from the files earlier in the day. Kate was going to check out each of the properties where there had been a murder. She'd just do a cursory walk by without Declan and then report back what she found. There was no point giving him any ammunition to wallow in his funk. If all the properties were gone, she'd break it to him gently.

She turned left on Iris Street and walked to the middle of the block and found the house still standing. She had no idea if the house was the original that had been on the lot at the time of the murder, but it certainly looked old enough. By the SUV parked in the driveway, she assumed new owners were living in the home. Kate kept the same pace as she walked by never slowing down or paying too much attention to the home.

She checked her phone and then walked a mile through the community to the next address and then the next. Once again, the lawn was manicured, the flowers lining the front stood in perfect order and a car in the driveway indicated people living in the home. Kate would have never guessed that the home had been the sight of a murder.

Kate didn't think that she could ever move into a home where such a tragedy had taken place, but some people weren't bothered by such things. She had seen far too much violence in her life. She wanted her home – her safe haven – to be free of it, even residually. At least, she and Declan would have a few scenes to work with if they needed them at some point.

Kate checked the last address on her list and then walked the five blocks to Lilac Lane. The house sat at the far end of the cul-de-sac on the dead-end street. Kate would have to walk down the road and then turn around. It was worth it though. She felt as if she were making some progress. The houses were still standing. She had memorized license plates and she could check the real estate history and current residents when she got back to the house.

Kate walked down the street with her head up as if she were out for a brisk walk. As she rounded a turn in the road and the cul-de-sac came into view, she assessed the four houses that made up the end of the street. She stopped dead in the road when she saw them.

Natalie and Andrew were in the middle of the front lawn near a maple tree locked in a heated exchange. Natalie's face was flushed and she waved her hand around wildly as she argued with her husband. Andrew stood his ground not backing down.

Kate wasn't sure if she should walk to the end of the road and determine which house was the one where the fifth murder had happened or if she should turn back and try another day. She watched them for a moment and then continued, her curiosity getting the better of her.

Kate glanced at each address as she walked and a sinking feeling consumed her gut. She told herself that it wasn't true, but when she stopped at the curb right in front of the house Natalie and Andrew were fighting in front of, she couldn't deny it. That was the scene of the fifth murder.

CHAPTER 19

Kate couldn't hear what Natalie and Andrew were saying to each other. Once she got close, she realized they were speaking in hushed tones, but their body language told the story of a couple fighting. Andrew caught sight of Kate and stepped back from his wife. He got Natalie's attention and pointed to Kate in the road.

Natalie's head snapped in her direction. "What are you doing here?" she asked, the anger in her voice rising.

"I didn't know you lived here. I was looking for an address." Kate didn't even have to lie. She knew right then that she'd warn Natalie about the house she was living in. "I didn't mean to interrupt you both." Kate made no effort to leave though.

"We'll talk later," Natalie said to her husband and then walked across the lawn to Kate. She stood at the edge of the lawn and glared. "I don't appreciate you coming here. I got in enough trouble talking to you the other day."

Kate held her hands up in surrender. "I didn't say anything, Natalie. I'm not that kind of person. We need to talk. Walk with me."

Natalie looked back at the house and at Andrew who stood on the front porch waiting for her. She turned back to Kate. "I don't have long."

"I'll be quick. Leave your cellphone here though." Kate caught the flash of recognition in Natalie's eyes. She already knew she was being bugged. "Is that why you're arguing on the front lawn?"

Natalie nodded. "How did you find out?"

"When Jack confronted me last night about our conversation, I knew you wouldn't have told him and I didn't tell him. I don't trust that man so it was an easy conclusion to draw."

Natalie seemed hesitant to walk. She'd take a step and then stop. She gestured toward the back of the house. "There's a path through the woods behind my house to a walking path that runs through the property. Let's walk there, it's more private. I don't want people to see me with you."

Kate followed Natalie up the driveway and around the side of the garage. Andrew watched them as they walked. Kate waved to him but he didn't return the gesture. When they crossed the property line in the backyard to the wooded area behind the house, Kate said, "Your husband doesn't seem to like me much."

"Andrew doesn't like anyone here." Natalie paused and corrected herself. "I'm not sure like is the right word. He doesn't trust anyone, and I'm quickly seeing his side of the argument. So many strange things have happened since we arrived."

Kate wasn't sure how hard she should push. She let her tone go soft. "If you don't mind me asking, what were you two arguing about?"

Natalie didn't respond as she kept her quick pace up the hill through the woods until they reached a small clearing and walking path. Once there and still surrounded by trees, Natalie threw her hands in the air in frustration. "Andrew was unfaithful to me. I never believed he could do that. I didn't even think it was in him to do that. Here I am trying to make myself more attractive to him and I catch him with a half-dressed woman on his lap. I know he blames me for bringing him here, but that's cruel. Andrew is never cruel."

"What did Andrew say happened?"

"What every man caught cheating says, Kate. That he didn't cheat. That she came on to him. That it wasn't what it looked like." Natalie shook her head furiously back and forth. "I'm not an idiot. I walk into the room and there is a woman with her breasts exposed straddling my husband. What am I supposed to think is going on?"

Kate read between the lines and a picture slowly started to emerge. "Were you at Jack's place when it happened?"

"Yeah, why? It was after our training."

Kate snickered and rolled her eyes. "Let me guess, you were pulled into another room alone and Andrew and maybe one of the guides were left alone."

Natalie narrowed her gaze at Kate and didn't say anything for a moment. "How do you know that? Were you there, too?"

Kate shook her head and explained the events of the other night. "Jack showed me on video, Natalie. He sent a woman in there with Declan to get him to cheat on me. Jack was surprised when Declan shoved her away. Monica was in the room with them. Was she with you?"

"She's the one who asked me to step out of the room so she could speak to me. We were in there for a few minutes and then she got a message on her phone. We wrapped up the conversation and I went back into the room. That's when I saw Andrew and that horrible woman." Confusion fell over her face. "Are you saying it was a set-up? Andrew did seem pretty freaked out and he kept yelling that he hadn't touched her."

Kate nearly held her breath when she asked the question. "Did you know the woman who was half-naked trying to seduce your husband?"

"That was the worst part of it. She had been so nice to me about an hour earlier."

"What was her name? The woman who hit on Declan was named Bridgit. We didn't get her last name though."

"Bridgit Taylor," Natalie explained and Kate tried to hold back her excitement. "She was initially introduced to us as a psychology student who was shadowing the guides as they conducted the training. The next thing I knew, her breasts were out and she was straddling my husband."

Kate had empathy for Natalie. As she had said the night before, she knew what she felt like watching Declan and she wasn't even in love with him. "It was hard to see. Try not to take it out on Andrew. It wasn't his fault. I don't know if they are testing us or trying to see our reactions. It all feels like one big game."

"That's what Andrew said." Natalie chuckled to herself. "I feel so stupid now. It was such a bad night all around. We arrived for our training session and Monica pulled me aside to talk to me about blabbing information to you. She threatened to sue me for the millions in the non-disclosure agreement." She looked over at Kate. "I assume you signed one of those."

"We did and the health waiver. If it makes you feel any better, we have officially been asked to join the program so us talking now might not be as big a deal as it was before today."

Natalie clicked her tongue. "I don't know how any of this works. It's all confusing. Did they start asking you for more money yet?"

Kate and Declan hadn't paid a dime yet not even for the introductory session. "They haven't mentioned money to us yet. How much more do they want from you?"

"Ten grand on top of the twenty-five we already paid for the first level of training. I don't want to give them more."

Kate's instinct was to warn her not to, but she didn't want to outright tell the woman what to do. "That's incredibly expensive. I had heard about the twenty-five grand for the training, but I didn't know it was only for the first level. Did they say what the additional money was for?"

"No, and that's another thing that's frustrating Andrew. He said if we give them more, nothing is stopping them from coming back and asking again. We are brand new to the program and haven't received much in the way of education unless you count what we endured last night. I'm sure if it was a test I failed. I threw a fit and screamed and yelled and then dragged Andrew out of there."

"Natalie, go easy on yourself," Kate cautioned with concern and sympathy in her voice. She angled her chin toward the sun and closed her eyes briefly as the sun warmed her face. "It's too much for anyone to take. You had a normal reaction any woman would have had in the situation. If Jack and his guides try to tell you otherwise, consider their motive."

"What does that mean? Their motive? They are here to help us be better people."

Kate sighed in a loud puff of air out of her nose. "Who tries to make people better by playing games with them emotionally? They are testing your boundaries and expecting you not to have any. Boundaries are healthy in relationships with other people."

Natalie stopped walking and sat down on the grassy edge of the woods along the path. She raised her eyes to Kate. "Let's sit a minute and talk this out. I can't walk, think and talk all at the same time."

"It's a lot to take on." Kate sat down next to her in the grass. She kicked her legs out in front of her and angled her head slightly so she could keep one eye on the woods behind them. She didn't like leaving herself vulnerable. "Even if Andrew said nothing happened, what you witnessed is still trauma. It's testing you and your marriage and the trust between you. I don't think that anything happened. Based on what occurred with Declan, I'm inclined to believe Andrew is telling you the truth, but it's okay to be angry and upset by it. Have you heard from any of the guides today?"

Natalie nodded. "Sadie has called me three times. I figured it would be Monica, but I think she's good cop to Monica's bad cop."

Kate smiled at the reference. She had an inkling of that the other night. Sadie had said only a few words to them the entire evening while Monica had been bossy and rude to them both. "If it were me, I'd take time to sort things out with Andrew and get on the same page before calling them back. You and Andrew need to be a team in this. If not, they will only work to split you apart."

Natalie turned her head. "You seem too smart and far too together to be in Jack's program. Why are you here?"

"I had hoped to work on some professional goals, which is what I thought the program could help me with. So far, it's been more personal than professional. Jack told me that I had to choose personal goals."

"You've had a lot of contact with Jack so far," Natalie said, surprised. She leaned back on her hands. "I've barely seen him outside of an initial meeting when he told me that I needed to go on a diet." There was an air of jealousy in Natalie's voice.

"Don't be envious of Jack's attention. It's not all it's cracked up to be."

"It's easy for you to say. You're the one getting the attention."

Kate would trade just about anything to not have Jack's interest. "We were invited to a welcome party tomorrow night. Are you attending?"

"If Andrew and I stop fighting." Natalie let out a groan of frustration. "Life wasn't perfect by any stretch of the imagination before we came here, but it seems much worse than it's ever been."

Kate had no words of encouragement for her. She didn't want to risk telling her to leave again. Although Kate assumed with Natalie's cellphone at home, they weren't being recorded.

"Give it time," Kate said instead. "You're in the thick of it now with Andrew. We can finish our walk and then you can go home and sort things out with him. Declan and I made a pact that no matter what was thrown our way, we had to stay a team in this. It's the only way it's going to work. He's the one person I trust among all others so when I saw Bridgit trying to grope him, I knew he didn't want it."

Natalie nodded along as if she agreed with Kate but she didn't offer a verbal response. She stood and brushed grass and dirt off the back of her pants. "You said you didn't come by to talk to me. You said you were looking for an address. Did you find it?"

Kate wanted to tell Natalie about her house, but she was worried about the woman's reaction to the news. She had to try a gentler approach. "What do you know about your house before you rented it?"

"Not much. Just that Jack had a few rental houses available and he offered one to us. It's a nice enough house though." Natalie peered down at her. "Why?"

Kate stood and leveled with her. "Declan's brother mentioned to us the addresses of the murders that happened here in Mulberry Grove. I hate to tell you this but your house is one of the houses where a murder happened."

Natalie drew back in horror, her face contorting in fear and disgust. "Does Jack know that?"

"I'm sure he does. It was his members who were killed." Natalie didn't react the way Kate thought she would. Instead, the woman had a look of curiosity. "Do you know something?"

Natalie shook her head. "I'm not sure. Andrew suspected something was strange about the house. He said he got a weird vibe about it. I thought he was being difficult since he didn't want to be here and then we found…"

"You found what?" Kate asked, growing concerned.

Natalie didn't respond, she took off in a run to her house with Kate right behind her.

CHAPTER 20

"Y ou are not going to believe what I found out today," Kate said as she entered the house and walked down the narrow hall to the kitchen. She slowed her pace when she heard the voices – one male and one female. Declan's voice was light and airy, not anything like when she had left him before her walk. Kate assumed he would have been napping with her gone.

She turned the corner from the hall into the kitchen and stopped short when she saw her. Long thin legs clad in tight red leggings that went all the way up to firm round buttocks protruding outwards as she leaned over the island in the kitchen. She wiggled her backside back and forth as she giggled and talked.

Declan cleared his throat. "You said that you had another reason for stopping by to see me other than asking me about the party. What did you want?"

"I wanted you all to myself," she cooed. "Your wife doesn't seem like much fun, and I can see that you're a man who deserves some fun."

"Kate's a lot of fun when she's around the right people."

"Am I the right people?" she asked, her voice flirty.

"Definitely not." Declan chuckled and then he grew serious. "You probably should be going. I don't want Kate to come home and find you here and get the wrong idea."

"She might get the right idea and realize that her husband could be stolen from her if she doesn't get it together. I've been told she's not a good wife to you."

"Kate's a great wife. You should go and not come back. I shouldn't have let you in to begin with." Declan's voice grew even more stern. "Nothing is ever going to happen between us, Bridgit. No matter what you do or say, I'm never going to betray Kate."

Bridgit stood up straight and kept her hands on the island. "I'm sure Kate doesn't meet all of your needs – no wife does. There are things you can do with me that I'm sure she won't let you do with her. We could have a lot of fun, Declan. Think of all the frustration you can work out with me. There's little I say no to."

Declan didn't waver. "You don't know anything about my relationship with Kate. She's all the woman I need."

If Kate hadn't known the truth of their fake marriage, she would have bought Declan's lie. She thought about walking into the kitchen but looked down at the journal in her hands and thought better of it.

"You need to go," Declan said again with more force.

Kate could tell he was losing patience with her.

"If you say so. Kate could have joined us when she gets home. I'm not against that kind of fun." Bridgit waited another moment, probably to see if Declan would change his mind. When it was clear he had nothing else to say, she shrugged. "I'll go then. You know where to find me should you change your mind. They always change their mind, Declan. No one says no to me."

"I'm not going to change my mind."

"Goodbye then…for now." She giggled.

Kate froze in place, deciding which direction to go. She slipped out of the kitchen and scooted down the hall to the stairs and then took them two at a time until she reached the top. She ducked into the bedroom and closed the door. She leaned against it to hear what was happening downstairs. It wasn't anything as dramatic as she had witnessed in the kitchen though. Declan and Bridgit said goodbye and then the front door opened and closed as she left.

Declan called out from the bottom of the stairs. "I know you're here, Kate. I saw your reflection in the microwave."

Kate had no idea she'd been seen. She opened the door and went to the top of the stairs and then walked down them slowly, carrying the journal Natalie had given her. "What was she doing here?"

"Trying to seduce me again. I'm just that irresistible. You heard how hard she tried. It's been a long time since a woman wanted me that badly." Declan smiled proudly at himself.

"I think it's her job to seduce men in the program." Kate watched as his face fell. She couldn't tell if he was seriously hurt or joking with her. When she reached the bottom of the stairs and stood at about his height, she leaned forward, resting her hands on his chest. "You're irresistible to all women except me, Declan. You always have been. I don't think you've lost your touch even though you're starting to prematurely gray at your temples."

Declan couldn't keep a straight face. "That just about killed you to say."

Kate held her hand to her throat. "I can feel the bile rising. All silliness aside, why was she here?"

Declan stepped out of the way and let Kate get to floor level. "Bridgit stopped by to see if we would be attending the welcome event tomorrow night, which I knew nothing about."

Kate grimaced. "We received the invitation as I was leaving earlier. You were in a bad mood and I figured I'd tell you when I got back. I assumed you'd be napping and sleeping off your misery."

"I was until Bridgit arrived and woke me up." Declan ran a hand down his face. "She told me about the party to get in here. I figured the kitchen was the safest place for us. She kept hinting there was another reason why she was here. You walked in when I asked her to get to the point."

Kate wanted to know if he got anything out of her, but her curiosity was piqued. "Are you attracted to her?"

He laughed. "Are you? As you heard, she wouldn't mind a threesome."

"I'm not into women. I can barely be friends with women." Kate walked into the living room and snuggled back on the chaise. "Seriously, Declan. I'm curious. If we weren't in this situation and she hit on you, would you go for it?"

Declan sat across from her on the couch. "Maybe when I was twenty and didn't have any sense. Not now though. She's attractive but not my type."

"What is your type?" Kate wasn't sure why she was suddenly so curious about Declan's attractions. It might be because he was getting divorced and would be back out in the dating world.

Declan breathed in and out slowly, watching her. Kate was sure he was wondering why she was interested. Finally, he shrugged. "I'm not sure that I have a type anymore. I'm looking for intelligent, kind, and accepting of my work. I just got divorced, Kate. It's going to be a long time before I even think of dating again. Women are the last thing on my mind."

"As we've said all along, this life isn't for everyone." Kate pulled a blanket from the arm of the chaise and wrapped it around her legs. She wasn't cold but there was something comforting about being wrapped in the blanket. "Did you find out anything about her that we can use?"

"Taylor is her last name. I don't get the sense she's being held against her will given she came here alone." Declan sank back and put his ankle on his opposite knee. "I didn't get a chance to ask her much else. She seems to enjoy doing whatever it is she's doing. Where were you? You've been gone for longer than I thought you'd be."

Kate held up the journal she had brought back from upstairs. "First things first. Natalie told me that Bridgit is a student interning with the guides. She also walked in on Bridgit sitting on her husband's lap. She was topless. I'm not sure what her internship is all about but it's not anything like the internships I've had. We can get back to that later. I found something far more interesting."

Declan hitched his jaw toward her. "What's with the book?"

Kate told him about walking the neighborhood and checking out the other properties where the murders had happened. Then she told him the most important detail. "Natalie and Andrew are living in the fifth murder victim's house, Declan. I almost lost it when I realized. I ended up telling her and you're not going to believe what she told me."

"I'm guessing it has something to do with that book."

"This is Amelia Beckett's journal. Amelia and her husband, Ben, were part of Jack's program. Natalie had no idea that Amelia had been murdered. Who wants to live in a crime scene?" Kate shuddered at the thought of it.

"It's not a crime scene now, Kate. Properties like that get turned over all the time and go on to be wonderful family residences despite their dark past. If we stopped living in places where people died, there would be lots of empty houses."

"Fair enough," Kate responded with an edge of annoyance in her voice. Declan knew exactly what she meant. "But you know what I'm saying. The murder happened a year ago and the Becketts were a part of Jack's program just like Natalie and her husband."

Declan nodded along with her. "Is Natalie freaked out now that she knows?"

"Probably less so than I am for her. She sprinted home and showed me this journal when I told her. She asked me the murdered couple's names and started putting two and two together. That's when we realized Amelia's journal might hold a clue to her death. Natalie never read the journal. She found it when she was moving her things into the closet. Natalie said she figured the last tenant had forgotten it. She didn't want to snoop into someone's private life so she put it back in the closet and that's where it's stayed."

Declan stood from the couch and walked the few steps to the chaise and reached his hand out for the journal. He looked at the flowered leather cover and then flipped it over. It had the same design on the back and a leather tie that loosely bound the book closed. He untied it and then flipped open the pages of scrawled black penmanship. Amelia had written the whole thing in neat cursive.

Kate was no handwriting expert but when she viewed the pages it was clear without even reading the words that Amelia had hope in the early pages of the journal and then her writing became forced, closed, and tight – revealing her anxiety and fear. A real expert could tell Kate even more but she didn't have access to one right now.

"What do you think?" she asked, wanting Declan's impression of the pages.

"The last few pages of the journal are barely legible. I can't even make out some of the words." Declan snapped the journal shut and handed it back to Kate. "I'm surprised Natalie gave this to you. How did you get it from her?"

"I had to use the same story about your brother. I don't think she'll tell anyone. Natalie has only been in the program a few months and is already starting to regret it. Her husband doesn't want to be there at all. I trust her about as much as I trust anyone here."

"I should make the effort to connect with Andrew. If Natalie is that talkative, Andrew might be willing to talk to me, too."

"That's a good idea," Kate agreed absently as she ran her hands over the journal. All she wanted to do was dig into the pages to see if there was any clue to her murder. She raised her eyes back to Declan. "Why don't you start some background research on Bridgit and I'll begin going through this journal. We need to talk about potential suspects."

"Do you have a list?" Declan had skepticism written all over his face and he didn't hide it in his tone.

Kate didn't have a specific list but that didn't mean anything to her. They had to start someplace. "We've met enough people that we can start jotting down names and digging into their pasts and current connections to see what we can find. We need to figure out what questions we might have before we implode our connection to Jack."

Declan sat down on the couch and leaned forward, resting his elbows on his knees. "Speaking of that – I agree it's the best plan. I'm just not sure that a welcome event is the best place to throw a fit and storm out of there. It might seem a little too forced."

"I agree with that. We are going to have to wait." Kate barely got the words out of her mouth when Declan's cellphone buzzed from his pocket.

He checked the screen. "Spade. He wants us to give him a call. I assume he's made contact with Det. Jerry Miller and wants us to set up a call."

Kate tossed the journal on a nearby table and got up from the chaise. She followed Declan into the office, closed the door, and sat down while he placed the call. One ring later, they were connected to Spade who wasted no time in barking orders to them.

"Det. Miller doesn't want to talk on the phone. He said he doesn't trust it. I asked him what he means and he wouldn't go into detail. He hung up and then called me back an hour later from an undisclosed number. He said if the FBI wants information beyond what's in the official reports, he'll meet face to face."

"How can we do that? We're supposed to be undercover," Kate protested.

Spade didn't answer her question. "You'll meet him tonight, at eleven, on Mulholland Drive. Miller said the road west of Encino Hills Drive becomes unpaved and nothing but dirt. It's closed to cars. He said to go about a half mile down the dirt path and he'd meet you."

Declan wrote down the directions. "Spade, I have the same concerns as Kate. We don't know anything about this guy."

"Bob trusts him and he's got a hard-on for Jack Harlow. He wants to bring him down if it's the last thing he does. Don't be seen by anyone else." With that, Spade hung up without further discussion.

Kate took a deep breath. "I guess we're going to Mulholland Drive."

CHAPTER 21

Declan drove the forty minutes to Mulholland Drive with both hands on the steering wheel and his back straight against the seat. Gone was his affable demeanor and laid-back driving style that usually made Kate feel like she didn't have a care in the world.

After the call with Spade, they debated the merits of meeting Det. Miller in person like two people who might have had a choice in the matter – which they absolutely did not. Spade said go, so they went. Kate didn't have too much of a feeling about it one way or the other, but Declan didn't know Det. Miller and therefore didn't trust him. He'd been undercover enough to know that an agent didn't blow their cover until the right time and place and possibly never. No matter how much Kate reassured him, he had remained on edge.

When Declan hit the end of the paved roadway, he pulled over on the two-lane road onto the gravel shoulder and cut his lights. "I'm not feeling any better about this, Kate."

Kate reached over and placed a calming hand on his thigh. "I doubt that the lead detective in two homicide investigations is going to out us. We should have met Det. Miller sooner than this."

Declan shook his head. "If he was safe to meet, we would have met him by now."

"Sitting in the car worrying about it isn't going to do anything."

Kate withdrew her hand, tapped the gun on her hip, and then opened her car door. The street was bathed in darkness and there wasn't a home in sight. They had passed the last residence a few hundred yards back. One lone street light cast an orange glow but wasn't enough to illuminate them or the dirt road ahead.

Declan got out of the car and then opened the back door. He grabbed a large flashlight and flicked it on in the direction they were going. He kept the light to the ground a few feet in front of them as they walked. They had to navigate around concrete barricades that were put up to stop vehicle traffic. After that, it was a wide-open dirt road in front of them. Kate hadn't seen any other cars parked near them so she had no idea if Det. Miller was running late or had parked someplace else.

They walked for a few minutes until the light from Declan's flashlight caught a pair of sneaker-clad feet. He shined the light up to jeans and then a blue windbreaker, not unlike the ones worn by the FBI.

"Det. Miller," Declan said quietly but loud enough the man heard him.

"Cut the light. You have no idea how far it can be seen up here in the pitch black. We don't want neighbors getting curious, or worse, calling the cops."

Declan did as he was asked. With the beam of flashlight gone, the only light was from the crescent moon overhead and a smattering of visible stars. They walked until they were practically toe-to-toe with the detective who stood about five-foot-ten and had short dark hair. He pushed a pair of dark-framed glasses up his nose and then extended his hand and introduced himself. Kate and Declan did the same.

"You must trust me," Det. Miller said nervously. "I heard that you're in Mulberry Grove undercover. I'm surprised you'd be willing to meet me."

"I don't trust you. Not yet," Declan said evenly. "It wasn't our idea to meet. You said you wouldn't speak on the phone so here we are. If we had it our way, we would have had a phone call where you never learned our identities."

"Fair enough." Det. Miller jammed his hands in his pockets and rocked on the balls of his feet. "Pretty gutsy of you two to go undercover. I'm glad the FBI is taking these cases seriously. I tried for more than a year. What do you want to know?"

Declan turned his head to Kate and allowed her to go first. "Det. Miller, we don't know much of anything so far. We had a briefing from our FBI contact and read the files. There are some gaps in information particularly from the early cases."

Det. Miller chewed on his lip and bobbed his head. "The first thing you have to know is nobody connected these cases until I had two in a row that looked nearly identical and then when I went back and found earlier murders, I connected them. No one else agreed."

"Were you unaware of the earlier murders at the time you got the case?" Declan asked.

"Yeah, I wasn't involved before that. Detectives with the LAPD have enough on their plates we don't go digging around in other investigations. I searched the community for recent criminal activity and the gun used in the murder, and I can't tell you the shock I felt when I found the two previous homicides. Then I went back even farther and found the stabbing case. That one didn't make a whole lot of sense to me at the time so I didn't connect it right away. Later though, when I realized they were connected to Jack Harlow too, I knew it had to have been the first. That makes five in all." He paused and then added, "Well, six with the one the other night."

Kate asked him a few questions about connecting the murders and then when she was done, she moved on to more specifics. "Walk us through the Amelia and Ben Beckett murder investigation. The fifth one, before this last. I've met the couple who is living in that house right now. They had no idea its history."

"They a part of Jack's program?"

Kate nodded. "Joined a few months ago."

Det. Miller took a breath and let it out slowly. He went over the basic crime scene details that Kate and Declan already knew. Ben had been shot in front of the television and Amelia on the threshold from the kitchen to the living room. A bottle of dish detergent was found near the body.

"There was still a sink full of dishes. The back door had been unlocked and no forced entry. The place had been wiped down. That made me wonder if the killer had been hanging around before the murder. There was a third plate in the sink I couldn't account for. Too many utensils to tell me one way or the other. Same with the cups. It was the third dinner plate that caught my eye though."

"Same with the first couple, right?" Kate asked, trying to recall the specifics.

"Right," Det. Miller said but didn't elaborate. "I found nothing other than shell casings to give me any clue to who killed the Becketts. They were good people caught up in Jack's program. I spoke to Amelia's sister, Cara. From what I understand Amelia and Ben were looking for a way out of Jack's program. In fact, they were making plans to move. The sister was the only person willing to speak to me and she was angry that we weren't doing more. I can't blame her though. Amelia was supposed to cut off ties with her, but the sisters were close."

Kate didn't want to tell Det. Miller that she had found Amelia's journal until she had a chance to read it. It was still technically an open homicide investigation and would need to be turned over. "We read in the report that no neighbors were willing to speak to you."

Det. Miller pinched the bridge of his nose. "That's not technically true. No neighbor was willing to go on record and make a formal statement. Two of the neighbors in the cul-de-sac spoke to me privately and told me that they saw a person running from the home shortly after the gunshots. I have a basic description of the shooter but their head was covered."

Declan turned to Kate with the same wide-eyed expression she had. "That wasn't in any record we had been provided."

"It wouldn't be. I didn't include it." Det. Miller seemed to be waiting to be chastised by one of them, but when no such dressing down occurred, he went on. "The reality is, like you, I didn't know who to trust. There are people in the department who view Jack Harlow favorably, so I didn't want to tip my hat in any official way and give a description of the killer. I didn't know who was going to have eyes on that."

It made a certain kind of sense to Kate, but it hampered the investigation. "I assume you want to tell us now. That's why we are here."

Det. Miller offered a wry smile. "I wanted eyes on you to see if I could trust you. My gut tells me you're on the up and up."

Declan reached out and squeezed the man's shoulder. "If there are any two people you can trust with this information, it's us. We want to bring down Jack Harlow or whoever is responsible for the murders. We promise you that we'll go wherever the evidence takes us."

Det. Miller took his hands out of his jeans pockets and folded his arms over his chest. He locked eyes with Declan. "I'm fairly certain that it is Jack Harlow, but I understand your hesitancy to pin the murders on him yet. The description I received was a person between five-foot-eight to five-foot-ten possibly taller. The witnesses were not able to see the person's face or hair or even build. They were dressed in black pants and a gray baggy sweatshirt with a hood up. It hid their face and frame although both witnesses said they thought the person was in shape. No one saw the person below the knees so they are unsure what they were wearing on their feet. They also didn't know if it was a man or a woman."

Declan pulled out his phone and jotted down a note of the description. "Where exactly did the witnesses see the person?"

"One witness saw the person step out of the back door of the home onto the porch close to five-thirty. Then about an hour later, another neighbor saw a person fitting the same description running from the back of the home towards the woods after the gunshots."

With urgency in her voice, Kate said, "I didn't think any of the neighbors called 911 or law enforcement."

"They didn't. The neighbor heard the gunshots, stepped out onto his back porch, saw the person running toward the woods, and went back inside. He knew the Becketts were involved with Jack Harlow and didn't want any part of it."

Kate could understand not wanting to get involved with Jack but to not even call law enforcement when there had been some kind of shooting was something she couldn't wrap her mind around. That went to a whole other level of either indifference or fear. "The neighbor was willing to speak to you later though?"

"That's right." Det. Miller caught the look on Kate's face. "I know what you're thinking. Sounds kind of callous not to call 911. Doesn't make sense why he'd talk to me days after."

"That's exactly what I was thinking."

"Fear is a funny thing, Agent Walsh. It got the better of him and then his conscience ate at him. When I interviewed him the day of the shooting, he didn't tell me anything, but then he called two days later and gave me a solid statement. I'd say his information was even more reliable than the other neighbor because he was on high alert because of the gunshots. They both said about the same thing though."

Kate and Declan took turns asking a few more questions about possible suspects in the Becketts life but came up short. Det. Miller had done a thorough investigation on the Becketts' case and the one before it. There were no suspects outside of the Mulberry Grove community.

"Were you able to interview Jack?" Declan asked when they had exhausted other questions.

"If you can call it that. He allowed me to come to his house and sat down with me but shared almost nothing. He made a big show of cooperating, but at the end of the day, his information yielded nothing more than I already had. I tried to press him on why the Becketts were leaving if everything was so wonderful. Jack acted like he had no idea they were leaving, but Amelia's sister told me otherwise. There had been a confrontation a few days before the murder. Jack wouldn't admit to that though and it wasn't enough for me to get a search warrant. I have no corroborating witness."

Kate couldn't fault him. It wasn't enough for a search warrant. Det. Miller's hands had been tied. "What about other people in Jack's program – Ethan, Monica, and Sadie who work as guides for him? Did you speak to any of them or any current members who might have had information about the Becketts?"

Det. Miller lowered his eyes to the ground and shook his head. "None of the members would speak to me. I heard word that they had been forbidden to get involved. Ethan and Monica refused to speak as well on the Becketts' case or the ones before them. Sadie must be new. She isn't a name I'm familiar with."

"How long have Ethan and Monica been with Jack?"

"They were among the first people in the program and the first to reach Jack's inner circle. They went to work for him after that."

"Both of them could also fit the description of the killer," Declan said, interrupting.

"I thought of that, but like with Jack, I didn't have enough to get a search warrant or even detain them for questioning. They both lawyered up quickly."

Declan cursed. "There doesn't seem to be any breaks on these cases."

"None at all."

Kate had a few more questions but wanted to change gears and ask something she was afraid she'd forget. She locked eyes with Det. Miller. "By chance do you know Alison and Liam Brady? I met Ali at the coffee shop and she warned me about Jack as soon as I met her. She said her father has been researching Jack Harlow."

Det. Miller's already pale skin drained of color. "Liam Brady was my only other suspect."

CHAPTER 22

"Suspect?" Kate and Declan asked at once, turning to each other to share a look of concern. Kate refocused her attention on Det. Miller. "Why would he be a suspect?"

Det. Miller raised one eyebrow and smirked. "Have you met him?"

"No." Kate wondered now what she had been missing as a sense of dread filled her. "I've only met his daughter who seemed a bit…"

"Off," Declan said, finishing Kate's sentence. "I don't have the relationship with Ali that Kate has started to develop. I only met her once and she seemed a bit off. It might just be that everyone we've met has been secretive, but unlike everyone else, Ali seems to have no problem standing up to Jack Harlow."

Kate didn't argue with his description. "The first day I met her she told me that since I was drinking coffee that I must not be in Jack's program. From there, she cautioned me against getting involved with him. That's unusual, to say the least for this neighborhood. I've not met Ali's father though, and she doesn't seem to say much about him even when asked."

"She won't," Det. Miller said, his voice strong. "Ali is a tough nut to crack and she has almost a parental role with her father. Liam was once a well-respected tenured professor and then he started investigating cults. He became particularly interested in Jack Harlow, quit his job, and moved out here. He teaches at a local community college to have enough money to pay the bills, but he's obsessed."

Kate didn't understand how that made him a suspect. "You said Liam was a suspect though."

"Getting to that." Det. Miller pulled out his phone, flipped through saved photos, and then turned the screen around so Kate and Declan could see it. "This is a photo of Liam and Ali from two years ago, shortly after the fourth murder – the first one I investigated. He fits the description perfectly and at the time he had interaction with the couple, trying to get them to leave the program. A neighbor overheard a confrontation between them the day before the murder. When I interviewed Liam, he explained that he was a deprogrammer and was trying to help them out of Jack's program and that's when the confrontation occurred. He had an alibi for the evening of the murder. I let it go at that."

Declan shook his head like he was missing a part of the story. "I assume something happened after that?"

"With the Becketts' murder." Det. Miller slipped his phone back in his pocket and rubbed his brow in thought. "I was probably about a month into the investigation and I got an anonymous tip to take a look at Liam Brady. The name was familiar to me so I searched my notes from the previous case and there was my interview with him about the confrontation with the victims. The caller didn't give me a lot to go on other than Liam was friendly with Amelia and Ben at first. Then the relationship grew contentious. Liam was seen on a walking trail in the community shouting at Ben. It escalated to shoving and then both men got into a fistfight. The caller said that was about a week before the murder. Then when the neighbors described a man who looked like him, I set up an interview."

"Did you bring him down to the station?" Kate asked.

"He refused that so I met him at his home. Liam is a charismatic and affable guy. He told me all he wants is for people to be free of

Jack Harlow and that he's doing everything he can to help with that. I asked about his alibi for the night of the murder and Ali said they were both home eating dinner that night." Det. Miller opened his eyes wide and gave Declan and Kate a knowing look. "Ali was also his alibi for the night of the previous murder. She gave a credible story and even when I pressed her, she didn't crack. I had nothing to prove otherwise so there wasn't much I could do."

Declan took an audible breath. "What about the fight with Ben Beckett? How did Liam explain that away?"

"Liam said it never happened. He explained that he had been friendly with the Becketts and that they had started talking about moving away. Liam had been providing them some counseling and support to make that happen when they were murdered. He swore up and down that there had been no confrontation."

"With no name of the caller who allegedly witnessed the fight, you couldn't follow up or verify the facts," Declan said, finishing Det. Miller's thought.

"Correct. I had no other evidence to prove it happened. No other witnesses. It was Liam's statement versus an anonymous tip. I knew from Amelia's sister that they were trying to leave and that they had help. It checked out. I couldn't find a reason he'd want to kill them, but still, there's something off about the guy and his daughter." Det. Miller opened his arms wide. "As you can see, I've been roadblocked in every direction."

Kate asked him a few more questions about Liam and Ali, but the detective didn't seem to know much more. "We haven't looked at Liam for these murders, but I think a meeting is in order at this point. As we said, I've been developing a relationship with Ali so I might have an in."

Det. Miller shook his head hard. "You're not going to have an in with either of them if you're cozying up to Jack. They won't trust you. The moment they suspect or know you're a part of the program, you're an enemy to them."

Declan turned sharply to Kate and gave her a look she understood. Kate opened her mouth to speak but a snapping twig and rustling of bushes drew her attention away from the conversation. She blinked off in the darkness, her heart starting to race.

Declan lurched forward at the sound and his hand went to his gun on his hip.

Only Det. Miller remained calm. "It's probably a coyote. They are common up here in the Hollywood Hills. Mountain lions too. They won't bother us if we don't bother them."

Declan kept his rigid posture but eased his hand off his gun and raised the flashlight in the direction of the noise. Det. Miller didn't stop him from shining the light. Kate followed with her eyes and caught two eyes staring back at her from the brush. It was mere seconds before the coyote turned and took off in a run up the side of the hill and out of sight.

"Guess you were right," Declan said, flipping the button on the flashlight and leaving them in darkness again. "I probably should have realized, but you don't get many coyotes in downtown Boston."

Kate stepped closer to both of them a little concerned about the potential wildlife at her back. "Det. Miller, before we go, we want to run something by you. Our initial plan was to get in deep into Jack's program and start connecting with people and gain their trust enough that they'd speak to us openly."

"That isn't going to work," Det. Miller said, interrupting but validating their thoughts.

Kate agreed. "We figured that out after going to the first information session. It was a disaster."

"I wouldn't say disaster," Declan said, reaching out and rubbing Kate's arm. "Jack came on to Kate a little too strong and then one of the young women who work for him tried to come onto me. I'll just say neither of us is compliant enough to fake this."

"Understood." Det. Miller rubbed the back of his neck. "He would have figured you out eventually once you started asking other members questions. The people who are loyal to him are unbreakably loyal. What are you going to do now?"

Declan turned to him. "We need an exit strategy and figured we'd cause a scene at one of the training sessions and quit but make a real show of it. Make it seem to everyone we think the whole thing is a big sham. If we cause enough of a commotion, his members might start talking about it. The hope is then the people on the fence about leaving the program might seek us out."

"Liam Brady might seek you out, too," Det. Miller reminded them. He mulled over their plan for several moments and then nodded his head in the way Kate had seen him do before. "That might work. I don't think I've heard of anyone leaving in quite that spectacular a way. Usually, people get hit up for more money, can't pay, and go away quietly feeling terrible like they missed out on their one chance at happiness. Others get so far in they can't leave – that's the murdered couples as far as I could tell. They were all in the program for two years or longer."

That reminded Kate of a question. "I had been wondering how long each of the murdered couples was a part of the program and what level they had achieved."

"All were at the highest you could go as far as I could tell. At some point, each of them decided it was time to get out – only I believe they knew too much and Jack wasn't going to let them go that easily."

Declan narrowed his gaze. "Were all of them at the point of leaving?"

"As far as I know. That was the other commonality among them. When I went back to the first and realized the connection to Jack and that they were ready to leave, I was sure that the murder was connected to the others. I couldn't get the detective on the case to believe me and he wouldn't give me much access to information, but I'd bet money it's the same killer."

Kate nudged Declan's arm. "Anything else before we go?"

Declan hitched his jaw toward Det. Miller. "How do you account for the drugs in the first murder case?"

"The psilocybin tea?"

"Yeah, that isn't a factor in any other murder and the victims weren't known to use drugs."

"The detective on the case never had an answer for that. I never had an answer for it either. I wondered if the killer drugged them to kill them or interrogate them."

Kate knew a hallucinogenic wasn't the best drug to use for interrogation. She knew of a slew of drugs utilized for torture – particularly getting someone hooked on something addictive and then delaying giving it to them as they entered into withdrawals. The United States had used their own truth serum and LSD in the 1960s that resulted in a suicide before the program was shut down. Kate had never taken psilocybin before so she wondered aloud if it would cause enough anxiety that it would get someone to talk. She asked Declan who knew more.

"It could," Declan said and then turned to Det. Miller who also agreed. "That would more readily happen under anxious conditions with someone who had never taken the drug before or known its effects."

"They could have been tortured then," Kate said more to herself as she thought through the night of the murder from yet another angle. "They might not have even known what they were ingesting and who knows what kind of reaction they had to it."

"That's what I always assumed," Det. Miller echoed. "The killer took their time with that one. I always assumed we might find a clue in that case that would break it wide open, but that hasn't happened yet. I'm starting to wonder how many more have to die before we find the truth."

They talked for a few more minutes and then Det. Miller started to back up. "We've been here too long. If there is anything else you need let me know. Otherwise, know that your cover is safe with me. I'm willing to do whatever you need to solve these cases. It's been going on for far too long."

Declan extended his hand to the man and they shook. "We appreciate that and we will be in touch if we need anything else. We are hoping to cause a scene soon enough and be out of the program. We may reach out if people want to leave and we need resources to help them do that. After what you said, I don't trust Liam Brady to help them with that."

"I wouldn't trust anyone in that entire community or even other law enforcement. Jack seems to have allies we don't even know about yet."

"Noted." Kate thanked him for taking the time to give them more information. "If you think of anything else we should know, call the number you called before. You'll be able to reach us."

Kate and Declan waited a moment and watched him walk away into the darkness. When he was out of sight, they turned back the way they had come in. They got about twenty feet and Declan had no choice but to flick on the flashlight. "Are you as freaked out as I am about the coyotes?"

"I don't plan on spending too much time in the dark up here in the Hollywood Hills. The whole area has a creepy vibe. What did you think of Det. Miller?"

Declan shined the light back and forth on the ground as they walked. "He was more credible than I thought he'd be. I don't understand why the LAPD didn't let him run with his suspicions. It sounds like they tied his hands."

Kate had thought the same, but she wasn't ready to put the full blame on the LAPD. "It sounds like he had a lot of off-the-record information and evidence he kept to himself. If anything, it sounds like he didn't trust the people he's working with at the LAPD so he might have hamstrung himself."

They were quiet the rest of the walk to the car. When they got in, locked the door and Declan turned over the engine, he looked over at her. "At least, we have a possible description of a killer."

"Except it could be anyone in Jack's program or even Liam. Even that doesn't help us narrow it down."

CHAPTER 23

At five-forty-five the next night, Kate descended the stairs in a short red dress that showed enough cleavage she'd get a few men looking and heels high enough that she held onto the banister as she carefully took a step at a time.

Declan stood at the bottom of the stairs, near the front door, fixing his cuff links on his new gray suit. He wore a white shirt under the suit and a striped tie that had the same color red as Kate's dress. Declan whistled when he saw her. "Are you planning to seduce every man at the party?"

Kate smiled as her cheeks warmed. "We need to make enough of an impression so when we cause a scene later people will remember us. I assume they will remember this dress."

"Honey," he said, holding out his arm so she could take it. "It's not the dress, it's the way you wear it. Everyone is going to remember you tonight."

Kate stepped down to the floor, thanking him for the compliment. "Remember you need to connect with Andrew tonight. He doesn't want to be here anyway so it shouldn't be too hard to make a connection with him."

Declan saluted her. "I have my marching orders, boss. Who are you talking to tonight?"

Kate wasn't sure. She'd get in there and read the room. "My goal is to make as many connections as possible and make sure everyone knows our names by the time the night is over. And stay away from Jack. I'm staying away from Jack."

"Maybe you should try flirting with Ethan a little and see if you can make any headway with him. We know Monica doesn't like you. I can attempt to chat up Sadie as well."

Kate shrugged and grabbed her clutch from the living room end table. "I don't know if there is any point. They have been with Jack for a long time. I don't know that it's even worth the effort."

Declan opened the front door and they stepped outside into the cool night air. It was warm enough that Kate wasn't wearing a wrap over her dress but she wondered if later on the way home she'd regret that decision. Declan would always give her his suit jacket if needed. They had planned to walk the few blocks to Jack's house. Kate made it about a hundred feet from the house and suggested they take the golf cart instead.

"I'm not going to make it there and back wearing these heels. I'm good in them but not that good." Kate's normally sneaker-clad feet had never quite grown accustomed to stilettos and that was fine by her. As Declan turned them around and headed back to the house, he stifled a smirk. He had more than once teased Kate about her tomboyish ways.

Declan opened the garage and pulled the key for the cart out of his pocket. "I assumed we wouldn't make it far," he said, waving the key in front of her. He started the cart and looked at her while waiting for her to climb in.

Kate slid into the passenger seat. "Just drive."

An hour later, they were standing inside Jack Harlow's home in a downstairs ballroom. They had both been taken aback when they realized the home had a basement – and calling it that didn't even do it justice. It was an entire bottom floor that opened onto a grand patio with a built-in swimming pool and access to the lake behind his home. The home had been deceptive in its design.

Kate had run into Natalie almost as soon as they arrived. She wore a tight-fitting purple knee-length dress and looked like she had already lost a size or two just in the few days that Kate had known her. It was unsettling and too much too fast. Natalie's cheeks had lost their rosy hue and her eyes seemed vacant.

They had spoken earlier in the day and decided that it wouldn't be a good idea to be seen spending too much time together. They made a quick introduction between Andrew and Declan and then went their separate ways.

Kate made her way through three circles of people who were drinking, eating hors d'oeuvre, and chatting amicably like they were all old friends. Kate introduced herself to all of them, explained that she and Declan were new to the program and then pointed him out across the room before moving on to another group of people. All the conversation she overheard was in praise of Jack or the success each individual had been making in the program so far.

Kate had been nursing a glass of water for nearly an hour and it had grown tepid. She set it down on a passing tray and waved to Declan. He pointed to the bar and Kate nodded. There was no alcohol being served at the party because, like caffeine, it wasn't allowed in the program. She wasn't sure what the bar was serving but trusted Declan to pick something for her.

"That's a magnificent dress, Kate," a voice said from behind her. "All the men have their eyes on you, some of the women, too."

Kate didn't need to turn around to know that it was Jack. She shifted her eyes and head slightly to the right. "Thank you. Declan liked it so that's what I wore."

"You're making progress then, Kate. It's good you wore something your husband enjoys. Your beauty is a reflection on him."

Kate had to bite the inside of her cheek to hold back what she wanted to say. Through gritted teeth, she said, "It's a lovely welcoming party. I've met quite a few people in your program. All have quite complimentary things to say."

"You'll be one of them someday soon. I promise you that." Jack turned his head in the direction of Declan. "I see he's met Andrew. As I'm sure you know from Natalie, her husband is resistant to the program and wants to leave. Is Declan open to learning?"

Kate didn't confirm or deny anything Natalie might have said to her. "Declan tends to keep an open mind until he has reason not to. I know that he's tired of dealing with Bridgit's advances. If she keeps it up that might be enough for him to decide this program isn't for us."

Jack tilted his head down to her and assessed her for several moments. "Is it Declan who is tired of it or you?"

"Declan finds it inappropriate and annoying." Kate held firm as she turned and looked up at him. "What is her role anyway? Is she a paid escort sent to seduce your members?"

Jack pulled back as if he'd been slapped. His indignation was clear in his tone. "She is no such thing. Bridgit is studying to be a sex therapist and intimacy coach and is a significant part of our program."

Kate was sure he believed the ridiculous words he was saying. "Sex therapists do not sleep with their clients. If it's some kind of test for us, it's not happening – whether that means we pass the test or not. There are loyal bonds between Declan and me that no one can break."

Jack stared at her for several moments like he was on the verge of saying something but never did. He left without saying another word and walked to the bar where Declan stood ordering Kate a drink. Jack didn't approach Declan but gestured for the bartender to stop what he was doing and meet him at the end of the bar. Once there, Jack said something to the bartender, who snapped his head up and looked out across the ballroom as if searching for someone.

"Are you having a good time?" a man said, suddenly next to her. "You look lovely tonight, but you looked lovely the other night, too."

Kate turned to her right. "Thank you. Yes, I'm having a nice time. Just waiting for Declan to bring me over a drink."

"Here he comes now." Ethan leaned down and spoke right into Kate's ear. "After he gives you your drink, excuse yourself because I'd like to speak to you alone."

Kate furrowed her brow uncertainly. "Without Declan?"

"Just you for now." Ethan turned and walked away from her, clearly expecting her to follow.

Declan handed her a drink in a copper mug. It smelled of lime and ginger. "It's like a Moscow mule without the vodka," she said after taking a sip. She drank more as they talked, enjoying how good it tasted.

"The bartender said they are popular." Declan glanced around them. "Seems like you've spoken to quite a few people. I couldn't get much out of Andrew. He's angry and ready to go. He told me not to tell anyone that he and Natalie are planning to leave soon."

"I'm not surprised." Kate wanted to discuss this more, but Ethan stood waiting for her by the door. "Before you came over here, Ethan said he wanted to speak to me alone. If I'm not back in twenty minutes, come looking for me."

"Do you think you should go alone, Kate?"

She raised her eyes to him. "I'm in a house full of people. I think I'm fairly safe. Be ready to come looking for me." Kate couldn't decide if being alone with Ethan worried her or not.

With her drink in hand, Kate made her way through a crowd of people. She nodded hello to those she had already met and joined Ethan in a hallway just outside of the ballroom. "Where are we headed?"

He extended his hand to her, but Kate didn't take it. "Jack's special library is down this hallway to the right. I thought it would give us a private space to talk quietly."

"Is there something you need to tell me?"

Ethan leaned in the direction he wanted them to go and then took a few steps, turning slightly to make sure Kate was right behind him. He wasn't going to answer her question so Kate had no choice other than to follow or walk away. The library was only a short distance from the ballroom but far enough the noise from the crowd had dulled. He pushed open a heavy oak door and allowed her to step inside. The room had hardwood floors covered partially by an oval woven rug of bright blues and reds, leather furniture, and oak floor-to-ceiling bookshelves that were filled with books, unlike the upstairs library.

"Take a seat," Ethan said, gesturing toward the couch.

Kate went over to the couch and eased herself down, taking another sip of her drink as she sat. She had nearly finished it already. "What is it you want to know?"

Ethan sat down next to her and leaned back, resting his arm across the top of the couch, not quite touching her. "I heard a rumor and was hoping that you'd clear it up for me."

"A rumor about me?"

"Your husband, really, but it involved both of you."

Kate tried not to show concern on her face. "I'll answer you if I can. If it's a rumor though, I'm not sure I can address it."

"We've been hearing rumblings that Declan's brother is a detective and that you both have been asking around about the murders that have happened here."

Kate sipped the last of her drink and then set the cup down on the table next to her. She turned to him, a smile on her face. "Yes, Declan's brother is a cop. We're both interested in true crime stories. There are several podcasts I listen to. The latest murder happened shortly after we moved into Mulberry Grove. As you can imagine, it sparked our interest. Is there something wrong with that?"

"It's not a pleasant topic, Kate, and not something we want you to focus on any longer if you're going to be a part of the program."

Kate was feeling brave. She turned slightly and locked eyes with him. "Is it because Jack is considered a suspect? Or possibly you are considered one as well?"

Ethan shook his head. "Neither of us had anything to do with their deaths."

"Are you sure? Each couple was a part of the program here, quite high up too, and then decided to leave. Maybe they had secrets about Jack or the program and someone needed to silence them."

Ethan's lips upturned into a grin. He lowered his hand from the back of the couch and squeezed her shoulder. "Kate, you've seen too many movies. I've heard the rumors that this is a cult. We all have. We try to dispel that myth, but it stuck. Yes, there are levels like in any educational setting. As you learn more, you become ready for more advanced training. It's no more or less than that." Ethan rambled on about the program and the success stories to the point Kate became bored. She wanted to get up to leave when suddenly Ethan stood from the couch, crossed the room, and pulled what looked like a photo album from a nearby bookshelf.

"What's that?" Kate asked, watching him.

Ethan walked back over with the album outstretched to her. "Take it. It's filled with individuals and couples that Jack's program has helped. We don't normally show this to brand new neophytes in the program, but you're different. You're going to take some convincing. If I didn't believe we could help you, Kate, I'd tell you and your husband to leave the program. You've both shown real resolve in meeting your goals so far."

Kate didn't address what he said. She didn't care enough to respond. She took the book and laid it on her lap and began to flip through it. There were couples, most looking gaunt and pale, offering stiff smiles at the camera. She got halfway through the book when a warm rush of energy jolted her body forward. Her skin prickled as if being gently caressed by a cool breeze.

Ethan laughed. "I guess it's starting to take effect. You must not have eaten much today."

Kate turned her head to look up at him and her eyebrows fluttered uncontrollably and warmth spread throughout her body. "What has taken effect?" she asked, even though she was starting to believe she understood.

CHAPTER 24

Kate had grown uncomfortably warm and her vision blurred. It was a bit like looking through Plexiglas. She shoved the album to the floor and licked her lips, suddenly dry. She reached for her drink on the end table and then stopped when her fingers closed around the cold copper handle. They had put something in her drink. Even as she thought it, she pushed the thought aside. Declan had gotten the drink at the bar and walked it over to her. He'd never drug her on purpose.

Ethan moved closer than he had been before. He ran a hand over her bare knee and she shivered at his touch. She didn't mind his touch and that bothered her. There was a niggle in the back of her mind, reminding her who she was and why she was there. Another voice in her head told her to shut up and let herself have some fun. She tried to quiet the urge but it grew stronger with each passing moment.

Ethan spoke to her low and sexy, a melody she didn't mind following. She fixed on Ethan's mouth as he spoke and she squelched an uncomfortable curiosity about how the man kissed. Kate shook her head to the side as if trying to shake something loose. But her eyes drifted back to Ethan's mouth. Kate swallowed hard and licked her lips. She parted her mouth slightly and let her eyes roam over his face. He was an attractive man – his jawline firm, nose straight and thin, and hair she wanted to run her fingers through.

As if watching herself from the outside, Kate ran her manicured fingers down his chest – that too was as firm as she had suspected. "I hope you don't mind," she purred. "I've wanted to do this since I saw you the other night."

"I don't mind at all, Kate. It's why I'm here." Ethan leaned into her and lightly traced her lips with the pad of his thumb. "Do you think your husband will mind if I kiss you?"

At the mention of Declan, Kate pulled back slightly. She recalled the words she had said not even half an hour ago to Jack – they didn't cheat on each other. Kate fought the feeling of desire rising in her belly. She struggled to stand.

"You're fighting it, Kate. Jack thought you might. We've never had a woman as strong as you in the program. You need to lean into the feeling. Let go for once in your life."

Kate had let go many times over the years. One-night stands and random hookups in other countries flashed in her mind. They had meant very little to her, nothing more than scratching an itch. Men could have meaningless casual sex and not be emotionally tied to the person. Kate could do the same, but she rarely spoke about it for fear of being judged. Kate seemed like an uptight shrew to many but some had seen her more passionate side – surprised by it in the moment.

A wave of heat and dizziness overcame her and she was forced to sit back down on the couch. Kate leaned into Ethan watching his mouth while having an internal argument about whether or not to kiss him.

Ethan captured Kate's hand with his own and guided it to the front of his pants. "I'm already hard for you. This is what you do to men, Kate. Let yourself enjoy it."

Kate's hand lingered even though a part of her knew she should pull it back and tell Ethan he was being inappropriate. The feeling of being wanted coursed through her body and she leaned in to kiss him. Before her lips could touch his, the library door flew open.

"Kate, what's going on in here?" Declan's voice, loud and booming, echoed throughout the room.

Like a kid who had been caught with their hand in the cookie jar, Kate's eyes widened, she drew back her hand and leaned away from Ethan. When she opened her mouth to speak though, she had nothing to say.

Ethan didn't change his posture. He simply turned his head toward the door. "I was getting her warmed up for you. Come on over. Kate's ready to have a good time."

Kate ran her hands down her thighs and realized how high her dress had ridden. She didn't make a move to pull it down. Declan noticed as his breathing became uneven.

Finally, with confusion in his voice, he asked, "Kate, what's going on?" When she didn't respond, he held out his hand to Kate. "Let's go home."

Kate didn't take his hand. "I don't want to go home. I want you to sit down," she said, fixing her eyes on him. She dragged her bottom lip through her teeth and pursed her lips.

If Kate thought she had been attracted to Ethan, her newfound lust for Declan simmered near a boiling point. She parted her lips, breathed in short choppy breaths, and roamed her gaze over him, seeing for the first time what other women saw when they looked at him - his tall muscular body, large strong hands that Kate knew were deceptively soft, and the chiseled features of his face. Even his boyish dark locks that always looked unbrushed begged Kate to run her fingers through them.

She stood from the couch, not bothering to adjust her dress back into place, and moved to within an inch of him. Kate angled her head back and looked up at him, hoping her eyes conveyed her desire.

Declan's concern softened his facial features even though he had no idea what was happening. He placed his hands on her shoulders.

"What's going on, Kate?" he asked again, searching her face for an answer.

"It's lust," Ethan said from the couch. "It's probably been a long time since you've seen that look. She wants you and she's ready for you. I assume you want some privacy?" he asked with a hint of disappointment as he stood to leave.

"We want privacy," Declan said, giving no room for argument. His focus wasn't on Ethan though. It was on Kate and the way she swayed her hips back and forth and wouldn't take her eyes off his. He swallowed hard as Ethan left the room and closed the door behind him.

"Now that we're alone, kiss me like you did the other day. You know we both want it." Kate stood on tiptoes and leaned her body into his, brushing her breasts against him.

Declan stared down into her face, his temptation growing. He shifted his eyes away from her to the bookshelf across from the couch and then at the light fixture in the ceiling. "I think we're being watched."

Kate reached for his hand, lacing her fingers through his. "Kind of makes it more fun that way."

Declan couldn't help but break into a smile. "I don't know what's gotten into you."

"I was hoping it would be you."

Declan let out a nervous gasp. "Let's slow it down." He glanced toward the bookshelf and then pulled Kate down on the couch with him.

She didn't waste any time hiking her dress up and straddling his lap. Declan placed his hands on her hips to steady her and she leaned down and kissed him on the lips.

He gently kissed her back and then turned his head to nuzzle her ear. He tried to ask her what was going on and if this was what she wanted, but she had nothing to say. She didn't want to talk about her feelings. She was ready to act.

"Unzip my dress," Kate said and then placed her lips on his. She slipped her tongue into his mouth and teased his. She tried everything she knew to elicit a response like the last time they had kissed. After a moment, Kate grew frustrated and pulled back from him. "Declan, I want you right here right now. I can't make it any plainer."

"Maybe we should head home and do this there." Declan eyed the camera again. His back was straight against the couch and his face stern. He didn't have the look of a man about to make passionate love to his wife in a stranger's library.

Kate reached behind to undo her dress. She didn't have the dexterity she normally had though and gave up, crushing her arms against his chest. "Undo my dress," she said again this time with more urgency.

Declan captured her wrists in his hands. "This isn't right, Kate. Not here. Not like this. If you truly want me, then let's go home and do this properly."

"Properly," she groaned. "I'm finally letting loose like everyone wants me to and my husband wants me to be proper. You used to be so much fun. All those girls you were with. What happened to that man? Did your ex-wife take your balls along with all your money? Back in the acad…"

In one swift movement, Declan stood, taking Kate with him. He clamped his mouth down on hers, kissing her finally with the level of passion she had been trying to coax from him. Kate wrapped her arms around his neck and her legs around his body while he turned them around. He leaned down onto the couch, gently placing her and then laying his weight on top of her. Declan kissed her more passionately, and when Kate guided his hand to her breast, he didn't resist.

"I can't believe this is happening," he said, out of breath dropping kisses all over her face.

Kate parted her thighs to allow him to position his body against hers. She ran her fingers through his hair and tugged his shirt out of his pants. She slipped her hands under his shirt to touch his bare skin and he shivered against her.

Declan kissed her again, swirling his tongue against hers and running his hands over her body. It was only when Kate reached for his belt buckle that he stopped them again. He kissed her sweetly one more time and then leaned into her and whispered directly in her ear, "We are being watched so I can't ignore the advances of my lust-filled wife, but you're not in your right mind. God help me I want you, but I don't want to take advantage of you."

There was enough distress in his voice that Kate finally gave him a break. She smoothed down his shirt and looked into his eyes. "You want me?"

"I've wanted you since the moment we met. I was sure you knew that."

Kate giggled and looked away from him. "I know I don't tell you this enough but you're really hot. I've always thought you were hot. I acted like you weren't when we first met because every other woman hit on you and I didn't want to be one more notch on your belt. Things have changed now."

Declan pulled back in surprise at her admission. Kate had always gone out of her way to make it seem like she had no attraction to him at all. His expression was uncertain. "Is this true or is this something you're saying because..."

"Because of our special circumstance right now?"

"Yeah, that." Declan cleared his throat. "Please let's get out of here. We can continue this at home."

"I may not make it all the way home though."

Declan leaned back and saw the smile on her face. He adjusted himself and shoved his shirt back into the waistband of his pants.

After a moment, he reached for her hand and they both stood. Kate wobbled next to him and nearly fell. Declan scooped her into his arms and carried her out of the library, into the hall, and then through the ballroom where all eyes were glued to them. Neither seemed to mind they were making such a spectacle of themselves. Declan walked up the wide staircase to the first floor before leaving out the front door.

Kate looked at him with admiration. "You're stronger than I realized."

"I don't think anyone is going to forget us after this party." Declan carried her through a maze of golf carts until he found theirs and then set her down gently in the passenger seat. He climbed in next to her, put the key in the ignition, and then backed out of the driveway.

Once they were on the road heading home, Declan glanced over at her. Her cheeks had the same flushed rosy glow as back in the library and her eyes darted all around them. "Kate," he said and waited until her eyes were on him and he had her full attention. "What's going on? I don't understand."

Her lips parted in a smile and she looked over at him, still feeling the same rush of desire as earlier in the night. She slid her hand across his lap and rubbed the front of his pants. "I can't help myself. I don't know what's come over me tonight, but I'm finding you quite irresistible."

"What happened when you were in the room alone with Ethan?"

Kate wasn't sure she should tell him. "We were talking and then I started to get warm. He flirted with me, and I'm sorry, but I flirted back. I know I had made a big deal about us not cheating on the other in this fake marriage."

"It's okay, Katie. Did he give you anything to eat or drink?"

"No, all I had was half the drink you gave me from the bar."

Declan navigated the side streets back to their house. "Something is off though, Kate. You nearly gave us away back there when you started to say something about me back in the academy. I told you we were being watched."

Kate's eyes narrowed their focus. She didn't remember doing that. "I didn't say it. Did I?"

Declan shook his head. "That's when I stood up and kissed you. I had to do something to shut you up."

Kate gave him a sideways glance. Her fun lusty feelings turned cold. "Then you don't want me? You only kissed me to shut me up?"

Declan pulled the golf cart into the driveway and put it in park. He turned, and with sincerity in his eyes, said, "I want you, but I didn't want to expose either of us in a room with cameras."

Kate's mood quickly shifted. "Then when we go inside the house, you'll…" She didn't finish her thought, feeling suddenly shy with him.

"I'll aim to please." He held his hand out to her and she took it. "You ready?"

Kate nodded slowly and looked past him. "I only have one question."

"What's that?"

"How are we going to make it past all the frogs to get into the house?"

Declan turned to look where Kate had been looking. "I don't see any frogs."

"They are all over, Declan!" she shouted and then quieted herself until she let out a moan. "I feel the blood rushing through my body. I can't wait to kiss you again as soon as we make it past all the slimy frogs. Maybe you can carry me again."

Declan slumped back in the seat and moved her hand off his lap, cursing the situation. He expelled a frustrated breath. "This is going to be a long, long night."

CHAPTER 25

Kate woke slowly like coming out of heavy disorienting slumber. She rubbed her fingertips across her brow line, trying to orient herself in time and place. She opened one eye and then the other and took in familiar surroundings. She was prone across the king-sized bed in the bedroom she had been sharing with Declan. Half her body was covered with the sheet and the other half had been left exposed to the cool air from the ceiling fan rotating above.

Kate looked down at her chest and took in one plump naked breast and covered it with her hand, reaching for the sheet with the other. "Declan," she said her voice coming out hoarse.

Kate eased herself into a sitting position and caught her reflection in the mirror. She grimaced at the sight of herself. Her skin had an unnatural pallor and her hair stuck out every which way with no rhyme or reason for it. Kate tried to pat it down with her hand and tuck strands behind her ears but it wouldn't be tamed. Only a shower would do that.

She turned her head to the bedside table and her eyes grew wide at the time. Two-fourteen in the afternoon. It had to be wrong. There was no way she had slept the entire day away. "Declan!" she called again, no louder than the previous try. Her heart began to race as she tried desperately to understand what was happening.

"You're finally awake," Declan said, suddenly appearing in the open doorway. He had on shorts and a tee-shirt and was barefoot. "I've only been up for about thirty minutes. I started some coffee if you want some."

Kate hugged the sheet tight to her naked body, realizing that she had called him into the room while she was still naked. "I don't understand what's happening."

Declan raised his eyebrows and stepped into the room. He eased himself into a corner chair. "You don't remember anything from last night?" He had an amused smile across his face that concerned Kate.

Bits and pieces of the evening before came flooding back to her. The party. Being alone with Ethan. Memories that simply couldn't be real. She looked at him with uncertainty in her eyes. "We didn't have sex last night. Please tell me we didn't have sex."

Declan laughed and grinned widely. "No, we did not. But not for your lack of trying."

Kate's eyes grew wide with disbelief. "I tried to have sex with you?"

"Several times and I nearly gave in once or twice." Declan paused for dramatic effect and watched Kate's face contort. He was having trouble holding back his laughter and she wanted to grab a pillow and throw it at him, but it meant exposing herself in the process.

"If you wanted to and I wanted to, why didn't it happen?" Kate said the words, but she didn't look like she wanted an answer.

Declan leaned forward in the chair and locked eyes with her. "What do you remember about last night?"

Kate reached up and touched her head. "It's fuzzy and all feels like a dream. None of it seems quite real to me – like the edges of my memories are blurred. I know that doesn't make a lot of sense."

"It makes perfect sense." Declan stood from the chair and sat on the bed with Kate, but she pushed him away and told him to sit back in the chair.

"I'm naked under this sheet," she told him, her voice growing stern. Kate tucked the sheet tighter under her arms.

"I've seen it all, Katie. Trust me, you have nothing left to hide."

Her cheeks flushed. "What did you do?"

Declan sat down in the chair and kicked his legs up on the ottoman. "I stopped you from getting naked at Jack's mansion and in the driveway. When I finally got you into the house, I unzipped your dress – which you had been begging me to do for about an hour – and you took everything off in the living room. Then you again tried to get me naked and have your way with me. I tried to slow things down and you kept at it. Then you decided you were thirsty and starving so you went into the kitchen and stood around naked drinking water and having a snack."

"Naked?" Kate asked, slamming her eyes closed realizing that part of her memory hadn't been a dream. Declan had sat at the table in the kitchen and watched her with a broad smile on his face. She had chatted with him like she hadn't been naked. "Why didn't you look away or make me get dressed?"

"I tried, repeatedly. You weren't having it. You were hot and horny and dead set on having sex. You said you had been wanting it for years and you weren't taking no for an answer. Trust me, I deserve a medal for turning you down. It wasn't easy by any means, and I'll probably live to regret it."

There was something about the way Declan said it, a frustration that still hung in his voice that Kate believed. Besides, it was how she had felt. She had been attracted to Declan but had never wanted him to know. Then after they became partners, there was no way she could allow any complication. She didn't understand something though. "If I wanted to have sex that badly and it was that difficult for you to say no, then why didn't it happen?"

"You don't remember?" Declan asked his tone incredulous.

"It's not that I'm missing memories or can't recall last night. It's that my head is foggy and I'm not sure what was a dream or what was real."

Declan locked eyes with her. "You were drugged, Kate. I don't know when it happened, but my guess is it was some kind of mix of ecstasy and a hallucinogen. When we got back to the house, I was considering it. I was, but then you saw frogs everywhere and felt your blood coursing through your body. That's when I realized that all your unusual behavior wasn't because you wanted me, it was because you were out of your mind. I can't have sex with a woman seeing frogs everywhere."

Kate remembered the frogs but hadn't thought they were real. She didn't remember them everywhere though just in front of the house. "Did I see them inside too?"

Declan nodded. "You had a ten-minute conversation with the one you said was on the kitchen counter. You told me his name was Gus."

Kate thought that had been part of her strange trippy dream. "I didn't drink anything last night other than the drink you gave me. How could I have been drugged? It doesn't make any sense but neither does my behavior."

"I don't understand how it happened. I must have given you the drink with the drugs in it."

Kate thought back to being in the room alone with Ethan. She couldn't remember if she had said anything inappropriate to him. "It was good you went in search of me and found me before anything happened with Ethan. I don't think he would have been as chivalrous as you."

"I think he wanted to watch us. I'm fairly sure we were being watched, which is why things went as far as they did last night between us. I felt bad taking advantage of you like that. I didn't know what to do though. I couldn't not kiss my wife when she wanted me so badly. I wasn't going to put on a show for them though."

All of it was so sick and twisted, mixed emotions surged through her. "For what it's worth, I appreciate how you took care of me last night and I'm sorry for being so much trouble."

"No trouble at all. I feel a little weird with how we left things though." Declan paused and waited to see if Kate had anything to say, but she wasn't sure what she wanted to tell him.

"I don't know what to say," she admitted, pulling the sheet tighter around her. "I need to think about it all before we talk."

"Understood." Declan's tone indicated he didn't want to let it go quite yet. He seemed to be weighing his words carefully. "I want to say one thing and then I'll drop it until you're ready to talk about it. I would have had sex with you last night had you not been drugged. It probably would have complicated things between us and wouldn't have been good for our friendship. I've wanted you from the first day we met. By what you said last night, you felt the same and that's okay. It doesn't have to be weird between us now. We're still just us, Kate. Okay?"

Kate nodded and smiled. Declan was trying to make her feel better about her crazy behavior.

Declan wasn't done though. "I know you might feel weird because I saw you naked for hours. If it makes you feel better, I have no problem walking around naked so we're even."

Kate couldn't help but smile. She held her hand up to stop him. "I think we've crossed enough boundaries for one twenty-four-hour period. I'll let you know if I change my mind. I have a feeling it's going to take me a while to sort out my feelings about last night."

"I assumed so." Declan's tone grew more serious. "We need to deal with you being drugged though. We can't just let this go. If you were drugged, then I'm sure other people have been drugged. Remember, the first murdered couple was drugged. I'm concerned."

Kate hadn't even thought to ask him if he had been. "Were you okay last night?"

"I was fine. I got us out of there as quickly and efficiently as possible. No one was going to stop me."

"Thank you." Kate took a breath and let it out slowly. "I should be drug tested to see what they gave me."

Declan nodded. "I called Spade last night as soon as I realized. He wanted to send someone to the house to test you, but I told him no. There was someone outside the house watching us last night. I couldn't see who they were, but they were standing down by the corner watching the house. I thought about going and confronting them, but I didn't want to leave you alone inside for that long."

"What did Spade say last night?"

"He was concerned but knew I had it handled. I didn't tell him everything you were doing. I just said that you had some of the signs of being drugged with ecstasy, like being hot, thirsty, and overly flirty, for lack of a better word. Spade set up an appointment for us at a lab today." Declan looked over at the clock. "Are you feeling okay enough to shower? Sometimes there's a downer effect of ecstasy the next day. You didn't go to sleep until five this morning. That's why you slept all day."

"I'll be okay. I'll try to be fast." Kate scooted to the edge of the bed with the sheet still wrapped around her. "Did Spade say how we should address this?"

"We can't go running in there telling them that they drugged a federal officer. It sets us up though for the confrontation that we planned to have anyway. At least, now we have a good reason."

"That's true," Kate said, not having thought of that. Her brain didn't seem to be firing on all cylinders yet. "Did I embarrass myself too badly last night at the party?"

Declan shook his head. "No one saw you except for Ethan and whoever was monitoring the surveillance camera in the room. I'm sure they drugged you hoping that you'd let loose a little. That's what Ethan kept saying. They wanted you to initiate sex with me. As I said though, even if we had, I wasn't going to let them watch."

Kate knew there was something else she should tell him. The memory was peeking behind the curtain of her consciousness. She closed her eyes and then it hit her all at once. Kate looked over at him. "Ethan knew we'd been snooping around asking about the murders. He had heard what we said about your brother with law enforcement. He cautioned me against continuing. He assured me that neither he nor Jack had anything to do with the murders."

"What else was he going to say?" Declan stood and went to the doorway. "I'm not worried about that right now, Kate. I want to know what you were drugged with and then plan how we are going to confront them and when. The sooner we get on the outside of this, the better off we are going to be. After last night, I don't even trust that I can keep us safe."

Kate could see the hurt on his face. "You did keep me safe. I'm safe right now, Declan. Don't be so hard on yourself. If they drugged my drink without you knowing then they are more skilled at it than we realized." She stood with the sheet wrapped around her. "Give me thirty minutes and I'll be ready to go."

CHAPTER 26

After a quick trip to the lab where the FBI lab technician drew Kate's blood, plucked a few hair strands, and took a urine sample, they promised results as soon as possible. The lab tech had been warned that the results were a priority over everything else they had been working on. Spade had grown concerned for Kate's safety and demanded nearly immediate results.

He called Declan's cellphone as soon as they were back in the car. What Spade couldn't understand was how, in a room full of people, could an FBI agent be drugged. "I don't get it, Kate. Nothing like this has ever happened during a case."

Kate didn't understand it either. Shame and embarrassment overcame her. "I'm sorry, Spade. I don't have an explanation for you. I wish I did. We were careful not to eat anything, but we would have looked strange had we not been drinking anything. I had water early on and then a non-alcoholic drink from the bar. That had to have been it."

Declan felt a need to defend himself. "I got the drink for her when I got my drink. I watched the bartender make it. He handed the drink directly to me and then I handed it to Kate. It either happened at the bar and I didn't notice or when Kate was in the room with Ethan."

Kate tried to piece together every moment the drink was in her hand. She concluded that it had to have been at the bar. "The warm euphoric feeling took hold about twenty minutes in and Declan said it was about an hour later that the hallucinogenic effects took hold. We're sorry, Spade. We just don't have a better explanation."

"Don't apologize, Kate. I'm concerned but not angry with either of you." Spade barked an order to someone on the other end of the line and then refocused on them. "Listen, this whole thing tells me they are more adept at what they are doing than I gave them credit for when I sent you in. It's time to cause a scene and get out of there. I don't care how you do it but don't blow your cover and set yourselves up in opposition to Jack. Then you're going to have to watch your back."

"Someone was watching the house last night," Declan reminded him. "What do you want us to do about that?"

"Did you catch them on the home's security surveillance system?"

"No. They were down the road and out of sight. I only noticed it when I went out to get something from the driveway."

"What did you have to get?" Kate asked and then regretted it when she saw Declan's face.

"Your shoes. You had taken them off to throw at the frogs." Declan pointed to her lap and mouthed, "Your panties too."

"I don't remember taking off my shoes." Kate didn't remember taking off her panties in the driveway either and would be fine if that memory never resurfaced. She appreciated Declan hadn't said that loud enough for Spade to hear.

"I'll call you with the lab results." Spade clicked off and left Kate and Declan sitting alone in a quiet car in the lab parking lot. The air felt heavy between them.

After a few moments of silence where they listened to each other breathe heavy sighs, Declan turned to her. "You know what I could use right now?"

"Enlighten me." Kate had no idea what he wanted, but she could use a hot bath, a glass of wine, and to forget the night before ever happened.

"A cheeseburger, fries, and vanilla shake." He raised his eyebrows in a question and when Kate smiled, he put the car in drive. "I know of a good dive diner in Hollywood."

Kate's stomach growled. "I can't even remember the last time I ate anything."

"Exactly. We can't solve anything on an empty stomach." Declan drove like he knew the area although Kate had never known him to spend much time in Los Angeles or Hollywood.

Close to an hour later, they sat back in the red vinyl booth and stared at each other across the table. Both had been well-fed and felt stuffed. They had devoured their food, washed it down with thick sweet milkshakes, and barely said a word while they ate.

Now that their stomachs were full and plates empty, Kate's mood brightened. "As you said earlier today, this does put us at an advantage. I'm going to call Natalie and ask to meet her. I think you should come with me and then we can tell them that I was drugged and make sure they are okay. Then we can tell them that we are going to confront Jack at the next training session. I want there to be a house full of members when we confront him and his staff. The more people that witness it the better."

"When's the next training session?"

Kate shook her head. "I have no idea. They haven't even asked for money yet. They have already gone back to Natalie and Andrew for more."

Declan toyed with his fork. "I wondered when they'd get around to asking us to pay for the program. I'm not even sure we are officially in. I guess we will be bailing before that happens. The FBI will be happy we saved them some money."

Kate hadn't understood the process either or the different rules for different people. "I'm mostly concerned for Natalie and Andrew. They are living in that house where a murder happened and Jack knows they are unhappy." She paused and let the words hang as a memory came back to her. All at once, it hit her when she had been drugged. "Last night, Jack came up to speak to me while you were chatting with Andrew. He mentioned how unhappy Andrew is. Then he went to the bar and spoke to the bartender before making our drinks. I bet he told the bartender to drug me."

"It's likely." Declan sat back and rubbed his full stomach. "How much longer do you think we are going to be stuck here?"

"Until it's solved." Kate took the last sip of her milkshake and then raised her eyes to Declan. "We need to regroup. Go over all the evidence we have and define a potential suspect list. Then start a plan of action for after we bail on Jack's program. I want to connect with Ali again and this time meet her father."

Declan agreed with her on all points. "Let's get out of here and get to work. I'm looking forward to being done and going back home." He smiled and shrugged. "Well, your home if you're still willing to let me live there after all this weirdness."

Kate hadn't even considered rescinding the offer. "I want you there. I also want the break that Spade promised me months ago. It will be good to get back home and do absolutely nothing for a few weeks."

"It's adorable you still believe that's going to happen." Declan laughed at her naivete and then got their check, paid the bill, and drove them home. When he pulled into the driveway, neither was happy to be back. The home they had been given to live in was starting to feel like a gilded cage. He cut the engine, checked his phone, and showed it to her. "Spade texted and confirmed that you were drugged. He wants to speak to us. I'll tell him we'll call from the house phone."

"I can't believe they got the information back that quickly."

"Spade gets whatever he wants. I don't think I've ever seen anyone question him."

Kate knew that to be true. She followed Declan into the house and to the back office. He clicked the numbers of the keypad and the door opened and then he swept the house for bugs. When he was done, he rejoined Kate in the office. Declan went behind the desk as he usually did and she took one of the chairs in front.

The phone barely rang when Spade answered with a gruff greeting. "We've got an issue here. This goes beyond you being drugged."

Kate and Declan shared a look. She leaned into the desk and rested her arms. "What was I given?"

"It was exactly what Declan thought – ecstasy and psilocybin. We know that ecstasy normally comes in pill or powder form that users rub on their gums or snort. It seems it was ground up into the powder and then mixed with liquid psilocybin that was made synthetically, extracted from the mushroom. It was made into a liquid substance and dropped into the drink. At least, that's what the lab tech believes based on their analysis."

"I've never heard of anything like that available," Kate said not hiding the shock in her voice.

"The DEA hasn't heard of it either," Spade confirmed. "I got off the phone with them before I called you and they are as stumped as we are. They are getting the report from the lab when it's ready."

Declan cleared his throat. "I assume that was why it was so easy to administer without anyone noticing. If it's liquid, it would have been easily mixed in. There was some non-alcoholic ginger beer and lime soda in the drink. It could have been in either of those bottles already without anyone noticing."

Kate hadn't thought of that. She had imagined someone making her drink and then adding it in after. Having it already mixed into one of the ingredients for drinks was diabolical and genius in being able to do it without anyone being the wiser. "That could mean far more people than just me were drugged last night. I wonder if this is a routine thing for them."

"It must be. The DEA agent I spoke to who is familiar with these kinds of drugs said that someone with a healthy knowledge of chemistry created this. He was sure of it given how the effects of the drugs happened and there wasn't an overdose. Someone knows what they are doing and this wasn't their first time. He told me he's seen this on the street recently. The DEA said they hadn't been able to confirm where it's coming from. They want in on this case."

"It wasn't my fault then." Declan's eyes softened when he looked over at Kate. "I've been blaming myself for not keeping you safe. It sounds like there is no way I would have been able to stop them."

"There was no way we could have known. It wasn't anyone's fault except for Jack Harlow and his staff." Kate knew he had been feeling bad, but seeing the relief he felt now, she realized how guilty he had been feeling. "What do we do about this, Spade? We have run some background data on some of his staff. Not nearly enough, but I haven't come across anyone with a chemistry background. I don't remember seeing that in Jack's history either."

"He certainly could pull a specialist in. One of the companies he invested in several years ago was a pharmaceutical company." Spade clicked on his keyboard and the sound echoed through the phone. "I know one of the board members. Let me make some calls and see what kind of relationship Jack has with them now."

Kate leaned back and crossed her legs. "Even if he doesn't have a current relationship, it doesn't mean he didn't meet someone back then who he stayed in contact with through the years. It had to have been someone willing to do something illegal."

"You have a lot of work to do. Let me know when you're confronting Jack." Spade didn't wait for a response. He hung up without saying anything else.

Kate had been thinking about something while on the call with Spade. She wasn't sure if it was a good idea or not.

"What's on your mind, Kate? I can see the wheels turning."

"The confrontation with Jack." Declan waited while Kate finished thinking through the particulars of her plan. When she was ready to explain, she turned to him, her eyes lighting up. "I think I have an idea that might work. Assuming we get an invite back, we should prime the pump a little before going in there and flipping out. This way, we can get a little information from his staff first and then go on in there and implode our relationship."

Declan raised his eyebrows. "What did you have in mind?"

Kate smiled and cocked her head to the side, knowing he wasn't going to like her initial plan. "You have a connection with Bridgit." Declan started to interrupt her but she told him to wait. "Hear me out before you object. All I want you to do is go to Bridgit and tell her that I was acting strangely last night and ask if maybe I had taken something. You don't even have to suggest I'd been drugged. I just want to see what she has to say. While you're doing that, I'll seek out Ethan again and play up that angle."

"He wants to have sex with you, Kate." Declan rubbed his forehead – his worry wrinkle that ran from hairline to hairline making an appearance. "I don't know that it's safe for you to be around him alone."

"It's about as safe as you being around Bridgit." Kate folded her arms across her chest, digging in. "I had an off night. I don't need babying."

"That's not what I'm doing. I don't want to deal with Bridgit."

"Pretend you're twenty and that you want her too."

Declan didn't argue with her. "We need to be invited back first."

"We will be." Kate checked her watch. It was nearing seven and she wanted to check on Natalie. "Let's go take a walk."

CHAPTER 27

Kate and Declan arrived at Natalie and Andrew's house in time to hear slamming doors and the couple screaming across the house at each other. "They are still going at it," Kate said, glancing at the house from the curb and then back at Declan. "It's definitely not a good time to interrupt." She started to turn back but Declan put a hand on her shoulder and stopped her.

"It's a perfect time. Emotions are up and who knows what they are willing to tell us. I'm sure they are wondering what happened to us last night. Are we telling them about the drugs?"

Kate shook her head. She had been considering this very question on the walk over. "I don't think we should act as if we know for sure. We can suggest that we are concerned it happened. I want to hear their experiences if any."

Declan took the lead and Kate followed him to the door. He knocked once and Andrew came to the door a moment later. His eyes rounded in surprise. "I was worried about both of you," he said, opening the door and letting them in. "You carried Kate out of there last night and I assumed something had happened to her. She didn't look well."

Kate lowered her head towards the floor. "It was a rough night, to say the least. That's partly why we are stopping by. We didn't mean to interrupt."

Andrew threw up his hands in frustration. "We are always arguing these days. We had a great marriage and then we come here to improve ourselves and it all goes down the toilet." He walked them into the home and offered them something to drink, which they declined.

Kate wasn't risking it even though of all the people in Mulberry Grove, she trusted Natalie and Andrew the most. She and Declan sat side by side on the couch. "Where is Natalie?"

Andrew flopped down on a nearby chair, causing it to inch back. "Probably upstairs exercising or not eating. She is obsessed with losing weight. Monica keeps telling her it's not enough and she's not making the progress she needs."

"I'm not doing well enough!" Natalie shouted from the stairs as she came down, her footfalls loud on the steps. "What happened to you last night? Andrew said he was worried."

Natalie looked smaller and smaller every time Kate saw her. It was concerning, to say the least. Kate wanted to address it but didn't want to start an argument with her as Andrew had done. "Did either of you feel strangely after the party last night?"

Natalie and Andrew looked at each other and then back at Kate, shaking their heads. Natalie took a seat on the floor, tucking her legs under her. "I was fine and so was Andrew. The party wasn't much fun though and we left shortly after you did." Natalie's eyes bore into Kate's. "What's going on?"

Kate raised her hand to her head and began to explain some of the events of the night before. "Once I got into the library, I'm not sure what happened. I grew rather warm and had a rush of feelings come over me. I'm embarrassed to say that I found Ethan attractive and started flirting with him. It was almost like I was drunk or not in control of myself. Luckily, Declan came looking for me and that's when he carried me out and brought me home."

Declan clasped his hands in his lap. "It didn't stop there though. Once we got Kate home, she started seeing things that weren't there.

We don't have any explanation for it at all."

"It sounds like you were drugged. It's not the first time I've heard this," Andrew said matter-of-factly. Kate urged him to explain and he continued. "Molly met one on one with Jack one night and then came home and jumped all over Frank. They had the best sex of their lives. Towards the end, she started seeing things in their room. She saw a bunch of stars on their ceiling and then she has a stuffed bear that sits in a chair in their bedroom. Molly insisted it came to life and was talking to her. Frank came over the next day and told me how sexy Molly was the night before, but then they both freaked out over her seeing stuff."

Natalie seemed to be taking in the information. Then she put Kate on the spot. "Did you and Declan have the best sex of your lives last night?"

Kate let out a nervous laugh and she reached for Declan's hand. "Not exactly. I was a little too out of it by the time I made it home. As soon as I pulled into the driveway, I started seeing frogs that weren't there."

Andrew laughed. "That's not exactly sexy."

Declan laughed along with him and then he got serious. "What do you both think of Ethan? When I found Kate in the library with him, I was sure he was hitting on her. Then he suggested he wouldn't mind joining us or watching. It creeped me out. That's why I scooped up Kate and got her out of there."

Andrew made a face of disgust. "I'm telling you, there's something not right around here. Natalie was telling me a couple was murdered in this house and then there are a few past murders that happened in this community. I bet you it's all Jack Harlow. He has serious control issues. Nothing here surprises me, and I've been here a short time. I don't know how so many people stay here so long."

Declan agreed with Andrew and they spoke for several more

minutes about their impressions of the community. While they were doing that, Kate got up from the couch and sat down next to Natalie.

"Have you had much interaction with Ethan?" There was something on her mind and Kate didn't want to waste any time getting to the heart of it. She could tell by Natalie's face as soon as Ethan's name came up that she had something to say.

"Let's go for a walk," Natalie said suddenly. She stood and interrupted Andrew and Declan and told them they were leaving and would be back.

Declan raised his eyes to Kate in a question and she offered a nod, letting him know without words that she'd be fine. After she and Natalie left out the back door and walked through the backyard to the walking path behind the home, Kate asked gently, "Did something happen between you and Ethan?"

"Not me, no. It was Molly on the night that Andrew told you about. She had gone to Jack's house late to meet with him and work on some script copy he had wanted to be included in the documentary that Frank is making. While she was there, she had a snack and something to drink, and then she said she started to feel different. Like letting go, Molly said. All of her self-consciousness was suddenly gone and she felt free."

Kate understood that feeling. In retrospect, it was what had happened to her. "Did it happen during her meeting with Jack?"

"No, it was after." Natalie quickened her pace and Kate walked faster to keep up with her. "Jack offered her the drink and snack after she was done working. He told her to relax and to take a break before going home. So, she went to the library room, and sometime after, Ethan showed up. He told her how pretty she looked and what a great job she was doing to help Jack. Molly said that he sat down on the couch near her and she was overcome with a feeling of wanting him. She said it was the strangest thing she had ever experienced but she couldn't fight the feeling."

Kate recalled the night before and shuddered. "It happened to me too. Luckily, Declan came into the room before anything happened."

"Molly wasn't so lucky." Natalie stopped walking and then turned to Kate, grabbing her by the arm. "Please, don't tell anyone."

"I won't. I promise," Kate assured her. "Declan and I came to see you both tonight because you're the only ones we trust." She wanted to tell Natalie what Jack had said about Andrew, but it would have to wait. "Did Molly have sex with him?"

"They started but didn't finish. Molly told me that right in the middle of it Jack entered the room and was talking to them. He was telling Molly that she was doing a great job of letting her inhibitions go and that she needed to hurry home and satisfy her husband."

Kate's mouth dropped open. "So, she stopped having sex with Ethan and went home and had sex with Frank?"

"Yeah, that's exactly what happened. If you knew Molly the way I do, this would be hard for you to believe. She's not like that at all. Frank is the only guy she has ever been with. They met in college and have been together ever since. She said she was out of her mind and didn't even remember what happened with Ethan until the morning. That's not the worst of it though."

A feeling of dread washed over Kate realizing what she was about to say.

"When Molly confronted Jack the next day, he told her that if she tried to tell anyone, he'd expose the video of her having sex with Ethan. Worse, still, the video showed her coming on to Ethan. She was the aggressor."

"She was drugged though."

Natalie waved her off. "That might matter in a legal case, but not in Frank's eyes. Not in the court of public opinion. She's terrified of Frank finding out now."

Kate looked toward the sky. She had been afraid of something like this when Declan told her about the video. She couldn't remember all the details of the night before but at least Declan had stopped them. Otherwise, she'd be standing there in the same situation as Molly. "If Molly wants to speak to me, I'm open to it. Maybe we can tell Frank together that it happened to the both of us."

"He wouldn't believe you. He's so brainwashed into believing that Jack Harlow is a god, he'd never believe that he drugged his wife and that one of his staff raped her. All the video is going to show is Molly initiating with Ethan and then being interrupted by Jack. She left and then gave her husband the hottest sex they ever had. Frank is going to think she used him to finish what Ethan started."

"This is so sick," Kate said mostly to herself. "We have to figure out a way to help her."

"You can't. I promised Molly I wouldn't tell anyone. She wants to leave and is trying to convince Frank that she wants to go."

"I assume he won't go?" They started walking again and Kate angled her head to look at Natalie who wasn't responding.

"Did you read the journal I gave you?" Natalie asked after a few moments of silence.

"Not yet. Why?"

"I was wondering if this is why the couples were murdered. Maybe this happened to the other wives and they threatened to expose Jack if he exposed the videos. Maybe that wasn't enough to keep them quiet. I wonder if there was anything in the journal that mentions something like this."

For a teacher, Natalie was incredibly perceptive and Kate told her as much. "I promise to read it tonight. I might not finish it until tomorrow."

"I just want to know so I can help keep Molly safe."

Kate reached for her arm and closed her fingers around it. "That's not your job. You can't keep her safe. You and Andrew should pack up and leave."

Natalie stopped dead in the middle of the path and turned around to walk back to the house. Kate kept in step with her. "I want to leave, but I'm making progress losing weight. It's hard to just give that up when it's finally happening for me."

Kate pulled back and looked her up and down. "Natalie, you don't need to lose another pound. What you're doing isn't healthy. If you want to focus on exercise and nutrition, find a trainer or nutritionist when you go home. This isn't the way. It's certainly not worth risking your lives."

"That's what Andrew said."

"He's absolutely right. Please, listen to your husband and pack up and go." Kate's cellphone binged in her pocket. She took it out to see who had texted her. It was a message from Claire letting them know that they had officially been invited into the program and that an initial payment of fifteen thousand dollars would be due before tomorrow night's training sessions. Kate responded probably too quickly that they'd be there with a check. She'd make sure the check wouldn't clear so they didn't waste the FBI's money. She put her phone back in her pocket.

"Who was that?"

Kate hesitated not sure she should tell her she got into a program that she was pleading with Natalie to leave. She opted for the truth or at least as much truth as she could share. "It was Claire," Kate explained after a moment. "She told me that we are officially in the program. Listen though, we aren't going to join. We are going to confront Jack."

"No, Kate, you'll put yourself in danger."

"We know, but it's going to be okay." As they crossed from the path back into Natalie's backyard, Kate stopped her. "Jack told me last night that Andrew isn't being cooperative. He was angry about it, and I truly feel you are both in danger. I hope you'll listen to me and leave. You have options – families who will support you if you leave."

"I can't leave Molly."

"Then take her with you."

Natalie shook her head. "I suggested that and she told me that she couldn't leave Frank. She won't leave without him, and he is obsessed with making this documentary. It's why we are all here."

Kate pressed her hands to her eyes and rubbed them. "We'll figure something out. I promise you that."

Natalie gave her a funny look. "Why does it matter to you? You only just met us."

"I'll explain another time." Kate walked off toward the house leaving Natalie to stare at her. All Kate wanted at that moment was to get Declan and go home to make a plan.

CHAPTER 28

"Molly was sexually assaulted, Declan," Kate explained as they walked back from Natalie and Andrew's house. To stress her point that they needed to leave, Kate had told Andrew that he needed to pack their things and get out of there as soon as possible – that night even. He needed to go even if Natalie refused. Kate stressed that she thought they were both in danger.

Andrew had agreed with her but said that there was no way he could leave without Natalie who remained steadfast that she wasn't leaving without Molly, who would not leave her husband behind. It all hinged on Frank who had been completely taken in by Jack Harlow, at least that's what Natalie said and Andrew confirmed. The couple was staying put for now against Kate and Declan's advice and Andrew's desires.

Kate had not told Andrew what had happened to Molly and she hadn't clued Declan in until they were in the street on their way home.

Declan had stopped in the street and turned to her. "What do you mean she was sexually assaulted and by whom?"

Kate relayed the story about Molly that Natalie had told her. Her voice raised a notch and she remembered they were in the middle of the street so she quieted down towards the end of the story. "It's the same thing that would have happened to me if you hadn't come into the room."

Declan remained quiet for several moments while considering what she had said. When he did speak, he immediately angered Kate. "I don't know that the case would go far in court."

"That's hardly the point, Declan. It probably wouldn't go far in court if Jack produced a video that showed Molly coming on to Ethan and she couldn't prove she had been drugged. I can prove I've been drugged, so we both know standing here what happened. Natalie wondered if this is the motive for the murders."

"I hadn't thought of that," he said, his voice low. "I didn't mean to upset you. I was thinking from a criminal perspective. I agree that what happened to her was wrong. Just like what happened to you was wrong. I wasn't trying to justify Ethan or Jack."

Kate knew that and appreciated what Declan said. "I'm being sensitive right now because it could have been me had you not walked into the room and protected me."

Declan looked down at the ground as they walked and became quiet. After walking about a block, he spoke so quietly Kate wasn't sure she had heard him. "Do you consider what happened between us last night an assault? Am I guilty of that?"

Kate cursed under her breath and reached out her hand to stop him from walking. She moved so she was standing right in front of him, her feet between his and their bodies touching. She put her hands on his arms and looked up into his eyes. "How could you think that? You'd never hurt me or assault me or take advantage of me."

"I know, Kate, but last night I knew something was off. When you tried to have sex with me in the library, I gave into it. I cared more about keeping our cover than what was happening with you. Then when we got outside and you still wanted me, I can't even tell you how it made me feel. I would have gone home and had sex with you even though I suspected something was off with you. I didn't know that you were drugged though until you started seeing the frogs. Then I knew and nothing happened between us even when you tried. I swear to you."

Declan's face crumpled and Kate was terrified he might cry, which was something she couldn't handle. She had seen him break down only once in their years of friendship and that was on a particularly difficult case where a child had been killed. They had gone to a local bar and Declan drank his sorrows away. The more he drank that night the more emotional he became until he was sitting in a back corner booth crying his eyes out. There hadn't been much Kate could say to console him and his tears caused hers. It was a messy night for them both and not one she wanted to relive anytime soon.

Kate laid the palm of her hand against his cheek. "You said it yourself. As soon as you realized I had been drugged, you stopped." The words did little to shift the mood though. Kate took a breath and blurted, "Drugged or not I wanted to have sex with you. I've thought about it many times over the years, but our friendship, and more importantly, our partnership, stopped me every time. The lust you saw last night was real, Declan. You kissed me and I enjoyed it. Nothing happened between us that I didn't want to happen."

Declan's eyes shifted back and forth and then he looked across Kate's head. She wasn't sure what he was looking at but his gaze remained fixed. Then all at once he leaned down, tipped her chin up, and planted a kiss on her that she wouldn't soon forget. He ran his fingers through her hair and cupped one hand behind her head and another against her back, drawing her even closer. Kate matched his passion but the embrace ended as quickly as it began.

"I see you two are still at it," Ethan laughed, approaching from behind Kate. "I thought you two would have been worn out after last night." He walked right up next to them like nothing had happened the night before. He reached out to Kate, but she stepped back.

Ethan bristled at her response. "What gives, Kate? You were

friendlier than I've seen you last night. Don't tell me you've gone back to being a cold shrew again. It's not attractive or welcoming."

Kate reached for Declan's hand, which he had balled into a fist. She was sure by his tense body language and expression that he was seconds from pounding Ethan into the pavement. "We need to talk about last night, but this isn't the time or the place."

"You can address this right now. As your guide, I demand you do so."

Kate held her ground. "Another time." She pulled Declan by the hand and led him away. Ethan called to them to stop, but they didn't listen and didn't even acknowledge that he had spoken. They walked back in silence.

When they entered the house, Declan went to the back office while Kate kicked off her sneakers and sat down on the chaise in the living room and wrapped the blanket around her. A swirl of conflicting emotions bubbled up inside of her. It was rare she felt real fear around someone during an investigation but Ethan and Jack triggered something in her. She wrapped the blanket tighter.

Declan came into the living room a few minutes later with Amelia's journal. He tossed it to her before snuggling up with her on the chaise instead of taking his normal spot on the couch.

"We're snuggling now?" Kate asked, teasing him. She didn't mind that he was sitting with her. She hated to admit it but his strong muscular body next to her provided the comfort and warmth she needed.

Declan put one arm across the back of the chaise and she snuggled under his arm and into his chest. He rubbed the back of her neck with his fingers. "I figured we both could use it. This has been an emotional day."

"Did you kiss me in the street because you saw Ethan approaching?"

"I kissed you because I wanted to kiss you." Declan breathed heavily but didn't say anything for a moment. "I know it took a lot to admit what you did back there in the street, and I didn't want you to feel weird about it. I appreciate it because after you told me Molly had been sexually assaulted it sent my mind reeling. I thought for a moment you had felt like that's what happened between us. If you had, I couldn't live with myself. When I saw Ethan approaching and I couldn't respond to the wonderful things you said, kissing you at that moment felt right."

Relief washed over Kate that kissing her hadn't been about Ethan and putting on a show as a married couple. "We are going to have a lot to unpack personally when this case is over, but we can't do it right now. I just need to make sure you know what happened between us was something I had wanted to happen between us."

"Understood." He reached over and tapped the journal. "Let's figure out if Natalie's theory is correct and the drugs and sex tapes are a motive for murder."

Kate opened the journal towards the back. She figured if there was going to be something about what caused the couple's murder it would be closer to the back than the front. She scanned through a few pages without finding much of interest. When she got to the third page from the last journal entry, she struck gold.

Amelia had been drugged three weeks before the murder. She detailed what she could remember about the evening and having sex with Ethan in the library. She had come home that night to an empty house, taken a shower, and went straight to sleep. She woke sometime later and thought she was having a horrendous dream. Ben, her husband, had been beside her and woke as she screamed and kicked. They were both unsettled to learn she hadn't been dreaming but had been having vivid hallucinations. Neither of them had understood what was happening.

A week later, Amelia admitted to Ben what had happened with Ethan that night. She explained how out of her mind she had been and thought she might have been drugged. Ben, having seen firsthand the hallucinations, confronted Ethan and Jack. They admitted it was all part of the program and Amelia and Ben vowed they were leaving and going to the police. Jack cautioned them he'd make the video public. They told him that they didn't care. From what Kate read, it had been what sealed their fate.

Declan cursed and pounded his fist down on the side of the chaise. "This is all so sick. Do you think it happened to the other couples?"

"I think it's fair to say that it's probable. I can see why Jack and Ethan wouldn't want that to be made public, especially if the victims didn't care if the video was out there."

"Even if law enforcement didn't take them seriously, then it would be enough to ruin Jack's reputation and derail the whole program – costing Jack millions and exposing him to an investigation by the DEA. It would at least get him on their radar."

Everything Declan said Kate had been thinking. There was only one thing that stumped her. "Amelia and Ben had been in the program for years, the same with all of the victims. Molly is only a few months in and we hadn't even officially been asked to join yet. Why risk it so early?"

"I have no idea. It makes sense if they were going to pull something like this, they'd do it with people who had succeeded in the program and trusted them. Doing this with people barely in the program seems riskier."

"Unless it's not," Kate said, trying to form the ideas rapidly coming to her. She pushed herself up a little straighter and turned so she could see Declan. "What if Jack realized that it was too much of a risk with people so entrenched and connected to the program? If they left and went to the cops, think about all the information they could share. At the point the murdered victims were going to flee, they had known Jack and his staff and the inner workings of the program for a couple of years. Drugging people barely in the program is like a test – if they tell, Jack can defend himself with video evidence, but they don't know much about the program. If they choose not to tell anyone and stay in the program, it's a sign of trust for Jack. He can do anything he wants and they aren't going to tell anyone anything."

"How many women do you think he's done this with?"

"What makes you think it's only women?"

Declan drew back in surprise. "I hadn't thought about that at all. There's nothing to say that it couldn't have been me that Bridgit drugged and then finally took what she wanted."

"Exactly."

"I don't know how many people," Declan said evenly, running a hand down his face. "You made a good point though about them changing tactics. Does it fit the profile you've done on Jack?"

Kate hadn't formally done a profile on Jack yet. She, against her own better judgment, had been taking this case by the seat of her pants. Undercover work wasn't something she had been accustomed to and it meant she couldn't dig in and interview him. Looking at his past and her limited interactions with him, she could safely say she considered him a narcissist. Anyone with an internet connection could have come up with that though. "I should probably give it some consideration before we make a plan for tomorrow night."

"What's tomorrow night?" Declan asked.

"I forgot to tell you. Claire texted me while we were at Natalie's and we are scheduled for our first training sessions tomorrow night."

Declan whistled. "We better prepare for the confrontation. Are we going to check out an official training session or go in and confront right away?"

"We need a plan." Kate's head spun with possibilities. The one thing she knew for sure though was if the other women really had confronted Jack about the drugs and then left the program, she and

Declan would be living at serious risk from that point forward.

CHAPTER 29

The next morning around ten, Declan left for a run while Kate walked to the coffee shop to get a mid-morning snack and a mocha espresso. She also wanted to see Ali. While focusing on Jack, they couldn't forget what Det. Miller had said about Liam, Ali's father. He had been a suspect in the murders and never technically cleared.

More than that though, Liam might be the only person who could confirm for Kate if the victims were leaving because of the suspected drugging and sexual assaults. Kate couldn't confirm that with any of the other victims except Amelia. It was a working theory with no real teeth.

The night before Kate and Declan had stayed up late researching Jack and his staff as well as coming up with a solid plan for that evening's training. Walking into the coffee shop, Kate had an air of confidence she hadn't felt in a while.

Kate sidestepped a woman trying to leave the shop with a bag tucked under her arm and two coffees in her hand. As Kate approached the counter, someone called her name from the side of the room. She turned to see Ali sitting at one of the tables with a book in front of her.

"Are you here for coffee or to find me?" Ali asked, her voice tinged with anger. She closed the book and raised her eyebrows expecting an answer.

Kate crossed the room so they wouldn't be shouting across the shop. "Are you angry at me for something?" she asked, taking a seat across from the young woman.

Ali sat back and folded her arms across her chest. "How many times did I tell you not to join Jack Harlow's program? I wasn't talking to hear myself speak. I was trying to keep you out of danger. It sounds like you walked right into it."

Kate watched her carefully, a bit taken aback by Ali's tone of voice. She wasn't sure how to address this and keep her as a confidant. Kate resisted the urge to snap at her and instead relaxed back into the chair. "I appreciate your concern. I think there's been some misunderstanding. We went to an information session and then a welcome event."

"For new members." Ali smirked and cocked her head to the side, looking at Kate as if she were an idiot. "I know once you attend that welcome event, you're in."

Kate took a breath. "As I said, Ali, I appreciate that you warned us. There were things we needed to see for ourselves. If it makes you feel any better, we will not be joining."

Ali pinned her gaze on her. "You're not?"

Kate shook her head. "We are going to a training session tonight but that is the last thing we will attend. We have a few things to say to Jack Harlow."

"Are you being honest?" Ali asked, her voice softening.

"I'm being honest. I have no reason to lie." Kate leaned in and rested her arms on the table. "I've never had reason to lie to you. It was our decision to make though."

In a matter of seconds, Ali went from rageful back to acting like she was friends with Kate. It unnerved her how quickly the young woman changed. "Did something happen to make you not want to go back?"

"It's not the program for us." Kate wasn't going to get into what had happened. She didn't want to play her cards too openly for now. There'd be a time and place to reveal what she knew. "There's something important I want to talk to you about though. I want to meet your father. Can you introduce me?"

Ali's jaw set firm. "Why do you want to meet my father?"

Kate looked around the shop and then leaned more into the table, gesturing to Ali to lean in as well. She dropped her voice low. "I heard your father can help people leave Jack's program, and I have friends who need help. It's delicate so I need to speak with him directly."

Ali considered that for a moment and then took out her phone and sent a text. She put the phone face down on the table and then looked over at Kate. "I trust you, but I don't know that my father will. I asked and we'll have to see how he responds."

That was all Kate could ask for. "In the meantime, can you tell me more about him? I don't know much of anything other than hearing he helped people."

Ali checked her phone and put it back down. "Where did you hear about my father?"

Kate struggled to remember what exactly Ali had told her. "You've said a few things," she said cautiously, "and then one of the victims' neighbors said that your father had been helping them leave. She was quite upset that the victims didn't get to leave safely. She said good things about him though and thought he might be able to help me."

"He probably can." Ali watched her.

Kate kept her body language open and her facial expressions neutral. "I know it might be hard to trust me given you don't know me, but remember you're the one who approached me first. You trusted me enough to tell me not to join Jack's program. We have friends who are caught up in it and we needed to see for ourselves what it was all about."

"You'd risk your safety to help a friend?"

Kate nodded. "That's why it's so important that we get some help. Declan and I truly believe that it's a cult and we are worried for our friends, especially given the murders."

Ali considered this and then reached for her phone and sent another text. "As you can imagine, he's reluctant to trust new people. He's been burned in the past."

"Has he had issues with Jack? Is that what you mean by being burned?"

Ali shook her head and looked away, all of a sudden too shy to speak.

"Ali, I want to be able to trust you and your father as much as you trust Declan and me. It's a two-way street here."

"What do you know about my father?"

"Not much," Kate reiterated. They hadn't found much about the man online. Most of what they knew came from Det. Miller, but they hadn't been able to corroborate it. Not that Kate didn't trust the detective. She liked hearing information firsthand. "I know what you've told me. He has been doing some research about cults. Then I heard he's helped some people out of cults as I told you. I figured if there was anyone around here who might be able to help me it was your father – especially given all the warnings you provided me about Jack Harlow."

"You didn't hear anything bad about him?"

Kate sat back and bit at her lip. "Ali, you're starting to worry me. First, you tell me he's been burned in the past and now you're asking me if I heard anything bad." She gripped the edge of the table as if to stand. "Never mind, I don't think it was a good idea to ask for help."

Ali gestured for her to sit. "I thought everyone in Mulberry Grove had heard by now."

Kate offered a nervous smile. "Ali, you're being cryptic. I'd appreciate open dialogue here or I can assume I'm wasting my time. If you have something to say, please say it."

Ali hesitated for only a moment. She checked her phone again and then dropped the phone to the table. "I'm surprised you haven't heard that my father had been questioned in the murders, and some in the community and Jack's circle suspect him. There is even a detective who suspected him."

Kate didn't hide her expression of shock. "Why would anyone suspect that your father had anything to do with the murders? He was helping those people, right? Why would he kill people he was trying to help out of a cult? That doesn't seem to make a lot of sense to me."

"Me either," Ali said, a hint of sadness in her voice. "It all went a bit bad. My father was trying to help them leave. That's part of why he moved here. He wanted to learn more about the inner workings of Jack Harlow and his cult, but he also wanted to lend support to people who wanted to get out. The people who were murdered had come to my father to ask for help and he had been helping them, causing us to be put on notice from Jack Harlow. He threatened legal action. He harassed my father. Jack did everything he could to make sure my father left Mulberry Grove, but my father wouldn't be driven away like that. He helped several people leave so he knew what he was doing and he was dedicated to his mission."

"What went wrong with the people who were murdered?"

"They decided not to leave. That's why people say my father killed them." Ali threw her hands up. "I don't know the truth. My father doesn't know the truth. He said those couples were ready to go. They were afraid and delayed because they were worried about what was going to happen to them. There is speculation that Jack got them to change their minds, and in a fit of anger, my father killed them. They say he is unhinged and determined to destroy Jack."

"Is any of that true – that your father is unhinged and will go to any lengths?" Kate assessed Ali's body language and she was sitting there with her hands on the table, relaxed back in the seat. "Ali, you can talk to me. Maybe I can help you."

Ali shook her head. "I don't need help." She didn't say anything for a moment, checking her phone again and becoming frustrated by the lack of response. "My father isn't always the easiest to deal with. It's his way or none at all. He's arrogant and people don't like that about him, but he does know what he's doing. He's helped so many people get their lives back."

"I assume if your father hasn't been arrested for the murders that people stopped believing he could be the killer."

"I gave him an alibi for all of the murders." Ali looked away again and toyed with a ring on her finger. She played with the stone and then wiggled the ring back and forth on her finger.

Kate knew she had been lying. "Ali," she said sternly, drawing the young woman's attention to her. "Was your father with you at the time of the murders?"

Ali wouldn't meet Kate's look. "He asked me to tell the cops that I had been home those nights. In truth, I don't remember where I was. I can't recall a single date the cop asked me."

That was perfectly normal. If nothing significant happened, no one remembered random dates from years ago. Ali would have no reason to remember what she had been doing unless she had kept a detailed calendar and even then it would be appointments noted. She might not even have a real memory of the time.

"Why did you lie?" Kate asked even though she figured it was a stupid question.

"I didn't know what was happening. My father told me that Jack was trying to frame him for murders he had committed so that he'd stop helping people. I knew my father was doing something good and wanted him to be able to continue. I knew that he'd never kill anyone so I lied."

Kate understood the reason, but the FBI agent in her wanted to come down hard on her. She had to temper her emotion. "This is serious, Ali," she cautioned. "Lying to law enforcement is a crime. Not to mention if your father killed those people, he needs to be stopped."

"My father didn't kill those people."

"How do you know that? You don't remember those evenings so you don't even know where he was at the time."

"I just know." Ali checked her phone and then looked up at Kate. "My father said he'd meet you tomorrow – if you still want to after this."

"Tell him I'll be there." They stopped the conversation they had been having to hammer out the logistics of the meeting. When it was confirmed, Kate refocused. "Ali, this doesn't change what we were discussing. You need to come clean about what you know and don't know."

"Are you going to call the cops on me?" Ali's tone gave Kate the feeling she wouldn't care one way or another.

"I'm not calling anyone, but I'm concerned about you. Have you considered that you've gotten caught up in something dangerous? This is your father's fight but it doesn't have to be yours. You have your whole life ahead of you."

Ali seemed to let Kate's words sink in. After a few moments of quiet, she pointed to her ring. "This is my mom's ring."

Kate knew she wasn't just trying to change the subject. "You've never mentioned your mom. Where is she?"

Ali finally raised her head and locked eyes with Kate. "She's dead. Jack Harlow killed her."

CHAPTER 30

"Jack Harlow killed Ali's mother," Declan said from the bathroom with disbelief in his voice. He was standing in front of the mirror, a towel wrapped around his waist, brushing his teeth. He finished what he was doing and then walked out of the bathroom. "What did you do after she told you that?"

Kate sat in the chair in the far corner of the room with her laptop searching for more information about the death of Ali's mother. "Ali got up and ran out of the shop. I tried to catch up to her, but she took off running and I lost her."

"You're getting soft in suburbia." He laughed showing off a row of white teeth. Water beaded on his chest and the patch of hair that ran from his belly to below his towel remained damp. "Kate, are you going to look at me or is this too much for you to resist?"

Kate had been averting her eyes, keeping them trained on her laptop since he had exited the bathroom. She didn't trust herself after what had happened the other night. Kate raised her eyes from her laptop to look at him. "I'm doing some research on Ali's mother. You being in a towel does very little for me."

Declan slipped his hand into the space where the towel had come together at his waist. "I can drop it right here for you if you'd like. You already showed me yours, it's only fair I show you mine."

Kate couldn't help but laugh despite wanting to remain serious. "Go get dressed."

He shrugged. "Whatever the lady wants…"

Kate waited until he retreated into the bathroom. "I lost Ali because I wasn't trying to chase after her. I followed her initially to see if she was okay, but it was clear to me she wanted to be alone. While Ali is open with me and forthcoming with information, she isn't someone you should push for information. She tells you what she wants to tell you when she wants to tell you. Otherwise, she will shut down and might not speak again."

"You don't know anything more than Ali thinks Jack Harlow killed her mother. Is that what you're saying?"

"That's why I'm sitting here researching, but I didn't even have the woman's name until a moment ago. Lydia married Liam Brady in 1991. They would have just celebrated their thirtieth wedding anniversary. Now that I have her name and date of birth, I can do other searches." Kate focused her attention on her laptop.

"It makes sense though if Jack Harlow killed her that Liam would have a mission to take him down. I want to know the details surrounding it."

As did Kate, which was why she was sitting there instead of getting ready for Jack's training. She had only about twenty more minutes before she'd need to be in the shower and didn't want to leave without the details. Kate put the date into another search engine and whooped with happiness when she found the information in seconds.

"I found a death certificate for Lydia. She died six years ago here in Mulberry Grove." Kate scanned down the newspaper article that didn't tell her much. "It says she was found shot to death in her house. I'd need the autopsy report to learn more."

Declan stepped out of the bathroom in tight black boxer briefs and a smile. He held his arms open to the sides and twirled once for her. "Is this more to your liking?"

"Declan." Kate sighed. "I'm talking to you about a woman's murder and you're wiggling around like a cat in heat. Be serious for five minutes."

"Gallows humor, Kate. It's how we all survive doing this job. Besides, you're not telling me anything for me to get emotional about yet." Declan's lips set in a firm line showing her he was trying to be serious. "If Ali's mother was murdered, I feel terrible for her. No one should have to go through that. I need details though, and that's going to have to wait until we implode Jack's training tonight. Your mind should be on that. It's going to take some acting chops."

Kate knew he was right about needing to focus. He was wrong about one thing though. She wasn't going to have to put on a show of rage toward Jack and Ethan. It had been simmering all day. She set her laptop on a nearby table and eased out of the chair. "I'll take a shower and get ready."

As Kate walked by him, he reached for her arm and pulled her into him. He kissed the bridge of her nose. "Are you ready for tonight? Once we do this, there will be a bull's eye on our backs. We won't be able to undo it. Are we sure this is the way to go?"

Kate allowed herself to be enveloped in his arms. She hugged him back. "Did you ever get a chance to speak to Bridgit?"

"No, she never returned my calls or texts and when I went by Jack's on my run, she wasn't there. Jack was curious why I was looking for her, but I said that she called me and I was following up. He seemed to buy that. I haven't heard anything though, which is rather surprising given how she had been acting towards me."

Kate patted his chest. "Sorry, kid, your girlfriend is probably out seducing someone a little more willing."

"Let's hope so, but she could have called me back. Are we good to move forward without speaking to her first?"

"See if she's there tonight and I'll see if I can get Ethan alone. Based on that and the events of this evening, we'll know the right time." Kate wriggled out of his arms but turned her head over her shoulder to look at him and was surprised by the desire in his eyes.

At six that evening, Kate and Declan dressed casually as had been requested for the training, and walked hand-in-hand into Jack's house. A few of the couples they had seen the first night were milling around in the foyer, talking in hushed rushed voices about what the evening's activities would entail. All eyes turned to Kate and Declan when they walked into the room.

"Whatever we did the other night worked," Kate said in a whisper as they took their place along the wall and waited. "Everyone is staring at us."

"That generally happens when a husband has to carry his wife out the door in his arms. Plus, that dress you had on was bunched up close to your backside. Who knows what kind of show you gave them?"

Kate blushed at the memory of it. "Try to find Bridgit before we get started."

Declan let go of her hand and started to walk away down the hall and out of sight. Kate stood there alone, waiting for the training to start. None of the other members approached her and a feeling of awkwardness took hold. She wasn't used to being an object of curiosity if that's why people were staring. Kate normally commanded the attention in the room because of her knowledge and leadership. She was out of her element.

Declan hadn't come back by the time Monica appeared and ushered them into one of the training rooms. She pointed at Kate. "Where's your husband?"

"He went to find Bridgit. She left him a message and he hasn't been able to get in touch with her yet. He thought it might be important or something we needed to know before we started tonight."

Monica pointed down the hall and instructed everyone to go that way and then get comfortable inside the room. She approached Kate who was the last in line. "I don't know why she called Declan, but it's not important now. Bridgit's gone from the program. If she has any further contact with you both, let us know immediately."

"What do you mean *gone*?"

"Jack fired her after the party the other night." Monica started to walk away like that was the end of the discussion, but Kate wasn't having it. She caught up to the woman. "Why was she fired?"

"I can't discuss that with you. It's none of your concern." Monica dismissed her and wouldn't say another word. Kate had no choice but to follow her into the room.

Kate took a seat in the far back left side of the room in the last chair in a long row. She pulled out her phone to text Declan, but before she could hit send, he walked into the room looking a bit flustered. He spotted Kate in the back and walked toward her.

Declan sat in the chair beside Kate. "Bridgit quit the other night after the event. She walked out and they haven't heard from her."

Kate turned her head to look at him, her brow furrowing. "Monica told me that she was fired. Who told you she quit?"

"Sadie and Ethan. I ran into them near the library and they asked me what I was doing. When I told them I was looking for Bridgit, Sadie started to say something but Ethan cut her off and told me she quit."

Kate had a sinking feeling in her gut she didn't like. She didn't like Bridgit but she didn't want anything to happen to the young woman. "Call it a hunch but it's not adding up for me."

Declan shrugged, seeming to brush off her concern. "Maybe there's some speculation about what happened and no one knows the real story. It could be nothing. Why are you worried?"

"The murders that have already taken place for one. Being drugged for two. Shady things are happening around Jack and I wouldn't put anything past him."

Declan glanced down at her. "You think something has happened to her?"

"I don't know. Maybe she tried to seduce the wrong guy. Maybe Jack didn't like that she wasn't succeeding in seducing you or maybe she did get fired or quit. It's anyone's guess." Monica had started to speak in the front of the room and everyone quieted. Out of the corner of her mouth, Kate said softly, "Let's put a pin in it and explore more later."

They both focused their attention on the front of the room where Monica stood. She wrote the title of the evening's presentation on a large Post-It and then ripped it off and stuck it to the wall. "We are going to focus on shame for this evening. When we feel shame for one reason or another, it often holds us back from accomplishing what we want in life. We are going to explore our shame tonight as a group. This will be uncomfortable for all of you, but it's the only way to get past it. Shame lives in secret. Tonight, we are bringing it into the light."

Everyone in the room glanced around at each other, worried expressions on their faces. No one, including Kate, wanted to talk about things they felt shame about in their lives – certainly not in a room full of other people. She crossed her arms and legs and drew back in her chair. Declan tensed his posture as well.

"Who wants to go first?" Monica asked, looking out over the crowd and roaming her eyes back and forth until she landed on a woman. She pointed at her and the woman squirmed in her seat. "Please rise and tell us what you hold the most shame for in your life and how it holds you back."

The woman stood tentatively and rocked back and forth on her feet. She introduced herself and her husband. "I have a lot of negative self-talk that is shameful to me. I don't know why I do it, but I constantly put myself down. As a result, I'm highly critical of others. Putting them down helps me to feel better. I've never admitted that before, but being so critical is impacting my marriage."

The woman sat down, thinking she was done but Monica gestured for her to continue to stand. "Thank you for sharing. I'd like you to dig deeper about why this is something you do."

"I don't know that I can." The woman had her hands at her sides and then clasped them in front of her. Kate could see that her knuckles were turning white.

"Give it a try. There are reasons why we do everything – most often it stems from childhood."

The woman was quiet for several moments and then her body shook. Kate wasn't sure if it was with fear or anxiety or sadness. It was clear as the quiet settled uncomfortably in the room that she wasn't going to respond.

Monica walked right up to her and grabbed her by the arms. "Maybe the negative self-talk is true. You seem a bit worthless and pathetic right now." She called the woman names until she began to sob. No one in the room did or said a thing and no one stopped Monica until Kate and Declan had had enough.

Before Kate could get out a word, Declan jumped to his feet. "That's enough. Don't speak to her like that. There's nothing wrong with someone who has boundaries and doesn't want to share their deepest secrets in a room full of strangers."

Monica froze and her cheeks flamed red. She had gone from cool and calm to anger. She left the woman and came right over to Declan and pointed a finger, shoving it into his chest. "You don't speak unless you are spoken to and I approve it."

Declan laughed right in her face and everyone in the room collectively gasped. "I'm not sure who you think you are, but I don't take orders from you."

Kate stood up from her chair in solidarity with him.

Monica looked from Declan to Kate. "I'm in control here."

Kate joined Declan in his laughter. "It doesn't look that way to me." She got right up in Monica's face. "If you want to talk about shame – let's start with the fact that you drug and rape women here. I was drugged the other night and I have proof."

Monica reeled back like she'd been slapped while the room erupted in sounds of shock and horror. A woman who sat directly in front of Kate turned to her with her eyes wide. "I knew I had been drugged the other night. I knew it and no one believed me."

The din of chaos and noise grew louder with no signs of ceasing. Monica had no choice but to run from the room in search of help.

CHAPTER 31

After Monica fled the room, Kate explained to everyone what had happened the other night at the welcome party. Most looked on in shock as she explained the details. Declan added to the story from his perspective. The woman, who also said she had been drugged, told a similar tale. She broke down crying but said she had some comfort knowing that she hadn't been imagining things.

This was not how Kate and Declan had planned to start this, but Monica had given them an opening by berating the woman. Declan apologized to Kate for going off-plan, but she assured him all was fine.

Kate couldn't help but crack a smile when moments later, Monica charged back into the room followed by Ethan and Jack. Both men had pained expressions. Jack darted his gaze around the room until he spotted Kate and Declan in the back.

From his position in the front of the room, Jack gestured with his hand for them to follow him like he was a principal who had entered an unruly classroom to drag students to his office. Neither of them budged. Kate and Jack locked eyes and both remained where they stood.

Jack capitulated first. He commanded, "We need to meet in my office about this allegation right now. Let's go now, please. I'm sure you don't want to embarrass yourselves in a room full of people."

Declan folded his arms across his chest and widened his stance in defiance. "We aren't going anywhere with you. Not yet anyway. Besides, they already know. Kate informed them about what happened to her. We all know Kate isn't the exception here, Jack. This is something you've done to a lot of women and possibly men."

"You are to address me as Luminary and do as I say when I say it," he snarled.

Declan laughed. "Not in your wildest dreams is that going to happen."

Jack marched down the aisle between the chairs and when he reached Declan, he made the mistake of trying to grab him by the arm. Declan took hold of the man's wrist, bent it back, and had him on his knees before Jack even knew what was happening to him. Ethan followed the same path Jack took, coming to his defense, but Kate stepped around the chairs and got between them.

"I wouldn't if I were you," Kate said, getting right up in his face. "No point causing yourself any more trouble than you're already in. It's a crime to try to have sex with a drugged woman, Ethan. She can't consent to what's happening."

Ethan smirked at her. "We have a video, Kate, of you aggressively coming onto me. You have no proof you were drugged. You're in here saying this now because you're embarrassed by what happened. You allowed yourself the freedom to explore your passion and now you regret it. It's all part of the program, sweetie. You need to learn to let go and explore your feminine side." He reached out to put a hand on Kate's shoulder and she pulled back out of his reach.

"Don't put a hand on her," Declan snarled, allowing Jack to finally stand.

Ethan heeded Declan's warning and pulled back from touching Kate. "As I was explaining, if you continue to go down this route, we will have no choice but to publicize the video recording of the other night. I'm sure you wouldn't want that to be made public. After all, it shows you cheating on your husband."

Kate stood with her head back, locking eyes with him. "I'm fine with it going public, Ethan. Those who know me will immediately see that it was out of character for me. All you'll be doing is handing over evidence of the sick twisted games you play here."

Jack's eyes darted to Ethan and then to Kate. He believed that she didn't care if the video was made public. His voice was suddenly calm. "I think there's been a lot of misunderstanding here. Please, let's go to my office and we can discuss this calmly. I'm sure we can figure out a way to make this right."

Declan glared at him. "What's to make right if you didn't do anything wrong?"

For the first time, Kate saw Jack visibly shaken. Beads of sweat formed at his hairline and he paled. He licked his lips and blinked rapidly several times. "I simply meant that I don't know what happened the other night, but that I'd be more than happy to get to the bottom of it and rectify any situation that Kate imagined might have happened."

"I didn't imagine it happening," Kate said, standing her ground. "The drugs didn't make me forget what happened. It may have caused me to lose control in the moment, but I remember every detail."

Jack tried to offer a smile but it fell short of that. "Of course, Kate. Poor choice of words on my part. I simply meant that something happened the other night that has you upset. That's something we need to discuss and figure out. This program is meant to challenge you and break you out of old patterns. I know some of our methods might not seem mainstream to you, but they are effective. I've been doing this for ten years and have helped thousands of people."

"I'd agree with you that drugging and raping women on video is not mainstream."

"Now just wait a moment," Jack said, holding his hand up to stop her. "No one drugged you or raped you. You had an experience where you were feeling free to explore your sexuality and you did that. As far as the video is concerned, it's a training exercise and we video all training."

Kate cocked her head to the side. "Then explain why Ethan just threatened to make it public if it's just a training exercise."

"Well," Jack said slowly, turning to look at Ethan. It was clear Jack wasn't happy he had said that. "You're accusing Ethan of something terrible. Something he'd never do. He is simply defending himself."

"I'm not the only one, Jack, and we both know it. I'm one of the lucky ones. Declan interrupted and brought me safely home and then spent the night awake with me as I hallucinated. Other women haven't been so lucky." Kate glared at him, hoping her meaning would come across.

Jack looked between them and hesitated, seeming unsure of what to do or say to deescalate the situation. "Can we please go into my office to discuss the misunderstanding? I'm sure once we talk, everything will become clearer to you."

Before Kate could respond, the heavy-booted sound of reinforcements came through the hallway. Sadie walked into the room on the verge of tears as she gestured toward Jack. "It's the DEA. They said they are here to search the property. They have a search warrant."

Jack looked between both Kate and Declan as his mouth hung open. "What have you done?"

Kate went to her chair and grabbed her purse. She pulled out her lab report, unfolded the paper, and then walked over to him. The FBI had the lab create two reports – one with Kate's real name for the official record and then one with a made-up lab's name with her alias to show Jack.

She slapped the report against his chest. "I was smart enough to get tested the other night. I guess what they found was something they have seen on the street recently and the DEA had an interest in. From what the lab said, the call to the DEA was protocol. We had no idea they were going to search you like this, but I'm quite glad I was here to witness the look on your face."

"You'll pay for this." Jack pointed at her, dropping her lab report to the ground. He hadn't even looked at it. He locked eyes with Kate long enough to send a chill down her spine. He turned and grabbed Ethan and they both headed toward the door. The room erupted in sounds of fear and disbelief. One woman grabbed her husband by the arm and dragged him out of the room.

"Listen," Declan yelled above the noise. "All of you who want to leave this program and are afraid to do so, this is your chance. Tell others you know that if they are trying to leave, we will help them, too. I'm not afraid to stand up to Jack Harlow. We have created a website where you can send us anonymous messages. After what he did to my wife, we will make sure that Jack Harlow never hurts anyone ever again. If we have to take down his whole program to do that – that's what we will do. It's time someone stopped this cult."

At the word cult, Jack turned on his heels, his eyes burning with anger. He didn't even try to settle the crowd down. "You have no idea who you're up against. I will not allow you to shut me down. You haven't even officially entered this program and you think you know everything. No one can stop me. And don't forget the non-disclosure agreement you signed. You'll be hearing from my lawyer."

Declan smirked. "You should probably call a few lawyers, Jack. You're going to need them."

At that moment, the DEA lead supervisor popped his head into the room and told everyone they had to vacate the building. Kate and Declan might not be able to stop Jack at that moment but a search for drugs certainly would. Kate hoped that the DEA found what they were searching for, but she had the sneaky suspicion that Jack would be smarter than that. She didn't think he'd leave a supply of drugs on the property.

Everyone in the room gathered their belongings to leave. As Kate and Declan passed by Jack, he issued another warning that this wasn't over.

"Seems pretty over to me, Jack. At least for today." Declan slapped the man on the back hard enough he lurched forward. "You might want to consider that you don't know who you're dealing with and watch your step."

"I'll drive you out of Mulberry Grove," Jack said as the DEA supervisor practically dragged him away.

Declan snickered like he didn't have a care in the world. "Drive us out, Jack, or try to kill us as you did with the others?"

Jack turned his head to look over his shoulder as he was being escorted away by the DEA supervisor. His look told Kate and Declan all they needed to know – they were now Jack Harlow's enemy and he'd make them pay one way or the other.

"That's one creepy guy," Declan said, walking with Kate through the main foyer of the home and outside through the front door. Close to fifty people stood around the front yard.

Kate glanced around at the mostly unfamiliar faces. "This is more people than I thought there'd be. Natalie said she had training here tonight, too. I wonder where they are." No sooner had the words left Kate's mouth when she heard her name shouted from behind her.

Natalie waved and came down the steps with Andrew trailing behind her. He took in the scene and shook his head in disbelief. "Kate, what is going on? Sadie ended our training early because she said the DEA was here to search the place. Did you have something to do with this?"

Kate feigned innocence. "I guess I did. When I went to get tested the other night to see if I had been drugged, and they found I had been, they said they were going to need to report it. I didn't know quite what they meant, but I guess this was it. The DEA means business. I hope they find the drugs so this doesn't happen to anyone else."

Andrew reached for Natalie's hand. "Is a drug raid enough to get you to quit now? I don't know how much more I can take."

Natalie turned to say something to her husband but stopped. She and Kate spotted Molly looking ashen coming out of the house. She had her arms wrapped around herself and her hair piled on top of her head. Strands fell in front of her eyes and she didn't bother to tuck them back in. She saw Natalie and came over to the group of them.

"I don't understand what's going on," Molly said as she approached. She looked to Natalie and then to Kate. "I was downstairs going through some of the videos that Frank has gathered for the documentary and next I knew a DEA agent was pulling me out of the room and told me I had to leave."

Kate explained what she had told Natalie. Then she leveled a look at Molly. "This has happened to several women. They must come forward. I've confronted Jack about it and even tried to show him my lab results. This isn't going to stop unless we stop him."

Molly raised her eyebrows. "We? I don't know what you're talking about. Jack has been very good to me and Frank. I'm sure he didn't hurt anyone. If you think you were drugged, that's your issue." She hitched her jaw toward Declan. "Maybe he drugged you to get you to loosen up. It wasn't Jack though. He'd never do something like that." With that, she turned and walked away not even waiting for Kate to respond.

"I guess she's been brainwashed already," Declan said, rocking back on his feet, eyeing Natalie.

Andrew let out a sigh and cursed. "He's got Frank, too. There's no hope for either of them. That's why we need to stop worrying about them and take care of ourselves, Nat. We need to get out of here."

Natalie shook her head, holding firm. "I'm not leaving her here."

"Then we are all doomed." Andrew threw up his hands and walked away.

When he was gone, Natalie leaned toward Kate. "You shouldn't have provoked her like that. She's going to think I told you."

"This is serious, Natalie. People have died because of this situation and I don't want to see Molly or you be next."

Natalie stared at Kate and then tucked her hair behind her ears and left in the same direction as Andrew.

"What now, Kate?" Declan asked when they were finally alone.

"Now, we wait. That's about all we can do. Word will spread about what happened here. The website that was set up hopefully will garner some tips and we keep watch." Kate looped her arm through his. "I'm starving. Creating utter chaos makes me hungry. Can we go home and have a quiet dinner?"

Declan patted his stomach. "I thought you'd never ask." He reached for her hand and they walked away from Jack's house and the chaos they caused without looking back. It was good that no one could see the smug smiles on their faces.

CHAPTER 32

ater that night after Kate and Declan had filled their bellies, they sat in the backyard talking about events from the day. Kate had a file folder on her lap that a courier had dropped off that evening. Somehow Spade had worked his magic again and secured a copy of the police and autopsy reports for Lucile Schaeffer, the young woman who had been drugged with heroin, and Lydia Brady, Ali's mother.

Declan sat with his laptop on a nearby table. One of the last-minute decisions before causing a scene at Jack's had been the creation of a website. It and calling in the DEA were the two tricks up Declan's sleeve that he mentioned in the final hours of preparation.

With the website, he wanted to create an online space that went right up to the line of libeling Jack Harlow without actually crossing the line and being sued. They could use it to collect anonymous tips, share information and track every IP address of those who visited. They hadn't even shared the website address with anyone yet but the FBI's tech team had made sure it ranked high on search engines for any searches of Jack Harlow. They had also informed Det. Miller.

Declan reached over and tapped a key and then squinted down at the screen. "Four hundred and fifty-seven views so far. This website is going to do the job for us."

Kate was surprised it had that many views. Not that she didn't like

Declan's idea. She didn't often rely on technology for an investigation. She was more hands-on with a witness or suspect in an interrogation room. If Kate was being honest with herself, she enjoyed the mental chess match a one-on-one interview gave her. Her heart raced and her skin prickled and she came most alive in those moments.

"What are we hoping to get from this?" she asked, taking a sip of water.

Declan righted himself in the chair and stretched his legs out. "I thought people might be willing to give us tips if they didn't have to share their names. Not that it helps us much since we won't be able to interview them directly, but given we will capture their IP address, we should be able to narrow down who it's coming from. Plus, we can track how many times Jack and his staff track the website. I flagged their IP addresses and they are already looking."

That did have a certain value Kate couldn't deny. "Sounds like a good addition to our plan then."

Declan rested his head back and closed his eyes while Kate flipped open the police report on Lucile. She had been in her twenties, in college locally, and had no history of drug use. The autopsy was a reflection of what had been in the news. There was no new information for Kate and the death hadn't made any sense to her. The only thing in the whole report that jumped out was the description of the man that had struggled with Lucile that night. Two homeless men in the abandoned building Lucile had been found in described a man who had striking similarities to Ethan. The detective assigned to the case hadn't followed up though and wrote off the case as drug connected. There were so many in Los Angeles that it slid under the radar.

Earlier when speaking to Spade, Declan and Kate had asked about progress in the Winnie and Ned Stockton investigation. They hadn't been talking about it much because they had no information. The FBI agent on the case hadn't found anything significant yet and like the rest, all roads led back to Jack Harlow.

Kate placed the files down on the ground and picked up Lydia Brady's file. Lydia had been thirty-six when she was murdered in a house in Mulberry Grove. She had lived alone in a rental owned by Jack Harlow. Her body was found in one of the two upstairs bedrooms, half-dressed and shot once in the head. There were signs of struggle and it looked to the investigators on the scene that she had fought with her attacker before the murder. She had defensive wounds on her hands and several broken fingernails. There were contusions on her face and a large gash at the top of her head like she'd been struck with a sharp object before being shot.

Spade had been able to get crime scene photos as well. Kate flipped through the file until she reached them. Her brow furrowed seeing Lydia's face. Ali resembled her. Kate flipped through each photo, her face contorting with each one.

The written report did little to indicate the true violence that had taken place in that house the night she had been murdered. The bedroom where Lydia had been found had been destroyed – lamps smashed, the bedding crumpled on the floor, and dresser drawers pulled out and tossed. It appeared the killer might have been looking for something. Even the dresser mirror lay shattered in pieces on the floor. Kate rearranged the photos as she had found them and then dug deeper into the report to find the detective's notes.

She reached that page, unclasped it at the top, and pulled it out of the file. She looked once and then again making sure she was seeing correctly. The LAPD detective had been Det. Jerry Miller. He hadn't said anything to them about this case nor had he connected the case to Liam Brady – Lydia's husband. Had it been an oversight or had Det. Miller not realized the connection himself?

Kate scanned his initial scene notes and it reflected what she saw in the photos and what the crime scene techs had written. He hadn't made much progress on the case, although it seemed from his witness list and notes, he had knocked on every door, shaken every bush, and did everything a detective should do on the case. There was one curious scribbled note on the bottom of the page that drew Kate's attention.

The ink on the page had faded over time and Kate had to pull the page closer to her face to read it. *Parents notified and will make arrangements for her body and personal items.*

Several questions swirled through Kate's head. She turned to look over at Declan and he was breathing lightly with his eyes firmly shut. She'd wake him when she was done reviewing to go over it all with him.

She reached for the autopsy file, hoping she'd find a clue to the killer within it. Kate scanned the medical examiner's findings and the blunt force trauma to the back of Lydia's head that she thought she saw in the photo was confirmed. The medical examiner noted that the cut had a sharp edge to it and indicated that a pointy object might be the weapon. Lydia didn't die from that though. It was the gunshot to the head that did it. The wound had entered behind the left ear and exited the front. The angle indicated that the killer had been to the back and slightly to the side.

Kate had seen kill shots like that before and almost always the victims had been subdued at that point and were no longer fighting or had been incapacitated to the point of not being able to fight. Kate tried to imagine the scene in her mind – the struggle first, the blow to the head next, and then the killer overpowering and taking the kill shot.

Lydia was found on the bed on her back. It meant the killer had rolled her over. When Kate was done reading the autopsy findings, she closed the file and dropped it beside her with the rest. She hated to wake Declan because he looked like he was sleeping peacefully, but she wanted to discuss the case while it was still fresh. She stared at him long enough that she wasn't surprised when he opened one eye and laughed.

"Are you watching me sleep because I'm so handsome?" He shook himself awake, stretched his arms overhead, and yawned loudly. "I'm still not caught up on the sleep. What's up?"

Kate moved her chair slightly so she was facing him. "I read through the case file on Lydia Brady and there are some curious facts I found. Det. Miller was the investigator on the case and he never said anything to us about that. Secondly, he indicated that he notified her parents of her death. They were the ones who handled everything. Thirdly, Lydia was shot but she was also hit in the head, and it appeared to me that the killer was searching for something."

"Is it possible Det. Miller might not have connected Lydia and Liam Brady?"

"I don't know how. I don't see why he wouldn't tell us if he had."

Declan shook his head as if not understanding. "I think we need to speak to him then. He seemed like a straight shooter. I don't think he hid it on purpose."

Kate didn't disagree with him. "There isn't even a hint of a suspect in the file – including Jack Harlow. What do you think about the killer looking for something?"

"Is there a chance it was a burglary gone wrong?"

Kate shook her head. "No forced entry and it wasn't that kind of scene." She reached for the file and handed it to Declan. "It looks to me like the person intended to kill her."

Declan opened the case file and started going through it while Kate got up, grabbed their glasses, and went inside the house to give him time. She refilled their drinks and then ripped off a piece of bread from the fresh Italian loaf Declan had bought at the store earlier. She pulled open the fridge, slathered it with a generous amount of butter, and then bit off a piece. Kate leaned against the counter enjoying each bite so much that she helped herself to another slice.

After enough time that Declan should be up to speed, Kate walked back outside to find Declan bent over the file folder examining a photograph. "I think I found the object that the killer used to hit her over the head."

Kate set down their drinks and then stood over his shoulder. "How did you find it when Det. Miller didn't and the medical examiner couldn't identify it?"

Declan turned his head to look up at her and winked. "I'm that good." He pointed to a photograph of the victim lying on the bed with a mess of clutter on the floor next to her. "See the blue glass sticking out of that pile?"

Kate had to lean down to study the photo. She squinted and still couldn't see what Declan was talking about. He pointed to a few pieces of the glass and it became clear. It almost looked like pieces of a mosaic tile.

Declan sat back in the chair and rested the crime scene photos on his lap. "I had a case early in my career and no one could quite figure out what had made such an injury to the victim's head. She had been hit with a vase made out of mosaic tiles. It was hard enough that it caused blunt force trauma like a heavy object but the abrasions to the head caused a bit of confusion. It turned out that it was this kind of tile and it split apart as it struck the victim."

"Wouldn't the crime scene techs have found blood on those tile pieces?"

"There's blood everywhere, Kate. They could have simply chalked it up to blood spatter."

Kate sat with that for a moment and then gestured for Declan to hand her other crime scene photos. She flipped through until she found the photo – there sitting on the dresser was a vase exactly like Declan had mentioned. It had been tipped over but hadn't rolled to the floor.

He raised his eyebrows. "You see its match, right? Same tile as the ones that make up the other vase on the dresser. I'm guessing it had a twin. There are too many pieces on the floor and mixed up in that pile of clothing and papers for it to have come from that vase though."

Kate stared at the vase. She didn't know how Declan did it. She was good at assessing a scene but his eagle eyes had picked out something she had missed completely. "I still don't think it was a basic burglary."

"Definitely not. Had it been all he needed to do was hit her with that. He didn't have to shoot her, too." Declan's mouth set in a firm line. "No, the person went there to kill her."

Kate started to respond but rustling noises on the far side of the lawn drew her attention. Her pulse quickened and her eyes fixed to the spot. The shrubs that lined the back perimeter of the yard rustled loudly once more and then stopped. It did it again a moment later.

Declan was on his feet with his gun in his hand faster than Kate.

"Wait here. I'll see what it is." Declan advanced with his gun leading the way.

"Please don't shoot," a meek voice said from the darkness of the yard.

"Identify yourself," Declan commanded, stopping in place.

Sadie made her way out of the shrubs with her hands up. "I have information that might help us both."

CHAPTER 33

Declan didn't change his posture. "Walk over here slowly into the light."

Sadie did as she was told with her hands still slightly raised. "I'm not here to hurt you or cause any trouble. I heard what you said when you were leaving Jack's today and I need your help."

Kate took a few steps toward the woman who looked visibly shaken at the sight of Declan standing there with a gun pointed at her. Kate didn't care if he caused her fear. They weren't taking any chances. It could easily be a ruse to get their defenses down.

Kate walked within a few feet of her. "How did you get back here?"

"I cut through the neighbor's yard behind you. Their gate was open and I was able to get through the shrubs."

Kate shared a look with Declan. She was concerned that Sadie had overheard them talking. "What do you mean you need our help?"

"I don't want to work for Jack anymore and I can't leave on my own." Sadie looked toward the ground and her voice cracked. "Over the years, he's found out secrets in my life that will be exposed if I try to leave. Others who have reached the highest levels have tried to leave and they are all dead now. I've been biding my time, acting like everything is fine. I don't want to be here anymore."

Kate and Declan shared a look and neither seemed to know whether to trust her. Declan took decisive action first. He nodded toward Kate to grab the files from the chair he had been sitting in. Once Kate had them, she went to her chair and placed them on the far side on the ground out of sight from Sadie. Once that was done, Declan waved the gun toward the chair for Sadie to sit down, which she did.

"I understand why you don't trust me, but I'm here to give you information." Sadie rubbed her eyes with her fingertips. "Jack is flipping out. I've never seen him so worked up. The DEA didn't find the drugs, but I know where they are kept."

Kate stood over her. "Where?"

"There's a house on Jasmine Lane. His chemist lives there and makes everything right in the basement. There is a false wall at the end of the hallway. If you move the panel just right the door will pop open. When a batch is ready, she brings it over to Jack."

It took Kate a moment to process what she was saying. "Are you talking about Claire Adler?"

Sadie's eyes opened wide and she looked up at Kate. "I didn't realize you knew her."

"I met her briefly but I thought she was Jack's business manager."

Sadie nodded. "She does some of that for him, but she's a chemist. That's her primary role for as long as I've been involved. Jack has known her forever. She used to work at one of the companies he invested in. My understanding is that they developed some kind of personal relationship early on and she came with him when he moved to Mulberry Grove."

That certainly made sense to Kate. "What do you know about the drugs?"

Sadie wrung her hands in her lap. "I never gave them to anyone. What Jack told us was that it would lower people's inhibitions and let them explore things they wanted to but stop themselves out of fear. He also used them to help people be more open to suggestions and changes in their lives. Psilocybin does have real uses in therapy for helping people with trauma and the psychedelic compound MDMA is being studied to help treat post-traumatic stress disorder."

Kate knew that but drugs were never administered without the subject's knowledge. "How does Ethan sexually assaulting drugged women come into play?"

Sadie held her hand up to stop Kate. "I never knew about that. I swear to you. I've never done something like that. Monica said she didn't know either. That was a shock to us both today."

Kate narrowed her eyes at her. "Why are you willing to tell us all this?"

Sadie dropped her head in her hands and started to cry. Kate was an excellent judge if a cry was genuine or fake and the way her body rocked forward with sobs, she was starting to believe Sadie's fear was real.

Declan lowered the gun to his side but didn't holster it. "How long have you been working with Jack?"

"Too many years to count." Sadie focused her attention on Declan. "I heard about Jack while at college. He was a serious investor who had a lot of fame for his business savvy. Shortly after graduating, I was having trouble finding a job and heard he had started a kind of mentorship program. To be honest, I didn't understand his program at first. I didn't know what it was all about, just that it focused on personal growth and achieving your goals. I needed that desperately and figured what could be the harm."

Kate clicked her tongue. "I'm guessing if you knew then what you know now, you'd think differently."

"Exactly." She sighed and shook her head. "I wouldn't have gotten involved. The first year I was here was fine. Everything was new and I was learning so much about myself, but Jack was starving me, making me exercise at all hours of the day and night. I kept getting sick and weak. When I started losing hair, I went to a doctor who said

I needed to eat more. He said I needed rest and recuperation. Jack wouldn't hear of it. He said I needed to push my body harder to have a breakthrough. He said I wasn't trying hard enough. I started sneaking food. By then, Monica had joined the program and Jack was focused on her more than me. He was also starting to recruit younger women into the program so all of his attention was on them. I finally got myself back to a healthy state and stopped listening to Jack's advice about losing weight."

"How did that sit with Jack?"

"He never said anything to me but he also stopped sleeping with me so I guess that's the answer. Younger, thinner women took his attention."

"You were involved with Jack?" Kate asked, not even bothering to hide the shock in her voice. "Is there anyone not involved with Jack?" She knew she shouldn't sound so judgmental, and in a normal interview she wouldn't, but Sadie had no idea they were FBI.

Sadie swallowed hard. "He seduced me a month after moving to Mulberry Grove. I was young and enjoyed the attention, but then I realized that it wasn't just me. He had several women and he cast them aside when he was done. After a while none of that mattered, I was learning things and moving up the levels of the program, and eventually, Jack asked me if I'd like to teach."

"Where did you get the money for the program if you were just out of college? It's incredibly expensive." Kate had no idea how most people paid for the program let alone a recent grad.

"It wasn't then. My father has money and he helped me for a while but then he got tired of supporting me for doing nothing, as he put it. Once I was on my own, I started doing odd jobs for Jack to pay the bills, but he let me live at his house so I didn't have many expenses."

Declan holstered his gun. "When did you start officially teaching for him?"

"I had been in the program four years when Jack asked me. I've been teaching for five."

"Right when the murders started," Kate said. "What do you know about the murders?"

"I don't know anything. I know the rumors are that it was Jack or one of his staff because those couples were pulling out of the program. I know that it made him angry, but Jack isn't the kind of man to get his hands dirty like that." Sadie looked between them. "I honestly don't know who is doing it, but it's probably someone close to Jack. Ethan or Claire. I know Monica seems like she has an anger issue, but I can't believe she'd kill someone."

"Why Ethan or Claire?" Kate asked, agreeing with Sadie that it probably wasn't Monica.

Before Sadie responded to Kate's question, she asked one of her own. "Who are you people? Everyone around here is asking. You showed up a few weeks ago, got invited into the program, and imploded everything."

Kate raised her eyes to Declan. "We are exactly who we said we are. Declan is an attorney and I'm a photographer. We joined Jack's program with good intentions, but when you attend a welcome event and are drugged against your will, you reevaluate your choices quickly. I'm not the kind of woman who is going to stand by and let him do that to other people. Jack needs to be stopped."

"I wish I had your kind of conviction early on." Sadie leaned back in the chair. "What do you want to know? I assume you can get the information to the right people who can help stop him."

Declan told her he could without explaining how. "That part is taken care of. We aren't afraid of him, Sadie. He has power over you because you fear him."

"For good reason," she said, throwing up her hands. "Part of getting to those highest levels is admitting things about yourself and your family – embarrassing and private things. Imagine telling Jack on video things about your life or about your family members that you'd never want public. I told him about my brother's early legal troubles. He's well past that now but would lose his job if his boss found out. I'm not just trying to protect myself."

"We understand, Sadie, but why did you tell Jack about it at all?"

"I know you don't understand." Her body tensed and there was an edge in her voice. It appeared to Kate that she was growing frustrated justifying her actions. "It was part of the program at the highest level. To access that knowledge, you had to prove your trust in Jack. That was the trust exercise. If you thought the initial questions were invasive, you would have freaked out at that point – only then you're in too far to quit."

"Why not lie? You could easily make up something that wasn't true," Declan asked with an air of arrogance he didn't have often. He was growing as frustrated with Sadie as she was with them. Kate shot him a look to ease up. He acknowledged he saw her, but she didn't think he'd comply.

"You can't lie." Sadie's voice grew louder. "Jack does background checks on everyone. Plus, you have to say this stuff while attached to a lie detector test. He knows if you're telling the truth or not. It doesn't matter though because, at that point, I would have done anything Jack asked of me. I was in that deep. You two don't get it. Jack's program helped me and countless other people. That's the weird thing about it – it helps you become a better version of yourself and get out of your own way. The cost is just too steep."

Kate knew she wasn't talking about the financial cost. "What was it like teaching for him?"

Sadie cast her eyes downward. "I thought it was going to be easier, but Jack is demanding of all of us. Moving from student to teacher is when the veil started to come down and we saw Jack's other side –

moody, violent, and obsessed with money. What struck me the most was that he never practiced what he preached. He advocated non-violence and while I've never seen him hit a woman, I heard rumors he had. He never hit me, but he was cruel with his words. There was a lot of negativity in a space where we were preaching positivity. It was a drastic night and day difference behind the scenes."

Kate sat down in the chair across from her. "If we help you leave, do you have a safe place you can go?"

She nodded once. "I'd rather not say where though. I can't risk it getting back to Jack."

Kate wasn't sure what she needed help with then. "Do you need money to get out of town? Is that what you're asking?"

"No, I'm never going to be safe until Jack Harlow is in prison and can no longer hurt anyone."

"That's going to take some time. It's not something that's done overnight," Kate said softly, meeting Sadie's gaze. She had to choose her words carefully. "We can help people find safe places to go and money if they need it while we work to stop Jack. If you're willing to help us, would it be safe for you to stay on the inside and tell us what's happening?"

Sadie shook her head. "It was dangerous for me to come here tonight. I can't do it again."

"Then it will take longer," Declan said. "Other than the drugs, do you know about any crimes Jack has committed?"

Sadie shifted her eyes to the side and wouldn't look directly at Kate or Declan.

"If you know something, you need to tell us or the cops. It's the only thing that's going to stop Jack," Kate urged.

Sadie raised her head to Kate. "You think the local cops can do anything? Jack knows them all. They won't do a thing."

"The DEA did," Kate reminded her. "What do you know? Maybe it's enough that we can tell the cops we know who are willing to help."

Sadie pushed herself up from the chair and stood there as if trying to decide what to do. Finally, after Kate had given up hope she'd tell them, Sadie said, "A few years ago, Ethan killed a young single woman who had been in the program. I didn't know what happened at the time, but I guess he had probably drugged her and sexually assaulted her. I overheard Ethan and Jack talking. Ethan followed when she left and then he took her someplace and killed her. I don't know the details. The newspaper said it was a drug overdose."

"Lucile Shaeffer?" Kate asked.

"That's her."

"You have to make a statement to the police," Declan urged.

"No. Not until I'm safe from Jack."

Declan and Kate started to argue with her, but Sadie held her ground. She started to walk away but turned and told them one more thing. "Bridgit, who you met, was a spy for Liam Brady. Ethan found out and told Jack. I saw her leave Jack's the other night and she looked terrified. No one has seen her since."

Kate tried to ask her questions but Sadie shut them down. She walked to the shrubs and disappeared the same way she came in.

CHAPTER 34

After Sadie left, Kate and Declan gathered up the files and went into the house without speaking. It was only after Declan locked the back door and Kate slumped down in a chair at the table, that he joined her letting out a string of curses. "This is insane, Kate. How can Bridgit be working for Liam?"

"I don't know, but it makes a certain kind of sense to me."

"It makes no sense!"

"Think about it. If Liam believes that Jack killed his wife and his sole mission now is to get people out of Jack's program and bring the man down, then it helps to have someone on the inside. It's what we just asked of Sadie."

"I guess so," Declan said with an air of frustration. He kicked his legs out under the table and slumped back in his seat, tossing his arm over the side of the chair next to him. "This is all too convoluted for me. We've got six dead couples, a missing person, drugs, two murders from years ago. What's next?"

Kate held her hand out to stop him. "Don't even ask that. I'm meeting with Liam tomorrow so I'll get to the bottom of what's going on with Bridgit. He might not even know she's missing. Let's contact Det. Miller and ask him to meet tonight to discuss Lydia before I go into that meeting. Then we can call Spade and tell him what we know about the drugs, Lucile, Lydia, and Bridgit."

Declan agreed with it all. "I never made contact with Jack's doctor," he said absently.

"Don't worry about it now. It's the least of our worries."

"Is anything making sense to you?"

"Some of the pieces. Liam's motivation for one. Before I had no idea why or how he chose to do his work here. Now we know. As I just said, it makes sense Bridgit might be his inside person. They all have a motive for the murders as far as I'm concerned, and Ethan has climbed to the top of that list. Maybe even higher than Jack."

"How so?" Declan waved his hand dismissively. "Beyond what Sadie said about him killing Lucile. What are his motives for the others?"

"Ethan is the one sexually assaulting women. He might not see it that way, but that's what he's doing. It's his life on the line if those women had gone to the cops. Sure, Jack might have done some time for it, too. It's Ethan though who'd be the primary suspect."

Declan raked a hand over his head. "I didn't think about it like that. They all had motivation to keep those couples quiet. Remind me what background we have on Ethan."

"Not much. He's been with Jack since the beginning. Met him right out of college much like Sadie. He joined the program and then was teaching with him shortly after. He doesn't have much of a background to dig into though. No real job before that. He comes from a fairly wealthy family out of San Diego. He's an only child. No criminal record. Much of his experience has been with Jack."

Declan considered all of this and then pulled out his phone and sent a message. "I'm telling Det. Miller to meet us back where we were the other night." After Declan texted, they sat at the table talking until Det. Miller responded and they headed out the front door to meet him.

Gravel crunched under Kate's sneakers as she walked the same dark path on Mulholland Drive. Declan walked to her left with a flashlight pointed at the ground. A moment later, a whistle was heard down the path and Declan clicked off the light.

"Det. Miller," Kate said when she reached the man. He had the same weary-eyed look he had before. This time there was curiosity mixed in. "It was good of you to meet us on such short notice."

Det. Miller assured them it was fine. "I didn't know that I'd ever see you two again. Did something happen already? Did you exit Jack's program?"

"We're out," Declan said, not revealing anything more. They had decided on the drive over to leave out the particulars for now. The last thing they wanted was to derail what should be a short conversation. "We came to discuss Lydia Brady."

Det. Miller sucked in a short breath. "What does that case have to do with anything?"

"You worked the case?" Kate asked and he confirmed. "It's Liam Brady's wife and the case was never solved. I believe it might be what brought him to Mulberry Grove and why he has such a vendetta against Jack."

Det. Miller stepped back, stumbling almost. "I don't understand. What do you mean she was Liam Brady's wife? Lydia was unmarried at the time. Her parents told me that. They never said anything about her being married or notifying a husband."

"You had no idea she'd been married?" Kate asked, narrowing her gaze at him.

"I swear to you, Agent Walsh. There was nothing in her home to indicate she'd been married. I didn't search for a marriage license because I had no reason to believe she had been married. Her neighbor told me about her parents but didn't have a number for them. All I had was a name. It took me a few days to track them down."

"It didn't occur to you that Lydia had a different last name than her parents?"

"Maybe it should have but it didn't. I would assume that if she had been currently married her parents would have asked me if I contacted her husband first or something like that. They didn't. I made the death notification and they said they'd be on the first flight. They are the ones who came to the morgue and collected her body and then cleaned out the house when the scene was cleared. The neighbor told me that Lydia had been seeing someone casually. I checked him out thoroughly and he had been out of town at the time and there was never any indication of domestic violence."

Declan looked to Kate to see if she had questions, but she was stunned into silence at the moment. He turned back to Det. Miller. "Did you suspect Jack?"

"Not back then, no. Hardly anyone knew anything about him other than he was a rich businessman who had set up what was then called a mentoring program in Mulberry Grove. The rumors and suspicions about him came much later. I knew that Lydia had met Jack and that she was in his program. He gave a short statement saying that he hadn't seen her in a few days, and I didn't have any information to indicate anything different."

Kate stopped him. "I didn't see all these notes in the file."

Det. Miller raised an eyebrow. "You have the file?"

"The autopsy report, too. Declan thinks he identified the object that was used in the blunt force trauma."

He turned to Declan with amazement in his eyes. "How'd you manage that? None of us had any clue."

Declan told him about the vase made of mosaic tile. "I saw it in another case. That's the only reason it jumped out to me so quickly. I saw all the broken glass among the items on the floor."

Det. Miller shook his head. "They were searched and there was no blood found on any of the pieces."

Kate jutted her chin forward. "Is it possible the killer took the bloodied pieces with him?"

"Anything's possible. It would explain why we could never find an object. We also can't explain how that vase was smashed. We figured it would leave a mark on the wall or desk or something. It was heavy. There was one like it on the dresser."

They discussed the crime scene some and it was Declan who had follow-up questions.

"I assume you didn't have any leads on a suspect," Kate asked when there was a break in conversation.

"Not a one. It was a frustrating case marked by a lack of evidence – eyewitness evidence as well as forensic. I know with a mess of a crime scene like that you'd expect that we would have found something. It was almost like it was too messy. No prints or anything could be found. Lydia seemed to lead a quiet unassuming life. I never found a motive for why someone would have wanted to kill her."

"The scene made me think that someone had tossed the place looking for something."

"We considered that but had no idea what it would have been. She had cash in the living room that hadn't been touched. Her credit cards and other valuables hadn't been taken. It wasn't a burglary."

"Maybe it was something specific that she had taken from someone."

Det. Miller stared hard at her. "Is this a guess or did you have something in mind?"

"It was just a guess."

"Take me back a minute." Det. Miller scratched the top of his head. "How did you figure out Lydia was married to Liam Brady?"

Kate realized then she hadn't explained that to him. "Liam's daughter, Ali, admitted to me that her father thought Jack killed her mom. I searched for other murders in Mulberry Grove and came up with Lydia Brady. Ali has a striking resemblance to her mother."

Det. Miller cursed. "I feel terrible now. I had no idea Lydia was married or had a child. I wonder who notified them. He never called me. No one, not even her parents, ever tried to follow up and see what was happening in the case. Normally, you can't stop the parents from calling. Some call every day and ask if the killer has been caught. The lack of follow up always struck me as odd."

"The whole case seems odd," Declan said, and Det. Miller agreed. "Is there anything else we should know on this case?"

Det. Miller thought for a moment but didn't have anything else to add. "I hope you're able to solve the case along with the rest of them. The murders in Mulberry Grove are my only unsolved cases."

Kate felt for the detective. She only had one or two cases hanging over her head that had never been solved and they haunted her at times. One was personal – the embassy bombing in Kenya that killed her parents weeks before she graduated college and a series of art heists where they knew the offenders but had never been able to catch them.

"We will do what we can. I don't want to leave all of this unsolved any more than you do." Kate looked to Declan and they were ready to go. She turned back to Det. Miller. "We may end up having some information about a missing person. We don't have a lot of details right now and we don't even know for sure that she's missing. The FBI may handle it as part of this case, but if not, can you take the case?"

Det. Miller looked like he wanted to ask a few more questions as any good detective would. Kate's tone didn't leave much room for discussion though. "Technically you'd need to call it in and a detective would be assigned. I'm not positive it would come to me."

"Our boss will make sure it goes to you," Kate assured him. "I don't want to work with anyone else at the LAPD."

"Let me know how I can help. Happy to meet with you at any time."

They said goodbye and Kate and Declan started the walk back toward their car. They got about halfway when Declan stopped in the middle of the road. "Does it bother you that he had no idea that Lydia was married to Liam Brady, especially since you found it so quickly?"

"It does and it doesn't," Kate said and then explained, "I was looking for it. I knew what to search. If Det. Miller had no idea the woman was married, there was nothing at the scene to indicate it, and her parents didn't mention it, he'd have no way of knowing and no reason to search for marriages. How many times have you searched for a marriage record for a victim?"

Declan breathed out slowly as if searching for the words. "I guess I don't. We run background on suspects but rarely on victims unless we need more information. I guess I can see how that can happen."

Kate started back toward the car thinking the discussion was over but Declan wasn't walking in step with her. She turned back. "Is there something else wrong? Do you not trust Det. Miller for some reason? I find him to be honest and his shocked reaction to learning that Lydia had been married to Liam seemed genuine. Plus, he was told that she had a boyfriend who he checked out. He hadn't heard anything about an estranged spouse. He had no reason to go digging further."

"I'm not sure what I'm feeling."

"Well, I'm exhausted. I'm going home to sleep and we can leave this for another day." Kate walked toward the car with Declan right behind her. She chalked up his concern to a lack of sleep. There was one thing that bothered her and it wasn't what Det. Miller did or didn't do on the case. She couldn't for the life of her understand why Lydia's parents wouldn't have mentioned a husband and a daughter.

CHAPTER 35

y mid-morning the next day, Kate was three hours deep into background investigation on the victims. So far, though, she wasn't finding anything that pointed to a killer. There were no real surprises in their financials, credit card statements, or credit histories. There was nothing in work histories either. All had been solid upstanding citizens before their lives seemed to take a turn after moving to Mulberry Grove.

She clicked out of one credit report and was about to look at another when her cellphone rang on the table beside her. Kate reached for the phone but didn't recognize the number.

"Hello," Kate said, hesitation in her voice.

"It's Liam Brady. We have a meeting today that my daughter arranged. Is there any way we can move that up?"

Kate checked the time. "Sure, is there a time that's good for you?"

"How about now?"

Even this morning Declan had been unsure if he should attend the meeting with Kate. They both figured she might get more from Liam if she were alone. "Is Ali available that early?"

"No, she's working at the coffee shop." Liam hesitated and then said with an edge in his voice, "That's not a problem, is it? I don't always have Ali involved in my work. She told me that you might need help getting friends away from Jack and that you had some questions. I'm happy to help if I can."

"Where should I meet you?" Kate had a lot to discuss with him but would have felt safer going alone if Ali had been present. She'd go to the meeting armed for sure.

Liam rattled off his home address which was the location Ali had provided to her. She told him that she could be there in thirty minutes but no sooner. When she finished the call, Kate called Declan and left him a voicemail message. He had gone out earlier in the day to track down blueprints of Claire's house to see if she had a basement and to dig a little into Bridgit to see if she was really missing.

Kate got herself ready for the meeting including her concealed sidearm and texted Declan the address where she was headed. She left out the front door and followed the directions on her phone to Liam's house. He lived in an older section of the neighborhood farther in the back of the development. Kate found the two-story white Craftsman. The blue shutters created an upbeat welcoming vibe. She assumed it was Ali who had put the sunflower garden decorations on the front lawn. All in all, the home did not appear to be the dwelling of a killer – then again, their homes rarely did from the outside.

Kate walked up the two steps to the wide front porch and knocked on the door. A moment later, a slight man with wavy brown hair speckled with gray pulled the door open and waved Kate inside. He pushed glasses up his nose and tugged a thread on his tan cardigan. His jeans had a hole in the knee and his slippered feet shuffled against the hardwood floor.

Liam led Kate past a formal dining room and into the kitchen. "I have coffee if you'd like some."

Wary about taking any drinks from strangers, Kate declined. Liam pointed to a long rectangular table with a window seat on one side and a bench on the other. Kate took the window seat so she could survey the room as she interviewed him.

Once they were settled, Liam started. "Ali explained to me how you met but I don't understand what you're doing in Mulberry Grove."

Kate smiled across the table at him. "I'm sure it does seem confusing. My husband, Declan, and I moved here a few weeks ago. We were settling in nicely when I heard about a photography job for Jack Harlow. That's kind of how this whole thing got started and spiraled out of control rather quickly." Kate gave him the rundown of everything that had occurred with Jack to date, including being drugged. It was central to the information she needed from him and there was no point hiding it. Declan agreed that the more eager Kate seemed about sharing information with him, the easier it might be for him to trust her.

When Kate was done, he leaned back and swiped an errant hair off his forehead. "That's a lot to unpack."

"According to Ali, you've been doing this for several years. Is this the first time you're hearing a story like this?"

"So early on, yes. I've unfortunately heard of other women being put in compromising situations. Some thought they might have been drugged but no one had proof."

"Compromising or sexual assault?"

At the words *sexual assault* Liam's head snapped up and he fixed his gaze on Kate. He seemed uncertain as to what to say so Kate answered his question for him.

"It's a crime to drug a woman and then have sex with her in the state of California. All fifty states and a good deal of countries, too. Drugging a person takes away their ability to consent. You do understand that, right?"

Liam offered a wry smile. "Forgive me, it's not that I don't agree with you. I've never heard any of the women articulate it in such a way. You caught me a bit off guard, but as you said, that is technically what happened."

"You knew about the drugs then?"

Liam nodded. "Suspected drugs for a long time but never had anything concrete. You said you got tested. What did they find?"

Kate described the drugs that had been used, leaving out that Claire had been suspected of being the chemist. "My report prompted the DEA to raid Jack's house, but my understanding is that nothing was found."

Liam toyed with the frayed cuff of his cardigan. "It doesn't surprise me. Jack has been getting away with criminal activity for a long time. I'm starting to believe that he is untouchable."

"Ali told me that you help people leave if they need help. Is that what you do?"

"Yes and no. It's a bit more complicated than my daughter explained."

"Could you explain what you do then? I'd like to understand."

Liam pushed back from the table and crossed his legs. He explained his background in researching cult activity and that he had taken courses in helping people to leave cults. "They call us deprogrammers. I help people to understand what has been done to them psychologically and undo some of that wiring. Leaving a cult is both physical and psychological. Even if people are physically free from the cult, psychologically the chain is still there. For others, they have to have a psychological breakthrough to acknowledge that they are in a cult and need to leave physically. It's more complex than you'd believe."

There was a part of Kate that wanted to disclose that she had a background in forensic psychology so what Liam was explaining wasn't that far from her training. She couldn't tell him though.

Kate wasn't sure if she wanted to get into the murdered couples first or his wife. It was like taking a swing in the dark which might get him upset and her kicked out before she gathered the info she needed. "You had been helping the couples who were murdered. Is that correct?"

Liam pulled back slightly and turned his head. "No one likes talking about their failures but, yes, that's true. Dealing with one person is hard enough but dealing with the dynamics of a married couple in a cult is something else entirely. In each of those cases, the work helping them leave had been going on for more than a year. In all of them, the wives were ready to leave before their husbands. It took some convincing."

"I assume all of the women were sexually assaulted?"

Liam seemed surprised. "How did you know that?"

"I've been doing research," Kate admitted. "We were living here when the most recent murder happened. It was shortly after we arrived. I've always been a bit of a true-crime buff and the cases caught my interest once I realized how many there have been over the last five years. I suspect it must be the same killer."

"I'd agree with that assessment. I didn't realize there was anyone else who knew the women had been assaulted, as you put it."

"There are people in this neighborhood who like to gossip. After it happened to me, I put two and two together. But that's a question for you. I don't have any facts to back up my assumption."

Liam's posture relaxed some into the chair. "Most of the women weren't sure what happened to them. I suggested being drugged before they did. As far as I know, you're the only woman to have been drug tested, which is why it's gone on as long as it has. A few of them approached Jack and Ethan for an explanation as to what happened to them, but their questions were brushed off. Each of those women became more insistent with Jack for answers. They were shown the video of themselves having sex with Ethan. Two of them also had sex with Jack on those evenings."

Kate's alarm bells went off. She hadn't been privy to that information. "At the same time?"

Liam nodded and then blushed. "It's sick stuff, Kate. Jack picks and chooses the girls he wants, has sex with them and casts them aside. It shouldn't be surprising. Cult leaders have been using sex and drugs as far back as cults go. This time it was under the guise of personal improvement. That's the sickest aspect of all. People came here to improve their lives. Instead, they were financially exploited, drugged, and used for sex. This is commonplace in cults. It's why I'll never understand how people can fall victim to it."

Kate knew that he hadn't meant that. Anyone who has researched cults knew exactly how people fall into it. "How were you helping the couples?"

Liam gestured with his hand as if Kate should have been able to guess. "Once the women realized what had happened to them, it shattered something inside. It was an immediate break of Jack's hold over them and then they began to try to convince their husbands they had to leave. Only one woman told her husband what had happened to her but even at that, it took some time for her to disclose it. Because their husbands didn't want to leave, they sought out my help. I'm somewhat known in the community for doing that. We had some deprogramming sessions and once I thought they were ready, I gave them some strategies to use with their husbands. Once the men started to come around, then I worked with them as a couple to get ready to take the step of physical separation from Jack Harlow and Mulberry Grove. None of them made it out."

"Do you have any idea who might have killed them?"

"It has to be connected to Jack. I don't have any doubt about that, but as far as who pulled the trigger, that's anyone's guess."

Kate leaned into the table. "You don't think Jack would have done that on his own?"

"Absolutely not. He might have ordered the murders, but he's not one to get his hands dirty like that. Not to mention, Jack is physically soft. He looks strong and intimidating but it's all words. His bark is more ferocious than his bite. If put to the test, Jack will crumble."

Kate stared at him with skepticism on her face.

"Look at me," he said, holding his arms open. "I'm a lightweight and I could take Jack in a fight. Jack wouldn't risk it."

Kate hadn't heard that from anyone else. "Did you tell the detectives that?"

"They didn't want to listen to me," Liam said, brushing her off. "There was only one detective who had any interest in what I had to say and the big dummy considered me a suspect."

Kate shook her head in disbelief, not because of the information. She assumed she'd have to confront Liam about being a suspect and here he was opening the door for her. "Why would they consider you a suspect?"

"Well, Kate, I'll tell you," he said with an edge of anger as he leaned his arms on the table. "I don't like people who waste my time and who are phony and every one of those couples fit the bill."

CHAPTER 36

Kate was struck by the immediate change of tone in his voice and by the anger that flashed in his eyes. "How did they waste your time if they wanted to leave?"

Liam smirked and sat back. "That's just it, Kate. I don't think they wanted to leave. They might have at first but then when it came down to it, they weren't following through on the plan."

"The plan for leaving?"

"No," he said stiffly. "The plan I had put in place for them to leave. They refused to do what I asked of them."

Kate had no idea what he was talking about. "I'm sorry, I'm a bit confused by what you're saying. Did you want them to do something specific?"

"I'm not doing this out of the goodness of my heart, Kate. I'm trying to stop Jack Harlow. I'm trained to get people out of this cult but it's hard, frustrating work. In return, I wanted these couples to bring back some intel on what was happening on the inside." Liam met Kate's eyes and must have seen the disapproval. "Don't judge me, Kate. There were no inroads into this cult. You have to remember that each of these couples was at the highest level possible. Some of these people were closer to Jack than his teachers. They had access to information I wanted in exchange for helping them."

"I need you to stop for a moment and help me understand how

exactly you were helping them." He seemed to be glossing over important parts of his process that Kate wanted to understand.

"What's the issue?" Liam asked with an edge of annoyance.

"I understand that the women all came to you wanting help to get out of the cult. They needed some strategies to help convince their husbands to leave, but beyond that, why couldn't they just pack up their stuff and go?"

"Oh, I see," Liam said with a snicker. "You have no idea how invasive Jack Harlow is with his members, especially ones that reach that level. These people needed to go into hiding, Kate. Their homes are bugged, they are mostly broke, having turned over their money to Jack. They are living in properties owned by Jack. For those that owned their houses, no real estate agent would help them because they were connected to Jack. How do you put your house up for sale with no help and with Jack looking over your shoulder? You can't. These people were stuck."

"How were you able to help them?" Kate asked for what felt like the fourth time.

Liam pointed to his chest as he spoke. "Not only could I prepare them emotionally, but I also have access to people with money who'd pay to help them leave, get them jobs, new cities to live in. I could even get them new identities if it needed to go that far. I could get them out of here in every regard and all I asked was for them to help gather some information for me." Liam grunted. "I hardly think that's too much to ask."

Kate thought it was far too much. "Liam, they had gone through serious trauma and you were asking them to spy for you. They were risking their safety. Have you considered that they found something they shouldn't and it might have been what got them killed?"

"They were as good as dead anyway if they tried to leave Jack."

Kate narrowed her gaze at him. "How do you know that? Until

this situation, Jack has never been accused of killing anyone that I'm aware of."

"That you're aware of," Liam said regretfully.

He had opened the door to talk about his wife, but Kate wasn't ready to walk through yet. She wanted to keep him focused on the couples. "To your knowledge did any of the couples start to gather the information you asked for about Jack or did they outright refuse?"

"That was the worst part of it. They all agreed and I started helping them and every time I asked if they had snooped around or what training materials they were going to provide or what Jack's plans were, they said they were working on it." Liam threw his hands in the air, his face reddening. "They were always working on it, but somehow never accomplishing it. I felt used."

"I'm sure it was frustrating after everything you were willing to do for them." Kate chose her next words carefully. "I'm wondering two things – how you responded to them and how you were able to continue your research on Jack?"

Liam looked away from Kate and sighed. "The research stalled for a long time and even now it's been hard to get information. I've created some channels but they haven't worked out as well as expected." Liam frowned and appeared defeated. "I'm close to giving up on Jack. That's why when Ali said you were looking for help but seemed like you might be able to help me, I took the meeting. As for the couples, there wasn't anything I could do. It was like I was in a tug of war with Jack and he won every time. The couples didn't bring me any information that I didn't already know, and in the end, I believe Jack convinced them not to leave."

"I'd have been furious. What did you do?"

"What could I do?" Liam stared over at Kate, but when she remained quiet, he continued. "I did nothing, Kate. I had a few angry words with them for sure. Jack had sued me unsuccessfully a few times to run me off, but it wasn't going to stop me. I let it go. That's why it both shocked me and made me chuckle when the detective showed up here accusing me of murder. I'm here trying to stop the bad guy and he's thinking I'm him."

There was something about Liam that struck Kate as a little off-kilter but nothing that indicated he could be a killer. "I assume if you weren't arrested there was no evidence to back up his claim."

"Absolutely no evidence at all. I was home here. There was only one thing about the whole situation that still bothers me today." Liam shook his head like he was dislodging an old memory. "I asked my daughter, Ali, to be my alibi because I had no one else. I'm here alone most nights and I couldn't remember the nights she was here or not. I know that I was home here for every night that there was a murder. I'm sure about that because that's where I am every night. By the time I was questioned, I couldn't remember if Ali had been home on those nights or not. I should have just told him I didn't know but that never satisfies a detective. Ali knows me and she knows I'd never do something like that. She stepped in and gave me an alibi."

Liam was so forthcoming with information, it caught Kate off guard. "Why are you telling me all of this?"

Liam shrugged. "You have one of those faces that disarm people. You're easy to talk to, and if you're able to truly help me take down Jack Harlow, then you deserve to know the truth about me, warts and all."

"How can you trust me so quickly?" Kate wanted him to trust her. That was the goal in any situation like this, but she was taken aback when anyone trusted a stranger too soon.

Liam looked over at her and called her out. "Don't be suspicious because I trust you. Ali said she knows you fairly well and trusted you early on and you've come through. Everyone in the neighborhood knows what went down at Jack's. You're the reason they were raided by the DEA. I knew that before you arrived today. You're one of the good ones, Kate. What I can't understand is why you took a meeting with Jack."

Kate started to remind him about the photography job, but he held his hand up to stop her.

"I know what you said. It's your story. Tell it any way you want to, but I've been a researcher and a professor for a long time and I'm not buying it. I don't know why you're in Mulberry Grove, but I'm not going to question it. What can I do to help you?"

Kate offered a smile and they shared a knowing look. He knew that she wasn't who she said she was and he was okay with not knowing the truth. "I want to see Jack and Ethan arrested and the cult dismantled. I've met some friends while I've been here and I need to make sure they leave safely. I haven't been able to convince them yet."

"You can send them my way," Liam suggested.

"I can try, but I don't think it will work."

Liam excused himself to get something to drink and again offered Kate, but she declined. While he stood at the counter pouring himself some tea out of a pitcher from the fridge, Kate said, "I want to ask you about something, but I don't want to upset you. It was something that Ali said to me the other day that I didn't quite understand. I haven't seen her since to be able to ask her. It upset her so I didn't want to push."

Liam looked across the counter at her with his eyebrows raised. "Ask away and I'll do my best to answer. Ali is a sweet kid, but she's been overly involved in my work. I've tried to discourage her because she is so sensitive, but she likes to feel like she's doing something to help."

Kate absorbed what he said. It was slightly different than how Ali had described her involvement in her father's work, but Kate could tell that the young woman had been eager to impress. "Ali told me the other day that Jack Harlow killed her mother. She ran out of the coffee shop right after she told me so I didn't know if that was true or not. I didn't understand what she had meant. She had never mentioned her mother otherwise."

Liam took a sip of his drink and his hand trembled as he brought the cup to his mouth. When he was done, he placed it on the counter and came back over to Kate. "My wife, Lydia, left us when Ali was young. She had heard that Jack Harlow was starting a community and she wanted to be a part of it. I didn't want to come with her. Ali was doing well in school and I had a great job. Our world collapsed when she left. Later, I came to learn what Jack Harlow was all about and it sent me into a spiral."

"How so?"

"It's the reason I pivoted my research and focused on cults. I was determined to get my wife free of him. She never filed for divorce and I hadn't either so we were in limbo. I came to learn later that she had been saying horrible things to her parents - that I wasn't supporting her financially and was trying to take Ali away from her." Liam slumped down in the chair and held his head with his hand. "Part of that was true. I had cut her off financially and I did tell her I was going to fight for sole custody. All the money I sent her went to Jack and there was no way I was going to let him anywhere near Ali. Lydia was a grown adult and could make whatever decisions she wanted to make for her life, but someone had to think about the health and safety of our daughter. The sick part is, I ended up here and am hurting my daughter by being here. She's the real loser in all of this."

Kate reached over and placed her hand on Liam's arm. She felt a surge of emotion for the man. It did seem like he had been a victim of all of this, too. She told him as much. "How did Lydia meet Jack and come to decide to move here?"

Liam patted Kate's hand and thanked her for her kind words. "Lydia was an only child to parents who were a bit cold and distant. She was always seeking something more even after we were married. I couldn't love her enough, and she knew it was something inside her that needed to be fixed. Ironically, it was her father who introduced her to Jack and he mentioned starting a community here. She begged me to quit my job and move. I wouldn't do it. We had a stable life and moving here didn't offer us anything. I got a call at work one day from our babysitter that Lydia had packed up her things and left. She refused to tell me where she was living. We spoke by phone a lot in the first year and I sent her money, but the things she was saying were getting crazier. She was becoming someone else and there was nothing I could say or do to help her. I even tried coming out here to get her to come home with me. It didn't work. A year later, she was dead."

"How did you find out about her death?"

Liam sniffled and wiped a tear from his eye. "Her parents called me. I asked why I hadn't heard from the detective directly and they didn't give me a clear answer. When I asked for the detective's name, they refused to give it to me. I called the Los Angeles Police Department who I assumed was investigating and never heard back. Her father didn't want me anywhere near the funeral. I didn't have the energy to fight it at that point so I stayed away from the home she died in and the cops, but it drove me to do what I'm doing today."

"You think Jack Harlow killed Lydia?" Kate asked but her tone was more statement than question.

"I'm sure of it. To this day I don't even know a lot of the facts surrounding her murder, but from what her parents told me, I can't imagine it was anyone but Jack."

Before they could continue there was a knock on the front door and Liam excused himself to answer. A moment later, Declan's frantic and angry voice echoed in the house. Their voices grew louder as they came toward the kitchen. Kate was already standing and walking toward them.

"What's going on?" she asked as Declan stepped toward her.

"Bridgit is missing and by all accounts, Liam is the last one to see her. She was attacked right after that."

Kate turned to him and didn't even need to ask the question.

He hung his head low. "There are things I need to explain."

CHAPTER 37

Declan grabbed Liam by the front of the shirt and walked him back right into a wall. "You used her, didn't you? What exactly was your relationship with her?"

Kate looked between Declan and Liam unsure of what was happening. There was a spark of anger in Declan's voice that Kate didn't understand. It was almost like he was jealous of the relationship Liam might have had with Bridgit. That didn't make any sense to Kate or reflect the annoyance Declan said he felt toward her.

Liam's tiptoes were barely touching the floor. Declan held the man with one hand. "Answer me!" he snarled.

Kate walked calmly over to the two of them and touched Declan's arm. "Let him go and we can talk about this. Scaring him isn't going to get you the answers you want. We were having a nice discussion before you showed up." Normally, she'd never scold Declan in such a way during an investigation but given they were undercover and he was interfering in her getting solid information, Kate felt she had no choice.

Declan dropped Liam and he staggered forward, fixing his shirt as he regained his balance. "What is wrong with you? You come into my home and accuse me of something like that. Bridgit was a graduate student. There was no *relationship* there. Don't be disgusting. She's barely older than my daughter."

"You know her then?" Kate asked, moving back over to the table hoping they'd follow. Her only goal was keeping Liam's trust and the openness they had before Declan showed up. When they sat down, Kate formally introduced them to each other. "Please let's talk calmly and figure this out. Liam, you know Bridgit?" she asked again.

"I know her. I've been worried about her, too. I haven't heard from her in a few days."

"That's because she's missing," Declan said again with force.

Kate shot him a look that he ignored. She turned her attention back to Liam. "Please, if Bridgit is missing and it has something to do with Jack, we need to sort this out before anything happens to her." Kate wanted to ask Declan what had happened earlier in the day, but she suspected he wasn't going to disclose that in front of Liam so she'd have to play catch up as they went along.

"Wait right here and I'll explain everything." Liam stood from the table and Declan got right up with him. As he did, Kate could see Declan's gun on his hip that had been hidden from view by his shirt. She didn't know what was happening, but he suspected Liam of something.

"I'm going with you," Declan said, his tone indicating that there was no room for argument.

Liam walked out of the room with Declan right behind him. Kate waited at the table, her heart beating a little faster. She hoped that Ali didn't return home until she got a handle on what was going on. As Kate waited at the table her cellphone rang. She reached for the phone and looked at the screen, hoping it wasn't important. It was Natalie and Kate didn't feel like she should let it go to voicemail.

Kate barely got out a hello when Natalie said, "I need your help. After you told everyone what happened to you, and Jack's place was raided by the DEA, Frank and Molly were back here at our house. Frank was flipping out that you were horrible people trying to bring Jack down like that. Andrew tried to talk to him, but he wasn't listening. Molly completely broke down and told Frank what happened to her." Natalie's voice broke and it sounded like she was holding back from crying. "It was awful, Kate. He believed her immediately and then she was crying and he was crying and I was crying. Then he got so angry and said he was going to kill Jack. He went storming back to the house with Andrew following him. The DEA was still there and Jack was being questioned. Frank ended up not seeing him and leaving. Molly called me and told me that he went after Jack again today and there was a huge fight. I'm so worried for them, Kate. I'm worried Jack and Ethan are going to retaliate. Frank and Molly have had a good deal of access to Jack. I'm worried about what they know."

"I'm in the middle of something right now, but I promise to come over there as soon as I can. Do you want to see if Molly and Frank will meet with Declan and me?" Kate checked her watch and wished she knew what was going on with Declan and what he knew. "Can we make it about an hour from now?"

"That's good. That's good," Natalie said, starting to mumble to herself.

"It's going to be okay." Kate wasn't even sure Natalie had heard her before she hung up. She took a breath and tried to even out her racing heart. Kate was thinking about what could be done about Frank and Molly when Declan returned with Liam, who had a file folder in his hand.

He dropped it to the table and slid it over to Kate. Pointing at the file, Liam said, "That's everything I know about Bridgit. She came to me about six months ago. She's the sister of Amelia, one of the murder victims."

Kate didn't understand. "We were told Amelia's sister's name was Cara. Is this another sister?"

"No, same person. Bridgit is her middle name and that's what she asked me to call her," Liam explained. "She is getting her Ph.D. and told me she wanted to work with me to break up the cult. I told her that she wasn't ready. She was highly emotional and made rash decisions. She was adamant that she'd do everything and anything to bring Jack down with or without my help. She blamed Jack for her sister's death. As I told you, I was having trouble getting any insider information so unbeknownst to me she went to Jack and told him she was fascinated with him and wanted to do an internship with him and study him. It was the magic words because he let her in and began using her within his program."

Declan folded his arms across his chest. "Use her for what, exactly? All of her interactions with me were highly sexual. It seemed to me they used her as a sexual prop."

"I know," Liam said, disgusted with the situation and seemingly himself. "I tried to talk her out of it, but she was gaining their trust and getting solid information. She was willing to do whatever it took, even have sex with Jack to get the information she needed. He pimped her out essentially to prospective members. The goal was to gain their secrets that Jack would use later to blackmail people into the program. You saw her. Few men could say no. But it gained Jack's trust and she was going through his house and files and trying to gather evidence. She called me the other night frantic that she suspected Jack had found out what she was doing."

"What did you do about it?" Kate asked, sitting on the edge of her seat.

"I told her to come here and that I'd get her out of the community and to a safe place. I know someone with a safe house outside of Los Angeles. She came here briefly and told me she was going back to her apartment near campus to grab a few things. I haven't been able to reach her since. I had hoped she was in hiding."

Kate raised her eyes to Declan. "How do you know she is missing and not in hiding?"

"Her mother called the LAPD. She was on the phone two nights ago with Bridgit and heard her being attacked. The line went dead and she hasn't been able to reach her daughter since. The police went to her apartment and there were definite signs of a struggle and blood droplets on the floor. She's an official missing person thought to be in danger."

There was panic in Liam's eyes. "I swear to you I had nothing to do with that. I didn't even know. I offered to get her far away from here."

Kate believed him. This was yet another woman thought connected to Liam who was in danger and she told him as much. "You need to help us figure out what could have happened to her."

Liam turned his head to look at Kate. "It had to have been Jack or one of them. Bridgit gained Jack's trust easily. She seduced him within days of meeting him. From then on, she did everything he asked of her. She reported back everything to me and she was getting close to some of the skeletons in his closet. She said she almost got him to admit to Lydia's murder."

"You had her investigating that?" Kate asked, her voice rising an octave.

Liam shook his head furiously. "No, I'd never ask that of her. I didn't even tell her about Lydia at first, but then we got talking one night and the story came out. I didn't say that Jack did it. I told Bridgit that Lydia was here with Jack and that she left our family. I told her that she was murdered in a home here. The case had never been solved. Because of what happened to her sister, Bridgit said it had to be Jack. She vowed to figure it out."

"And you were all too willing to let her do it," Declan said with disgust in his voice.

Liam wouldn't even look at him at this point. He kept his eyes on Kate. "I couldn't have stopped her even if I wanted to. She was getting good information."

Kate offered him a sympathetic look. "Did she hear anything about Lydia's murder?"

"She might have." Liam reached up and rubbed his fingers on his temples. "It wasn't enough to do anything with, but one night Jack told her that a woman betrayed him early on and he had to take care of it. He said it was an unpleasant situation. Bridgit tried to ask more questions, but he wouldn't say more." Liam fixed his eyes on Kate. "Can you imagine anyone using the word *unpleasant* to describe a murder?"

Kate didn't have to imagine. She had interrogated killers colder than that. She couldn't tell Liam that though. "You don't know that he was talking about Lydia though."

"No, but Jack had hinted about a woman around Lydia's age who had left her family, even her young child, to learn from him. She became one of his lovers and then she stole something of value and he had to get it back. When Bridgit asked what, Jack refused to say. When she asked what happened to the woman, Jack said that he thought she was dead now. He wouldn't say more."

Kate thought back to the crime scene and her first instinct had been that the killer was looking for something. She looked up and caught Declan's eyes. He was thinking the same thing.

Declan wasn't going to let Liam off the hook that easily though. "Was there anything else she found out?"

"Jack showed her some of his financial documents and where money was being funneled to. Jack had offshore accounts and even a plan if the whole thing went south." Liam dropped his head into his hands and began to cry. "She knew too much. I told her she had to be careful because she was getting in too deep. She wasn't trained for this. I don't know what she thought he was going to do. He was never going to confess that he killed her sister."

Kate acknowledged for the first time she doubted that Bridgit was still alive. If Jack found out what she was doing, he had every reason to kill her. "Did she find out anything about the drugs I mentioned earlier?"

With his head still in his hands, Liam sniffled. "Bridgit told me that Jack's chemist has the formula and all the materials hidden away. He told her that he doesn't keep any product on hand at his house unless it's being used. Jack once bragged to Bridgit that he could put an end to his program and sell the drugs to suppliers on the street and make millions upon millions. She didn't know if he was serious or not. When you told me you were drug tested, that's the first proof I ever heard that this was all true."

"Do you have any idea where Bridgit could have gone if she was in hiding?" Kate needed to ask the question but there was no conviction in her voice.

Liam used the back of his hands to wipe his eyes. "I'd say with her mother, but if she's the one who called in the missing person's report then I have no idea."

Declan's cellphone buzzed and all eyes turned to him while he checked it. He read the message and then looked to Kate. "Det. Miller with LAPD has officially taken Bridgit's case."

Kate felt relief, but when she looked at Liam, his eyes were focused on the table. Then he slowly raised his head to look at her. "The same Det. Miller who thought I was guilty of killing those couples?"

"It would appear that way," Declan gestured to Kate and then toward the door. "We need to wrap this up as we are needed elsewhere."

Kate asked Liam if there was anything else he wanted to tell them. When he declined, she promised to be in touch and then followed Declan out of the house.

CHAPTER 38

Kate waited until she was far away from Liam's house before she spoke. When she did, she tried not to have an edge of anger at Declan for the way he barged in. "What has you so worked up?"

"Bridgit played us for one. Liam used her for two and now she's missing and probably dead. I'm not sure why I feel such a huge responsibility for that, but I do." Declan cursed and shoved his hands into his pockets. "I can't believe I missed the signs."

"What signs, Declan?" Kate couldn't believe that he was blaming himself for Bridgit's stupidity. "We thought she was part of Jack's program. She did an excellent job of that including sleeping with him. She threw herself into the role and there wasn't much to indicate she wasn't being real with you. I'm sure given the opportunity, she would have slept with you, too, hoping to get close to you and get any information she wanted."

"She was a college student, Kate. Don't you feel bad at all?"

Kate didn't and she didn't even feel guilty that she didn't. "Absolutely not. Bridgit had no business doing what she was doing. I understand why she did it but she wasn't trained to do it. She took huge risks and frankly could have damaged any criminal case she uncovered. She went in there acting like she was a sparrow for the KGB and went full-on sexpionage. She's lucky she didn't get found out sooner."

Declan's body remained tense as they walked back toward the house. "I got the plans for Claire's house. There is no basement and no ability to build a basement. Sadie wasn't correct about that, but I did notice something odd. There seems to be a room off a long hallway that isn't there in the final plans submitted after it was built. Like the room was planned for and then walled off later."

"Do you mean she built a smaller house than planned?"

Declan shook his head. "Not exactly. The house should have five bedrooms. The main bedroom suite is upstairs and then downstairs there should be four bedrooms off a long hallway from the family room. There are only three and then a space where a room should be. The size of the house remained the same but it looks like it's just an empty space that was never built out. The two plans don't add up. I don't know that anyone would have noticed it though. I studied the plans for a while and I didn't even notice it right away. We need to get into that house and check."

"How are we searching without a warrant?"

Declan blew out of a frustrated breath. "I already talked to Spade and after the fiasco of sending in the DEA to search Jack's and coming up empty no one is going to try that again unless we get something more solid. I need to see if the room is there. We are going to have to go in and then you distract her while I search the house."

It wasn't the worst idea Kate had heard. "Maybe I can appeal to her as a woman and try to see what she knows about the drugs without directly calling her out on it. She was the first contact I had so it might seem plausible I'd go to her to try to understand what's happening especially since the DEA didn't find drugs."

"That's good. That's really good," Declan said and stopped dead on the sidewalk. "Should we go back to the house and talk or go directly there?"

Kate turned her head to look up at him. "What's the plan, Declan?

You came charging into Liam's house like a man on a mission. I assumed you had a plan." Kate started to tell him about Natalie's call but Declan cut her off, saying he couldn't deal with that right now. It would have to wait.

Declan raked a hand through his hair and then jutted his chin toward the house. "Let's go back and talk first. I want to know about your conversation with Liam."

Kate agreed because she wasn't sure that they were both operating from the same information. Once they were inside the house and Declan did the sweep for bugs, which was starting to grate on Kate's nerves, they sat down in the living room to talk.

She sat on the edge of the chaise and looked over at Declan whose eyes were starting to darken underneath. The case was taking a toll on him physically. "Did you think that Liam killed Bridgit? Is that why you came into the house as you did?"

"I didn't know what to think, Kate. When I found out that he was the last one to see her alive, I lost it. Det. Miller connected me with Bridgit's mother and she explained to me that Bridgit had last been with Liam and then she was attacked right after... all sorts of things ran through my head – especially given Det. Miller still believed that Liam might be a suspect. That coupled with his wife's death, I didn't know." Declan raised his eyes to her. "Do you think he killed his wife?"

"No, I don't. Liam, at least then, was as much of a victim of Jack's as anyone else. Only now, he is taking all that anger and trying to do something good with it. He was forthcoming with information. His body language and tone of voice indicated he was being honest with me. He held back about Bridgit, but I hadn't asked about her." Kate wanted to phrase her thoughts exactly because she didn't want confusion. "I can't rule Liam out of any of the murders, including his wife's or Bridgit's disappearance, but I'd be shocked if it was him. He didn't indicate that he was responsible. I think he's genuinely here to help. He's desperate for information."

"Desperate enough to send in Bridgit," Declan said and then stopped himself.

"It wasn't Liam's first time."

"What's that mean?"

"The couples," Kate said, her voice tightening. "Liam told me that in exchange for helping them out of Jack's program he had asked them to gather information for him. He asked them to spy. They all either said no or said they were working on it. None of them got him anything usable, but I'm worried it might have led to their deaths."

Declan cursed again and he kicked the edge of the coffee table leg in anger. "They are all responsible, Kate. Every single one of them."

Kate couldn't argue with him. Even if Jack hadn't murdered anyone, he had set the wheels in motion to their untimely deaths. "We still have no stand-out suspect among them. Do you have a feeling either way?"

"I don't know, Kate," Declan said, throwing up his hands. "I've had enough of this case, living in this fake house and pretending to be someone I'm not. I want to go bust down some doors and make people talk."

Kate was surprised to hear him talk like that. He'd always been an exceptional undercover agent. "You never have trouble with undercover work."

"Yeah, when it has a purpose. This hasn't had a purpose. It's been a waste of time."

"That's not entirely true." Kate didn't finish because her cellphone rang from her pocket. She lifted the screen to her eyes and softly cursed. "It's Natalie again. As I started to tell you, she called me while I was meeting with Liam. She told me that Frank found out about what happened to Molly and he went after Jack. I don't know the full details yet but it sounds like he's going off the wall over there."

"Good. Maybe all four of them will pack up and leave."

Kate shook her head. "I said that to Natalie and she insisted that Frank was out for blood. She wanted me to come over right away but I couldn't." Declan peered over at Kate and their eyes locked. He offered her a knowing look and her stomach dropped. "You think the killer may go after them next?"

"Why not, Kate? Think about it. They fit the profile of the other murder victims. They haven't been here as long as the others, but Frank is probably as close to Jack as them."

"We need to get over there then and speak to them."

Declan pointed to her phone. "Text her and tell her we will be over there as soon as we can but it may still be a while."

After a quick change of clothes and a short walk, Kate and Declan stood on Claire's front porch and knocked. Kate had rehearsed what she'd say to the woman, but the longer they stood there, the more she grew worried they wouldn't be able to speak to her at all.

Declan didn't waste any time though. "Wait here," he said and then left the porch and headed across the front lawn toward the side of the house.

Kate assumed he was going to check out the part of the home that didn't match up to the architectural plans. Her heartbeat thumped in her ears. The last thing they needed right now was to get caught snooping around before having a chance to snoop around inside.

Kate tried knocking one more time and then stepped back from the porch, giving up that Claire was home. She started down the driveway toward the road when she heard her name called. Kate turned to see a flustered-looking Claire standing in the open doorway.

"Can I help you with something?" Claire asked, her voice serious. "I don't normally have visitors at my home without an appointment."

Kate took a deep breath and turned around, showing vulnerability on her face but confidence in her posture. "I need to speak to you, Claire. I'm sure you heard what happened to me the other night."

"I did and you stupidly called the police. Why would I ever speak to you now?"

"I didn't call the police. The lab that did my test said they had to call it in. I had no idea what they meant." Kate took a few steps toward her. "I need to understand what happened to me and thought as a woman you might understand how I'm feeling."

Claire narrowed her gaze. "Are you alone?"

"No, Declan was just here. He said he had to run back home for something." Kate turned her head to see Declan walking down the road. She breathed a sigh of relief that he wasn't on the property. She waved to him and then turned back to Claire. "There he is now. It won't take long. I'm trying to decide my best course of action."

Claire pursed her lips and stepped back. "Wait here a moment and then we can speak but only briefly." She turned and quickly went into the home and shut the door behind her.

"I assume she was in her lab," Kate said quietly to Declan as he approached.

"I'll know soon enough once I get inside the house. It's an anomaly that should be easy enough to spot. Sadie said that if you press a part of the wall a door opens. Maybe she assumed it went to a basement instead of a closed-off room in the house."

"Easy enough mistake," Kate said and then stopped speaking as the door to the home opened and Claire waved them in. She had smoothed down her hair and adjusted her shirt and appeared far more put together than when she first came to the door.

Kate and Declan followed her into the home through the living room to the home office. As they went to sit down, Declan cleared his throat. "I'm sorry but could I use your bathroom?"

Claire looked like she wasn't sure what to say but then dismissed him with a wave of her hand. "Down the hall. Second door on the right." She sat behind her desk and turned her attention to Kate. "I'm not sure what you'd like me to tell you. I don't know anything about you being drugged, but if you were, then it was part of the program and what you signed up for. Consider it a life lesson."

Kate crossed her legs. "I hardly think being drugged and sexually assaulted is a life lesson."

Claire dared to smirk and it took Kate everything she had not to leap across the desk and smack it off her face. "Dear," she said condescendingly, "you were not sexually assaulted. You were the aggressor. I saw the video. The DEA saw the video, too."

Kate cast her eyes to the floor in a bid to seem embarrassed. Spade had already informed the DEA of what had happened. The fact that they saw the video was proof of what Kate had explained. "If you're trying to embarrass me, you've accomplished that. I don't see how this can be okay for you. You're fine being connected to a program that does this to women."

Claire ignored Kate's plea. "Where is your husband? He should be back from the bathroom by now." She stood from her desk as Kate's eyes shifted toward the door. "I don't like people out of my sight in my home."

"Why not?" Kate said. "I thought this program was built on trust. Is there a reason we shouldn't trust you? I came here because I thought you'd be the one person I could trust." Kate was stalling for time and it worked. There was something in Kate's tone that struck a nerve.

Claire laid her palms flat on the desk and peered over at Kate. "Monica said that you weren't to be trusted. She knew it from the first moment she laid eyes on you, but Jack wouldn't hear of it. He said you had potential. He sees now that you don't. You're like every other non-believer out there. Feel free to go live your mediocre life. You'll never be what you could have been if you had committed to the program and done the work, Kate. You need to leave now."

Kate slowly rose from the chair and was about to respond when Declan stuck his head in the doorway, drawing their attention. "She's right, Katie. We are a couple of losers. Let's go live our loser lifestyle in peace and leave these smart people alone."

Kate tried not to smile as she turned to leave. As she stepped out of the office, she put her hand on Declan's chest and he patted it with his. Declan wasn't done though. He peered over at Claire. "Speaking of losers, you might want to watch your back. I heard karma is a real…" He turned and pulled Kate with him without finishing his thought.

"Do you think antagonizing her like that is a good idea?" Kate asked once they got out to the road. Declan took the lead and Kate followed behind him as they walked from Claire's house toward Natalie's.

"Not now, Kate. Let's get farther away and I'll tell you what I found." Declan reached out and grabbed her hand and then turned back to look over his shoulder. "We are being watched."

Kate didn't question him and kept walking. Once they were two blocks away from Claire's house, Kate turned around and saw that no one was following them. There wasn't a person in sight. "Can you tell me now? I don't feel like we accomplished much of anything other than learning that Jack showed the video of me with Ethan to the DEA. I acted like it wasn't a big deal, but my professional reputation is on the line here, especially since they didn't find the drugs."

"They found the drugs in your system though. No one is judging you." Declan kept walking but didn't offer more until they were another two blocks away. Even at that, he didn't say anything. He let go of Kate's hand and pulled his phone from his pocket and handed it to her. "Take a look at my recent photos."

Kate took the phone and stopped walking, but Declan nudged her to keep going. She wasn't sure how she could walk and look at photos at the same time. Declan slipped his hand around her back and guided her forward. She'd have to trust he wouldn't let her trip.

Kate clicked his photo app and the first photo was of Claire's hallway with blue walls on top and white wainscoting on the bottom. Three doorknobs poked out of the frames. Kate stared at the photo but wasn't sure what she was supposed to be looking at. She turned her head up to look at Declan in a question.

"Look toward the bottom of the photo near the floor."

Kate did as he instructed and that's when she saw it. Light coming through the bottom of the floorboards and scuff marks along the bottom of the white wainscoting. There was also the faintest discoloration on the hardwood floors. Kate assumed this was the spot that the wall opened and each time it dragged along the floor, it left a permanent discoloration.

She flipped to the next photo and now stopped dead. Declan had managed to open the wall several inches, enough to stick his hand through with his phone and snap a photo. Kate flipped to the next photo and then the next.

Claire had a full working lab inside her home. The photos didn't allow for much detail to be seen but there was a beaker sitting on the edge of the table with clear liquid in it. Kate wondered if Claire had been in the lab when she had initially knocked on the door.

"This is proof enough," Kate said, handing the phone back to him. "We are going to have to speak to Spade about the process for getting a warrant for this. I'm not sure about the legal process since we are undercover."

"Not something we need to worry about. I was wandering around her house and stumbled upon it." Declan turned to her and Kate offered him a skeptical look. "There's something else."

"More than finding the suspected drug lab?" Kate couldn't imagine there could be much more in the short time Declan had been out of the room.

He scrolled through the photos and stopped at one. "What does that look like?"

Kate leaned over him to look at the photo. It was taken inside a simple wooden jewelry box. It took her a moment to scan through the earrings and necklaces to see the one item out of place. Once Kate saw it though, she couldn't believe her eyes. "Is that a piece of the blue mosaic tile from the vase Lydia was struck with the night of her murder?"

"I can't be certain it's the same, but it certainly looks like it."

"Where is this jewelry box?" Kate had no idea how Declan had searched around so much.

"It's in a spare bedroom right across from the bathroom. It's luck that I found it. I didn't even see it at first. I was in that room before I saw the space on the floor and figured out the entrance was at the end of the hall. I thought maybe it might be built into a closet in one of the nearby rooms."

"Sadie said it was in the hall."

"She also said it led to a basement." Declan slipped his phone back into his pocket. "I didn't put too much stock into what Sadie said. Besides, it's good I searched that room and found this."

"It doesn't mean Claire killed Lydia. We don't even know what that's from."

"I don't believe in coincidences like that." Declan looked down at Kate walking beside him. "Didn't we hear that Claire has been with Jack since the beginning? If that's true, then she knew Lydia. She just happens to have a broken piece of a vase from the crime scene? It's more than coincidence."

Kate wasn't much in the mood for speculation. She remained quiet the rest of the walk mulling over the next steps. When they reached Natalie's house, Andrew and Frank were on the front lawn deep in discussion. They saw Kate and Declan and stopped talking long enough to meet them at the edge of the lawn.

"We need to get out of here," Andrew said with panic in his voice.

Declan agreed. "As soon as possible."

Frank crossed his arms over his chest. "I'm not leaving." He let out a string of curses and colorful language describing Jack and Ethan. "I'm not letting them get away with this."

Declan reached his hand over and gripped his shoulder. "Frank, I get it. I understand completely. As you know, they tried the same thing with Kate. I…"

"Yeah, and you were there to rescue her," Frank spat, interrupting Declan and shoving his hand off him. "I couldn't protect Molly then, but I'm going to do it now and no one is going to stop me."

"You already tried that with Jack and Ethan and it didn't get you anywhere," Declan said, trying to reason with him.

Kate didn't know how true that was. She hadn't heard the full story from Frank who seemed like he needed to vent. "Frank, tell us what happened with Jack and Ethan when you confronted them."

Frank sat down on the curb and cradled his head in his hands. "After Molly finally told me what happened, I lost it. They say you can go white-hot with rage and feel completely out of your body and that's what happened. I stopped thinking rationally. The first time I went there, the DEA was still there so I couldn't get near the place. I went back though. I stormed over to Jack's house and just tore through the place – breaking things and knocking over tables and such until I found him. I didn't even say anything to him. I grabbed him by the throat and slammed him into the wall. I swear I thought I might kill him, but Ethan pulled me off and we got into it. He was stronger than me though and pinned me to the ground." Frank rocked back and forth.

"Did you say anything to them?" Kate asked, wanting to comfort him but knowing how important the details were.

"Yeah, but it didn't do any good. I yelled and screamed about what they did to Molly. Jack didn't deny it and neither did Ethan. They said it was all part of the program. They said it was helping Molly be a better wife to me." He raised his eyes to Kate. "How is drugging and sexually assaulting my wife making her better? I'm going to kill them."

Kate sat on the curb with him. "Frank, you can't kill him. I know you want to but Molly needs you and there's no point going to prison over this."

"It would be worth it." Frank dug the palms of his hands into his eyes. "I told Jack I was going to expose him. I have all the interviews I've done with him and information he's shared that shouldn't be made public. I know where he keeps the videos."

Kate put her hand on his arm. "Of the assaults?"

Frank nodded. "They are all stored on Jack's computer. It's the only computer in the place that connects to the security system. He's the only one with the log-in information. I don't know the passcode, but I know you have to be on Jack's computer to access it."

"Frank," Declan said, his voice firm. It drew everyone's attention to him. "You need to get Molly and leave Mulberry Grove right now. You cannot stay. This is exactly what happened to the other murdered couples. Each of the women was targeted by Jack and Ethan, and later, their husbands found out. We don't know all the details, but what we do know is all the couples ended up dead. You need to leave right now. Go back to your house, do not speak about leaving or where you're going. Turn music on and pack as much as you can and get in your car and go."

"Where?" Andrew asked, his face giving away how overwhelming the prospect of doing that would be.

"I know someone. I can get you accommodation for as long as you need until Jack is neutralized."

Andrew's eyes grew wide. "Are you going to kill him?"

Declan shook his head. "No, but I promise you he will be held accountable for what he's done."

"I'm not going," Frank said, digging in. He shook his head and cursed some more. Kate and Declan continued to try to convince him that they had to leave. Even Andrew tried to no avail. There was no way Frank was going to leave even if it meant his life was in danger.

Kate looked up at Declan and mouthed, *"We need to tell them."*

Declan nodded once in agreement and understanding. He looked around the cul-de-sac and then pulled his badge out of his back pocket. He held it covertly in his palm and flashed it to Frank and Andrew who stared at him in disbelief. He put the badge away. "Please, do as we ask. I cannot keep you safe if you stay. Don't tell anyone what I'm telling you. We have been working here undercover for the past couple of weeks. Pack your things and go. I'll have another FBI agent contact you and get you into a safe house."

Frank and Andrew shared a look. All at once, Frank's body deflated in defeat. "We'll go. What do you need us to do?"

Kate stood and offered her hand to Frank. "Where is Molly?"

He pointed back to Andrew's house. "She's inside with Natalie."

"I'll go in and bring them out." Kate turned to Declan. She didn't trust that Frank and Molly or even Natalie and Andrew could pull this off on their own. "You go with Frank and Molly and get them packed up to go and I'll stay here and help Andrew and Natalie. Then text me when and where they should meet."

"Sounds like a plan." Declan walked off to call Agent Bob Carver, who Kate was sure would arrange for them to give detailed statements to a local FBI agent and find them a safe place to stay.

Kate turned to Frank. "Is all the video you've taken at your house or at Jack's?"

"At my house. I've been working from home and have all my

equipment there."

"Good. I need you to bring everything you have against Jack and Ethan with you. Even if you don't think it's important, bring it. When you're inside your house, do not speak about leaving or what you're doing. Don't breathe a word about the FBI or police or anything. Make casual conversation like you invited Declan over for dinner. Talk about football, the weather, movies. I don't care what subject you choose – do not mention that you're leaving."

"Why?"

"I believe your houses and phones are bugged. When you go, leave your cellphones. We can get you new phones when you're safe."

Neither of them argued with her. Declan returned a moment later and confirmed that Agent Carver was more than happy to help. He didn't disclose the plan right then but said he would when they were both ready to go, which Kate thought was smart. He promised to let her know the details as soon as Andrew and Natalie were ready – this way no one could slip up in conversation inside the house while they were packing.

As Kate started up the driveway to get Natalie and Molly, it occurred to her that Frank had spent considerable time at Jack's. She turned back to them. "Frank, do you remember the last time you saw Bridgit?"

"The other night when she left Jack's."

"Did she leave alone?"

"I thought so at first. She seemed pretty upset when she left. Jack and Ethan followed her out but then came back in after that without her. It sounded like she was heading home for the night. But about an hour later, I heard Monica say that she had to meet up with her at her house. I thought it was kind of odd because they never saw each other outside of Jack's. None of them do."

"Do you know she's missing?"

Frank sucked in a sharp breath. "They told me she was home sick for a few days."

"She's missing and the police are looking for her," Kate said and then turned to go into the house, leaving them looking weary and shellshocked.

CHAPTER 40

Later that night nearing midnight, Kate and Declan sat in the office updating Spade about everything that had happened. Spade assured them he'd work on getting a warrant to search Claire's house and confirmed that Natalie and Andrew and Molly and Frank had made it to the safe house and had given detailed statements to a local FBI agent. Frank also turned over all the information he had been collecting and recording for the documentary. It would take some time to go through.

Given the information that Frank had provided, Spade requested a warrant for Jack's financial documents both personal and for the business. He told them he had an FBI forensic accountant waiting in the wings to begin to dig into Jack's financials once they were received. It was a long game that might prove an easier case than the murders. Many big-time criminals were taken down for white-collar crimes when other felonies wouldn't stick. Kate felt like the wheels were finally in motion to bring Jack to justice.

"I hate that you had to blow your cover, but I get why you did it," Spade said, nearing the end of the call.

Declan leaned in toward the phone. "We didn't have a choice. Kate and I felt that ensuring their safety and getting them out of Mulberry Grove was more important than keeping our cover. We were with them the whole time though and took their phones. I'm not sure who they could or would tell."

"There's not much left for us to do anyway. This spiraled once we pulled the plug on Jack's program," Kate added. She knew that Spade wasn't angry but given this was her first undercover assignment, and hopefully the last, she felt the need to explain herself.

"Do you have any leads on a suspect?"

Kate gnawed at her bottom lip. They didn't have anything positive to tell him. "We have no evidence pointing to anyone specifically. There are several people on the list though – nearly all of them connected to Jack's program. I don't see why anyone from the outside would do such a thing and given the common victimology, we aren't dealing with a random offender here."

They had already explained the mosaic tile that Declan had found in Claire's house and passed on the information that Monica had been headed to Bridgit's apartment the night she disappeared.

Spade grunted. "You have more work to do then."

Declan shook his head and sighed loud enough for Spade to hear him. It was what Kate had felt like doing, but she wasn't as bold as Declan. He asked, "What exactly would you like us to be doing? I feel like we might get a better response from the neighbors if we could identify ourselves and sit down and interview them."

Kate agreed but Spade shut that down quickly. "Figure it out and call me back when you have something." He slammed the phone down before they could argue.

Declan shoved the phone away and sat back. "I'm getting sick of working for him. He asks the impossible and will not listen to reason."

"When has Spade ever been wrong though?"

Declan couldn't argue with that. He got up from the desk and came around to where Kate was sitting. "There's not much we can do tonight. We have no more answers than we had earlier. At least we made sure a few people got out safely and Det. Miller should be running down the lead with Bridgit." He held out his hand to her.

Kate took it tentatively and eyed him suspiciously. "What did you have in mind?"

"I never got the pizza and beer you promised me the other night. Let's pick some up and talk about the case." He grinned at her. "Unless you have a more interesting plan."

Kate felt her cheeks blush. It was strange to be under Declan's gaze in such an intimate way. They both knew what he meant and they both knew they couldn't proceed. It was a sexual stalemate for both of them – right back to where they had been, only now the years-long desire had been expressed. "I never have a more interesting plan. Pizza and beer sound fantastic."

Later in the evening, they sat at the kitchen table with slices of pizza on plates and bottles of beer in front of them. Declan leaned back in one chair and had his long legs kicked out in front of him. Kate sat with her feet propped on the chair next to her. She devoured the delicious cheesy goodness and didn't even mind that the sauce wasn't as good as what they had in Boston. The food was hot and comforting and the beer cold. There wasn't more she could ask for at the moment – outside of a solid lead on the killer.

Declan took a bite of pizza and then washed it down with beer. "All right, give it to me straight. It's just you and me. I know you have a feeling on the killer."

Kate finished her bite, pulling off the string of cheese that lingered and popping it into her mouth. "I don't have a lead on the killer. I do think I understand the motive and that might help us narrow down the list. Let me say first that I agreed with you about interviewing the neighbors as FBI agents rather than doing it undercover. That's the biggest drawback since we got here. I can't do what I do best and we have zero credibility. I know Spade shot you down, but I wanted you to know I'm on your side with that."

"I appreciate that. I know we disagree on approach sometimes, but it's good we are on the same page now. Not that it's going to get us anywhere with Spade." Declan set down his beer and gave Kate his full attention. "What's the motive?"

"Let me clarify something first. I think I know the motive for the cult not necessarily the motive for the murders, but I could venture a solid guess." Kate took another swig of her beer. "At first, I thought it was about Jack running a cult and keeping himself in power. The more I heard though I think ultimately it's about money and relevancy. Jack doesn't have the same ideological motives as Jim Jones or David Koresh. He didn't have the criminal background of Charles Manson. When he was in business, Jack had a ton of money and relevancy, but the more I studied his background, at the time he started the cult, he had made some poor investments and his notoriety had been fading. He could have gone several different directions, but he came here, set up a community when he was famous enough that people still thought he was a genius, and began taking money off unsuspecting people who were looking for a self-help guru. Then we have the added drug factor, which even the DEA said is making someone rich. Jack has investment properties here and has grown an empire. I don't think he wants to see that all come crashing down. He doesn't want that cash cow to go away."

Declan considered that for a moment and didn't disagree. "He's guilty of blackmailing people that's been clear. The price Jack charges is outrageous and only gets more expensive the higher people go in the program."

"Right. By the time they are at the highest levels, he's bled them dry and collected enough dirt on them to make sure they won't leave the program, leaving them forced to keep paying him to keep their secrets buried."

Declan took another sip of his beer, his gaze indicating he was mulling things over. "Do you think that means that Jack killed these people?"

"I don't think he did it." Kate saw Declan was about to debate the point so she asked him to hear her out. "He may have had knowledge it was happening. I don't think it was him at the crime scenes though. His psychological profile doesn't indicate that he'd be willing to get his hands dirty like that. Plus, I think Liam was right when he said that Jack wouldn't risk the fight. You had him on his knees in seconds. He's not a physically tough guy."

"It doesn't take toughness to shoot someone," Declan countered.

"I agree with that. I haven't ruled out that the killer is a woman, but I don't believe it's Jack."

"What about the sexual assaults? He was willing to rape women who had been drugged."

Kate had considered it. Sexual assault wasn't that big a leap to murder, but she had an answer for that. "Like most powerful men who sexually harass and sexually assault women, they don't see it as wrong. They see themselves as entitled to it. I think that's where Jack is coming from. He's a rich powerful guy and assumes everyone wants him. If it takes some drugs to get them to let their guard down or as he said to me let my wild side show, then it's a part of the process. We've heard that from people a few times – it's all part of the process. Like he's doing the woman a favor."

Declan nodded along as she spoke. "What is the motive for the murders?"

"Protecting Jack and the empire he's built. Ethan, Monica, and Claire seem fairly devout and devoted to Jack. I can see Ethan doing everything and anything to protect Jack and protect himself. Plus, he probably killed Lucile. Jack may survive the sexual assault allegations, but Ethan doesn't have Jack's background and fame. I think he knows that if it came down to it, Jack would throw him under the bus in a heartbeat."

Declan raised his eyebrows. "So, you think it's Ethan then?"

"I'd say if anyone stands out among the crowd, it's him. He's familiar with all of the couples, he's been with Jack since the beginning and he's directly involved in the sexual assaults."

"Let's focus on him tomorrow and talk to some neighbors and see if any of them saw him around before or after the murders. We've run background on him and nothing comes up, but maybe we need to dig deeper."

Kate agreed and nudged her empty plate forward. "I'm exhausted. I'm buzzed from this beer, full of food, and sleepy. I'm heading up. We can tackle this in the morning."

They said goodnight and Declan said he'd be up soon. He wanted to do a sweep outside to make sure no one was watching the house, make sure the doors were locked, and then set the alarm. Kate got up, took their plates, and ruffled Declan's hair before going to the sink. She said goodnight again and then retired upstairs.

At two-thirty that morning, Kate woke with a start. It wasn't so much that she had heard someone but felt them nearby. Seconds ticked by as her eyes adjusted to the darkness. She ran her hand over Declan's side of the bed to rouse him from sleep but found his spot empty and cold sheets under her touch. She turned her head sharply to the doorway and found it closed. Her heart raced. On instinct, Kate reached for the bedside table for her gun.

"I wouldn't make any sudden moves if I were you," a voice said from a chair in the corner of the room.

With exhaustion dulling her senses, Kate couldn't identify the voice on hearing alone. She turned to where the voice came from and blinked her eyes several times until they came into focus. When Kate saw Claire sitting there with her legs casually crossed holding a gun pointed at her, she wasn't even surprised.

Kate threw off the covers and swung her feet to the floor. "What are you doing, Claire?"

"I should have killed you in your sleep, but I have a few questions your husband wouldn't answer."

Kate lurched forward, remembering that Declan wasn't beside her. "What did you do to Declan?"

Claire smirked. "He's dead in the backyard. Well," she paused dramatically, "he might not be dead yet. A shot to the chest might take some time to kill him. He never saw it coming. A shot to the leg brought him to his knees and then when he wouldn't tell me what I needed to know, I finished him off."

Kate's throat constricted and she fought back tears. "It's you. All these murders. It was you?"

Claire waved the gun at her. "I'm the one asking the questions here."

"Then ask." Kate started to stand and Claire aimed the gun right at her. She lowered her bottom back to the bed, her hand inching slowly toward the nightstand. "What do you want to know?"

"Who did you tell you were drugged?"

"I told you it happened at the lab. I knew that night something was off and so did Declan." Kate's voice cracked even mentioning his name. She swallowed hard fighting emotion. "I'm smart enough to get drug tested."

"Did you make a police report?"

Kate studied her face trying to figure out if she was serious or playing her. "No. I told you the lab called the DEA. I had to give details to the lab where I was and what I thought had happened. They told the DEA."

The answer seemed to satisfy her. "Where are Natalie and Andrew and Molly and Frank? I went to their houses tonight and they were empty. I assume you made good on your threat and helped them leave. You're going to tell me where they are."

"Why, so you can kill them, too?"

Claire didn't say anything for several moments, then she raised her voice. "You'll tell me where they are or I'll kill you."

"I'll tell you," Kate said, stalling for time. "We both know you're going to kill me, so at least let me die knowing why you did it. You already killed my husband. I have nothing to live for anyway."

Claire didn't speak but there was a flash of emotion in her eyes that Kate thought she understood. "You're in love with Jack, aren't you? You were protecting him. Does he even know it's you?"

Claire didn't say a word but she leaned to the side and wobbled slightly.

Kate knew she had to keep talking. "Claire, you're not getting enough credit. You're making him the drugs and he's using them to seduce and have sex with other women and you're cleaning up his mess. I bet he doesn't even appreciate you."

"You don't know anything about our relationship."

Kate shrugged. "Some relationship. You're doing all the work and he's screwing other women. I must be losing my touch. Of all the reasons I thought these murders were being committed, I didn't account for a jealous pathetic woman cleaning up after some loser guy. You're even protecting Jack. You're mostly protecting Ethan who is the one assaulting women. Tell me you're not in love with him too."

Claire's body tensed and her mouth set in a firm line. She thrust the gun forward. "Shut up! Where is Frank? Tell me now!"

"Did you kill Lydia Brady?"

Claire cursed and called Lydia a foul name. "She showed up here in Mulberry Grove and thought she was going to take over. She stole Jack from me and then stole the formula for the creation I made. She threatened to go to the cops with it. Jack would be nothing without me. Lydia had to die and I took pleasure in making her suffer."

Kate inched her hand closer to the end table where her gun had been stashed. She had to move slowly not to arouse Claire's suspicion. "Did you stab the first couple, too?"

"I did what had to be done."

"You shot Lydia. Why change to drugging and stabbing them? It makes no sense."

"I didn't want to kill them," Claire said, growing flustered. "I thought I could get the truth out of them, but then the truth confirmed they needed to die. The knife was all I had."

"Too messy for you." Kate grimaced, trying to figure out her next move.

"Who are you? You're not a photographer." Claire stood. "No more games. Tell me right now where Frank and his wife are. Tell me or I'll shoot you and let you bleed out right here."

Kate slowly counted to three. She calmed her heart rate and evened out her breathing and then all at once she yanked open the end table drawer, drew her gun, and fired one shot at Claire, hitting her stomach. Claire dropped her gun and put both hands on her stomach to stop the blood from gushing. Her eyes closed in agony and she dropped to the floor, writhing in pain.

Kate stood with the gun trained on her and kicked Claire's gun across the room. She leaned over her. "I'm FBI Special Agent Kate Walsh and you're under arrest." Kate said the words, but she knew that Claire would be dead long before an ambulance could show up.

Kate started toward the door to find Declan when she heard Claire's strained voice. "You couldn't protect Declan and you can't protect Bridgit and…"

Kate leaned over hoping to hear the rest of the sentence, but Claire gasped three sharp breaths and then died right there in front of her. Kate turned and ran out of the room to find Declan.

CHAPTER 41

Barefoot and still wearing pajamas, Kate raced through the house, down the stairs, and through the kitchen to the backyard. She flung open the back door and ran to the yard. With a gun in hand, she scanned the yard until she saw a figure lying in a heap at the far corner near the fence.

"Declan!" Kate screamed his name as she ran to him, her feet growing damp on the wet grass. Declan was lying on his side facing away from her. She dropped to her knees and turned him slightly and pulled back in horror at the amount of blood on his clothes and the ground near him.

Kate leaned over him checking to see if he had a pulse and if he was breathing. Hot tears spilled down her face when his breath swept across her face and his pulse faintly beat against her fingertips. He had lost a lot of blood but was still alive.

"Declan," she said more softly this time. Blood dripped from a hole in his thigh. Kate had nothing but her clothes and didn't want to leave his side. She ripped off part of her pajama top and tied a tourniquet around his leg. Then Kate unbuttoned his shirt and saw the bullet wound to the side of his chest, closer to his shoulder than his heart. She had no time to waste. Kate grabbed for his pocket where she knew he kept his phone. She dropped her gun next to her on the ground and called 911 with one hand while the other applied pressure to the wound on his upper body.

"We have an FBI agent down with two gunshot wounds. He is unconscious but breathing. Pulse is faint. Please send help quickly," Kate stammered out the words and then gave the address and location where Declan could be found in the backyard. She didn't want to leave him but he was bleeding too much. She needed something more than her hand to apply pressure. She darted into the house to grab some dishtowels from a drawer near the door.

Kate went back to him and dropped to her knees again using the towels to apply pressure to his wounds. "Declan, I'm here. Help is on the way. Please hang on. I can't lose you. Please…" The tears came hot and wet down her face. Her voice creaked and she choked back sobs. They stayed like that until the paramedics arrived and they forced Kate to leave Declan's side so they could work on him. They shouted questions about what happened and his allergies and a range of medical questions Kate scrambled to remember the answers to.

Kate stood off to the side watching them do their work. She wrung her hands hoping he'd wake and say something to reassure her that he was going to be okay. After it seemed like time had stopped, the paramedics placed Declan on the stretcher and wheeled him out of the backyard, shouting information to Kate about where they were taking him. She wanted to follow but she was wearing ripped-up bloodied pajamas and there was a dead woman in the bedroom.

Kate grabbed Declan's cellphone from where she had dropped it on the ground and called Spade. She left him a detailed message along with the hospital information. She'd have to call Declan's parents but she couldn't do that just yet.

As she turned to walk into the house, trying to remember if she had told 911 that she had killed a woman, sirens wailed off in the distance and then grew closer. Kate looked down at herself, Declan's blood still on her hands and clothes. She'd need to make a statement and probably have her clothes taken for evidence. It was the last thing she wanted to do.

"Kate," someone shouted from the side yard as they came through the gate. Agent Bob Carver rushed to her. "I heard what happened. What can I do? LAPD is in the front yard."

Kate took a deep breath. "I want to get to the hospital and be with Declan."

"Understood," he said, looking at her with sympathy in his eyes. "You have to talk to the locals first."

Kate hung her head low. "Let's get that over with."

Later, after Kate had given a statement to the police and crime scene investigators had combed through the backyard and the bedroom and the medical examiner had retrieved the body, Kate had received word from the hospital that Declan was in stable condition. He had been shot through both his thigh and near his shoulder and wouldn't require surgery. He'd had a blood transfusion, his wounds cleaned and stitched up and he was resting comfortably drugged with painkillers. The doctor said he had come to briefly and asked for Kate to make sure she was okay. The doctor confirmed that Kate was fine and then he passed out again.

Relieved, her body finally relaxed as she stepped into the shower. While she was washing her hair, Claire's words about not being able to save Bridgit drifted through her mind. She had only been focused on making sure Declan was okay and had forgotten the woman's last words. Kate made a mental note to call Det. Miller after her shower.

Kate let the hot water beat against her back and then she turned the water off and wrapped herself in a towel. She was in the spare bedroom and had grabbed her clothes and phone earlier. She'd never return to the main bedroom if she could help it. While Kate felt no guilt in killing Claire, she didn't want the visual reminder. All she wanted right now was to get to the hospital.

Kate walked into the bedroom, dressed, and towel dried her hair. Once she was presentable, she checked her cellphone and saw that she had missed three calls from Liam all within the last thirty minutes. It was five in the morning and she couldn't imagine what was so urgent. She listened to the voicemail messages and stumbled back when she heard his words. Ali was missing. She hadn't come home the night before. He only noticed this morning that her bed hadn't been slept in. His voice frantic in the first two messages and the third shook Kate to her core.

Jack had called and left Liam a taunting message that he had both Bridgit and Ali and would kill them both if he didn't come to the house immediately. Kate called him back.

"Liam," she said, her voice rushed and loud, "do not go to Jack's house alone."

"He'll kill her, Kate. I can't lose my daughter."

"He'll kill you both if you go." Liam confirmed for her that he hadn't called the police yet because Jack had told him not to. He was to go alone and bring all of his research and information about Jack and his program with him. Jack promised a trade – Ali's life for the research and assurance that Liam would leave him alone.

Kate did not doubt that Jack would get his hands on the research and then kill both Liam and Ali. She told Liam she'd be right over to help and not to do anything until she got there. He balked but Kate insisted and finally, he said he'd wait.

Kate called the only person she knew who could help – Spade. Even though he was thousands of miles away and she had already spoken to him about Declan's condition, she knew he'd know what to do. He answered on the first ring and they got down to making a plan.

Not even thirty minutes later, Kate arrived at the front of Jack's house with Liam standing beside her. She had a gun on her hip hidden under a long shirt and another gun strapped to her ankle. As discussed with Spade, FBI SWAT was assembling out of sight around the perimeter. Kate saw this as her last chance at getting a confession from Jack or potentially his other staff. She had no idea if Claire acted alone or if this was a conspiracy to commit murder. With Claire dead, this might be the only way to bring Jack to justice for anything.

She knocked once and then waited. Beside her, Liam bounced on his feet and wrung his hands. The poor man had been amped up since Kate arrived at his house to tell him the plan.

"You need to calm down," Kate reminded him. "Just follow my lead inside."

Liam nodded once but didn't say anything. Kate wasn't sure if he was going to be able to follow any directions with his daughter's life hanging in the balance. He was the wild card in the plan and she had initially wanted him to stay home. Spade insisted she bring him.

A moment later, the door opened and it wasn't Jack but rather Ethan who stood on the other side. He locked eyes with Kate. "What are you doing here?"

"Liam told me that you have Ali and I'm here to make sure they both leave alive."

Ethan smirked and started to laugh, but the look Kate gave him made him rethink that. "Ali is fine and unharmed. She's downstairs sitting in the library room with Bridgit. You remember that room, Kate. We had some fun there."

Kate wasn't going to let him throw her off her game. She didn't have to pretend to be a photographer anymore. She wasn't going to tell him she was an FBI agent, but she was going to go after him with every weapon in her arsenal – especially if they were involved in hurting Declan. "Lead the way and we'll follow."

Confusion fell over his face as Kate presented herself with more confidence than she ever had in his presence. "Whatever," he said but did as she asked.

They went downstairs, through the ballroom, and entered the hall. As the doors to the library room opened and they stepped into the room, Ali was already up. She ran to her father and threw her arms around him. Then she looked to Kate with her eyes wide in a question.

"It's going to be okay," Kate reassured her. Bridgit sat on a far couch. She had a bruise under her left eye and her lip had been split. Her usual demeanor had been replaced by a frightened young woman uncertain about the choices that had led her there. She raised her eyes and Kate offered her the same reassurance she had with Ali.

Kate turned to Ethan. "Liam's here now. He's got his laptop and removable drive with all the research in the bag in his hand. You're getting what you want. It's time to let the girls go."

Ethan took a menacing step toward her but Kate held her ground. "You're mistaken if you think you're in charge of this."

It was Kate's turn to smirk. "You're one of Jack's lackeys. You have no power here. Let the girls go and then we'll show you the research. I wouldn't press the issue too much, Ethan. I know about Lucile."

Ethan pulled back, his face growing red with anger. "I don't know what you're talking about."

Kate ignored him and pointed toward Liam to set the bag down on the floor. "Take it, but we are leaving."

Kate gestured toward Bridgit to get up from the couch and walk over to them. She looked to Ethan but slowly rose from the couch and walked to the front of the room near the door. Kate stepped out of the way and was about to escort them to the front to safety but as she stepped through the doorway, Jack stood there staring down at them.

"You're not going anywhere. Back inside."

Kate looked to both Ali and Bridgit. "Don't listen to him. Run to the door and keep going."

Bridgit hesitated but Liam encouraged Ali to leave so she took off in a sprint. Jack stared after her like he wasn't sure what to do. Ethan tried to make a move to go after her and Kate blocked his path. When Bridgit saw that they wouldn't do anything, she took off too. Once outside, Kate knew the SWAT team would bring them to safety.

Jack held his arms wide. "Okay, I let them go. See, Kate, I'm not a bad guy. I didn't harm one hair on their heads while they were here, but I accomplished what I wanted."

"What was that?"

Jack walked over to Kate and put a hand under her chin tipping her head up to look at him. "I wanted to bring you here. I don't care about Liam's stupid research. He doesn't have anything on me, but I've been watching you and I knew that Liam would call you and tell you I had Ali and you'd come running. I'm just disappointed your husband isn't here."

Kate couldn't believe he still didn't know that she was FBI. She was equally surprised he didn't know about Declan being shot. "Declan is taking care of other things right now."

"He seemed like a wimp," Ethan said, "leaving his wife to take care of things for him."

Kate studied Ethan's face and believed he, too, didn't know about Declan. "Liam, go and leave me alone with them."

Liam hesitated and Kate reassured him again. Jack and Ethan made no move to stop him.

"Go ahead, Liam, I think Kate wants to have a little fun with the both of us this time," Ethan said, snickering like a boy. "Don't you, Kate," he said, grabbing himself lewdly. "You didn't quite get your fill the other night."

It wasn't the time now, but when the time came, Kate would hurt him and she'd enjoy it. "Not quite what I had in mind. This time, it's all going to be about my pleasure." She told Liam to leave again and although he seemed uncertain, he did as he was told – again, following the plan.

When Liam left the room, Kate stepped toward it and closed the door. It clicked firmly into place. Then she turned with a broad smile set across her face and her eyes shimmering. "Okay, boys, I want in on this racket you have here. Declan and I know you're making bank on the sale of drugs and scamming these idiots out of their hard-earned money and we want a piece of the action."

CHAPTER 42

Jack shared a look with Ethan and then turned back to Kate, seeming not to understand what was happening. "You were trying to take me down, Kate. Why the change of heart?"

Before Kate could answer, Ethan reached for her. "I don't believe this b…"

He didn't get much more out of his mouth because Kate took his hand, snapped back his wrist, and then punched him squarely in the face, bringing the man to his knees. "Don't ever touch me again."

"Go," Jack told him. "Clean yourself up."

Kate brushed past Jack and then took a seat on the couch, making sure her pant legs fell below the gun. She scooted back and got comfortable. "We had to make it look good. If you were dumb enough to keep the drugs here, then you'd be too dumb to partner with. But you did well. I'll give you that. I assume you keep the drugs off-site and bring them over for a party. Declan, once he got over being angry about what happened to me, figured the street worth of those drugs would be worth partnering with scum like you. We talked and want part of the action."

With uncertainty and a little fear on his face, Jack sat in a chair across from Kate. "What about the website and helping people to get away from me?"

"Thinning the herd of detractors, Jack. You have people here who don't want to be here. If you get rid of them, you're going to have a lot less hassle on your hands. I mean, Jack, come on. You can't keep killing off your members. The cops are getting suspicious." Kate locked eyes with him. "This is all a money racket, right? It's a way to continue your empire. Only you're making poor business decisions. You can't rape your members and then expect them to still pay you."

Jack waved his hands. "Ethan gets a little out of control at times. It's not all about the money, Kate. I do good work here for people. That drug helps women let go of their inner inhibitions. Look at what it did for you."

Kate laughed. "Is that what you tell yourself? Please, Jack, you are trafficking in girls here for your pleasure and then letting Ethan run loose all for the sake of wellness and personal development. He killed a girl, Jack. Did you know that?"

Jack didn't say anything but he didn't have to. His look confirmed that he knew.

Kate waved her hand at him. "Tell me what the end goal is if it's not making money. What you set up is amazing. You're tricking smart wealthy people who are unsuspecting. What you need to do is stop drugging your members, get a network to get that fantastic good time drug on the street, and then bilk your members out of money another way. The blackmail is genius. The cops are getting suspicious though."

Jack folded his hands in his lap and assessed her. Kate remained quiet and let him ruminate over what she was saying. The way his eyes flickered and the silence in his stare told her she had him. He was buying every word she said.

Kate leaned forward on the couch. "Jack, I don't even understand why you're trafficking women in here. You're a good-looking guy. You can get any woman you want. I understand wanting a variety, but again, high risk."

"You think I'm attractive?"

"Extremely." Kate batted her eyelashes at him. "I was disappointed it was Ethan in here with me that night instead of you."

"I didn't think you liked me."

Kate smiled. "When has that ever stopped you?"

Jack nodded his head to the side. "I'll give you that one. You're much different than I realized. I assessed you all wrong and it's fascinating to me." He held his arms open wide. "You can have me anytime you want, my dear."

Kate threw up a little in her mouth, but she got the confession she needed. "Business first. Pleasure second."

"A woman after my own heart."

"Declan and I have one hang-up though, Jack. We don't want to be in business with killers."

"I've never killed anyone," Jack said evenly.

"I believe you, but we know Ethan has killed at least one girl. Is he responsible for the couples?" Before Jack could answer, Kate hitched her thumb over her shoulder. "Ethan is out of control. How do you know he's not out there killing?"

"I thought about that, Kate, but he was with me on the nights of the murders."

"What about Monica? I heard she roughed up Bridgit to get her here."

Jack shook his head. "That was Ethan. Monica surprised Bridgit and then Ethan did what he had to do to subdue her. Monica would never kill anyone."

Kate nodded as if she understood. "Well, someone is killing people, Jack. We need to figure it out."

Jack shrugged. "I don't know what to tell you. It's not me or anyone connected to me."

Kate knew that was untrue, but given Jack seemed to know nothing about the events of last night, she had to take him at face value. "Fine.

Let's put a pin in that for now. Tell me what distribution networks you have set up for the drugs. Declan has some ideas, but maybe not as good as yours."

Jack's face grew animated and he detailed for Kate all the ways that he and Ethan pushed the drugs to the street. They were selling quite well already. "It can always be improved upon."

"What can you tell me about the structure of the program? I'd love to learn more about that."

Jack shook his head. "I have to keep some secrets to myself. Besides, if you and Declan want to work with me, then you need to commit to the program. Everyone does it. There's no way around that. Once you are at the top, then I'll tell you."

"The program is a bunch of crap, Jack."

"It's really not." Jack shifted in his seat and Kate could tell she shouldn't push the issue anymore.

"Tell me about Claire," Kate said, her voice calm and steady.

"Claire is my right-hand woman. I probably should call her if you're serious about talking business."

Kate shook her head and frowned. "I don't think she likes me much. She tried to kill me in the wee hours of the morning."

Jack furrowed his brow. "What are you talking about?"

Kate leaned forward and rested her hands on her knees. "Claire came to my home, shot Declan in the backyard, and then came into the house and surprised me in my bedroom."

"That's not funny, Kate. You shouldn't joke about things like that."

"It's not a joke." Kate paused for dramatic effect. She enjoyed toying with him. "She's dead, Jack. I killed her."

Jack froze in the chair and his mouth hung open. "No," he said in disbelief, shaking his head. "No. You couldn't have done that."

Kate nodded her head. "Right after she confessed to the murders. She did it to protect you. She even killed Lydia Brady all those years ago. You were getting too close to her."

Jack's hand flew to his mouth. He wasn't acting. He was clearly in shock at the news. "I don't believe you." He stood quickly and advanced on Kate who got to her feet just as quickly. "Ethan!" he called and then called again.

"Sorry, Jack, there's no one here to rescue you. They are all in FBI custody. All of your bank accounts are frozen, too. Even the ones offshore that you think no one knows about."

Jack turned toward the door and then back to Kate. "What are you talking about?" He was so frantic he didn't know where to look. His body jerked in every direction.

Kate put her hand in her pocket and pulled out her badge. "I'm Special Agent Kate Walsh and you're under arrest." She pulled up her shirt and put her hand on her gun. "I'd hate to have to kill you too, Jack, so drop to your knees and put your hands behind your back."

Jack took a few steps back, horrified as he realized what was happening. Kate had tricked him, got him to confess in the comfort and safety of his own home, taken out his chemist, and succeeded at destroying everything he had worked so hard for – doing it all from the inside.

Before Kate could say anything else, the SWAT team stormed in and put Jack in cuffs while they read him his rights. They had already been in the house waiting. Kate's main job had been to distract Jack and get a confession if she could. She managed to do both while the FBI brought Jack's staff into custody. Spade had secured a warrant immediately after finding out what had happened to Declan.

Jack was dumbfounded. His face was ashen and his eyes roamed over her.

"It's okay, Jack. Maybe you can teach prisoners some personal development lessons." When Jack was gone, she breathed a sigh of relief and then remembered Declan. She raced out of Jack's to the hospital as fast as she could get there.

Kate sat at Declan's bedside. He had on a hospital gown and bandages wrapped around him. An oxygen sensor was hooked to his index finger and an IV was in his arm. He was heavily sedated, and in and out of consciousness. The monitor next to his bed showed his blood pressure, oxygen, and other stats that didn't interest Kate. He was alive and would be okay. That's all she cared about.

Kate leaned onto his bed from her chair, took his hand in hers, and rubbed the pad of her thumb over the back of his hand. "Declan, I was so scared I lost you. I have no idea what I'd do without you. You're the most important person in my life." She tried to choke back the emotion as she sat there watching him sleep. Eventually, she laid her head near their hands and dozed off.

Sometime later, Declan wiggled his fingers against hers. "Will you give me a sponge bath if I ask nicely?" he asked, his voice hoarse and weak.

Kate raised her head and saw that he had his eyes open and a smile on his face. She stood and leaned over and kissed him right on the lips, lingering for just a moment. Embarrassed by her display of emotion, she pulled back. "I was so worried."

He didn't seem to mind that she had kissed him. "I think this means we get our vacation now."

"Don't joke, Declan. I thought you were dead. Do you need anything?"

Declan shook his head, and Kate sat back in the chair. "She took me by surprise, Kate. I was walking the perimeter of the yard and suddenly Claire was right there. She called my name and as soon as I turned, she fired a shot at me that hit me in the leg. She kept screaming questions at me that I didn't even understand. I went for my gun, but she fired off another shot that hit me in the chest, or at least that's where I thought she hit me." Declan looked over at Kate.

"How am I alive?"

"It was inches from your heart but missed everything important. It will take a while to get full use of that arm again and your leg. You're looking at significant recovery time."

"She didn't hurt you. Did she?"

"She didn't hurt me, but she was upstairs in the bedroom when I woke. She confessed to all of the murders." Kate went into detail about everything that Claire had told her. She ended the story with how she was forced to shoot her. "I don't know how I didn't hear the gunshots outside."

"She had a suppressor on the gun, Kate. She came prepared," Declan said. "You got to me in time. Did they find Bridgit?"

Kate didn't recall seeing a suppressor on the gun but it had to have been that. She filled him in on everything that happened that day including the arrests of Jack, Ethan, Monica, and even Sadie. Spade thought they'd probably let Sadie and Monica go given they couldn't directly tie them to any crime, but Jack and Ethan would be fully prosecuted for their crimes. So far, no evidence had been found to tie anyone but Claire to the murders, but the drugs and sexual assaults would send Jack and Ethan away probably for the rest of their lives. Spade didn't know if Ethan would ever be prosecuted for Lucile's murder. There just wasn't enough evidence.

"In the end, saved a few people and solved the murders. Even Liam and Ali found some justice." Kate gestured to his broken state. "Other than you, it was a job well done."

Declan grimaced. "Do I still get to live at your house?"

"Of course. Someone has to nurse you back to health, but we need to rein in pretending to be married..." Kate trailed off hoping he got the message.

Declan bit his lower lip and eyed her suggestively. "You know what I want?"

"What?" Kate asked tentatively.

"That cheeseburger, fries, and vanilla shake we had the other night." Declan turned his head toward the door. "I'm allowed to eat, right?"

Relieved, Kate laughed. "I'll smuggle it in if I have to." Kate's phone rang. She looked at the screen and answered. "Spade, any news?"

"Case is wrapping up nicely. Everyone is turning on Jack and it's the end for him. I think this calls for a celebration of a job well done."

Spade never celebrated. "What do you have for us?"

"How's a three-month vacation sound? That's about how long it should take Declan to recoup and get back to desk duty. There are two plane tickets for you both to anywhere around the globe once he's feeling better."

"Are you serious?" Kate asked, barely believing him.

"You both deserve it. Tell Declan I hope he feels better soon." Spade hung up before Kate could say anything else.

She slipped her phone back in her pocket and turned to Declan who stared at her with the same apprehension she had felt moments before. "You're going to have to get shot more often," she teased. "We got our vacation!"

"I told you."

Kate sat down in the chair and took his hand again. "Let's just focus on getting you better first."

"Right after you go get us dinner."

"Anything for you," Kate said, already feeling the stress releasing from her back and shoulders. She was going to enjoy every minute of the next three months.

About the Author

Stacy M. Jones was born and raised in Troy, New York, and currently lives in Little Rock, Arkansas. She is a full-time writer and holds masters' degrees in journalism and in forensic psychology. She currently has three series available for readers: paranormal women's fiction/cozy mystery Harper & Hattie Magical Mystery Series, the hard-boiled PI Riley Sullivan Mystery Series and the FBI Agent Kate Walsh Thriller Series. To access Stacy's Mystery Readers Club with three free novellas, one for each series, visit StacyMJones.com.

You can connect with me on:
- http://www.stacymjones.com
- https://twitter.com/SMJonesWriter
- https://www.facebook.com/StacyMJonesWriter
- https://www.bookbub.com/profile/stacy-m-jones
- https://www.goodreads.com/StacyMJonesWriter

Subscribe to my newsletter:

✉ http://www.stacymjones.com

Also by Stacy M. Jones

Watch for FBI Agent Kate Walsh Thriller Series Book #4
   THE FUSE - Fall 2022

Access the Free Mystery Readers' Club Starter Library
   PI Riley Sullivan Mystery Series novella "The 1922 Club Murder"
   FBI Agent Kate Walsh Thriller Series novella "The Curators"
   Harper & Hattie Mystery Series novella "Harper's Folly"

Sign up for the starter library along with launch-day pricing, special behind-the-scenes access, and extra content not available anywhere else. Hit subscribe at
   http://www.stacymjones.com/

Please leave a review for Mad Jack. Reviews help more readers find my books. Thank you!

Other books by Stacy M. Jones by series and order to date:

FBI Agent Kate Walsh Thriller Series
   The Curators
   The Founders
   Miami Ripper

PI Riley Sullivan Mystery Series
   The 1922 Club Murder
   Deadly Sins
   The Bone Harvest
   Missing Time Murders

We Last Saw Jane
Boston Underground
The Night Game

Harper & Hattie Magical Mystery Series
Harper's Folly
Saints & Sinners Ball
Secrets to Tell
Rule of Three
The Forever Curse
The Witches Code
The Sinister Sisters